Wet
Grave

BANTAM BOOKS

New York

Toronto

London

Sydney

Auckland

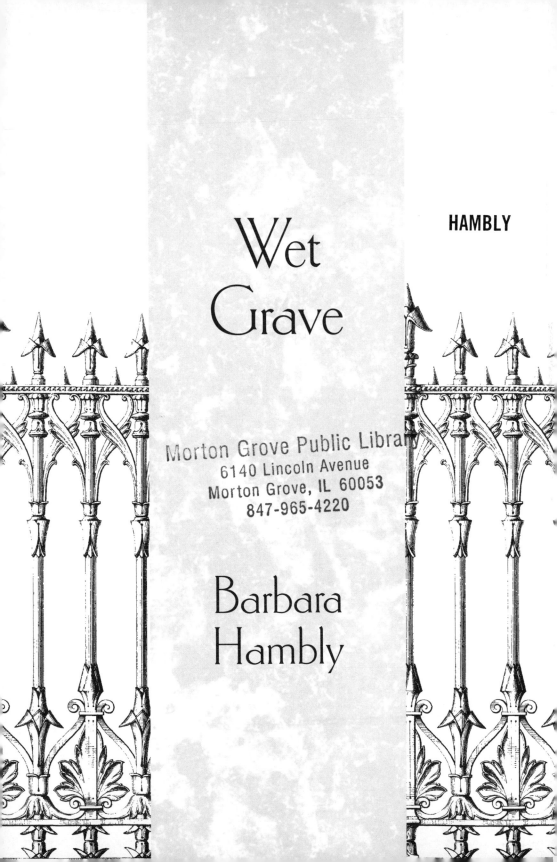

Wet Grave

Barbara Hambly

WET GRAVE

A Bantam Book / July 2002

Library of Congress Cataloging-in-Publication Data
Hambly, Barbara.
Wet grave / Barbara Hambly.
p. cm.
ISBN 0-553-10935-9
1. January, Benjamin (Fictitious character)—Fiction. 2. Free African Americans—Fiction.
3. African American men—Fiction. 4. New Orleans (La.)—Fiction. I. Title.

PS3558.A4215 W48 2002
813'.54—dc21   2001043401

Published simultaneously in the United States and Canada

PRINTED IN THE UNITED STATES OF AMERICA
BVG   10   9   8   7   6   5   4   3   2   1

For Jill and Charles

Special thanks are due
to Pamela Arceneaux and all the staff of
the Historic New Orleans Collection;
to Andy and Sue Galliano; to Jessica Harris;
to Mary-Lynne and Lou Costa; to all the folks
at Le Monde Creole and at Lucullus;
Kate Miciak and Kathleen Baldonado of Bantam Books; and
to all my friends for their patience with me.

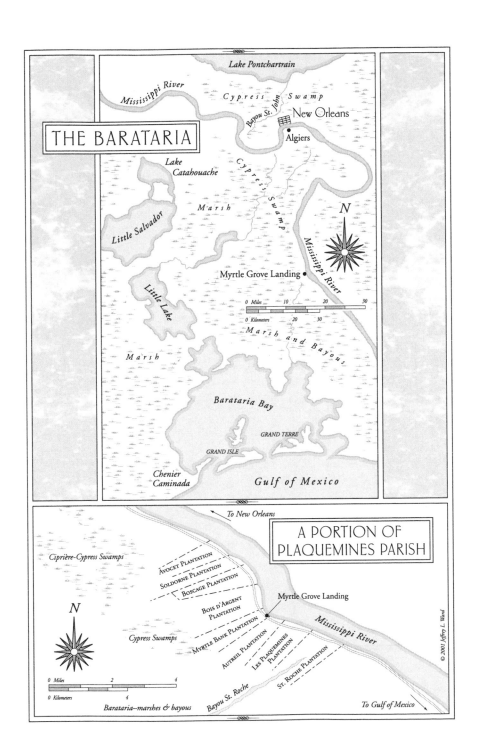

THE BARATARIA

Lake Pontchartrain

Mississippi River

C y p r e s s S w a m p

Bayou St. John

New Orleans

Algiers

Lake
Catahouache

C y p r e s s S w a m p

M a r s h

Little Salvador

N

Mississippi River

Myrtle Grove Landing

Little Lake

0 Miles	10	20	30

0 Kilometers	20	30	

M a r s h a n d B a y o u s

M a r s h

Barataria Bay

GRAND TERRE

GRAND ISLE

*Chenier
Caminada*

Gulf of Mexico

To New Orleans

A PORTION OF
PLAQUEMINES PARISH

Ciprière-Cypress Swamps

AVOCET PLANTATION

SOLDORNE PLANTATION

BOSCAGE PLANTATION

BOIS D'ARGENT
PLANTATION

Myrtle Grove Landing

N

Cypress Swamps

MYRTLE BANK PLANTATION

AUTREIL PLANTATION

LES PLAQUEMINES
PLANTATION

Mississippi River

ST. ROCHE PLANTATION

Bayou St. Roche

0 Miles	2	4

0 Kilometers	4	

Barataria—marshes & bayous

To Gulf of Mexico

© 2001 Jeffrey L. Ward

Wet Grave

———⊗⊗⊗———

Howdy! Hola! Bonjour! Guten Tag!

I'm a *very special book*. You see, I'm traveling around the world making new friends. I hope I've met another friend in you. Please go to

www.BookCrossing.com

and enter my BCID number (shown below). You'll discover where I've been and who has read me, and can let them know I'm safe here in your hands. Then... *READ and RELEASE me!*

BCID: 585-16277046

The only time Benjamin January ever actually exchanged words with Hesione LeGros was when they were both hiding behind a piano in a New Orleans hotel hoping they wouldn't be massacred by pirates.

It wasn't a long conversation.

She said, "I'm gonna shoot that fuckin' man of mine for this."

And January—who had just turned nineteen and was hoping to make twenty—replied, "What makes you think any of us will live to see you do that?"

As it happened, someone else shot her man a number of years later in the Yucatán, but at the time January hoped that the dark-eyed little African Venus beside him would have that honor, and fairly soon. The man certainly deserved it.

The whole debacle began, tamely enough, with the arrival in New Orleans of Major-General Jean Robert Marie Humbert, formerly of the Grand Army of Napoleon. Humbert, in that year of 1812, was avoiding Napoleon's various domains because of opinions he'd rashly expressed after the Little Emperor had relieved him of command. Some said this was because Humbert's army had ignominiously failed to re-conquer the island of Saint-Domingue from rebelling slaves. But January's mother—a clearinghouse for gossip concerning both the white and the free colored communities in New Orleans—was of the opinion that Humbert's affair with Napoleon's sister had something to do with it.

"Though I don't see why Napoleon should cut up stiff over Humbert," Livia Janvier had added, pinning an aigrette of diamonds to the confection of rose-colored silk and plumes that covered her hair. She studied the result critically in the mirror. "The woman's slept with his entire general staff, most of his marshals, and is now working her way down through the colonels. I can't imagine how she keeps their names straight when she encounters them at military reviews."

She propped an elbow on the dressing-table and held up her hand peremptorily for her maid, who'd been gently dusting talcum powder into the fingers of a pair of long white kid gloves. Livia Janvier didn't even glance at the maid as the young woman set to work easing and moulding the soft, close-fitting leather over her mistress' knuckles and palm. When January's mother was dressing to meet her protector—the man who had bought her and her two small children from slavery eleven years previously—she displayed a meticulous patience, a concentration like an artist's that January found fascinating to watch. "Don't you stay out late after you get done playing tonight, p'tit," she added. "And make sure that M'sieu Davis pays you. Promises are cheap."

It went without saying that January's mother, slender as a bronze lily at the age of thirty-six, would not give her son so much as a nod when they separately reached the Marine Hotel. January would be present at General Humbert's birthday dinner strictly as a hired musician, a profession he'd worked at since the age of sixteen concurrent with such medical studies as were available to a young free man of color in that time and place. St.-Denis Janvier, his mother's protector, was one of the guests, a select gang of the wealthier businessmen of the town assembled to honor the elderly war-horse. Most of them would be accompanied by their mistresses. It was not the sort of party to which one brought one's wife.

And Livia Janvier—she'd taken her protector's name, as many free colored plaçées did—wasn't the sort of woman who'd admit to being the mother of one of the musicians. This would have been true even if her son hadn't been all of nineteen years old, six feet three inches tall, and very obviously the offspring of an African rather than a white man. As the guests came into the hotel's dining-room that night, to the bright strains of a Mozart overture, it was St.-Denis Janvier, and not Livia, who caught January's eye and smiled.

January knew most of the other guests by sight. In 1812, New Orleans wasn't that big a town. The women present were mostly friends, or enemies, of his mother. These ladies of the free colored demimonde were by and large plaçées—*placed*—with a single pro-tector, though one lady he recognized as a highly-paid courtesan. About half the men were businessmen and planters: he noted the tall, powerful form of Jean Blanque the banker, whose name graced nearly every financial transaction in the town and whose young and beautiful wife (not present) was the daughter of Barthelmy de McCarty, brother of the wealthiest planter in the district. De Mc-Carty came in just behind Blanque, joking with his brother Jean Baptiste. Both of their mistresses, exquisitely-gowned women of color, wore silk tignons—headscarves—that were plumed and jew-eled mockeries of the law that forbade women of African ancestry, slave or free, to go about in public with uncovered hair.

Bernard Marigny was there, a lively little French Creole planter notorious for his gambling and his duels. As he came in he was laughing over something with a tall, black-clad gentleman whom January recognized as Jean Lafitte.

If you wanted anything in New Orleans, duty-free or difficult to obtain, you could probably get it through Jean Lafitte. Four years previously, when it became illegal to import slaves into United States Territory, Lafitte had surfaced, lounging around the black-smith shop he and his brother owned on Rue Bourbon or drinking with businessmen and planters in the Café Tremoulet. Somehow, the handsome young Gascon always had a slave or two to sell. Of course these slaves were always warranted born in American terri-tory. Of course the sales were private, between gentlemen, nothing on the open market. Lafitte sold brandies, too, and fine French silks. . . . In fact, anything you might want.

And cheaply, as if United States customs duties did not exist.

Though Lafitte didn't have a mistress with him, he didn't arrive at the birthday dinner alone. In addition to Marigny—who was friends with everyone in town except his own wife—Lafitte entered with his usual coterie of "friends": a planter named Huette, who had a place on Bayou St. John where boats could be landed that came off the lake; the fair-haired Pierre Lafitte, his newest mistress on his arm; a dark little man named Laporte who kept the books for the Lafitte brothers; and Jean Baptiste Sauvinet, one of the most prominent bankers of the town. Lafitte moved in the highest circles of French Creole society, among the men, at least.

There were others, less respectable, whom January had seen only at a distance in the cafés and the market. The fierce and jovial sea-captain Dominic Youx. Cut-Nose Chighizola, whose face was a mass of scars—at the moment he was explaining in voluminous Italian-accented French to a planter named St. Geme how he'd lost his nose in battle against the Spanish. The dark and sinister Captain Beluche, of the "Bolivian" privateer vessel *Spy*. Vincente Gambi, another Italian, strode along on the outskirts of the group, glancing at the silverware and the cut-crystal pitchers on the tables as if calculating their worth. He had, January noticed, what looked like a couple of fresh cuts on his face, superficial but adding to his appearance of coarse menace.

The plaçées of these "friends" drifted behind them, gowned in silks and chattering among themselves. They were less fashionable, more sumptuous, and far more heavily jeweled than their town counterparts. Down on Grand Terre, where Lafitte had his headquarters these days, the free colored ladies lived with their men openly, as wives, instead of keeping separate establishments as the town plaçées did. January noticed that his mother and her friends kept their distance from them, not in open enmity, but with a cool politeness that spoke volumes for what was going to be said about their dress, speech, and taste in ornamentation over chicory-laced coffee the following morning.

Hesione LeGros was one of these Grand Terre ladies.

January noticed her because she was one of the youngest, probably his own age, and also one of the darkest. Among the free colored community, as among the whites, dark skin and African features were not admired. January had grown up with the knowledge that his own huge size and African blackness were a reminder of the slave father whose name his mother never spoke, and this knowledge was ground in upon him every time any stranger, white or colored, heard the delicate strength of his piano-playing and looked astonished.

From the first time he'd played a recital, he'd been aware that they would not have looked so surprised if he were fair-skinned or white.

Most of the plaçées were quadroon or octoroon, complexions shaded anywhere from soft matte walnut to the hue of very old ivory. A few, like his mother, were mulatto, of African mothers and white fathers. The wealthiest businessmen of the town favored the lightest-skinned women: fairness itself was a commodity. Hesione—though January didn't learn her name until years later—was richly dark. Unlike most of the others she pointed up undeniably African features by wearing a gold silk gown so vibrant it bordered on rust, a color no white woman would have dared to put on. A necklace of topaz and citrine ringed her throat like a collar of fire, and plumes dyed gold and black blossomed above her tignon. As January played—Mozart rondos and snippets of Rossini, light-handed on the five-octave Erard in the corner of the Marine Hotel's dining-room—he looked out over the jostle of heads and backs and saw that nodding explosion of sable and flame, like the single oak on a little island in a marsh.

The tables were set out in the old-fashioned French manner, sparkling with the hotel's very fine silver and Limoges-ware dishes. Oysters in lemon, gumbo of shrimp, Italian pâtés and vol-au-vents; artichokes and turkey-poults and turtle roasted *en croute.* As the hotel servants went around with the wine—which the new owner, Mr. Davis, bought from Lafitte at a substantial discount—the conversation grew louder. The bankers speculated as to what full statehood in the United States was going to mean now to Louisiana and freely slandered the new Governor Claiborne and all his works. The planters cursed what the war between the Allies and France was doing to sugar prices. January heard for the first time about the sinking—by pirates—of the American brig *Independence,* a subject brought up by a pink-faced British planter named Trulove and hushed at once by Jean Blanque: "The less said of that," the banker murmured with a glance toward the table of Lafitte and his cronies, "the better for all it will be." News had reached New Orleans only that day of the *Independence*'s destruction, brought by a man named Williams, the sole survivor of the massacre.

"What I want to know, is," persisted Trulove, who like everyone else in the room was fairly drunk, "what was a dashed Massachusetts merchantman carrying from Africa to Cuba in the first place, eh? Dashed Americans complain about Lafitte and his men smuggling slaves in through the Barataria marshes, and what are *they* buying along the coast of Africa, eh? Bananas? Tell me that!"

"I shall tell you nothing of the kind," replied Blanque gently, laying a restraining hand on the young Englishman's arm. He hadn't anything to worry about, really, for Lafitte and his men were roaring with laughter over Dominic Youx's tale of the Bishop of Cartagena and a shipload of whores from Port-au-Prince. January let his hands float from song to song, alternating popular overtures and opera-tunes with the quadrilles and cotillions that he'd play when hired by the wealthy for balls. Though he was studying medicine with a surgeon named Gomez, he had always loved music, and St.-Denis Janvier had paid for him to be taught by one of the best instructors in town. That instructor, an émigré Austrian named Kovald, was only lately dead. January played the antiquated airs of Pachelbel and Purcell that the grim old musician had loved, sadness in his heart that his teacher had not lived to return to Vienna. Had not lived to see Napoleon defeated and cast out, as he must, January believed, one day be.

With the after-dinner cognac came the cigars, the ribald laughter, the sly jests. In short order there would be trouble. For twenty-two years France had been torn by violence, Europe subjected to bloodletting and fire. There were men in the room whose fathers had been beheaded in the name of the French Republic, whose family fortunes were destroyed by the Revolution and by the Emperor who had climbed to power in the wake of chaos. Any minute now, he thought, someone was going to say *regicide* or *Corsican upstart*— or accuse someone of having the manners of an American. . . . January knew the signs.

"Now that Bolívar's in in the south, the whole Spanish empire's going to crumble," prophesied Joffrey Duquille. He was a big, robust, saturnine planter, with the obligatory reputation as a womanizer and a duelist. "A man can get letters of marque in Cartagena, and go after anything flying the Spanish flag. . . ."

"Lafitte should have known better than to go after an American ship, slaver or no slaver. . . ."

The air condensed to a golden roux of wine and food and pomade; the candles in the wall-sconces burned low, and the crystal-hung chandeliers dripped wax onto the tablecloths. The great dining-room seemed stuffy and close. A servant opened the long windows that looked down onto Rue Chartres and January slid into "Childgrove," a country-dance tune that could be endlessly embroidered. His mother, at Blanque's table with St.-Denis Janvier, flipped open her sandalwood fan and looked down her nose as Cut-Nose Chighizola's mistress took the scar-faced privateer's pipe from his mouth and blew a cloud of smoke herself. Chighizola gestured extravagantly, and shouted to Hesione LeGros how he'd lost his nose escaping from an Algerian dungeon. . . .

Talk pattered on all sides, like summer rain.

"Shut up, you fool, he'd never have done something that damn-fool stupid! Sink an American ship? He knows what side the bread's buttered on. . . ."

"It's all Spanish prizes of war, after all . . ."

". . . a giant black, six, seven feet tall and as wide as a door, coming down upon me with a battle-ax . . ."

". . . pegged the interest at ten percent, plus an additional two percent the first two years. . . ."

The voices were getting louder. The Italian captain, Gambi, announced into a momentary hush, "Privateer this and privateer that, bah! Like there was any disgrace in being a pirate! Pirate is what I am and I don't care who knows it! Nobody tells me who I'll sink and who I'll spare!"

"I hear there's a new cargo come in down at Big Temple. . . ." St. Geme's voice determinedly overrode Gambi's.

"Hardly pays to go down there anymore," remarked de McCarty with a laugh, "now that Lafitte's got a shop on Royal Street as well."

"Still, you get the best, going down there, or to Grand Terre. Used to be you'd have to deal with this smuggler or that smuggler, and run all over town trying to get the best deal. I will say for Lafitte, he organized them all under one leader. . . ."

"Like the American Washington?"

"A toast." Blanque got to his feet, wineglass lifted so that the topaz liquid caught the molten hundredfold amber of the candle-light. January ruffled a little fanfare borrowed from Rossini, then stilled his hands on the keys. Just as well, he thought. The piano was going out of tune anyway. These little square ones did that in the damp of New Orleans. "To our guest of honor."

In his big chair at the head table, General Humbert half-rose, creaking a little in his blue uniform, and inclined his graying head.

"A man whose victories in the field put such amateurs as this American Washington to shame. A man who truly knows the face of war; who has carried the war against England onto their own conquered soil in blood-soaked Ireland; whose boldness in the attack at Landau is legendary; whose courage and intrepidity were key elements in the pacification of uprisings in the Vendée. A true soldier, a true warrior, whose vocation has been the sword and whose duties he has always acquitted with honor and dignity. . . ."

Perhaps because he was taller than any man present—or maybe only because some of the banqueters had shifted their chairs a little—January could watch the General's face in the candle-light as Blanque spoke. And from a drunkard's fatuous smile, he watched the man's expression change.

He's drunk himself sad, January thought. *Or drunk himself philosophical, which is worse. . . .*

". . . carried the banner of the Republic against all odds, caring nothing for his own safety; caring nothing for the politics and the quibblings of politicians. . . ."

Slowly, Humbert surveyed the room, and with a flash of insight January guessed what he saw. In New Orleans, this was the top level of society. Perhaps not the highest born, but the wealthiest, the men who moved events in the town. But even as young as he was, he'd seen how the Frenchmen of France regarded their Creole French cousins, when they came to balls. He was familiar with that polite expression that said, *This is all very well for the New World, but in PARIS . . .*

He could almost see General Humbert asking himself, *Who are these people? Is this what I have come down to?* In Paris, thought January, this graying old lion would have been entertained by his brothers of the regiment, most of whom, despite the Revolution, had some trickle of noble blood in their veins. Not by bankers who financed shady deals in Indian land and smuggled slaves. Certainly not by a raffish gang of privateers who ran in goods for illicit sale.

"Let those who wish to, speak of armies and of supply-lines!" Blanque, clearly a cognac or two beyond the frontier of careful thought, had fallen under the spell of his own oratory. "It is personal courage, personal command, which broke the rabble in the Vendée. It was the sheer bravery, the audacity, of the commander, which delivered victory to the Republic's banners at Landau—"

"Enough!" With a crash the armchair at the head table was flung back. Humbert stood swaying on his feet, face crimson, eyes blazing in the candles' liquid glow. "Enough of this praise! Your words remind me of what I was—of what I am. And I will not remain here as an associate of outlaws and pirates!"

Captain Beluche, also an alumnus of Napoleon's army, lurched to his feet. "Pirates, is it?"

"Pirates!" bellowed Humbert, who had never liked Beluche. "Call yourselves what you will, and fly what flag you find it convenient to buy, what are you but thieves who take the goods of other men and sell them as your own? You, who only yesterday sent an American ship to the bottom without a thought, without a blink— yes, and paraded yourselves the next day in full view of the town, like whores, like dogs!" His hand smote the table with a noise like a gunshot, making all the tableware jump. "I spit upon such men as you!"

This was the point at which January went behind the piano. Even Captain Gambi, who generally didn't care who called him a pirate, was on his feet with a table-knife in his hand, screaming "Pig of a Frenchman!" and Beluche started straight over the table that separated him from Humbert, cutlass drawn—God knew where he'd had it during dinner—and nearly foaming at the mouth with rage and alcohol. Men yelled something about the *Independence;* women screamed. Hesione LeGros, quicker-thinking than most, plunged behind the piano, all her black-and-gold plumes askew, cursing at whichever of the several captains was her protector at the moment, and pulling from her tignon a very long and very businesslike stiletto. Her face was calm, her rosebud mouth almost smiling—January noticed she had a small mole in one corner, like a beauty-patch. The other Grand Terre girls clumped like scared sheep in the corner and shrieked like parrots in a storm, and January's mother, a chunk of sugar halfway to her coffee-cup, regarded the whole eruption with an expression of disapproval and disgust and didn't stir from her chair.

As it happened, Livia was the only person in the room who had an accurate estimate of Jean Lafitte's presence of mind and power over his men. The smuggler-boss was on his feet—without toppling his chair—and across the dining-room in three long strides, outstripping even Captain Beluche, who had a few yards' lead on him. Reaching Humbert's side, Lafitte held up his hand—with no appearance of hurry, or of fear. It was how January remembered him best, in later years: a tall, black-haired man in a black long-tailed coat, hand upraised, the other hand resting gently on the furious old general's shoulder. As if to say to both Humbert and the enraged and thoroughly inebriated corsairs, *Let's all be quiet and think for a moment before this goes too far.*

Humbert turned to him and burst into tears, laying his head on Lafitte's shoulder.

And as gently as if he had been the old man's son, Jean Lafitte led General Humbert from the room.

Slightly more than two years later, when the British attempted to seize and hold New Orleans as part of their long struggle against Napoleon, Jean Lafitte—rather to everyone's surprise—turned down a cash offer from the British General Pakenham and volunteered his services to the American forces under General Jackson instead. Benjamin January, twenty-one by then and as well trained a surgeon as was possible for a young man of color to be in New Orleans, fought in the free colored militia in the ensuing battle. Though the Americans won—and the British ceased boarding and seizing the crews of American vessels—it was still several years before either he or St.-Denis Janvier deemed it safe for him to risk a sea journey to France to continue his medical studies.

He was in France for sixteen years. For the first six of those years he studied medicine, and worked as a junior surgeon, at the Hôtel Dieu. St.-Denis Janvier died in 1822, but the little money he left his plaçée's son would not stretch to cover the expenses of buying a practice. Moreover, it was quite clear to January by then that even in the land of Liberté, Egalité, and Fraternité, no white man was going to hire a black surgeon to cut him open if he could find a man of his own color to do it instead. January tried not to be troubled by this, accepting it as he'd accepted the fact that in his former home he'd had to step off the banquette to let white men pass. . . .

And then he'd met Ayasha. And understood that if he wanted to marry this very young and very competent Berber dressmaker—at eighteen she had her own shop, her own small clientele, and looked like a desert witch inexplicably trying to pass herself off as a Parisian artisan—he'd need money.

That was when, and why, he went back to music.

For ten years he played for the Opéra, for the balls and parties of the restored nobility who'd returned to Paris in the wake of Louis XVIII and of the wealthy who'd founded their fortunes on the wreck of Napoleon's empire. For ten years he and Ayasha lived in happiness in a little flat on the Rue de l'Aube near the river. In the newspapers he followed the careers of Lafitte, and Humbert, and those privateer captains who'd once had their fortified camp on Grand Terre. His account of General Humbert's birthday dinner became an after-dinner tale for his musician friends, when Humbert became Commodore of the Navy of Mexico, or when word got out concerning Dominic Youx's participation in the plot to rescue Napoleon from St. Helena and spirit him away to live out his days in a comfortable town house in New Orleans.

The American Navy ran Jean Lafitte out of his new headquarters on the Texas coast in 1821. Rumors swirled about what became of him, but no one knew for sure. René Beluche became the Commodore of the new nation of Venezuela. Vincente Gambi, and Antonino Angelo, and Lafitte's captains met their fates variously at the hands of the American Navy or the British campaign against pirates and slave-smugglers. Some simply encountered those deaths that awaited so many white men in Louisiana: yellow fever, malaria, typhus.

In 1832 the Indian cholera reached Paris.

Ayasha died.

January returned to New Orleans—to the town he had hoped never to live in again. To the only family he knew.

To a city he had left while it was still an outpost of France in the New World. But he found, on his return, that the city had been inundated in his absence with Americans intent on making a profit from slavery, from sugar, from cotton, and from everything else they could lay their hands on. Much of the city was now the province of upriver Kentuckians whose rapaciousness made Lafitte and his cronies look modest and whose manners made even such hard-bitten souls as Cut-Nose Chighizola appear refined.

For a few years January lived in the garçonnière behind his mother's house, the small separate chamber traditionally given to the growing son of the household. His mother had married a free carpenter of color upon St.-Denis Janvier's death, and was now a respectable widow. January made new friends, and renewed his ties with old. He played at quadroon balls and at the Opera, and at the parties of Americans, free colored, and Creole French alike; he found refuge in the familiar joys of music from the almost unbearable pain of loss in his heart.

He met a young schoolmistress named Rose Vitrac, Ayasha's opposite in nearly every way: erudite, gawky, bespectacled, and so heart-scarred and frightened of men that it was nearly a year before she could endure the touch of his hand without pulling away.

He learned, a little to his surprise, that it was possible to love passionately without lessening for a moment the ache of the love that had gone before.

And in all those years since 1812 he never so much as remembered Hesione LeGros' face, until one day in the summer of 1835, when he walked into a shack near the back of town and saw her dead body, with her head in a puddle of blood.

TWO

"When you a woman and black—not to mention dirt poor, God forbid"—the mocking sparkle in Olympe Corbier's dark eyes was like the flash of dragonflies over a bitter lake—"there ain't a man in this town'll smirch his boots crossin' the street to save your life. What makes you think anybody'd come out here after she's already dead?"

Kneeling on the floor beside the body, January looked up at his sister, who had knocked at the door of his lodgings an hour after sun-up, asking him to come with her here. He knew she was right.

Olympe was his full sister, by that African field-hand his mother never spoke about. When at sixteen she'd run away to join the voodoos, her mother hadn't even troubled to look for her. Her work as healer and midwife among the poorer artisans, laborers, and freedmen of the town had given her scant respect for the whites who made the city's laws.

Still it angered him that the City Guards hadn't troubled to send an officer out to this straggle of shanties, shelters, and one- and two-room cottages huddled on the fringe of the still-more-unsavory district of town universally known as the Swamp. It wasn't more than half a mile from the turning-basin of the canal that connected New Orleans with the lake, and probably less than a mile from the river itself. Although one of the liveliest and wealthiest cities in the United States lay so close, oaks and cypress still grew among the wretched dwellings here; reeds and marsh-grass stood thick just outside the door.

It wasn't nine in the morning and the heat was like a hammer. Flies crept thick over every splash and puddle of the blood-trail that started by the shack's upstream wall and ended under the body. The cloud of insects overhead, up under the shack's low roof, made a dull droning, inescapable as the stink of sewage or the sticky creep of sweat behind January's shirt-collar.

Heat, stink, flies. Summer in New Orleans.

"I heard how you not supposed to move somebody who been killed," said one of the neighbors, peering in around Olympe's slim, tall form. A square young man, he wore the numbered tin badge of a slave whose master let him "sleep out"—find his own room and board in exchange for a percentage of what he could earn as a laborer. At this time of year, there was little work to be had, even on the levee or the docks. "How you supposed to not touch nuthin' till the Guards had a look." His ungrammatical French was the fluidly sloppy get-along speech of an Anglophone who has made his home among French-speakers for a few months, not the half-African patois of the slave quarters. Born in the eastern states, January guessed automatically, and sold down the river . . .

"I sent Suzie right away downtown to the Cabildo." The young man nodded back at a girl of sixteen or so who crowded up behind him. "I did look around, see if I could find some kerosene or pepper or somethin' to keep the ants from comin' in. But they's all over the place already. Hessy been dead awhile. Else I wouldn't a' left her just lay on the floor."

"What'd they say at the Cabildo?" January tried to move the arm of the woman who lay sprawled in the gummy pool of drying gore a few feet from the front door of the shack. The muscles were hard as wood. Most of the blood had soaked into the dirt floor, and the smaller patches were already dry. The smell was indescribable, early decay mingling with the metallic sharpness of blood and the reek of piss and the spit tobacco with which the floor was liberally daubed. Ants streamed in inch-thick black ribbons from three or four directions, under the shack's ill-fitting board walls. Unlike the patient flies they went about their business, as ants do, unimpressed by humankind.

"That they send somebody by'n'by." The girl spoke Creole French, slurred and sloppy, the kind January's mother and January's schoolmasters had beaten out of him by the time he was nine. She seemed in awe of him, maybe because he wore boots in the summertime and spoke with authority. Maybe because he was Olympia Snakebones' brother.

"They'll send along the Coroner." Olympe's sweet, deep alto was like bronze and gravel. "He'll come an' he'll say, *Yep, she dead all right*. Takes a white man to figure that one out."

There was a chuckle among the neighbors clustered around the front door or peering in the back, men and women who made this shabby corner of the town their home out of poverty or stubbornness or unwillingness to be too closely scrutinized by the minions of the country's various laws. January turned the corpse over, and it came all of a piece, like a plank. She must have been dead some hours before midnight. She'd been stabbed three or four times in the chest, and once in the side. Her throat had been cut, probably at the point of death or just afterward, when she'd quit fighting. There were cuts on her palms and fingers as well.

The whole front of her faded, twice-turned, ill-fitting charity-bag dress was sheeted with blood, and moving with ants.

The half of her face that had lain in the drying blood of the dirt floor was unrecognizable. The other half, with all its wrinkles smoothed away by death, touched his memory: the full pouting lips, the neat, small upturned nose. The tiny mole, like an old-fashioned beauty-patch, just below the corner of the mouth.

The mole touched a memory in his mind.

He'd seen her, January knew, around the levee. In almost three years back in New Orleans, he'd seen just about everyone in town at least once or twice, as he'd crossed beneath the shade of the plane-trees on the Place d'Armes, or walked along the boisterous chaos of the river-front among the cotton-bales and hogsheads of sugar and molasses. He'd noticed her because she wrapped her tignon like an island woman, not in the usual New Orleans style. The faded old

Turkey red dress she wore was the same every time. Sometimes she'd be sitting under the plane-trees, braiding little animals of straw or folded tin, giving them to passers-by. Other times, drunk, she'd sit cross-legged on packing-boxes and call out to the deck-hands and stevedores in a sing-song rasp. Once January had walked past her and she'd said, in a perfectly conversational tone, "I let you fuck me in the ass if you buys me a bottle."

"What was her name?" he asked now.

"Hessy," answered Suzie. "Hessy LeGros—Hesione. An' she wasn't so bad, you know, 'cept when she was real drunk. She tore up Richie here pretty bad last month when she got the horrors. . . ." She nodded to her young man, who did indeed have a healing cut on his right hand. "Who'd a' done this?"

Who indeed?

"Could you good people leave us for a few minutes, Olympe and me?" He sat back on his heels and straightened his back, looked around at the neighbors. "I want to take a better look at her, see if the bastard did more than kill her."

There was a murmur and they backed away, so that Olympe could close the rickety doors. Moving carefully—he could already see the dirt floor was scuffed all over with tracks around the body—January turned up the tattered skirts. It was difficult to tell because of the fluids and matter leaking out of the corpse, but he didn't think the woman had been raped, either before or after death. Her bodice waist hadn't been torn open, only ripped on one shoulder, as if she'd thrashed away from an attacker's grip.

Dribbles of tobacco-spittle, old and new, stained the front of her dress.

He got to his feet, and wiped his hands on a bandanna handkerchief from his pocket. "What do you know about her?" he asked his sister. Voodoos could generally be counted on to know whatever there was to be known.

Olympe shrugged. "That she was a drunkard; that she was poor; that she didn't deserve to live this way. Or to die this way." In the morning heat, sweat already blotched his sister's faded calico bodice. "She was a free woman. No family that I know of. She claimed she used to be Jean Lafitte's mistress, but I don't think that was true."

"No," agreed January, suddenly realizing where he'd seen that neat little mole before. "But she was mistress to one of his captains." And as he moved cautiously around the room examining the criss-crossed tracks, and the contents of the room's single shelf, he recounted the events of General Humbert's birthday dinner, twenty-three years ago.

"Here's her visitor, look," he said, crouching to show Olympe the print of a wide, square-toed boot. A notch had been scored in the heel, as if the wearer had trodden on something sharp. The tracks led from the rear door—which looked out into the woods—to the chair beside the bed, near a packing-box on which a burning candle had been set. The candle stump remained, in a messy dribble of pale brown "winding-sheets," themselves already sagging with the heat.

Scratches in the dirt floor marked where the chair had been knocked over and later set back on its legs. Deep heel-gouges showed where the visitor had sprung, strode, struggled among the vaguer scuffings of Hesione's bare feet, all covered and mucked over by the first great splash of blood. A yellow-and-green tignon lay trampled there, too.

Blood and tracks crossed the floor to the body.

The man's tracks continued. Beside the bed, which was planks on a frame nailed to two walls and a bedpost in the corner—the moss mattress was rucked a little, but hadn't been turned or had the lumps shaken out of it in months and it crawled with bedbugs and fleas. Along the wall, where a shelf held three dirty and louse-ridden tignons, an assortment of unwashed gourd dishes, four braided-straw cats and horses, a lot of whiskey-bottles and a nearly-empty sack of coffee-beans. Beans scattered the shelf and the table beneath it, which also bore a dirty cup and bowl, and a basket of strawberries creeping with flies. A small handful of beans scattered the floor immediately underneath. When January crouched beside them he observed that they were shiny, without dust.

In the dirt of the floor beside the beans, two small round blobs of white candle-wax gleamed, also dustless. Under the table, under the bed, around the scraped slots near the table that marked the chair's usual place and all throughout the weeds that poked in under the shed's walls, the unclean debris of a hundred frugal meals de-cayed: bread-crumbs, fruit-cores and pips, the knuckle-bones of sheep and pigs, picked clean by ants. These were mingled with wads and stains of chewed tobacco of varying ages, though a considerably larger number of these—fresh—splotched the dirt floor around where the murderer had sat in the chair by the back wall.

"He searched the place," said January.

Olympe looked around at the jumbled bedding, the neglected dishes, the whiskey-bottles gleaming in the weeds, and gave a mirth-less chuckle. "Like you can tell?"

"Oh, yes," said January. "You can follow his tracks, for one thing. Look, he carried a candle, a wax one, not the tallow one on the box there, so he must have looked around after she was dead. Were the shutters open or closed when she was found?"

Olympe frowned, and glanced at the single window. "They was open when I got here." They were open now, and between two cy-presses another shack could be seen, a ramshackle cottage pieced to-gether from bits of old flatboats, with chickens scratching around its rear door.

January looked back at Hesione LeGros' body. At her dirty dress and dirtier gray hair, and the bare feet whose toenails had grown out into curving horny claws. He recalled the parure of topazes she'd worn with that gaudy red-gold dress: that gorgeous necklace, ear-rings, bracelets the size of slave manacles. The glint of the stiletto in her hand, and the smile on her lips. *I'm gonna shoot that man of mine for this. . . .*

The ground here was low, close by the cypress swamp that lay all along the back edge of town. In the winter it would be freezing cold, and there was neither stove nor hearth. A ragged mosquito-bar hung over the bed, torn and looped carelessly back. By the number of bites on Hesione's face and neck it couldn't have done her much good. But then, she was probably drunk most nights, by the time she slept.

He let his breath go in a sigh. He hadn't recognized her when he'd seen her on the levee, inebriated and foul-mouthed and already grown old. Hadn't connected her with that bright-eyed girl in the defiantly gaudy dress.

Life battered the poor.

Olympe came back to his side. "What was he lookin' for? She didn't own but the clothes she wore."

"Maybe some of her neighbors can tell us."

He started to cross toward the door, but his sister stepped in front of him: "You ain't just gonna leave her lay?"

The flies had settled again. The body, which he'd returned to its original position face-down, looked as if it had been covered with a shroud of black lace, one that moved and glittered in the morning light.

"Whoever the Guards send to look at the place, he'll want to see it as it was when she was found." Even as the words came out of his mouth he felt like a simpleton, and Olympe's eyes jeered at him, at his trust in the white man's laws. Two years his junior, she had known from earliest childhood, perhaps even before he had, that their mother had no great regard for her slave husband's African-featured children, lavishing her care instead on their lovely lace-trimmed half-sister by St.-Denis Janvier. Now she didn't even speak, only looked at him with that combination of incredulity and scorn.

"I'll go down to the Cabildo," he said, "and see they send someone."

"Oh, I'd go along to watch *that,* brother," retorted Olympe. "Only I got the ironin' yet to do this morning."

Still, she settled herself on the edge of the filthy bed to wait for him as he went out into the yard.

Summers, New Orleans slowed, like a stagnant river sinking in the heat. Sugar harvested in November, a desperate race against frost. In December, slaves dragged the long, coarse sacks through the cotton-fields before the bitter-cold first light dawned and picked the sharp, dry boles with chilblained fingers that bled. First frost brought the businessmen back to New Orleans from their country places in Milneburgh or Mandeville by the lake, brought the steamboats downriver in droves with the winter rise. Flatboats came in from Ohio and Kentucky, loaded with pumpkins and pigs and corn and tobacco-spitting Kaintuck louts who gawked at everything they saw. Harvest and business and trade and sales, ships coming in from the Gulf, Christmas and Carnival and Mardi Gras . . .

Summers, everything stopped. The wealthy families—the Destrehans and de McCartys, the Bringiers and Livaudaises—fled the gluey heat that settled on the town, fled the clouds of mosquitoes that hummed over every gutter and puddle and the riotous proliferation of gnats and fleas and immense brown palmetto-bugs. Fled the reek of the gutters and the swollen carcasses of dogs, rats, horses rotting for days in the mud. Many years, they fled worse things as well, yellow fever some years, sometimes cholera, too.

The only people left in town were the poor and the relatively poor. Little business was done. The markets were quiet, the teeming levees nearly still. Even the gambling-parlors were a little subdued.

So nobody in Hesione LeGros' neighborhood was in any tearing hurry to get anywhere.

They waited for January in the shade of the rickety gallery of the cottage visible from Hesione's window: Suzie and Richie sitting side by side on the steps, another couple a few years older—the woman with a baby at breast—and two or three single men lounging in the cypress-tree's shade. January guessed that some were runaways, picking up a few cents a day at whatever inconspicuous jobs they could find and sneaking out to the plantations from which they'd escaped to visit their friends and families when they could. There were many such, in New Orleans.

"Who found her?" he asked.

Richie raised his hand tentatively, a little uncertain if that was the question that had been asked, and January inquired in English, "When was that?"

"Just after sun-up, sir." The young man seemed relieved to be able to reply in his native tongue. "I was on my way down to the levee to see could I get loadin' work, an' I saw five or six dogs, diggin' at the wall of the shack. Two of 'em was Doc Furness' dogs from the Swamp, but the rest was wild ones, that live in the woods. You don't usually see 'em around folks' houses by daylight. It didn't look right to me."

No, thought January. And the dogs would smell carrion even above the general fetor of privies and garbage and back-yard pigs that hung over the neighborhood in the heat.

"Was the shutters open or closed?"

Richie looked a little startled at the question, but shut his eyes a moment to picture it, then answered, "Closed, sir. I opened 'em up, to see."

"They's open when she come home last night," added the other man on the porch, taller and stringier than Richie and without the tin slave-badge. He spoke French, but January had seen his eyes, knew he'd followed the discussion in English. "I remember thinkin' how the place would be just roarin' with mosquitoes inside."

"But you didn't see a light burning?"

The tall man shook his head. "I walked back with Hessy from town, round about full-dark. She'd been down the market, pickin' up what she could from the market-women that was closin' up. She had a couple baskets of berries, just gone off a little an' mushy. She asked me if Titine here would like some." And he patted the slim sloped shoulder of the woman with the baby on the gallery's single broken-down chair at his side. "She give 'em to me just there where the path splits."

He pointed toward the weedy track that led from the end of Perdidio Street. The ramshackle saloons and whorehouses of the Swamp, which lay farther off in that direction, looked even dirtier and somehow more sinister under the brute glare of the late-July sun. Their stillness was deceptive, like a corpse teeming inside with foul activity.

"I hadn't made much on the levee—things is so slow—but I give her a couple bits for 'em. I know she didn't have nuthin', an' ol' Mulm that owns the Nantucket Saloon pays her for cleanin' up there with liquor instead of money. I had to just about twist her arm to take it."

"It's funny," said the woman Titine, with a shy gap-toothed grin. "Some days she'd come here beggin' an' cryin' to me an' Gali, 'cause she needed money for rum—that's when she was too drunk even to work for Mulm. An' last month, like Suzie said, she cut Richie up bad when she was off her head. Other days she'd give you whatever she had in her pockets."

"And she went on into her house?"

The man Gali nodded.

"Did you see any light burning later? Any of you?" January looked around at the little group on the gallery.

"I had the shutters up already," said Suzie, and nodded back into the cottage.

"Hot nights like these been," explained Richie, reaching over to rub Suzie's knee, "Suzie shuts up the house the minute the sun goes down, 'cause of the mosquitoes. Seems like no matter what M'am Snakebones give her, lemon or camphor or juju oil, they still come after her like buzzards on a dead cow. She just so miserable these nights I want to weep for her, and they don't bite me at all."

"But Suzie an' me, we was finishin' up the cookin' an' puttin' up the chickens for maybe an hour before that." Titine hoisted her tiny daughter, naked and plump as a little loaf of brown bread, onto her shoulder, and stroked her back. Baskets dangled from every rafter-end along the cottage roof, the African way of cooping chickens away from the depredations of foxes and rats. "We'd a' seen if somebody came into Hessy's house 'fore then."

"But not after you went in and put up the shutters?"

"No, sir."

"Anyone else around?"

Suzie and Titine looked at each other for a moment, then shook their heads. "No, sir."

Had Hesione let her killer in? Or had he come in and waited for her in the dark? In either case, a candle had been lit, and had been let burn for fifteen or twenty minutes. . . . January didn't even consciously think, *It had to have been last night.* No tallow drippings would have remained standing upright after a day as hot as yesterday had been. The same way he didn't consciously think, *I'll bet the man was American,* after seeing the extra tobacco around where the chair had been.

She hadn't dropped the berries on the floor in surprise, upon entering. Yet neither had she carried them over to the chair, or dropped stems or leaves in eating any.

"You hear anything later in the night?"

The two men looked at each other, self-conscious. Then tall, thin Gali gave an embarrassed chuckle. "This gonna sound stupid, an' I'm purely sorry for it, because if either of us had thought . . . See, we both heard a woman scream, Titine an' me. I thought it was Richie takin' out his mad for somethin' on Suzie, like every man does now an' then. An' he thought it was me hittin' Titine. Or maybe Titine hittin' me."

Titine poked him hard in the ribs. "You'da screamed louder than that, an' more than once, my friend."

He mouthed a kiss at her.

"She cried out only once?"

All four nodded. "Damn, I wish we'd a' gone to look." Richie's bulldog face twisted with distress. "We might a' been able to stop him, or do somethin' to help her."

January thought of the wax-drips of the search, and the deliberate final cut across Hesione's throat. *No, you'd only have bought your own death by your helpfulness.*

He said nothing.

By noon no one had yet come from the City Guards. The air cooled a little, as it does afternoon summers when the black clouds thicken for the daily thunderstorm, and the roar of the cicadas in the trees alters its note. January took the path that skirted the worst of the Swamp's taverns and boarding-houses, circled behind the new cemetery, and followed the unpaved track that became Rue St. Louis on the other side of Rue Rampart. The streets in the old French town were hushed, reeking heat lying like a dead thing between the pastel stucco walls of shuttered-up town houses, cottages, shops. As usual, the companies hired to clean the municipal gutters were behind on their work, and the stench of sewage and offal hung over everything, as if the town were sunk to the roof-line in a cesspool. Bloated with gases, a dog lay dead in the middle of Rue Rampart—swarms of gnats, mosquitoes, and fat black greasy flies hung over the brown standing water in gutters and streets, slashed through by the gunmetal wings of dragonflies.

Even the Place d'Armes before the Cathedral, usually alive with the traffic of the levee and the markets which bounded it, seemed to sleep. The few steamboats at the wharves lay lifeless, like stranded whales. The only animation was that of a man in the stocks before the Cabildo: he wept with frustration and pain as he tried to jerk his head away from a persistent horsefly as big as January's thumb.

The blue shadows of the prison's stone arcade held heat, not coolness, as January crossed through them to the open double doors. Voices echoed in the flagstoned watchroom inside, where the City Guards had their headquarters. A knot of well-dressed gentlemen clustered around the desk of the man January had come to see. All of them babbled and gesticulated in fury.

White men—January recognized one of them as Arnaud Tremouille, Captain of the City Guards, and resigned himself to wait.

"Bertrand Avocet claims he was out searching for a runaway slave at the time of the murder," Tremouille was saying, presumably to Lieutenant Abishag Shaw, whom January could not see beyond the crowd of backs.

"He lies, then!" interrupted another man, tall and stout and sweating profusely in a blue coat and a high scarlet neck-cloth. "His shirt was found in the woods, entirely soaked with blood!"

"Do you say my client is a liar, M'sieu Diacre?" demanded another, whose old-fashioned pigtail was so tightly braided as to curl up over the back of his musty black coat.

"I say that your client had every reason to wish his brother dead and himself in charge of the plantation, M'sieu Rabot."

A squirt of tobacco was spit from behind the desk, missing the sandbox a few feet away: the stone floor all around the box was squiggled with syrup-brown gouts and the whole watchroom smelled like a cuspidor. "Anybody ask where Guifford Avocet's wife was 'long about the time Guifford was kilt?"

The question, framed in Lieutenant Shaw's appalling French, acted upon the well-dressed French Creoles like a fox thrown into a henroost. Tremouille, the two lawyers, and the State Prosecutor Cire all burst into speech at once, while Shaw—visible now that everyone had drawn fastidiously aside from the path of further expectorations—calmly drew a notebook, a carpenter's lead-pencil, a measuring-tape, a small silver-backed mirror, and a pair of long-nosed tweezers from various drawers of his desk and secreted them in the pockets of his out-at-elbows coat. The lawyers and the Captain of the Guards, January noted, all shouted at one another, but none seemed willing to lower himself to shout at a greasy-haired American who looked like he'd come down from Kentucky on a flatboat. Shaw started to rise, bethought himself of something else, dug through another drawer, and pulled out a fresh twist of tobacco.

Then he stood, six feet two inches of stringy scarecrow homeliness, and said, "Maybe we better go have a look at the place? Maestro," he added, surprised, seeing January for the first time. " 'Scuse me just a moment, iff'n you would, sir," he told Tremouille, and slouched over to January.

He smelled like his shirt hadn't been washed in weeks—January didn't know if he owned another besides that faded yellow calico—and his long hair straggled over his shoulders, ditchwater brown where his hat usually covered it, bleached to the color of tow-linen farther down. With his rather cold gray eyes, his linsey-woolsey trousers tucked into high-topped boots, and his skinning-knife sheathed at his belt, Shaw looked like any of the thousands of keelboat owl-hoots who populated the taverns of the Swamp or the whorehouses of Gallatin Street, looking for liquor to drink and trouble to make. January's mother wouldn't have had him in her house.

"What can I help you with, Maestro?"

"A murder." January's voice was dry. "Out in the shanties, past the Swamp. According to the neighbors, it was reported just after sun-up. The victim's friends would like to get her body up off the floor and wash the ants off it so they can bury her. Sir." He knew he was taking advantage of Shaw's tolerance in speaking this way: Shaw was, in fact, one of the few white men in New Orleans who wouldn't hit him a few licks with a cane for being uppity, and he guessed the delay in sending someone to Hesione's shack wasn't the Kentuckian's fault. But he was very angry, at Tremouille, at police in general, at Americans, and at the white French and Spanish Creoles who were becoming more like Americans every day: who looked at free men of color now as Americans did, as so much money loose on the hoof, money that could be going into their own pockets.

Angry that it was so.

And angry at Olympe, for being right.

"God bless it." Shaw spit again, this time with no particular target. "I am sorry, Maestro. You talk to DeMezières about it. . . ."

The lieutenant caught the eye of the burly desk sergeant, pointed significantly to January, and signed that DeMezières should do as January asked.

"I should be back into town tonight," Shaw said, and scratched under the breast of his sorry coat—January could only guess as to whether his concern was fleas or prickly heat. "You still boardin' with M'am Bontemps on Ursulines? I'll be to you then."

As Shaw ambled from the watchroom in the center of the little troop of Creole gentlemen, the backwash of their rising voices swept over January: ". . . attempted to alienate twenty arpents of land . . . quarreled with his brother . . . account-books . . . had a favorite slave of M'sieu Bertrand's sold. . . ."

White men with money, thought January bitterly, returning to the cool ozone-smelling tension of the pre-storm air. He would have bet, had he had any money of his own, that Shaw wouldn't return until well into the following day. Avocet Plantation, if he remembered his mother's gossip correctly, was forty miles away in Plaquemines Parish. Not in the jurisdiction of the New Orleans City Guards at all.

But somebody wanted a policeman more expert than the sheriff of Plaquemines Parish, and that somebody was almost certainly related to somebody on the City Council to whom Tremouille owed a favor. . . .

And Hesione LeGros could lie in her own blood and rot, for all anyone cared.

Only when the white guests were done eating did the slaves get the leftovers, if any.

And with justice, thought January, as with food.

Lightning flickered above the trees in the direction of the lake; thunder distantly growled. In his years in Paris, this was one of the things January had never forgotten about the home he hoped he had left forever, that forerunning cool kiss of warning wind, and the smell of the lightning. His dear friend Rose, he thought, smiling, would check her barometer and make notes about the direction and strength of the wind. . . . He wondered if the man in the stocks breathed a prayer of thanks to the gods of the upper air.

Hesione LeGros, washed of blood and filth, lay on her bed beneath a clean sheet obviously borrowed from somewhere else. Flies clung to the mosquito-bar, swarmed around the bloodied dress where it lay wrapped in a newspaper outside the shack's rear door. The storm-shadowed interior of the little building reeked of the kerosene and pepper that had been sprinkled all around her to keep the ants away. Through the dirty scrim of the netting January saw that she still lay in the position in which he'd seen her on the floor, one arm flung above her head and the other tucked beneath her breast. Someone had combed out her hair. When the rigor wore off, he knew, her neighbors would dress her in a nightgown, probably not her own, and collect what money they could among themselves so that she would not be buried in Potter's Field.

Standing beside the bed—dripping on the scuffed and trampled floor, for the rain had caught him just the other side of the Swamp—January could feel his sister's eyes on him, waiting for him to say something, so that she could lie and tell him the Coroner had come after all. Thunder boomed and the damp wind flowed through the shed, bellying the mosquito-bar. The cypresses and oaks outside made a rushing noise, like water through a millrace. Around the front door, Gali and Titine and their neighbors were drinking ginger-water and trading stories about the dead woman on the bed, the woman who'd glowed with topaz and flame-colored silk and that tower of black-and-golden plumes, who'd died so poor, she'd spent the last evening of her life scrounging leftover vegetables from the market-women . . . and had insisted on dividing them with a neighbor who had a child.

I'm gonna shoot that man of mine for this. . . .

Twenty-three years, thought January, since she'd pressed beside him in the shelter of the piano, a stiletto in her hand and a smile on her lips. Twenty-three years during which he'd become a doctor, and played at the Paris Opéra; in which he'd loved and married, studied and traveled. . . .

"Michie Janvier?"

He opened his eyes, looked down to see the woman Suzie beside him. Her faded dress was soaked from the rain, which was pouring hard now. She must have just come across from her house. In her hands was the apron Hesione had worn, tattered and filthy where it wasn't brown with blood. "I was takin' her clothes to the trash-heap," she explained, "when I found this. It was in her pocket."

She held out her hand. In it were two cut pieces of a silver Spanish reale—bits, they were sometimes called, eighths of a reale sliced up to make change. Pieces of eight.

With them was a whole silver double-reale, a doubloon.

Enough for a poor woman to live on for months.

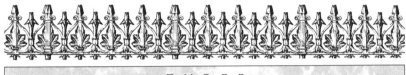

THREE

"And did anyone ever come?" Rose Vitrac glanced back over her shoulder at January, who had loyally accompanied her into the kitchen of the St. Chinian town house on Rue Bourbon to make coffee.

And in fact, with the first cool of evening already drowning the high-walled courtyard in shadow, the kitchen wasn't nearly as infernal as it must have been in the hot part of the day. How old Martine—Veryl St. Chinian's cook—had endured turning out a full-on Creole dinner in this weather, January couldn't imagine. Frequent trips outside to chop vegetables or roll pastry on the table under the pepper-tree, probably. But now that most of the work was done, Martine was prepared to tolerate Rose coming in to make coffee.

The cook was dearly fond of old St. Chinian's nephew Artois, and extended this benevolence to Artois' tutor, even if she didn't think it quite right that the tutor was a woman. If Michie Artois was happy, it was well with her.

January shook his head. "No one came," he said. The last sunlight gilded the roof-slates and fleckered the pepper-tree's feathery leaves. A rust-red dragonfly darted into the kitchen, perched briefly on Rose's tignon, then whirled away.

"It isn't as if they're inundated with work at this time of year."

Rose said nothing. She concentrated instead on the slow turning of the roaster crank, and paused to push up her spectacles and wipe the bridge of her nose with a corner of the apron she usually wore to teach. Most of the dinner was done, and the coals that had been heaped around the iron dutch-ovens on the hearth cleared away to simmer sauces in the line of stew-holes on the other wall. Rose had begged a shovel-full of the still-radiating coals to pile around the coffee-roaster. Martine herself was in the house, helping St. Chinian's valet—the only other servant the reclusive old gentleman possessed—to set the table. The courtyard between house and kitchen was a jungle of banana-plants and resurrection fern, of oleanders decades untrimmed and pavement-bricks so heaved and buckled with water-damage as to be worse than bare earth would have been. The carriageway out to Rue Bourbon rivaled most attics January had seen in both quantity and variety of clutter.

The old man's family, one and all, considered Veryl St. Chinian mad.

"Is that M'sieu Janvier?" called a youth's voice from the flag-stoned room next door that had once been a laundry. "Shall I put in more water for him?" Without waiting for yea or nay, Artois St. Chinian came into the kitchen with a yellow pottery jar, and ran a couple of cups of water into it from the big glazed-clay water-purifier on the shelf.

Artois was sixteen. Since April, Rose had been the boy's tutor, hired by Artois' uncle in the face of the absolute incredulity of the family that a woman could either hold such a position, or teach a youth anything of value. By the tangle of wires, pots, cranks, and bottles spread over the big worktable in the former laundry, January guessed the subject was still electricity, as it had been for weeks. Nothing that would be of any use to a student preparing for the University in Lyons, of course, but it was a treat that both Rose and Artois indulged each other in after they'd finished the day's ration of Latin, mathematics, and Greek.

"I really will have to talk Uncle Veryl into getting gas laid on, at least in part of the house," sighed Artois, drawing the gallows-iron of the kitchen fireplace to him with a poker to add the water to the pot. "This is just impossible."

"Making coffee over a spermaceti lamp in the workshop?" January grinned in spite of his day-long, weary anger at the injustice of the world.

"Heating anything over a spermaceti lamp. I'll bet Michael Faraday didn't do his experiments by heating his wires and solutions over . . . over *bonfires* in the middle of the laboratory floor." In spite of a white linen shirt, the silk waistcoat, and the sky-blue cravat of a young dandy, Artois St. Chinian still had a schoolboy air. His curly hair, halfway in color between molasses and honey, tumbled loosely over his forehead; his eyes were the hue of pale tourmaline. His mother had been fair, too, January had been told, with nearly European features, and the planter Raymond St. Chinian had lavished as much care and attention on his plaçée's child as he had on the daughter of his legitimate, white wife.

Only at Raymond St. Chinian's death had the care stopped. Had Raymond's uncle Veryl not stepped in, January wasn't sure what would have become of the boy Artois. Apprenticed out as a clerk, he supposed—to waste that shining intelligence copying bills of lading or columns of figures in a bank for the rest of his days.

"Between Creole family politics and low water in the river, I'd be surprised if Shaw returned any time before tomorrow night," January went on as Artois fetched down the coffee-grinder and perched on the table to adjust the rather delicate, fiddly rollers to his favorite consistency. "There aren't many boats coming upstream from Plaquemines Parish this time of year. From curiosity I might see what my mother knows about the Avocet family when I go out to Milneburgh tomorrow afternoon to see Dominique."

"You think she'll know?" Rose's eyebrows quirked above the gold rims of her spectacles. "It sounds like whichever brother it was got himself murdered only last night."

"*My* mother?" January chuckled without particular mirth. "She'll have heard everything about it before the family lawyers got to Shaw."

"There is much in what you say." Rose shook the roaster and tonged the lid aside to check the color of the beans. January fetched the pot from its shelf and went to the wide-open arch that looked into the courtyard. Relative coolness aside, the kitchen was still stifling.

"Would your mother be able to tell you something about Hesione LeGros?" Artois was a good-looking boy, his golden fairness melding oddly with the features of an African prince. "You said she was at General Humbert's birthday party with her."

"Being in the same room with her doesn't mean she'd speak to her," said January, returning to the kitchen. "You should have heard my mother on the subject of the smugglers' women, the day after the party. And I doubt she could tell me much that Olympe didn't know."

"You think the doubloon might have been a souvenir from her days with Lafitte?" asked Rose. She wiped her face again with her apron—as befit a tutor, she dressed in a frock of dull pink chintz, the apron she wore for experiments as spotless as her white tignon. "And that was what her killer came to get?"

"If the money was what he came to get," said January thoughtfully, "why didn't he get it? If that was what he was searching the house for, he'd have searched her body, too. And I doubt anything—money or jewels or pirate treasure from her glory days—would have survived a decade or so of hard drinking."

"True." Rose nodded, thinking—as January was thinking—of their mutual friend Hannibal Sefton, whose few possessions, with the exception of his books and his violin, had been constantly in and out of every pawnshop in town. Most of the books now resided in Rose's cramped little room on the Rue des Victoires. The violin had gone with Hannibal when he had, rather unexpectedly, run off to Mexico with a soprano from the Opera last winter. "And if she'd had it on her, she wouldn't have been begging for food from the market-women."

"If she'd had it on her," said January, "she wouldn't have gone home. She'd have walked on over to the Nantucket in the Swamp, which, I understand, sells liquor out the back door to anyone who comes down Gravier Street."

Rose shivered. "I'm astonished no one ever kidnapped her to sell as a slave. You told me yourself that happens fairly frequently, down in the Swamp."

"It happens to people who're worth money." January's voice was dry as he held the coffee-mill steady for Rose to pour in the beans. "Hesione was almost past child-bearing and so clearly a drunkard I doubt even a cotton-planter from the Territories would buy her. She was worth nothing to anyone."

"Then why would anyone kill her?" Artois followed them out to the table under the pepper-tree, took his turn at the coffee-mill's crank. James, Veryl St. Chinian's valet, emerged from the loggia at the back of the house looking flustered, Martine at his heels. Together they crossed the courtyard's primordial wilderness to the kitchen, and brought out chunks of wood and bunches of damp lemon-grass to put in the iron flambeaux near the dining-room's rear windows. Veryl St. Chinian seldom had guests, and the dinner party scheduled for tonight was an occasion of major upheaval. Mostly the old man lived in two cluttered rooms in the book-choked, dusty old house and consumed a little soup without ever looking up from the *Eclogues*.

It was, January had heard, considered an absolute scandal in the family that the son of his nephew's plaçée lived in an attic bedroom in the town house, and not in the garçonnière behind it—a wing which had been shut up for decades and was now buried under three storeys of feral jasmine.

"Why indeed?" January shook his head. "I'm guessing the killer came into the house sometime between the time Suzie and Titine went inside and closed the shutters, and Hesione's arrival. He searched the place neatly—the mattress was rumpled rather than thrown on the floor, the coffee-beans pawed through, not dumped out. That means he expected her to see what the place looked like when she came in. He brought his own candle and kept it shielded with his hand as he searched, then blew it out once he sat down—I found the spatters on the arm of the chair. Only after Hesione came in did he, or she, light one of her own candles, tallow rather than wax, and whatever they talked about for the ten minutes or so the candle burned, it was so interesting that neither of them thought about trimming the wick."

Rose said, "Hmn," and her eyebrows peaked up again above the small oval lenses of her spectacles. Steam blurred the lenses as she poured the boiling water, a few tablespoonsful at a time, into the top half—the *grecque*—of the coffee-urn, and the smoky perfume of the coffee rode above the damp green smell of the leaves matted in the bottom of the fountain's basin. Like all courtyards of the old French town, this one was designed to be aromatic as well as cool, protected from the stench of the streets as well as all but a few hours of direct sun by the towering walls. The afternoon's rain had brought out the smell of the orange-trees, the jasmine, and the sweet-olive. It was quiet, too, save for the drumming of the cicadas in the trees. In the dimming light January saw, to his distress, how the elbows of Rose's simple frock were worn threadbare, and how faded the skirt was, and beginning to fray at the hem.

Two years ago Rose had fallen afoul of a powerful French Creole matron, whose subsequent machinations had robbed her of the girls' school that had been her sole property, her livelihood, and the focus of her life. Since that time Rose had made a sort of living correcting Greek and Latin examinations for a number of the boys' schools in town, the way another woman would have made a living sewing—and it paid the way sewing would have paid. In some cases January knew she was far more fluent in Greek than the instructors she worked for, but it would never have occurred to anyone to hire a woman, much less a woman of color, to actually teach.

Yet he himself made too little to say to her, *Marry me . . .*

And he suspected she would rather starve than wed a man simply to keep from starving. Even a man she loved.

Maybe especially a man she loved. If indeed Rose was capable of fully loving, fully trusting, any man, after what one man had done to her long ago.

"So it was somebody she knew?" Artois' voice broke January's troubled reverie.

January thought about the woman's hoarse voice, offering her body in trade for liquor on the wharf.

"Maybe not," he said.

They drank their coffee, Artois excusing himself once or twice to go to the back door of the house and ask James if he needed help getting the dining-room in order. He came back both times, shaking his head: "I've told James my lesson is done for the day. It won't make a servant of me to help him hang the lusters back on the chandelier. He's too old to be standing on that ladder."

"If he won't let *me* touch it," sniffed Martine the cook, crossing back to the kitchen, "he sure as heck won't let *you*. . . . The stubborn old mustard-plaster."

"I didn't think anyone was left in town," remarked Rose as the three of them went into the workshop to tidy up. She had to strike a light and set candles around the darkening workshop in order to check her barometer one final time. "Anyone who would be dining with your great-uncle, that is."

"Anyone who is anyone, as they said in Paris." January thought of Hesione's neighbors out in the Swamp, and his own landlady, patiently sweeping the hearth each evening and fetching water from the cisterns to do her own laundry. "Anyone but the poor."

Artois glanced at him, troubled at the tone of his voice: guilt in his eyes at his own white shirt and silk waistcoats, his gold watch-chains, polished nails, tutor-perfect French. But seeing that January's bitterness wasn't directed at him, the boy said, "They're coming in from Mandeville to call on him—you never heard such a fuss. Why didn't he leave town like *they* did, and get a place out on the lake? How can he possibly inconvenience them like that? Because, of course, my sister has to call on everyone in the family before she gets married, and Aunt Marie-Agnes is insisting the wedding be next week, because she claims she's going to die."

By "sister," January knew Artois meant his half-sister Chloë, the legitimate daughter of Raymond St. Chinian, and heiress to the considerable family fortune.

As he and Rose picked their way down the carriageway half an hour later he had a chance to glimpse Chloë St. Chinian when she arrived. All the debris that ordinarily choked the carriageway had been moved back to the inner half of the passage, on the courtyard side of the doorway that led into the town house itself, the front portion of the building's ground-floor being occupied, as was usual in New Orleans, by a shop. Cressets had been lit on either side of the house doorway; when the carriage drew up before the archway out onto Rue Bourbon, January and Rose withdrew, with instinctive good manners, into the jumbled shadows of the inner end as the occupants disembarked.

It would never do, reflected January wryly, to have the white gentleman's guests encounter a mere tutor—and that tutor's still-more-mere sweetheart—on their way in to the obligatory pre-nuptial dinner.

Thin, fair, and small of stature, January had heard Chloë St. Chinian likened to a mermaid—not the sweet ones sailors dream about but the other kind, the ones who have no hearts. In her white gown and pale-blue ribbons, she seemed chill, self-possessed, and distant, far older than her barely-seventeen years, like a little creature of glass and diamonds. Uncle Veryl bent and kissed her hand, firelight brightening his long white hair, and escorted her inside, followed by her lumbering fiancé, a tall, fat, bespectacled planter named Henri Viellard.

It was to Henri Viellard that January's sister Dominique was plaçée.

"How is Dominique?" asked Rose after several minutes of quiet while they walked together down Rue Bourbon. It was dark by now and the night air was like warm glue. Palmetto-bugs the length of Rose's fingers lumbered aside from their feet. Blue-uniformed lamplighters at the intersection of Rue Toulouse were refilling the iron lantern there with oil, the crossed chains that supported it hanging slack from the corners of the buildings. Rose and January ducked as they crossed the plank over the brimming brown gutter, the iron pattens on Rose's shoes scraping and clattering on the muddy brick of the banquette. As the lamplighters hoisted the lantern to its place again, gold flecks of brightness caught in the lenses of Rose's spectacles, on the freckles that dotted her nose, and on the white tignon that framed her long, rather narrow face.

She looked tired, but the harried look she'd had in the springtime had disappeared. January blessed Veryl St. Chinian for hiring a woman to teach his grand-nephew and at the same time cursed the poverty that dogged them both. Between playing for the Opera and for balls—white and free colored, private and subscription—and teaching piano lessons, he had saved enough the previous winter to live on through the slow times when the town lay half-dead in summer's heat. But it was not enough to support two people. Nor would Rose allow him to pay her shot at the cafés or the gumbo-stands.

Since Veryl St. Chinian had hired her, Rose had been able to allow herself one night a week at the Buttonhole Café, and an occasional Italian ice.

"My sister's well," said January. "As well as she can be. Henri gave her that cottage by the lake, you know; it's hers, as well as the house here in town. According to her, he still goes to see her whenever he can."

"With the wedding in a week," remarked Rose, "I don't imagine that can be often. Do you think he'll be able to go on seeing her—let alone supporting her—once he's married? Many men do, you know."

"Many men aren't married to Chloë St. Chinian." January put a hand under Rose's elbow to help her across a plank that bridged a gutter and nearly dumped her into the brimming ooze when a mosquito tried to fly up his ear into his brain. The insects swarmed like dust-motes in the lamplight; January swatted at them ineffectually, and they both hastened their steps. "By every account she has a cash-box for a soul—according to not only my mother, but to Olympe as well, she sold her own nurse to the dealers the minute her father was dead, and the woman's child with her. Not a wife to take kindly to her husband lavishing money on a mistress, or on that mistress' child."

Neither spoke of the possibility of Henri simply continuing to keep Dominique in the face of his new bride's objections, as so many men did. They both knew the lazy and malleable Henri too well.

Over the past two years, January had reflected a great deal upon the nature of love. There had been a time when he did not think he would ever open his eyes from sleep again without the stab of renewed pain in his heart, without realizing—each time like the first time—that Ayasha wasn't beside him. That she never would be beside him again, ever. The first time he'd dreamed of Rose, of the

scent of her flesh and the silky texture of her hair beneath his fingers, he'd waked up shocked, as if he'd betrayed his wife in her life-
time, turned from her fiery sweetness to another's arms.

But he knew, each time he was with Rose, each time his whole
body kindled at the lightest brush of her hand on his, that he could
not go on loving a ghost. And as his love for Rose—gentle and
quirky and so different from Ayasha's passionate sensuality—deepened, he ceased to compare the two women.

Not long ago he'd dreamed of Ayasha. Dreamed of fog beside
the Seine, and of the great dark stone buildings of Paris dripping in
the early-morning silence; dreamed of the smell of moss and vapor
and stone. They stood together on the bridge at the head of the island, at the place where January had pitched into the river the trunk
holding all Ayasha's clothing, lest, in giving it to the poor, he might
be surprised one day by the sight of some beggar-woman wearing
her dress.

"And what do you think, Malik?" Ayasha smiled up at him sidelong with those dark, slanting eyes. "That I'm going to pitch *you*
into the river so I don't have to see some other woman holding your
hand?" Her black hair hung down over her shoulders, as it used to
when she'd comb it out by the window, and gold earrings flashed in
it, hidden treasure in an ocean of night.

And to January's own surprise he laughed in the dream, like one
caught out in a foible of no great moment, though at the time he'd
thrown away the trunk his world had been a bleeding wound whose
pain filled earth and sky. "I did what I had to, my nightingale," he'd
replied, and kissed her. Her lips tasted as they always had, salt and
sweet together. It was as if she had never been gone. "I do love you.
And will, forever."

"Ah, Malik," she murmured, "of course. Of course. It is only
marriage that there is none of, in this dull Christian Heaven of
yours. Marriage and being given in marriage. Of course there is and
always will be love."

He'd waked in the darkness, smelling the sandalwood in her
hair. Then the scent was gone, leaving behind it not desolation as
before, but—finally—peace.

"When is she due?" Rose's sweet alto broke the memory of the dream. January returned to the present, looked down at the woman walking at his side.

"Early September."

By which time, January thought, Dominique might very well be alone.

Not as badly-off as Rose, of course. Dominique would at least have the house and the cottage, and, in a pinch, the jewelry Henri had given her. She might even seek another protector, returning to the Blue Ribbon Balls that were given nearly every week in the wintertime for the benefit of the wealthy white men of the town and their free colored mistresses. But it would be a rare gentleman, reflected January, who would take on another man's child.

And it would all be easier, of course, if Dominique didn't love Henri.

Over supper at the Buttonhole Café, he and Rose spoke of Dominique and Henri, and of the law under which the Viellard family holdings were a business, operated by Madame Viellard, to which Henri had and would have no access until he had done his family duty by marrying and producing an heir. Even then, there was nothing that said he would be chosen over one of his sisters to have control of the family corporation when his mother died.

His bride was an heiress, but January knew Chloë had control of her own property. Her father had died suddenly, leaving her half-brother, Artois, at the mercy of his mother's vagaries, as Chloë had been left to her guardian aunts. "Not that Uncle Veryl grudges taking him in, of course," smiled Rose. "I gather Veryl St. Chinian has acted as a schoolmaster-general to the boys of the family for years. But I think he's a little nonplussed that, having found at last a true scholar to help, Artois prefers optics and electricity to Thucydides and Livy." She spooned rice into the aromatic mixture of chicken, shrimp, and vegetables, and gently poked a bay-leaf out of the way: "That's a cup of coffee you owe me."

"That's the third time this month. I'll have to talk to Cora about that." Their eyes met, laughing: it was a game between them that whoever got a bay-leaf also got a cup of coffee the next time they were at one of the coffee-stands that clustered beneath the market arcades. Cora Chouteau, owner of the Buttonhole, had grown up with Rose on Grand Isle, south in the Barataria marshes, where Rose's father had had a small sugar plantation, after Rose's plaçée mother had died.

Perhaps, he reflected, that was why Rose and Artois had recognized each other as kindred souls. The children of plaçées might be educated by their white fathers, but it was generally expected that they would be educated to fulfill some useful and subservient role: a clerk or a craftsman if a boy, or, like himself, a musician. Generally the girls went on to become another generation of plaçée.

No one appreciated the quest for knowledge for its own sweet sake if the seeker happened to be of African descent. Even January's own training in surgery, excellent as it had been, had not been able to surmount the barrier of his appearance.

What would happen to Dominique's child if he or she happened to be charged with that wondrous, deadly Promethean fire? Particularly if by that time Dominique was struggling only to keep a roof over their heads.

For that matter, he wondered suddenly, what had happened to the children that the pirates' bejeweled women had borne twenty years ago in Lafitte's palmetto-thatched village by the Gulf? What *could* become of them, being what they were?

Certainly they wouldn't have the education a "respectable" man of property usually bestowed on his plaçée's children.

And what might they think—or know—of their mother's death?

"Would your brother, or your sister-in-law, down on Grand Isle, know anything about the remains of Lafitte's crew?" he asked Rose, startling her from scribbling notes about the properties of heated metals on the margin of a piece of newspaper. "Or did *you* ever hear anything about them while you were there?"

"Oh, half the islanders claimed descent from them." The dim candle-light warmed the reminiscent smile in Rose's eyes. "They were Portuguese and Cubans and Spaniards, and a lot of English as well. Buccaneers have been putting up at the Barataria islands pretty much since Blackbeard's day. There's still a tremendous amount of

smuggling going on through there—you didn't think all those fishermen actually made their living from fishing, did you? And after
the British finished dealing with Napoleon and started really turning their attention to pirates, a number of Lafitte's crew went into
running guns. All the rebellions in New Spain were just starting up
right about the time the Americans burned Lafitte out of his camp
on the Texas coast. They had the ships, and the connections in
Havana and Cartagena and here."

January smiled, seeing her growing up in those flat, endless
marshes, like Artois, with her nose in a book.

"Would you write to your sister-in-law, Alice?"

"I could," replied Rose judiciously. "But I doubt that it would
do any good. My brother's father-in-law was a good French Creole,
him"—her voice dropped into an imitation of the archaic French
spoken in the Barataria—"and he didn't believe in reading and writing for his daughters. Just makes women discontent, that book-
learning, and of what use is a discontented woman? Who you could
talk to, though," she added, returning to normal speech, "would be
Cut-Nose Chighizola."

"Cut-Nose? Lafitte's captain? Is he still on Grand Terre?"

"He's on Grand Isle. He and his sons have orchards and gardens
there; they bring the produce up to town every few days. He'd know
about Hesione LeGros if anyone would."

The Cathedral clock was striking nine when they finished their
coffee. Cora and her husband were already clearing up, for the café
was frequented mostly by free artisans and craftsmen of color, and
curfew was at ten for anyone of African descent. Despite the screens
of pink mosquito-bar tacked over the windows, the little room was
both stuffy and humming with insects around the few sconces and
oil-lamps, and the night outside was nearly as airless. January and
Rose made their way roundabout through the quieter streets of the
French town, seeking to avoid the infamous gauntlet of Gallatin
Street, which ran behind the downstream wharves. Even so,
nowhere near the waterfront was particularly safe for men and
women of color walking abroad after dark. Even in this slow season,
sailors of all nationalities came ashore from the deep-water ships

docked below the Place d'Armes, and the deadly currents of the river's bend. Above the Place, steamboats and keelboats disgorged their crews in quest of drink, whores, and trouble.

Cressets and flambeaux cast a hectic light against the masts visible down the cross-streets, but the young moon was setting behind patchy cloud and even a few streets back it was pitchy dark. Moths and roaches swarmed around the lights, where geckos waited on the walls to snap at them. A pair of fair-haired English sailors staggered by, faces burned red as brick. In the abyssal shadows, January heard a male voice ranting incomprehensibly as he pounded the shutters of a small house: "My name is Garfield J. Maverick and I eats broken glass an' Indian babies for breakfast! I can take on a steamboat in a fair fight an' I killed more men than the cholera! Come outa there, you French sons a' hoors! Come out an' meet a real man!"

Rose drew closer to January's side.

"Hey, Peaches." A man blocked the banquette in front of them, no more than a faceless shape. "What's Sambo there got that I ain't, hah?"

The building behind him was a tavern, and January saw smoky light inside, the color of raw amber. Tobacco-stink, smoked and spit; the vast reek of stale whiskey. He tried to draw Rose away and cross the street, which was without gutters here and almost without banquettes, just a mire of clayey mud. Two other men jostled out of the tavern behind the first.

One of them caught Rose by the arm, tugged her toward him. January's fist bunched and even as he thought, *Here's where I get killed for being uppity and striking a white man,* he was stepping forward. . . .

Rose flung back her head and screamed.

It wasn't a woman's shriek of protest or alarm, half-stifled with shock. It was a full-throated scream like a steam-whistle, and it so startled the Kaintuck that he dropped her arm and stepped back. Rose sprang clear the instant she felt herself free, and January swept her across the mud street and into darkness. Behind him he heard the three men laughing. . . .

"C'mon back, honey, I'll make you scream another tune!"

"You holler like that when ol' Sambo's on top o' you?"

Rose stumbled, but pulled sharply clear of his steadying grasp. January could feel her trembling as they turned the corner onto Rue des Victoires.

He was shaking, too, with rage and panic and emotions impossible to name. In any neighborhood in the city, a black man who struck a white one would be lucky if he lived long enough to be whipped at the Cabildo. Here, near the wharves, the action would be suicide, especially at this time of night, with every man in the tavern half-drunk and eager for the excitement of legitimized brutality. What would have happened to Rose in the melee he didn't even want to think.

"Wait." She stopped, leaning against the wall. He heard her gag, fighting not to be sick. Struggling to breathe, hands pressed to her corseted sides.

"Rose, we've got to get you out of here," he said, not meaning the immediate vicinity of the alley but the whole neighborhood in which she lived: he felt her stiffen under his hand.

After a few more breaths, she straightened and walked on. They were only a few score feet from Vroche's Grocery, behind which she lived in a rickety outbuilding that housed the kitchen and a laundry on the ground floor, and four rented chambers above.

Tallow candles and a lantern burned in the yard, for the fire in the kitchen had been banked. Around them a gaggle of men were drinking, two of Rose's fellow lodgers and their friends. Though free colored—*libres*—weren't allowed to buy alcohol, the beer-stink was strong, and a man's voice ragged drunkenly about how that lout Shreve had cheated him out of his share of the cargo, cheated him like a dog. January felt Rose try not to flinch at the slurred rage in that declaration.

"I'll be tutoring Artois for another year." Her voice fought for its usual matter-of-fact tone. "Until he goes to University. By Christmas I'll be able to afford—"

"You can't put up with this every night until Christmas!"

"It doesn't happen every night. Or every other night, even." She stopped on the rickety gallery before her door. "And right now I don't have any choice in the matter."

In the next room, Marie-Philomène groaned, "Oh, give it to

me! Give it to me hard!" The French doors were open; the creak of the rope bed was audible, the smell of the room salt and beery and foul.

Rose's hand fumbled with her latchkey, dropped it with a tinny metal clink onto the gallery planks; she bent swiftly to retrieve it before January could do so. In the shadow of the abat-vent above, her face was hidden, her tignon only a white blur framing a fleeting flash of oval glass.

January caught her hand. "Rose . . ."

She pulled away, hard, almost wrenching it out of his grasp. "Good-night," she said quickly.

The door closed.

FOUR

"What the *hell* does she think *I'm* going to do?" demanded January after he'd told Dominique about it the following day. "Rape her too? Beat her up?"

"Yes," said his sister simply, and January, furious and caught off-guard, stared at her open-mouthed.

"You're not serious, Minou."

"It's not what Rose thinks, p'tit." His youngest sister folded her slender hands over her belly and sat back in her chair of white-painted willow, her dark eyes sad in a face too thin, January thought, for a woman in her eighth month with child. "It's what she *feels*. What she fears."

"Are you telling me Rose is afraid of me?" All the exasperation he felt poured out of him like blood from a severed artery. He remembered how for so many months she'd drawn away from his touch, how warily she'd kept her distance from him. . . . After months of gentle patience he had been rewarded by the touch of her hand, only to have her turn cold on him and draw away once more. Last winter they had kissed, with tenderness and passion, for the first time, and he had forced himself to patience while longing to crush her to him, to taste not only her lips but her throat and her breasts.

And then she would shy off yet again, for no reason he could discover, like a bird deciding not to come to hand after all.

Sometimes he would go home angry, as he had last night. Angry and baffled and wanting to shake her, to shout at her, *I'm not the man who hurt you! Don't keep punishing me for what that other bastard did!*

Wanting to tell her, *We can't go on this way. Make up your mind.*

But he knew it wasn't her mind that made her thus, but her heart. And if he said, *Make up your mind,* she would turn away in that furled silence of hers, and that would be the end. He knew that as surely as he knew his name.

But the thought that she might fear him was a dagger in his heart.

Dominique's cottage stood on the shore of Lake Pontchartrain in a grove of cypress and willows. Shade dappled the back gallery that stood out over the water, and veiled his sister's face and hair like Venice lace. Across a curve of the water the red roofs and white-painted galleries of the Washington Hotel showed through the trees, and voices carried to them from the ninepin alleys and the kiosks where girls sold Italian ice.

The world smelled fresh here in Milneburgh. A mockingbird sang in the trees. The smells and heat of town, the clattering wagons and drunken Kaintucks and gritty filth of steamboat soot seemed part of another world.

As did last night's threat of violence, and the broken sleep and angry dreams that had run in its wake.

"I thought she was over it," said January quietly. "Her fear of men."

"Oh, p'tit." Dominique put out her hand, cool and slim, on his.

He had taught his piano-lesson that morning to the daughters of a plaçée who was grooming them in "accomplishments" with an eye to attracting protectors of their own as soon as they were of an age for it. It was one of two weekly lessons that continued into the summertime, the woman's protector having left her in town while he himself went to stay with his wife and white children at one of the stylish residential hotels by the lake. Riding out to Milneburgh on the steam-cars—in the last car of the train, which the free colored were welcome to share with the servants of the whites who occupied the rest of the equipage—January had felt only a kind of exhausted anger as he watched the green monotony of cypresses and magnolias pass by.

Anger at himself that he had not sprung instantly to bludgeon the man in Rose's path before he so much as touched her *(and that would have accomplished what?)*. Anger at the faceless shadow in the tavern door, reeking of forty-rod and spit tobacco, who'd assumed he had rights over any woman of color who came his way. Anger at Rose, who had repeatedly refused his offers to lend her the money to find other quarters than those she could afford. Who had closed the door behind her last night without even saying *Thank you, Ben.*

Anger that the world should be as it was.

I should never have come back from Paris.

Or, since he would have gone mad from grief in Paris, he told himself, he should have gone elsewhere: Venice, Naples, Vienna, Milan. Anywhere but back here—

—where Rose was teaching her school, and studying electricity and Homer and how to make mummies and bombs. Alone and aloof and as unconscious of his presence in the world as he was of hers.

He closed his eyes, letting the cat's-paw breezes trail over his face. Seeing her as first he'd seen her, a stranger—a tall, thin woman in the heat and stench of a cholera ward, who moved as if she was always about to trip and never did: *I need a doctor,* she'd said. *Three of my girls are down sick. . . .*

Her beloved students, all of whom had died. He tried to imagine what it would have been like to gather up the strength to start fresh in an unknown city in the wake of Ayasha's death rather than come back to this place, where there was a woman named Rose whom he'd never met.

I did what I had to. . . .

Tried to imagine not knowing Rose. Not seeing her every day.

He couldn't.

"Last year," said Dominique, "when you were trying to rescue Rose's friend Cora from her masters, and were beaten, and hurt . . . suppose that instead of just beating you, they'd cut up your manhood with a knife? How long would it have taken you to stop having nightmares?" She leaned forward in her chair, one hand resting on her swollen belly. "Or suppose that instead of dying, your wife had . . . had run away with another man? Not only run away with him, but stolen all the music you'd written, and given it to that other man for him to publish as his own?"

January's eyes flared in surprise. Dominique had been only four when he'd left their mother's house to go to Paris. He didn't think she'd remembered that he used to write music.

"How long would it be, before you trusted a dark-haired woman again? Or any woman, ever?" Dominique looked up at him gravely, all the lightness, the frivolous patter that characterized her absent now as she willed him to understand. "And if you did fall in love with some dark-haired lady, and she wore the same perfume as Ayasha did, or liked the same colors . . . Wouldn't the pain come back and hit you sometimes, when you didn't expect it, and undo everything *she* was patiently trying to heal in *you?*"

January turned his face away. Two boys rolled hoops along the shell paths by the lake. Under a tree a little girl served imaginary tea to her friends and their dolls.

"Does it take so long?" he asked.

But he knew that it did. He knew there were women who never got over being raped.

Dominique broke a tea-cake in two, crumbled half of it into bits that she dipped into her tea and then left untasted on the edge of her plate. "Honestly," she said, and her voice regained its old bright chattiness, "the way people tiptoe around me, you'd think I was the first woman in the world whose protector took a wife! Iphigénie and Phlosine were here this morning"—she named her two best friends, plaçées whose protectors likewise had bought them cottages on the lakeshore—"and to watch them fetching tea for me and glancing at me sideways whenever they thought I wasn't looking, you'd have thought I was going to hang myself from the rafters the moment they turned their backs."

She laughed, but her laughter was brittle, as it had been since she had first learned of Henri's engagement.

"Poor Henri! When he was last here he looked just *wretched.*

And who wouldn't be, who has to visit every single member of *that* family before the wedding? I wonder if he even got in to see their crazy old uncle Joffrey? I understand the man hasn't been off his plantation in twenty years—literally twenty years, p'tit!—and is crazy as a banana. . . . His sons, too. No one in the family has seen any of them since I don't know when. And that *dreadful* grandmother of Henri's . . . the one who insists she's about to die and has to see her niece and her grandson married right this minute, before she goes, and never mind that everyone has to come into town again, because God forbid any grandchild of hers should be married by anyone but the Bishop—and I'm sure His Excellency would much rather stay out here at the lake as well. Do you know she has four footmen to carry her around in a palanquin like a Roman empress? It's the truth, p'tit, I've seen her. She has two or three of the things—palanquins, I mean—all of them draped in black, to match her dresses. . . . Not that she has a gown newer than the reign of Napoleon, honestly! I can't imagine what she's going to wear to the wedding. . . ."

January let her chatter, drank his tea, and listened, knowing that it was all that he could do. Her friend Iphigénie, he guessed, had been full of advice—as far as he knew she was still trying to get Dominique to abort the child that would certainly be a desperate liability should Henri in fact be forced by his new bride and her family to repudiate his mistress. And Phlosine, with her own second child on its way, was a wellspring of well-meant tricks to hold Henri and deceive his wife. And their mother, January knew, would be no help. Other people's problems bored her, except as a source of gossip with her own friends.

So he listened, hearing how many times Dominique spoke Henri's name, as if repetition would serve as proof—or conjuration—of his continued devotion. And he wondered where hope ended and folly began. His own love for Rose, maintained in the face of her fear that might prove too strong for him—or her—to conquer . . . What of that? Was it madness to love a woman who could not respond?

Would that love turn to hate when he finally came to understand that there truly was no water in that well?

But there is, he thought, recalling the passion of her kisses when times were gentle and good. *I know there is.*

"I was saying to Henri only . . . only last week"—her voice hesitated a little—"that there's no reason on earth for his poor sisters to be stranded all the way downriver at Bois d'Argent for the summer. Poor things, they're all starting to look *exactly* like his mother's sisters! The family has four plantations, after all, and Viellard itself is only across the lake. And Henri agreed with me that the older three are *never* going to be married if their mother *persists* in dressing them in that petunia-colored gauze. . . ."

Before he left Milneburgh, January walked along the lakeshore to the handsome boarding-house where his mother rented rooms every summer, so that the lakeside cottage St.-Denis Janvier had given her could be let out to a white sugar-broker and his wife. His mother had offered to let him stay in her house in town—at only the smallest of rents—and could not understand why he had refused, any more than he could understand, he supposed, why Rose would not be beholden to him, who loved her.

"Oh, it's Henri this and Henri that now," sniffed Livia Levesque, after January had delivered an account—unsolicited—of how he'd found his sister. "Sneaking away from that mother of his, and the St. Chinian girl, to see her. They'll put a stop to that, and so I told her, though, of course, she wouldn't listen."

She fanned herself with a round of stiffened and painted silk, as beautiful as she had been on that night twenty-three years ago when she'd dressed before her mirror for General Humbert's birthday dinner. There were more lines around her enormous pansy-brown eyes, and at the corners of her wide, secretive mouth, but a steady regime of crushed strawberries and wafer-thin slices of raw veal had so far held Time's more serious graving-tools at bay. She dressed as exquisitely as ever, in delicate shades of turquoise and buttercup—she'd worn mourning for the late Christophe Levesque for precisely the prescribed year and then had put it aside with the comment that black did not become her—and still kept the slender upright figure that was the envy and despair of her contemporaries. The only difference between that slim, elegant plaçée and this slim, elegant widow lay in her eyes, and the briskness of her voice and movements, at variance with the languid gait and murmur of a rich man's concubine.

Livia Levesque was her own woman now, well-off and beholden to none.

"If Henri Viellard thinks that marriage is going to give him one pennyworth more say in the ordering of the family plantations, all I can say is he doesn't know that mother of his particularly well. She ruled old Jean-Charles Viellard like the Empress of Russia, and you can see what she's made of her son: a bag-pudding good for nothing beyond reading books by heathens and deists and picking out waist-coats for himself. Minou will be well shut of him. Drink your tea, Benjamin. It's first-rate China green at a dollar and seventy-five cents a pound and it'll be completely useless if it gets cold."

January drank his tea. The gallery of the Louisiana House over-looked a small garden that ran down to the lake; on the lawn two bluejays tormented a stout gray cat, one of them hopping about in front of it exactly a quarter-inch beyond the maximum strike of its forepaws, the other stationed behind, pulling tufts of fur from the end of the cat's thrashing tail. January could almost see steam com-ing from the exhausted and exasperated tom's ears.

The Widow Levesque dropped a chunk of white sugar into her tea with the silver sugar-tongs, and did not offer the plate to her son. "I went to the trouble of finding a woman in St. John Parish who'll take that baby and nurse it for a dollar a month—when every slut in town is charging two dollars and some of them more—and all I got from your sister was a lot of eyewash about Henri Viellard's child, as if he won't be getting a dozen like it onto the St. Chinian chit. Well, I wash my hands of her."

She shook her hands illustratively. Well-kept hands, thought January. Smooth as a girl's and the color of walnut-hull dye, the nails kept like jeweler's work. Only a scar just below the little finger of the right one marked where a sugar-cane had gouged, in the days when she'd dragged bundles of cut cane to the mill like any other slave-gang girl. Once she'd become St.-Denis Janvier's plaçée she'd never spoken of those days. When January or Olympe mentioned them, she would turn away from them in cold silence, as if they had ceased to exist.

On the night of General Humbert's birthday dinner, the topaz set Hesione LeGros had worn could have bought Livia's cottage and everything in it—Livia and her children as well, had they still been on the open market. January had seen what became of freebooters' women when they ceased to be young and fiery and gay, when childbearing and drink began to mark their faces and their bodies. It was the clever women like his mother who spent their money not on Italian silks but on creams and paints and Olympian Dew to prolong their youth, investing not only in their own beauty, but in property, slaves, mules, shares of cotton-presses and steamship companies.

For those who loved, and who gambled on a man's love, the damage and the pain were perhaps the worst.

Livia had little enough to say about Hesione LeGros. "Of course I remember her! Who could forget those hideous old-fashioned topazes—which I'll go bail were paste—and feathers like she'd bought out a hatmaker's shop?" She selected a beignet from the plate Bella brought out to her and considered the question. Bella had been the slave who had, twenty-three years ago, helped her on with her delicate kid gloves. These days she looked ten years older than her mistress, though in fact they were both fifty-nine.

"I think she came to one or two of the Blue Ribbon Balls, got up in the most antiquated crimson taffeta polonaise and jeweled like a shop window, but I don't recall anyone giving her a regular place or so much as thinking of it. She looked haggard even then and she spoke the most awful French, blast this and blast that and blast your eyes out. . . . Men laugh at that sort of thing but they don't buy cottages for it. I think she whored for a little while on Tchoupitoulas Street." She sounded pleased about that, and brushed powdered sugar from her fingers.

"Did she have family, or particular friends?"

"Good heavens, Ben, I don't know! This was years ago. And any man with silver in his pocket—or copper, later on—was Hesione's particular friend, I daresay."

She shrugged impatiently, the curious features of Hesione's

death meaning as little to her as they apparently meant to the City Guards.

But when January mentioned, in frustration and in passing, that Bertrand Avocet was supposed to have murdered his brother Guifford, and this case was taking up the whole attention of the City Guards, his mother was avid with attention.

"Absolutely common tradesmen," she sniffed, which was a little high in the instep, January thought, from a former field-hand. "The father came from France with a shipful of shoes and married old Tileul's daughter—the bossy one—and got her father to give them the place down in Plaquemines for their own rather than any share of the family holdings. . . ."

Olympe was right, thought January again, even more annoyed than he had been in the Cabildo the previous day. His mother wouldn't have gotten her skirts dirty to cross the road to look at Hesione's corpse, but produce the smallest shred of gossip concerning the lives of the white and wealthy and she would let herself be trampled by wild horses in her rush to demonstrate how much she knew about them.

". . . barely a hogshead of sugar per acre, and the swamp so far off across the open marshes that the wood-gangs spend half their day dragging fuel. What with the one brother spending every cent that came in on this and that newfangled scheme to get rich, and marrying Claud Houx's widow earlier this month into the bargain—a flighty piece of work if ever I saw one—and the other brother undercutting him and trying to force him to hold household *and* carrying on an affair with his brother's new wife. . . ."

"I ought to introduce you to Lieutenant Shaw," remarked January bitterly, after his mother displayed—as he had predicted— an exact knowledge of every clue surrounding Guifford Avocet's death in the marshy clearing behind the Avocet sugar-mill: the bloody shirt, the broken watch in his pocket whose hands marked half-past nine, the parlor clock likewise inexplicably stopped, the discrepancy in Bertrand's tale of a runaway slave when no slave had been missing from the quarters. "He'd appreciate your information."

"Don't be silly, Benjamin." She didn't even speak sharply, and the indulgent chuckle in her voice told him just how much she regarded the thought of *her* conversing with Shaw as simply a jest in doubtful taste. It was as if he'd suggested that she go into real estate partnership with one of Dominique's pet finches: something unthinkably foolish, not even considered.

As if he'd suggested that the City Guards *actually investigate* the death of a drunken black woman who owned nothing.

"Mind you," she added, as January prepared to depart, "I expect you to let me know more about the Avocet murder, as soon as you hear anything from that flea-bitten American animal you consort with . . . Not that *he'll* speak a word of the truth."

Exasperated, January returned to town by the steam-train, to find "that flea-bitten American animal"—his mother's favorite term for Lieutenant Shaw—still absent from the Cabildo.

The rainy afternoon streets were quiet as he walked back to Rue des Ursulines—too light for a real storm, and afterward the steaming dampness would render the heat ten times worse. Shuttered shops and shuttered houses, except for the gambling-halls on Rue Royale, which Death on a Pale Horse itself couldn't have closed. As he climbed the garçonnière steps he could hear Madame Bontemps talking with her protector as she swept the back gallery, in the flat, queer accents of the almost-deaf. The fact that M'sieu Bontemps had been dead for a number of years did not seem to bother the stooped little woman any more than did the rain that spattered in under the gallery's wide roof. When he'd come to board here, after one too many of his mother's acts of emotional blackmail, January had negotiated the use of Madame Bontemps' parlor in which to teach his piano students, and even in their summer absence he kept up his payments to her, so that he could have an hour or two a day uninterrupted of playing his piano for the sheer joy of it.

In many ways he felt most himself—most real—at such times. His enormous hands floated lightly over the keys, his mind and heart engaged, both producing the music and listening. Playing the cotillions and mazurkas, the quadrilles and waltzes, that were his livelihood: arias from Rossini and Meyerbeer, overtures and ballet interludes. Playing, too, the old-fashioned pieces that were no longer in demand, but whose clockwork precision rejoiced his heart:

Mozart marches, concertos of Bach and Vivaldi. Playing, too, the songs he'd heard the stevedores sing on the levee, with strange strong rhythms like the surge of the moon-called sea, and African words that no one any longer understood.

Songs his father had whistled, walking out to the fields in the black dark of winter mornings during the harvest, swinging his long cane-knife in his hand.

The stuffy heat of the little house seemed to dissipate when he played. The parlor had a ghostly feeling, with its chandeliers and mirrors shrouded in tattered gauze to keep the flies away, a sense of floating between times or worlds. Dominique had spoken of the music he used to write, and he played now the tunes he'd made in Paris, marveling a little that they could have come from his own mind.

They weren't at all bad.

He finished one of them—a Kyrie he'd made with the intention of writing an entire Mass—and turning, saw Rose standing in the parlor's long window.

He got to his feet. As a tenant he couldn't go to greet her through the bedroom, as was considered proper, and it was bad manners to come through the tall French windows straight into the parlor—like most Creole housewives, Madame Bontemps put chairs in front of them. Rose vanished, going through the narrow passway by the house around to the back, and January crossed the back parlor in three strides to meet her as she came up the gallery steps: "Are you all right?" Her fingers closed around his offered hands, and did not withdraw as she looked up into his face.

"Yes." He hadn't asked in the polite tone of commonplaces, nor did she answer so. The fear that had caused her to thrust him away last night and flee had receded to its lair in the darkness of her inner heart. "I never said thank-you last night for whisking me away so quickly. In fact, I was so shaken up—so frightened—I know I behaved like an absolute toad. . . ."

"You behaved like a woman who'd been attacked," said January, and gently took her into his arms. His words of last night—*You can't go on living there, let me help you find somewhere else, I can contribute something*—these jammed against his teeth so hard, he had to clench his jaw. In his silence she relaxed against him, her cheek to his chest, and he thought, *Minou was right. Patience. For however long it takes.*

And if it takes longer than my life?

Then I will still have this knowledge: that she has come to trust even a little at all. That will have to be enough.

Shaw came after Rose had left. If Madame Bontemps had glared at Rose when she saw her sitting beside January on the piano bench, she flatly refused to have the Kentuckian in the house at all. "M'sieu Bontemps does not like Americans," she declared, peering malignantly up at Shaw from beneath the fantastically-twisted monstrosity of her green-and-orange tignon. Marie-Claire Bontemps was a tiny woman, well under five feet tall, and her stout body had an air of crookedness, as if the floor she stood on partook of a geometry and a gravity alien to that used by other folk. Like most women, she sewed her own garments, choosing cheap, garish calicoes and styles anywhere from two decades to four centuries out of date. This one was purple, with red trim and sleeves that trailed the floor. "He fought against the Americans when they invaded, and drove them out. They're all spies, he says."

Shaw had encountered January's landlady before, and had heard all about the delusional American invasion and its various and ever-altering repercussions. "That we are, m'am," he agreed, placing his verminous hat over his heart. "But I was captured, an' am here on parole to deliver a message for Mr. January." He looked tired, as if last night had been a sleepless one. His gargoyle face, and his wrists where they dangled from his ill-fitting sleeves like rope and bones, were spotted red with mosquito-bites, and January remembered his mother informing him that Guifford Avocet's body had been found in marshy, low-lying ground behind the plantation sugar-mill.

Madame Bontemps regarded Shaw for a long time with her brown, slightly bulging eyes, as if she didn't quite understand his French—no surprise, reflected January, given the Kaintuck's idiosyncratic non-command of that language. "You can't come inside.

He can't come inside," she added, to January. "He'll put a mark on the house."

January didn't even want to inquire what kind of mark she meant.

At the end of Rue des Ursulines the river glared with molten gold behind scattered groves of masts. Blue shadow already filled the street, and mosquitoes hung above the gutters in whining brown clouds. Shaw and January had to walk down toward the market to be free of them. Had they halted, the insects would have settled on Shaw and devoured him alive.

"I come to ask if'n you'd be game to help me out," said Shaw as they walked. "I just got back from Avocet"—indeed, January had already observed that Shaw wore the same sorry yellow shirt he'd had on yesterday morning, though given the Kaintuck's sartorial habits, that didn't necessarily mean he hadn't been home—"an' the whole set-up there stinks like a basket of last week's oysters."

He slouched, his hands in his pockets, spit a line of tobacco-juice in the direction of the gutter, and rubbed his unshaven jaw. "That shirt they found—it's Bertrand's, all right, an' it's bloody, I got no argument there. Soaked all over in blood, like somethin' out of a Gothic novel. Trouble is, the wound that killed Guifford was made by a thin-bladed knife: it's deep, but it's small, and there'd a' been a lot of blood in a small area, not sort of enthusiastical like that. An' then again, how'd he get his shirt bloody an' not the coat an' waistcoat on top of it? They wasn't even lines down the breast where a man's braces woulda stopped the blood."

January glanced sidelong at him, his mind darting over the lies and planning that Shaw's observations implied, but he said nothing. They were close enough to Gallatin Street that occasional drunken cries and shrieks of female laughter could be heard; two men staggered by on the opposite banquette, arguing loudly in English—"... damn you, the fuck you callin' me, hunh? The fuck you callin'. ..." He felt more than saw the change in Shaw's stance, the way the backwoodsman's gray eyes seemed to triangulate the situation, aligning the anger in the voice with the probable results of alcohol on their potential attack-speed and the distance across the street. Was aware of Shaw's awareness of the diminishing threat as they walked away.

"Guifford's watch was broke at nine-thirty: his wife, M'am Vivienne, his an' Bertrand's sister, Miss Annette, an' M'am Vivienne's daughter from her first marriage was all together in the parlor till after ten. Laurene, the girl's name is, pretty little thing, dark like her ma. Guifford was gonna adopt her but hadn't done nuthin' about it as of yet. The parlor clock was stopped too, later on in the night. The ground where Guifford was found was too wet to hold tracks an' the path from there to the mill was tracked up an' scuffed by half the slaves on the place. The Barataria marsh comes right up behind the plantation, with smugglers an' slave-stealers an' trappers an' runaways an' who-all comin' an' goin'. . . ." He shook his head, and stepped easily across the wide gutter of Rue du Levee with his long legs.

"An' not a soul of 'em tellin' me the truth, 'ceptin' maybe the girl, Laurene. An' her mama haulin' her away from me like she thought I'd scalp her an' cook her up for breakfast. An' to complete the picture, last night their overseer run off—didn't take nuthin' but the horse he was ridin' the fields with."

They had reached the market, a long, open shed whose brick pillars supported a tiled roof. Breezes blew through from the river, dispersing the mosquitoes, but the flagstoned floor reeked of soured vegetation, trampled fragments of spinach and tomatoes, the juice of broken pineapples and mangoes, all mulched together with the soapy stink of the sweepers' brooms. Geckos fleeted along the heavy beams overhead. Most of the market-women had packed and gone home, and except for the few coffee-stands on the far side, closer to the river's cool, the enormous space was quiet.

Too late for flies, and too early—but only just—for the rats.

Two slaves with brooms were down at the far end, the scrape of coarse straw on wet paving-stones loud in the shadows. One of them was singing, the other joined wailing on the final line:

> *Chink, pink, honey, oh Lula,*
> *Chink, pink, honey, oh Lula,*
> *Chink, pink, honey, oh Lula,*
> *Wash that kerchief in the bayou.*

"Will you come?" Shaw glanced sidelong at January under thin lashes the color of old tow. "Far as I can tell, between Bertrand an' Guifford cheatin' each other an' keepin' slave mistresses an' sellin' off the slaves they was payin' to spy on each other—an' I understand Raffin the overseer wasn't helpin' the situation none—I'm not gettin' a straight story out of anyone on the place, white or black. I don't even know if the overseer disappearin' had anythin' to do with Guifford's murder or if one of the field-hands just sort of took advantage of everythin' bein' at sixes an' sevens an' put him to bed with a shovel: it wouldn't surprise me none, from what I've heard. I would purely appreciate havin' a man at my back I could trust."

Shaw's light, rather scratchy voice was noncommittal, but January heard in it the wariness of a man who knows himself to be going utterly alone into enemy territory: a Kaintuck, hated by French and Africans alike. It was clear too from what Shaw said that he did not believe Bertrand Avocet to be the killer—which meant that there was a good chance the true killer would be waiting to stick that thin-bladed knife between Shaw's ribs as well.

His mother, January reflected, would be outraged if he did not take the opportunity to get a first-row seat on the Avocet melodrama of passion, money, and blood.

He said, "No." And heard in his mind the leaden roar of the flies in the hot shadows of a shack on the edge of the swamp, smelled rain and blood and the turpentine laid down in a vain, belated effort to keep ants from the body of a woman that the City Guards hadn't even bothered to view.

Anger flared up in him briefly, like kindling. But like kindling it ignited a bigger log, an anger that did not leap and glare but that burned slow and deep and hot.

"I know you have better things to do in town than go chasing around Plaquemines Parish so that your Captain can look good to the City Council," January said. "And I know that you're doing your duty, and going where you're sent. But the fact remains that nobody from the City Guards is going to make the slightest effort to find out who murdered Hesione LeGros. And I think she's as entitled to justice as a rich white man is. Or she should be, anyway."

Shaw said nothing, only chewed his tobacco in silence, pale eyes catching the last glints of light between the pillars. The last of the market-women gathered their baskets and left. A couple of men over by the coffee-stand scraped their rush-bottomed chairs close together, so that the brims of their high-crowned beaver hats almost touched. "I can let you have it for three hundred," murmured one of them, "plus the balance at five percent on the fifteenth. . . ."

"She is as entitled, Maestro, yes," replied Shaw. "If it's justice you're after, an' not revenge."

"Sometimes it gets hard to tell the difference, if you haven't had a look at either one for a while."

"Chink, pink, honey, oh Lula," sang the sweeper, his voice fading as he put his broom on his shoulder and walked away toward the levee. *"Chink, pink, honey, oh Lula. . . ."* Shadow flowed out of the east in his wake. In the plane-trees of the square, the cicadas roared.

Shaw said, "You know I'll do what I can to help."

"I know," said January, and held out his hand. "Thank you."

But as he watched the gangling shape depart, silhouetted against the orange flare of the cressets along the levee, January reflected that he himself was probably the only person in New Orleans actually interested in bringing either justice or vengeance to the shade of Hesione LeGros.

January dreamed that night about the man who'd raped Rose.

Rose's white sister-in-law Alice had told him once that this man had been a planter on Isle Dernière, a free man of color: *Big like you,* she'd said. *Lighter, of course . . .*

(*Why "of course"?* he'd wondered. *Because people don't come much DARKER than me?*)

No wonder Rose sometimes shied from his hand.

In his mind he'd constructed him, enormous and swaggering and arrogant—well-dressed like the quadroon boys who'd called him *country* and *cane-patch* in his days at the St. Louis Academy for Young Gentlemen of Color. Grinning with big white teeth as he dragged Rose to the bed in her little room behind the grocery, though of course the rape had taken place years ago, most probably in the woods on Grand Isle.

Still he saw it taking place in her room. He saw this man—Mathieu was his name—strike her and throw her down on the bed, and January shouted, shocked and sickened; saw Mathieu tear her bodice open, drag at her skirts. Heard him laugh as she screamed, as she sobbed *No, no, please . . .*

And January, dizzy, confused, overwhelmed with a desperate disorientation, laid hold of this man, tried to drag him off her, tried to strike him. In the manner of dreams he could not, for his arms had been hurt trying to help Cora, and his hands had no more strength in them than a child's. He could only shout *Stop it, stop it,* and Rose thrashed her head back and forth, weeping, *No, no. . . .*

Never saying *Ben.* Never calling on him for help.

Why not?

She had a knife in her hand, the thin-bladed paper-knife she used to slit the pages of her books, and she stabbed at Mathieu's back, unable to strike a genuine blow. January wrenched the knife away from her and buried it between those wide, dark shoulders. Stabbed again and again, the knife releasing spraying fountains of blood, as if the heart itself had been punctured or the throat cut. Mathieu reared back and rolled onto the floor, and January fell on his knees over him, straddling him, burying the knife in his chest again and again—chest and face and belly, slashing and cutting, with blood everywhere and the smell of it choking, like the nights at the clinic of the Hôtel Dieu in Paris, when there'd been a riot at some tavern in the Saint-Antoine district and they'd brought in corpses.

(Shouldn't I help Rose? But he kept on stabbing Mathieu, shaking with relief that his helplessness had been conquered, that he could save her.)

While he was stabbing Mathieu, Rose got up off the bed, blood on her clothing *(Mathieu's? Her own?),* her hair straggling over her shoulders, her face streaked with tears and gore. She got off the bed, weeping, and walked past January and out of the room.

Down the stairs.

Across the yard.

Away . . .

Rose? January got up, ran to the door. *Rose!*

He could hear her crying but she didn't turn her head. She left bloody footprints across the dirt of the yard.

He looked back and Mathieu was gone. Flies crawled on the splattered crimson on the sheets, the floorboards, the paper-knife. Down in the yard he saw Mathieu, bleeding, grinning, stride across the yard in pursuit of Rose. . . .

ROSE!!!

. . .

During the days that followed, January undertook as systematic a search as he could manage for information concerning the last days of Hesione LeGros. In those dog days of summer there was little else that required his attention. He had saved enough to live carefully till the frosts brought commerce and entertainment back to the town, and unlike the previous two summers, neither the yellow fever nor the cholera demanded skilled hands in the hospitals.

He was aware that his quest was a quixotic one. Even if he could learn who it was who had waited for the weary drunkard in her shack that night, he was almost certain the City Guards would be as lax in their prosecution as they were in their investigation. And if, as he suspected, her killer was an American, even an arrest would very likely be followed by an acquittal.

Yet he felt drawn to the search. Perhaps the sense of helplessness he'd felt in his dream drove him, the anger and the desperation to save Rose—to save Hesione—even though his gesture would be as futile as it was in the dream. He could not change the past; he could not bring back the dead.

At other times he wondered whether he acted purely from self-interest. As a child he'd been taught to love justice for its own sake, and with each person who abandoned the ideal of justice, he sensed that the cold night of absolute cash-down callousness drew nearer. His life had touched Hesione's, long ago. He had seen her as she had been, and had seen, too, what time had made of her. She was owed some little justice for that lost beauty, for that abandoned life.

Or maybe, he reflected, he just didn't want the jeer in Olympe's eyes to reflect the truth.

"Do you think your landlady might know something about her?" asked Artois St. Chinian as he followed January into the market on the morning after January's talk with Shaw.

The difference from last night's stillness and shadow was striking. Plank tables glowed with the fruits of summer: tomatoes, eggplants, squashes brilliant as jewels. Frilly bushels of lettuces, spinach, kale, like green and purple petticoats. Piles of beans, thin as thread or thick as a man's finger; aureate-bearded corn. Fuzzy peaches and dark-shining plums. Early sun splashed the gutters like a blinding scatter of coins. A beggar played the same eight bars of the overture from *The Barber of Seville*—badly—on the cornet, and against it the charcoal-man's wailing song lifted to the rafters: "My horse she white, my charcoal black/Get your charcoal, five-cents sack/Chaaaaaaar-cooooooal. . . ."

The levees might be still and the town half-sunk in feverish summer doldrums, but at this sunrise hour of the morning, there was always something going on at the market.

"She might," January agreed. "But I'm not sure how much of what Madame Bontemps knew would be true."

Artois laughed, and gazed around him eagerly, like a schoolboy despite the dandyish adult costume of nip-waisted blue jacket and silk vest. Rose had told January recently that prior to his father's death the boy had led a sheltered life.

Thinking of her words—thinking of Rose at all—brought last night's dream back to him, and with it a sense of panic and guilt, as if it had really been true.

And it was true, he remembered: Rose really had been raped, and had tried to kill herself as a result.

And he, Benjamin January, love her though he did, could do nothing. . . .

"But your landlady was a plaçée, wasn't she?" Artois' clear voice called back his thoughts from the smell of blood, the red-daubed tracks of Rose's bare feet across the yard. . . .

"She was. But I don't think she was even out, the year Hesione was coming to the Blue Ribbon Balls. And then, Marie-Claire Bontemps was one of the town ladies. She'd no more have spoken to a Grand Terre pirate's woman than your mother would have."

"Well, that's true." Artois smiled ruefully. "But my mother will barely even speak to *your* mother, because she was the plaçée of a businessman and not a planter."

Having been snubbed at his mother's house in the past by the beautiful Coquelicot St. Chinian, January knew this was true. In the wake of her protector's death, Raymond St. Chinian's mistress had immediately converted the house and the lakeside cottage he'd given her to cash and had removed to Boston, where she was reputedly passing herself off as a Spanish countess, which, being fair-skinned and fine of feature, she was easily able to do. Artois, just as light-complected but unmistakably of African descent, had been put in the boarding-school for young free gentlemen of color from which his great-uncle Veryl had rescued him: sometimes January shook his head wonderingly that after such treatment the boy was as happy and peaceful-hearted as he seemed to be.

Cut-Nose Chighizola wasn't at his stand in the market: "Gran'père, he only come here one, maybe two times in five." The swarthy young man behind the mountain of velvet-green haricots shrugged with a resigned grin. "Used to be he'd come up here every other load, from the farm on the island; come up, and work the table, him, the biggest farmer in the Barataria. Come up through the bayous in the pirogue, sell here in the market till it was gone, then head back down for another load while Papa brought up his load. And *fast!*"

He shook his head wonderingly, and glanced past January to give a grin and a wave to a bandy-legged Greek lugging a rush-basket dripping with salt-water and shrimp. "It takes my Papa two, sometime three days to get up here, across the Bay and up through the trembling lands. Sometime up Bayou des Familles or Bayou St. Roche or the Little Barataria, depending on where the water is. But Gran'père . . . he leave Grand Isle before the wasps wake up, as they say, and I swear he be setting out his tomatoes here in the market next morning! That's what it is to be a pirate, eh? He can run his pirogue on dew, an' I swear he gets the birds in the trees to tell him how much water's in Bayou Segnette, or whether he needs to come through Lake Catahouache this time, and which way's the fastest to-day. I tell you, Governor Claiborne couldn't beat my Gran'père, an' the American Army couldn't beat my Gran'père, an' the British couldn't beat my Gran'père. Not on the marshes."

And he chuckled, with a glint of the old pirate shining in his eyes.

"I ask him once, I say, 'Gran'père, why you go all the way up the bayou to town with the fruits, eh? Why don't you stay here and be comfortable, 'stead of squishing round the trembling lands and gonna get eat by an alligator.' An' he say, *Jean, when I was a gentle-man . . .* ' They all call themselves gentlemen, you know? Lafitte's boys that camped on Grand Terre. My Gran'mère just roll her eyes an' say, 'Gentlemen my cat's left hind leg!' But Gran'père say, 'When I was a gentleman, I know everyone in town, and everything that go on there, same way as I know the marsh. I see one glance, I hear one whisper, and to me it's like I see whether the elephant-ear growin' thick or puny at the head of Little Barataria Bayou. It tell me is there water there this week or not, like M'sieu Blanque not sayin' *Hello* to M'sieu Dutillet in the market tell me whether steamship stocks are up or down. But to know this, to see this, you gotta go up check that bayou pretty often. And you gotta go up see the faces in the market, an' know who's in town an' whose servants are wearin' new shoes.' "

Jean Chighizola laughed. "My Gran'père, he's an honest man now, but he don't forget."

"Did your Grandpère bury treasure?" Artois was fascinated at this insight into the workings of the piratical mind.

"Pff!" The young farmer was a few years older than Artois, his beard making him appear older still; short and stocky in a faded smock of blue-and-pink-striped homespun. *"What the good buryin' treasure?* my Gran'père say. Everybody who come to the island, they always ask about buried treasure, and they always ask Gran'père, 'cause he there. But the Boss—that what they call Lafitte in them days, the Boss of the Barataria—what the Boss steal, it's always stuff he could turn around and sell right away, and he put the money in a bank. Only an idiot bury his money in the ground."

January stepped back as a well-dressed housewife came up, the sort of French Creole matron who bedizened herself "with four pins," as the Creoles said, to go to the market, and who circulated among the stands as if she were doing the Stations of the Cross, haggling over every bean. While Jean Chighizola and this lace-bonneted Madame engaged in war to the knife over the value of the onions, January selected a couple of eggplants and some tomatoes, explaining to Artois, who had never shopped for his own meals, how to tell if melons were ripe and what to look for in strawberries.

"You come back an' look for Gran'père next week," advised young Jean when the housewife's servant had stowed the contested vegetables in her basket and the two women departed in quest of tomatoes. "I tell him you asking for him, he make sure to be here. He know everything, Gran'père." And he wisely tapped the side of his nose, whose size and aquiline arch spoke volumes for the organ that his progenitor had lost.

January's inquiries about Hesione's customers, and the events of her last day on earth, were similarly inconclusive. A number of the market-women remembered her prowling among the bare stands Thursday night, reeking of cheap rum and ramblingly begging for either leftover vegetables or a few reales to buy bread: "Not that bread was what she woulda bought with it if I'd a' given her money," added a vendor in a purple tignon. "But that ain't my business." January gathered that toward evening, the market-women frequently saw Hesione trolling for customers, either in the market or on the levee beyond.

"She'd take 'em on sometimes two an' three at a time," said another vendor, shaking her head sadly: an elderly former plaçée called La Violette. "Sailors, mostly, or men too poor to pay what the younger girls charges. Or those the younger girls wouldn't go near, the dirty ones or the mean ones or the ones drunk themselves on whiskey and laudanum, and dangerous. When she was sober Hessy'd just about kick 'em to pieces for speakin' to her, spittin' an' cussin'; but when she was drunk, or needed bad to get drunk, she'd pull up her dress in an alley for a glass of rum."

"But she had no money that night?" Beside him, January was aware of Artois' expression of sickened pity. Studious and rather shy, the boy had lived in the shadow of his father's wealth for most of his life, and of his mother's finicking insistence that he was a gentleman and the son of a gentleman. Only since Rose had become his tutor—and since meeting January through her—had Artois begun, like Siddhartha Gautama before him, to encounter the class of persons who didn't leave New Orleans for the lakefront every summer.

La Violette shook her head. "Hessie said as how she'd been drinking at the Nantucket that afternoon. Some men there had promised to 'lend' her some money, white men, keelboatmen, but they cheated her of it in the end, she said."

She asked January then after his mother, and Dominique, and how was Dominique's health; after Artois' mother Coquelicot, although January would have been willing to bet Coquelicot St. Chinian would never have passed the time of day with an old market-woman who peddled coffee. The whole subject of Henri Viellard's marriage to Chloë St. Chinian was brought out, aired, shaken, and re-folded like clothes in a hamper. It was summer, after all, and no one was in any hurry to get anywhere or do anything, and in parting La Violette gave Artois a white praline fragrant of coconut, and a flirtatious smile.

"It's come back to me twice, since the night Rose was attacked," said January, folding his hands between his knees and not meeting Olympe's eyes. "Thursday after I spoke to Shaw, and then again last night." The parlor of his sister's cottage was dim, with the shutters still closed to guard the morning's vanishing cool. Through the dining-room the yard could be glimpsed, where Olympe's husband, Paul, worked fitting legs to a cradle for Dominique's baby. In the rear bedroom, young Zizi-Marie told her small sister Chouchou tales of magical princesses and talking dogs as they made the beds.

This front parlor was where Olympe met with those who came to her for gris-gris—for balls of black wax and pins to make an enemy go away, for jack honeysuckle and verbena to uncross the spell of a jealous neighbor or malicious rival in love. Shelves on one wall held the stock of her trade, bright-colored tins or stoppered gourds of willow-bark or comfrey, pottery jars of gunpowder, a dish of mouse-bones, squares of red flannel or black. Bunches of herbs hung drying from a string. Banners of cut paper surrounded a bottle painted black and glued with beads. Cowrie shells strewed around a glass jar of ashes that contained fragments of bone.

"I try to pull him off her, and I can't." January didn't look at Olympe as he spoke, staring down instead at his own hands, conscious of the gray cat watching him from the cold hearth and wondering why he'd come to his sister with these visions at all. But he knew of no one else he could take them to, and after the second time of dreaming, he knew he had to take them to someone.

"I stab him, over and over, and while I'm doing it she just gets

up and leaves, crying. Then he gets up and follows her, and I can't
kill him again because he's already dead."

He looked up at her then, seeing her not as the skinny little sister of his plantation memories, or the furious, foul-mouthed urchin
whose silent hatred of their mother and their mother's protector had
earned her so many beatings. Seeing rather the healer of bodies and
minds, the priestess of an ancient faith: a servant of God by one of
His alternate names.

"And what does Rose dream?" asked Olympe, and January was
so taken aback by the unexpected question that for a minute he
didn't answer.

"About me? Or about Mathieu?"

"About herself," said Olympe. "And about what she wants out
of life."

"I don't know." And as the words came out of his mouth he felt,
instead of anger at himself that he didn't know, or anger at Rose for
not speaking to him of her dreams, an understanding: *She does not
speak of her dreams because she does not dare.*

*Maybe because it has never occurred to her that anyone would be
interested in the secrets of that walled garden within her mind.*

He was aware of Olympe's eyes on him then, speculative under
lowered lids: velvety, like African night. Gauging him, putting together pieces of information and coming up with . . . *What?* "What
do *you* dream?" he asked, curious, and her smile widened and softened, and he came away from that conversation into the slamming
heat of the forenoon a little wiser, a little bemused, and with an in-
explicable sense of peace.

Was it Rose he dreamed of saving, he wondered, as he turned
his steps toward the Swamp, or was it Hesione, with her gaudy dress
and brilliant smile?

Or did it matter, to his dreams? They had both deserved rescue
that, at the time, no one arrived to give.

And he, Benjamin, could only give them now what he had.

In going down to the Swamp, January had long ago learned to pick his time. By noon, the keelboatmen, filibusters, and roughnecks who inhabited its coarse boarding-houses and canvas-roofed taverns were awake and stirring but not yet drunk enough to make trouble. This may have been because at noon on an August day it was simply too hot to get into fights over nothing. Early evening was the danger time. The bearded and filthy river-rats who came down the Mississippi with cargoes of skins or corn or rawhides spent most of their days in New Orleans drinking, aware that they were despised by the regular inhabitants of the town and aware, too, that any money they were paid for their goods was almost immediately taken from them again by town gamblers and town whores and town tavern-keepers. By early evening, liquor had fueled their sense of grievance to the point of striking out at anyone who came to hand. Even each other, if they were in the mood for an all-out fight.

If they simply wanted the savage pleasure of beating up some-one who was legally prevented from fighting back, anyone black would do.

Clouds were moving in from over the lake as January walked out past Charity Hospital and along Perdidio Street. His broken-down rawhide "quantier" shoes slurped in the mud: he'd clothed

himself at a slop-shop, and walked with a slouch, like a man who's
tried to find work on the levee in the morning cool but has given up
for the day.

He wasn't the only such—black or white—loafing along here.
Unceiled, unpainted, ramshackle buildings gradually replaced the
brick or wood of the new American business section of town. The
unpaved street narrowed to a track; taverns straggled among the
trees, and rough-built whorehouses consisting of single lines of
rooms, each room's long window opening straight onto the mud
street to display an untidy bed and an untidier woman: "Fuck you,
bitch, are you sayin' my perfume stinks?" screeched a voice from one
of them, and January leaped aside as someone hurled a chamber-pot
that barely missed his shoulder.

Sewage, stale liquor, and livery-stable muck-heaps freighted
the air.

Legally, of course, men of color—slave or free—were forbidden
to be sold alcohol, and even if it had been allowed, there wasn't a
tavern or barroom in New Orleans that would permit a man of
African descent to drink with whites. But many of the taverns and
half the groceries in town routinely sold liquor out the back doors
to all comers, and January knew the practice was nearly universal in
the Swamp. He asked—cautiously—the whereabouts of the Nantucket, aware that if Hesione had been killed by a customer whom
she'd injured or insulted, it wouldn't do to have word get around
that a six-foot-three-inch Congo-black Negro had been making inquiries. The saloon in question was, in fact, one of the larger and
newer ones of the district, boasting at the moment only canvas for a
roof, a rather large stable, and four sheds that evidently served as
whores' cribs.

Two men—one of whom wore the tin badge of a slave earning
his own keep—loitered on the rude plank bench outside the saloon's
back door, talking in the desultory fashion of those whose hopes for
day-labor have already been crushed and who have a day of heat and
idleness before them. A sort of abat-vent made a patch of shade,
though the Americans clearly had no idea of the French Creole skill
in manipulating shadow and breeze. The yard, with its steaming
puddles and reeking mire around the outhouse, was hot as a

bake-oven at an hour when any courtyard in the French town would still retain at least a little of the night's cool.

January made the obligatory queries about was it so that a man could get a drink here, and for half a reale received a gourd cup of liquor so mouth-wringingly vile, he wondered that the place had customers at all, ever. Another man—a runaway, he guessed—showed up, and one of the local whores in her sweaty gimcrack finery, and when rain started to fall at about one, everybody took whatever liquor they'd bought and retreated under the eaves of the stable, which did have a roof. It was a long, idle, unproductive day.

Hesione had been there, January learned, and had picked up a pair of beaver-hunters, brutes who skinned for the Rocky Mountain Fur Company and boasted of the half-breed girls they'd raped in the villages north of Taos. She'd paid Franklin Mulm, the Nantucket's owner, fifty cents for the privilege of receiving her customers in one of the cribs—"The one back of that tree there, that he rents to girls who don't work for him regular," explained the badged slave, whose name was Cuffee—and there'd been an altercation over the rest of the money owed her. "Talk about cussin'! Mr. Burke, that works for Mr. Mulm, couldn't shut Hessy up, an' ol' Mulm himself come out, madder'n piss 'cause he had a customer with him. . . ."

January shot his eyebrows up and asked, "What, they got white folks here who didn't know what Hessy could say when she got a head of steam?"

And the men laughed. Mr. Mulm checked his stride on the way across the yard to the privies, and cast a glance at them lounging in the shelter of the stable doors; the laughter ceased instantly and everyone gave the tavern owner smiling, easy greetings, which didn't appear to fool him in the least. A lean, tall Yankee with a jawline beard so thin and fair it reminded January of socks on a clothesline, Mulm dressed immaculately, his narrow black cutaway coat and dark waistcoat giving him the appearance of an undertaker rather than a publican. He carried an ivory-handled English umbrella as he crossed the yard, to keep dry his clothing and his tall-crowned silk hat.

"Well, hell, I had him give me a lick or two with that cane of his for sayin' damn," mused the runaway man. "For a man as crooked as a snake's hard-on he sure doesn't hold with cussin'. But I think he was mostly pissed 'cause old Sangre bargained him hard over that day's cargo. . . ."

"Other way around," contradicted the whore, taking a bottle of laudanum from her reticule and dosing her whiskey with it. "Sancho Sangre's buyin' these days, not sellin'. Runnin' guns down to the rebels in New Grenada an' makin' the poor bastards pay double for rusty old blunderbusses you couldn't kill a dog with, less'n you whacked it over the head with the butt." She scratched down the front of her emerald silk gown, tattered and soiled and sloppily laced over her bare flesh: it was amply evident she didn't even have a chemise beneath, let alone a corset. "Sangre still screwed Mulm good over the deal, though. I thought old Wispy-Whiskers would get his bully, Burke, to have a little word with Sangre on the way out, but Sangre brought three or four friends of his own. . . ."

"I'd still have give a lot to hear Hessy when she got cussin'," sighed January as a way of steering the conversation back to the original topic, and the others laughed.

"Hessy shouted down Burke," agreed Cuffee. "That takes some doin'. He's a big bastard. Mulm finally give her a couple drinks to shut her up. I don't think she ever did get money outa them two fellas."

"Went to the same place, anyways." The woman Zulime shrugged. "I come on her later that day, sleepin' behind the privies, an' woke her when it start to rain. She give me a *milagros*—one of those blessin' things she made—to put up in the church. . . . See?" From her shabby reticule the whore produced a tin amulet of the crescent moon and a star, pinched and twisted of wire and scraps and fragments of dirty lace. "What a damn shame, that anybody'd hurt her."

And presumably her dissatisfied customers had had plenty of time to take revenge on her if they'd wanted it while she was sleeping, reflected January, turning the little blessing-sign in his hands.

A crash in the saloon brought all their heads around. "You suckass hound, I can fuck an alligator in the ass an' I ain't about to be cheated by no lousy pimp like you!" Voices bayed, slurry with liquor and the quick rage of those who live by violence. Chairs rattled and scraped. Then a man came rolling, hurled out the back door and into the mud, a big-bearded keelboatman in heavy boots. The next second Mulm strode out the door and was on top of him, swift and smooth as a rattlesnake, his lead-headed cane in his hand.

Before the Kaintuck could get to his feet, Mulm kicked him, hurling him into the mud again, and proceeded to beat him with the leaden end of the cane: savagely, brutally, and without change of expression, his face calm, as if he were reading a shipping invoice. Twice the Kaintuck tried to get up and twice Mulm shoved him down again. The dull whump of the blows resounded across the yard like a steam hammer striking a pile of hides, while the rain sluiced them and mud and blood splattered like sea-spray.

In a few minutes the keelboatman's upraised hands fell. Mulm went on beating him, like a woman beating a carpet. "He gonna kill him," whispered the whore Zulime.

The runaway only said, "Looks like."

Thunder boomed and the rain redoubled, gray, blinding sheets of it. Mulm, thin fair hair hanging soaked about his ears, kept up with his beating as if contracted to deliver a specified number of strokes. When he finished he went inside, calling for a clean hand-kerchief to wipe his spectacles—January wondered where he'd get anything clean in the Nantucket. His victim lay in the mud without moving, until men came out from the saloon and dragged him away.

January left soon after that. The rain was easing. Men who'd spent the afternoon getting drunk would soon be in the streets. He didn't want to ask more questions about Hesione, knowing how such things got around. He had learned pretty much what he'd set out to—that the two men she'd quarreled with that afternoon had had no reason to seek her out that night.

Or no reason anyone drinking in the yard was aware of.

There were other customers, of course. And there were men in New Orleans perfectly capable of murdering a woman because they imagined she'd passed the clap along to them, though he couldn't imagine any man who wasn't a poxed degenerate in the first place coupling with Hesione. He made his way through the weedy wilderness of broken-down shacks, with the hot damp of the rain rising back out of the sodden ground and the drumming air thick with green scents, and wondered what his course of inquiry would be if Cut-Nose couldn't provide him with information about a child or sibling from Hesione's Grand Terre days.

Not a sparrow falls, Jesus had said, whose death God does not mark.

Perhaps he, January—and Hesione—would have to be content with that knowledge.

In the meantime the summer days lay hot on the town. With most of his pupils away, January had the leisure to read, and sleep, and play music for his own pleasure. Evenings of walking with Rose, or Rose and Artois—aimless, peaceful walks along Bayou St. John or under the plane-trees of the Place d'Armes, with talk of music or books or the good-natured gossip of friends. Artois gesturing, pouring out his speculations about why thunderstorms formed or what scientists like Redfield and Brandes wrote about them, and how barometers could be improved; Rose smiling, more like a friend than the boy's teacher. Pralines and coffee in the market stands. Rose's calm profile in the evening light, and the smile that came and went.

January asked her what she dreamed, and she tucked away her smile and glanced aside, and said, "Terribly ordinary things, I'm afraid: gardening—I miss having a garden—and counting gloves."

"Counting gloves?"

"My mother would never wear a pair again if they got the slightest spot on them; I inherited them, in every color one could imagine. . . . I don't know why they fascinated me so, because after I was about ten my hands were too big to fit into them. She had dainty little hands, my mother, and let me know in no uncertain terms that no true lady had big, clumsy paws and long fingers like mine."

Her hands were big, true, but they were long and supple, like those of a Renaissance portrait; January took one and brought it to his lips, seeing as he did that the glove she wore had been mended, not once but several times. Her mother, like his, had been a plaçée: she had undoubtedly been expected to become one, too.

A few days after his talk with Olympe, January got a job playing for a cotillion at one of the big hotels in Milneburgh, and rode out in the steam-cars with the other musicians, walking home late along the shell road beside Bayou St. John with the cicadas rattling in the trees. That Friday he took the steam-cars again to give a lesson to the Saulier girls, daughters of a Frenchman who stayed in town to mind his importing business and entertain his mistress during the week; January would see the man sometimes on the Rue Burgundy, where M'sieu Saulier's placée had her house. That Friday, too, he walked from the Sauliers' cottage to Dominique's little lakeside dwelling, and drank lemonade with his sister on the gallery over the water, and talked of the affairs of the town.

Dominique was quiet, and when she talked, she spoke in a bright, airy, brittle voice of what Henri had said to her, or the gifts he had given. But it was clear to January from stories repeated, and the hesitancies while Dominique counted up days in her head, or from the way her maid would look at her mistress when Dominique's head was turned, that she had seen Henri seldom lately, and not for any long period of time. "Poor thing, his mother is driving him absolutely *distracted,*" she said, fanning herself with a circle of stiffened silk. "My heart *bleeds* with pity for that *horrid* girl he's marrying, who'll have Aurelie Viellard for a mother-in-law, which nobody deserves, even a girl who sold off her nurse and half-sister, not to mention spending the rest of her life trying to find husbands for those *ghastly* sisters of Henri's. . . . Do you know they're trying to make a match with old Theobald Trudeau for Manon? He's a perfectly nice man, of course, even if he does charge two dollars a pound for quite ordinary China tea. . . . Not that the way the girls look is their fault, of course. And sheep are actually quite amiable creatures, unless one has to marry a girl who looks like one. . . ."

When it began to rain, and Phlosine Seurat appeared with a rosewater jelly to tempt her friend's appetite, the three of them went inside and January played for Dominique and her guest—after a short delay to tune his sister's little six-octave piano, which as usual had succumbed to the damp. Afterward he tried to find out what the plaçées knew of local rumor, but like his mother, neither Phlosine nor Dominique had the slightest interest in the murder of Hesione LeGros and were instead consumed with questions and gossip concerning the baroque details of the Avocet scandal.

"Darling, of *course* Vivienne Avocet and her husband's brother were lovers! Everyone in *town* knows that!"

"I've heard she just about bankrupted her husband Guifford, too," added Phlosine, a slim young woman whose nervous, fairylike beauty always reminded January of jasmine blossoms. "Not that there was much money there to begin with. And Guifford himself was an absolutely pestilent man, not that Bertrand is any saint. And that poor little dab of a sister of theirs, caught between them and being treated like a servant by both."

"You know what I find suspicious about the whole story?" Dominique set her tea-spoon down, and widened her eyes. "That Vivienne was sewing in the parlor with Sister Annette at the time of the murder. Because according to Thérèse's cousin Louise, who knows the sister of the cook on Avocet, Annette Avocet *hates* Vivienne. She calls her 'that French imbecile' and to get back at her Vivienne makes Annette repair her dresses and wear her cast-offs. . . ."

"Marie-Ursule—that's Guifford's plaçée," explained Phlosine, as if it were the most natural thing in the world for a nearly-bankrupt planter who'd been married less than a month to have a town mistress, "—says Guifford and Bertrand tried to get their sister into a convent so they could each have a bigger share of the plantation. Bertrand tried to get up an affair with Marie-Ursule, too: just to enrage Guifford, Marie-Ursule says."

"Really, p'tit," sighed Dominique, shifting her aching back a little within the shaped cage of her "motherhood" corset, and tucking a pillow behind her, "I don't see why you don't help M'sieu Shaw with finding proof that Bertrand did it, instead of wasting your time about that tiresome woman in the Swamp."

No, thought January later, as he rode the steam-cars back through the stagnant heat toward the city again, *no, she does not see.* . . . And indeed, he could understand her puzzlement. A drunk old woman was dead—so what?

But though he jotted notes of everything the two young women had gossiped about the Avocets, to pass along to Shaw the next time he saw him, he felt a great sense of impatience with the affair, and a great sense of distance. For most of the week, he knew, Shaw had been down in Plaquemines Parish, patiently quartering the plantation for some kind of physical evidence to add to the slim facts he'd been able to glean, or for some indication of what might have become of the missing overseer.

Yet as January printed in his notebook *Mistress Marie-Ursule—Bertrand tried to seduce...* the obviousness of Guifford Avocet's death, in its tangle of money, passion, and family hatreds, faded before the maddening question of why the man with the gouged bootsole would *lie in wait* to murder a woman of no value. . . .

Guifford Avocet, from all January had ever heard, sounded like a completely unpleasant man who had all but asked for the blow that had ended his life. Hesione LeGros had owned nothing, had presented no threat to anyone . . .

Or had she? A jolt of the train made his pencil veer—*Well, that looks enough like "bankrupt" for me to remember what it is when I see Shaw. . . .*

He gazed past the thinning cypresses, to the first wretched gaggles of tents and shacks and pigpens that gradually gave place to the rude board houses, then the low-built pastel dwellings of the French Town, the clapboarded wooden houses of the American; the walled cemeteries and muddy streets and overwhelming privy-reek of New Orleans, simmering under the molten weight of the afternoon sun.

There's something about Hesione's death that I'm not seeing. Something behind it, that will make it make sense.

And Guifford Avocet, with his new wife and his mistress in town and his two stopped clocks and his missing overseer—the man had been replaced already, according to Shaw, by someone just as capricious and heavy-handed as the missing Raffin—*can rot, for all of me.*

He wondered if Shaw felt the same.

SEVEN

On the day of Henri's marriage to Chloë St. Chinian, January went again to Dominique's, accompanied by Rose and, at the last minute, by Artois. January wasn't certain how his sister would react to the presence of the octoroon half-brother of Henri Viellard's bride in her home, but Artois was virtually the only member of the family not invited to the wedding—and, it turned out, January had greatly underestimated his sister.

She met them on the shell path down to her door with eyes wide in mock astonishment, crying, "P'tit! Why, today of all days! *What* a surprise!" And laughed gently at his well-meant concept of her overwhelming distress.

Dominique took to Artois at once. The two of them compared notes about the family and laughed hilariously over coffee and gingerbread about the procession from town and the reception at the Viellard "cottage." "What did they think I was going to do?" demanded Artois when Dominique referred to their gathering as the most distantly separated table at the wedding-breakfast. "Stand up and make a speech? Demand to escort my sister down the aisle?" He gestured with his coffee-cup, spilling coffee on his sleeve.

"Benjamin was offered five dollars to play at the wedding-breakfast," put in Rose, something January hadn't intended to mention.

"Oh, you should have taken it, p'tit!" cried Dominique. "Then you could tell us what it was like! I wonder if they really did dig mad old Uncle Joffrey out of his plantation to come."

"They didn't manage that," grinned Artois. "But Gran'mère Marie-Agnes was there, in full mourning. . . ."

"At a *wedding?*"

"Obviously her grief is more important than her grandson's good luck," remarked Rose.

"How unkind of you to cavil!" declared Artois in mock reproof. "If the old lady has any gowns that aren't black crepe, they'll be the kind with the big skirts and panniers. I think she's been wearing mourning since Napoleon left for St. Helena—and claiming she's going to die for at least that long. We saw the wedding procession coming out from town. . . ."

"And I owe you an apology, Minou, for not believing you," added Rose, passing Dominique the bread-and-butter. Breezes floated across the lake and its waters murmured around the piers beneath the back gallery on which they sat; music from the Washington Hotel colored the warm air. "Not only was Henri's grandmother immured like a Turkish lady in crepe and jet jewelry and lockets made of her dead husband's hair, for all I know, she actually did have four servants—also in mourning livery—following her carriage with a carrying-chair to get her in and out of the Cathedral and the cottage for the breakfast, all draped in black like a catafalque. I thought you had to be making that part up. . . ."

"Darling, who could make up a story like that?"

January smiled, listening to them, hearing his sister laugh for the first time in weeks. Grateful that the day of the wedding, which he knew Dominique had been dreading, had been turned, by company, into an occasion of laughter and coffee.

Had Dominique watched the wedding procession, too, coming along the shell road that was visible from the gallery where they now sat? Henri Viellard, enormous in a gray satin coat and knee-breeches, blinking myopically through his spectacles and not looking at his bride. The bride herself, a chill, pale girl of barely seventeen, gazing straight before her with enormous china-blue eyes, her arms full of flowers. Aurelie Viellard, Henri's formidable mother, in the same carriage, immense in plum-colored silk and reminiscent, with her Roman-nosed arrogance, of a huge and highly-bred sheep; the unmarried Viellard daughters clumped in the next equipage, all five dressed in extravagant lilac gowns that suited none of them. Eloise Viellard de McCarty and her husband in the carriage behind them, with their children, the whole tale told right there, thought January: Henri must marry, and must produce an heir, so that the four plantations, the town houses, the sugar-mills and the hundreds of slaves would remain in the control of the Viellards and not be dispersed among sons-in-law.

And every child Henri might father upon a mistress, his mother—and his wife—would see as seed robbed from the legitimate line.

The rest of the procession had been, as Artois described, the usual French Creole gallery of types: bachelor cousins and old aunts. Uncle Veryl, resplendent in knee-smalls and a linen cravat tied in a *trône d'amour* style such as January hadn't seen in public for twenty years, in a decrepit phaeton far back in the line of carriages, driven by the valet James. "Everyone in the family thinks Uncle Veryl's hopelessly eccentric to live in that big town house with only a valet and a cook," said Artois.

"And here I've been unable to hold up my head all this time," sighed January, "because I have only a valet, a cook, a footman, and a gardener."

Artois flashed him a grin. "James and I hunted all over town for a suitable wedding-gift. We got a pair of Sèvres soft-paste candlesticks—Louis Fifteenth—which I hope Uncle will recognize when he sees them at the wedding-breakfast."

"We'd best go inside," said Rose at the grumble of thunder above the lake. Lightning flickered among the gathering black clouds. "Water conducts electricity."

"From how far away?" inquired Artois at once. "If the lightning struck three miles out, could it kill us here?" He didn't sound particularly worried over the possibility, just curious.

"If water conducts electricity, why wasn't Mr. Franklin electrocuted when he stood out flying his kite in a storm, like an imbecile?" objected Dominique. "And more importantly, why didn't he catch his death of chill? What did his wife have to say about him coming home soaking wet and spending the next three days demanding foot-baths and blancmanges and fortifying steams?"

"I don't think he had a wife," said Rose.

"And a good thing, too," sniffed Minou. She broke a croquette in half and left it untasted on the edge of her plate; her condition, though gracefully concealed by the raised waist of her gown and a lace-ruffled pelerine, made her peckish. "If he left a great clutter with kites and keys and parts for his new stove and spending all his time at philosophical societies and scribbling the Declaration of Independence, hmph!"

Thérèse brought more coffee and croquettes, and Artois took out the red-bound commonplace-book that never left him, and made notes about the waterspouts that wavered far off over the dark surface of the lake. As on the previous occasion, they all went inside and lit the candles, and the rain drummed gently on the lake and the gallery and the willow-trees. January played Purcell and Artois studied Dominique's cageful of German finches: "Uncle Veryl's paying for my education," he said when Dominique asked him how Rose came to be his tutor. "Poor Uncle Veryl. He has no children of his own, and the Perrets and Picards—my grandmother's family— are all as stupid as owls. The Viellards, too, except for Henri, who comes over all the time to borrow Uncle's books, you know. I think what Uncle Veryl really wanted was to be a teacher himself, but of course the family wouldn't hear of it any more than they'd hear of Henri becoming a scholar."

"And I suppose the whole family is up in arms now." Dominique rolled her eyes. *"How can he pay to educate the son of That Woman . . .* do they call your maman *That Woman,* cher? I suppose they call me that, too. *How can he pay to educate the son of That Woman and not our own dear little Gnat-Brain and Sheep-Biter?"*

"Ah, that's his strategy in hiring me," smiled Rose, cradling her coffee-cup between her palms. "By employing a Mere Female as a tutor he evades the entire question."

"Nonsense." Artois ducked his head shyly. Like Chloë St. Chinian, he had sky-blue eyes, but his were startling against a complexion like old ivory, and his dark, curling lashes made them stand out like jewels. "My uncle's strategy in hiring you was that he wanted me to have the best."

Later, when the rain cleared and Dominique went to lie down for her rest, January, Artois, and Rose made an expedition along the steamy lakeshore to test the skyrocket propellants Rose and Artois had been working on in the laboratory behind Uncle Veryl's town house, shooting rockets out over the restless surface of the lake. This was how Artois had joined the party at Dominique's in the first place, carrying his rockets in a satchel which January had insisted he leave in the outhouse during their visit. It still raised the hair on his head to see Rose casually tinkering around with artillery of that kind—not to mention wading in the ooze of the lakeshore in the habitual haunts of gators and snakes—but he knew it gave her pleasure.

So he carried the satchel, and helped her and Artois set their charges, and held his peace.

Needless to say, their activities that afternoon had been wildly illegal. No person of color, slave or free, was permitted to handle firearms anywhere in the United States after the big slave revolts in the east a few years ago, and January couldn't imagine Captain Tremouille of the City Guards stretching the point for experimentation with rockets. Hence the choice of venue, among the cypress-knees and stands of sedges far from even the optimistic stakes of land developers.

"You have no idea how grateful I am," sighed Rose as they made their way back toward town at day's end, "every time you *don't* say what a woman should and should not do." Her face was smutted with soot where she'd wiped sweat from her forehead, and the hem of her dress was muddy. Behind her spectacles her eyes sparkled bright.

He grinned. "I didn't think you saw me getting ready to die in your defense every time I glimpsed some keelboatman or filibuster in the distance, wandering along the path from town."

He spoke lightly, but in fact he felt drained by his nervous readiness, watching both in the direction of town and all around in the mucky green monotony of the swamps. Rose, from her days on

Grand Isle, knew all about snakes and alligators, and had more than once dragged Artois back from cheniers or deadfalls and made the boy probe them with a stick before he set foot on them. And January knew his own fear stemmed from something else: fear of losing this second treasure, just as he had lost Ayasha.

And that, he supposed, was the true source of his unquiet dreams.

"I've spent most of my life being told how I'll feel or what I'll think, if only I do as I'm told." He heard Rose try to make her voice light as she said it. *You'll feel differently about wanting an education when you're married.* That was my father's favorite. Would you—or anyone—say such a thing to a boy? *All any woman really wants is children of her own.* I don't know how many times Papa and his wife said that to me. My own mother, too, before she died. And that . . . that *pitying* expression in their eyes when I'd cry and cry and tell them they didn't understand."

She looked up into his face, her hazel-green eyes not velvety with the softness of a lover, but clear with a friend's joy in friendship. "You understand. I don't think you realize how rare that is."

"You forgot *You'll look back on this when you're older and thank us,*" put in Artois, skipping back to them from where he'd gone to see if that was really a baby alligator he'd glimpsed in the ditch beside the shell road—it hadn't been, to his disappointment and January's vast relief. The boy had shed the trim coat of gray superfine he'd worn to Dominique's, and the yellow silk waistcoat; his sleeves were rolled to his forearms and he was licking up the half-melted remains of the Italian ice he'd bought back in Milneburgh, out of its little rolled-paper cup. "I think the nitrate of potassa gave the most distance, don't you? The oil of vitriol by itself in the propellant didn't seem to make much difference one way or the other."

And he skipped forward again to catch a better view of the great mounds of cloud slowly dispersing over the lake.

"Yet my father wanted me to be happy," continued Rose quietly. "Even when he was trying to force me into marriage with Mathieu Patric, he honestly believed that I would 'learn to love,' and be happy."

Hearing her speak the man's name touched a fire in January, as when she had touched a burning match to the fuse of Artois' rocket; red heat went up through his body and into his head.

"He would say that to his own daughter about a man who'd . . ." He bit the words off, remembering that Rose had never told him what Mathieu Patric had done. For a few moments he said nothing, his whole body hot, fearing that she would shrink from him, and from the memory and the shame.

But she only regarded him with those hazel-green eyes, a slight smile on her mouth: "Who told you?" she asked at last.

"Alice. Your sister-in-law." He felt he could barely get the words out. "And I would never have . . ."

"Oh, I certainly guessed you knew." Rose took his hand, those long fingers firm and confident now in his. "And believe me, I appreciate Alice for letting you know—and you for not saying anything of it before. I find it doesn't . . . I'm glad to know that you know."

There was nothing he could think of to say, and this, it seemed, was the right thing; her grip tightened, then she sighed, and shook her head. "Father . . . had no imagination. He wouldn't have admitted that he wanted to get me off his hands—but he wanted to get me off his hands. If I would marry someone and be happy it would mean he'd done well, and could think well of himself. He never could understand why I wanted to go to school. Mathieu was . . . an easy answer to his dilemma."

Even though Mathieu was the kind of man who believed raping a woman was the best way of forcing her father's consent to their marriage.

January asked instead, "Was there money to send you to school?"

Her smile glinted, swiftly tucked away as she guessed his line of thought: that marrying this troublesome daughter to Mathieu Patric, besides allowing him to "settle well" a girl who was now damaged goods, would be cheaper than educating her.

"There was and there wasn't," she replied, and turned her head to watch Artois, a hundred feet ahead of them on the shell path, stooping over the roadside ditch to investigate something there: gecko, snake, turtle. "There would have been if he didn't get new mules. Which is nearly always the case," she added, "when it's a daughter asking for schooling, and not a son."

The day after this, January sought out Marie Laveau on the subject of Hesione LeGros and what family she might have left on Grand Terre. Sundays, the voodooienne could be found in the market the slaves held in Congo Square across the street from where the old city walls used to be. Summer afternoons, the market was quiet, the slaves from the plantations along the lakeshore, or those who managed little garden plots near the city itself, setting out their wares on old blankets or squares of straw matting: corn and eggplants, fat red tomatoes and baskets of ground-nuts and okra, foods most white folks and certainly most Americans had no idea what to do with. "Is it good?" asked Artois a little hesitantly, bending over the okra, and the woman who was selling it grinned up at him.

"Depends on who's cookin' it, Blue-Eyes."

They sold fish there, and game, squirrels and possums and alligator. Snakes, too, hung up by their heads, and baskets woven from braided Spanish moss. Women sold pralines, brown sugar and pecans, or white sugar and coconut, or coconut dyed pink with cochineal, the smell of them vying with the stench of the cemetery a few dozen feet away behind its walls. Others had little fires going and sold coffee by the cup, or gumbo, or coarse stews of shrimp and tomatoes and rice. Artois gazed around him in astonishment, but January smiled to hear him modulating his Parisian-perfect French when he spoke to the vendors, and calling a worm a *loulou,* as they did, and greeting this man or that by January's slangy inquiry *How's your green-beans?* rather than the formal *How do you do?*

When the sun went down and the dense, thick heat cooled a little, someone began playing the drums. More fires were built, to light the space between the trees.

There was a time when January had avoided the dancing in Congo Square.

Although not as sheltered as Artois, he'd been rather strictly raised. Once his mother had been bought, and freed, by St.-Denis Janvier, she'd done her best to eradicate any trace of the heritage of slavery into which she and her two older children had been born. As a child, January had risked a beating if he went to the slave-dances, or even to the market here at the edge of town. His confessor, too, had frowned on it, saying quite rightly that the dancing was wild and inflamed the passions, and adding, with equal truth and considerable insight, that it masked the worship of the old gods, the alien gods who by rights should have been left behind in heathen Africa. The fact that those gods were now given the names of saints didn't fool the old priest, or excuse young Benjamin's attendance at the dances.

And of course his teachers at the St. Louis Academy for Young Gentlemen of Color had argued that association with slaves had an appalling effect on anyone's French.

But returning from sixteen years in France, January had come to see the markets in Congo Square with different eyes. He had been young when he'd left—in his early twenties—and eager to put this land of injustice and grief behind him forever. Only with Ayasha's death had he understood how much of himself was rooted here, in this low green marsh, among these pastel walls. Returning to find his family, he had found his people: the music of the tribes blending, in his heart, with Mozart and Palestrina and Pachelbel in a way that had been impossible during his days of foreign flight.

And as the dancing commenced, the men laughing as they turned the women under their arms, the women flourishing their skirts and tossing their tignoned heads, January saw all this reflected from Artois' wondering blue eyes.

Saw the French boy look into the mirror at the reflection of an African man.

Twilight transformed the sky to a shining topaz. Cicadas roared, and the earth gave back its scents in a deep musk of wetness and sweet-olive. In the wild firelight Marie Laveau the voodooienne appeared, stepping up on a platform of boxes, a tall, handsome woman in a skirt made of red bandannas, her head adorned with a tignon worked into seven points, like flames around her dark, Indian-boned face.

Men shouted, and sang her song: *Oh, yes, yes, Mamzelle Marie/She know well the Grand Zombi. . . .*

And in Laveau's arms the Grand Zombi was lifted up, a

seven-foot king snake with a darting tongue and wise copper eyes that seemed, in the firelight, to be more than the eyes of a reptile.

> *I walk on pins,*
> *I walk on needles,*
> *I walk on gilded splinters. . . .*

People came up to her in the firelight, reached out their hands to her, seeking by contact with her Power to absorb a little of the dark brilliance that seemed to shine from somewhere just beneath her skin. Under the plane-trees, men pranced and leaped and kicked, the bells they wore around their ankles jangling bright as gold. But when Mamzelle Marie danced, she danced as they dance who sing for the dead, only her body moving, sinuous as the snake's. Her eyes were shut, her face at rest, and yet somehow ecstatic under its sheen of sweat: January had seen her at early Mass that morning, praying before the Virgin's altar with that same intense stillness, that same burning peace.

After the dancing, people came up to her. Market-women gave her lemonade or pralines, or bits of callas for the snake. Shopgirls or young wives sought advice from her, or asked for gris-gris to bring to them men they sought. An old woman with country-marks on her face blessed January with spears of gladiolus dipped in a bucket of water; there was laughter and the smell of tafia rum from out of the dark under the trees. Runaways from the woods whispered bits of news and information about things seen in the ciprière, and servants came with other tales to tell, of the doings of their masters whose *blankitte* wives might well visit Marie Laveau in secret and marvel at how much of their doings she already knew.

The voodooienne was the queen of the voodoos, and those Mamzelle Marie didn't rule by friendship and mutual aid, she ruled by secrets and knowledge and fear.

"This is my friend Artois," said January, and the voodoo queen regarded the youth with those bright, sleepy, dangerous eyes.

"Coco's son." She smiled her sidelong smile. "I hear tell you're a pride to any mother's heart that's got a lick of sense. That you're learning the names of all the stars, and all the secrets about how the world is made."

"I have a good teacher," said Artois, which warmed January's heart.

"We're here looking for a secret or two," said January. "You heard about Hesione LeGros being killed, and the Guards not doing a thing to find who did it."

"I heard." She tilted her head to one side, and on her shoulder the Grand Zombi regarded January also, and moved his great smooth narrow head back and forth.

"Did she have family?" asked January. "Or any who knew her, back from her days on Grand Terre, who'd have reason to seek her out now?"

Behind them the drums knocked out a contest of rhythms, a back-and-forth rallying, like a conversation: the deep-voiced barrel-drum grumbling, the little double-headed tenor tapping quick and impudent, like Compair Lapin running circles around ugly Bouki the Hyena, fooling him cross-eyed and getting away with his coat and his supper and his wife.

"What is it to you?" Mamzelle Marie asked January. "Hesione LeGros was nothing to you."

"Hesione LeGros was nothing to anyone," replied January. "None of us are."

"You think a child of hers, or a sister or a brother, would know who came into her house that night and cut her to pieces?"

"I think they might tell me who might have wanted to," he answered. "Who tears down a fence that's in ruins already? Who walks out of their way to break open an empty box? The Americans in the Swamp, that go around beating up each other and the Indians and the slaves who can't defend themselves, they don't lie in wait. They don't cover their tracks and hide in the darkness. It takes hate to plan like that. Hate or greed."

"Or madness." Mamzelle Marie regarded them with wise, cynical eyes. "The madness that sees one old woman and thinks she's another who did a man wrong—his mother, or his aunt, or someone who hit him when he was young. There's crazy men in this town, and men just this side of crazy, who'll go over the edge when they've had a drink or three."

It was a possibility January had considered, too. But something about the spatter of wax on the floor by the chair, that spoke of careful planning, something about the length of charred wick—ten minutes' conversation—spoke to him of other things. Hesione had known her killer. Of that he was sure.

The drums changed their rhythm. Couples paired off again to dance. Firelight dyed the sweaty faces, gleamed liquid gold in dark eyes. They were waiting, January realized, for Marie Laveau to climb back on her box and draw them on with the electric flame of her presence.

"I'll ask around," Mamzelle Marie told him. "I don't go down much to Grand Terre, but there's them that do. Hesione LeGros had three children there, one by Vincente Gambi, another she claimed was Lafitte's; another woman raised them up as hers. Those three are still there, far as I know, and nothing heard against them, but I'll ask. But you steer clear of that Mulm. Keep away from the Nantucket Saloon."

And when January frowned his puzzlement, she shook her head. "Mulm's like a hunter, looking at tracks in the dirt. He's a bad man, a blackmailer, living by secrets and putting together this little fact and that little fact, to wring money out of people. He's a slave-dealer and a thief, and he's always watching, always looking. Men have hanged themselves from knowing him. You watch your back around him, lest you find yourself in more trouble than you counted on."

January stepped back, reflecting that Mulm wasn't the only person who lived by putting facts together—how did Mamzelle Marie know he'd been to the Nantucket? She turned to go, then stopped, looking at Artois, who had put out his hand to touch the great king snake's blunt nose.

The boy snatched his fingers back guiltily, and Marie smiled at him, and brushed her fingers gently against the side of his face.

"I think you better stay out of this, too," she told the boy. "There's no good for you—no good for anyone—in askin' after that poor woman's death. You got a good home, and an uncle looks after you, and gives you all you want. What do you seek in ugly places and unpleasant things?"

"You yourself said why, Mamzelle," Artois replied. "I want to know how the world is made."

"So do we all, my friend." She sighed, and gazed searchingly into his eyes. "So do we all." Her smile faded into an expression of sadness, as if she looked off a great distance, into space or time. Seeing what? January wondered. The woman who styled herself the Contessa d'Ernani, who had left her son in a school full of strangers rather than admit to African blood in her veins? Hesione herself, lying in the pool of blood beneath a glittering shroud of flies?

Then she was gone, and standing on her platform with the Grand Zombi twining around her bare shoulders in the firelight as the drums rattled louder and the great brown-winged palmetto-bugs dove rattling into the flambeaux.

> *Hé hé, Bomba, hé hé,*
> *Canga bafio té!*
> *Canga moune de le,*
> *Canga do ki la. . . .*

"Could the man who killed Hesione have been . . . well . . . Lafitte himself?"

Artois spoke hesitantly, glancing up at January as they slipped through the iron gates of the palisade that surrounded the square, and crossed the stinking dark of Rue des Ramparts. "I mean, no one knows what became of Lafitte after he was driven out by the American Navy. And Hesione did claim she used to be his mistress."

"He could have," agreed January slowly. The drums rose behind them, an insistent throbbing that moved the bones within the flesh; faster and faster, like the pounding of a lover's heart at the strong caress of a hand. Bells jangled on the ankles of the dancers, and already men and women both were *mbuki-mwuki*: throwing off their clothes, the better to dance. He himself had lived his early years on a plantation, and thirty-five years ago the thin veneer of Christian conduct had been even thinner than it was among slaves today. He found himself a little worried after Artois' encounter with Mamzelle Marie.

That the boy would incur harm or sin? he asked himself. Surely not.

That he'd be shocked?

And he realized that the way the voodoo queen had looked at the boy had troubled him. The sadness in her eyes. The regret.

He pushed the thought away. As queen of secrets, Mamzelle Marie might very well have known things about Coquelicot St. Chinian that would make anyone sad for her child. "From everything anyone ever said of Lafitte—those who knew him, I mean— he wouldn't have harmed an old woman."

"Even if Hesione knew something that would compromise him?" asked Artois. "She could have recognized him, you know. If he'd changed his name and gave up smuggling, after the United States Navy burned him out of Campeche, and has been living in hiding all these years, she could have threatened to expose him."

"To whom?" countered January. "And why? Half the French Creoles in town would invite Lafitte to supper if he turned up on their doorsteps. . . . AND ask if he'd happened by any promising bits of goods lately. If Hesione recognized him, and threatened to expose him, he'd be far more likely to buy her off than to murder her, unless there was some enmity between them. And my understanding is there were few women the Boss couldn't charm."

He recalled the Boss encountering an American banker and a staff Colonel of the American Army and their wives on the street, one day just before the war while the army was still engaged in trying to find a way through the swamps of the Barataria to end Lafitte's smuggling ventures. The officer especially had looked tired and disgruntled, since every trapper and fisherman in the marshes knew the thousand tiny waterways of the trembling lands and could relay information about troop movements to Lafitte hours before the soaked and exhausted American invaders arrived at whatever tussock or chenier Lafitte was supposed to be occupying that day; if looks could kill, the gutter of Rue Bourbon would have run crimson.

The Americans had glared, and had passed without a word. But

January had seen how the smuggler-boss removed his hat and placed it over his heart, to bow to the wives of banker and Colonel: graceful as a dancing-master, or as a man must be who lives by his physical strength and speed. And he'd seen the faces of the two women, and how they'd looked back over their shoulders before hastily averting their forgiving eyes.

He and Artois crossed Rue des Ramparts, made their way down Rue d'Orleans, with the iron lanterns flaring on their crossed chains above the intersections, the moths and palmetto-bugs roaring and clattering around the lights. On both sides of the street, shutters stood open to whatever cooling breath might be available. The candle-light within showed simple rooms, simply furnished, and the shadows of men and women thrown huge against ochre or yellow or persimmon-red walls.

"Lafitte might not have had any choice if he was involved in smuggling something important," argued Artois, who had clearly been reading *The Corsair.* "You said people like Mr. Mulm at the Nantucket and Mr. Shotwell at the Blackleg finance gun-running to the rebels in New Grenada. If Hesione had recognized Lafitte, and talked about it to the wrong person, it could have been Mr. Mulm or Mr. Shotwell who went to her place to kill her. You said, because of the tobacco, that the man with the nicked boot-heel was probably an American."

"Except that Shotwell's about five feet five, and we worked out that the man in the nicked boot has to have been six feet," said January. "Mulm's a few inches short of that. And if Hesione had been talking about recognizing Lafitte, I think the folks at the Nantucket, or one of her neighbors, would have overheard some of it."

"Maybe." Artois didn't sound satisfied, and walked on, hands in pockets, frowning.

A frog hopped from the gutter and bobbled across the banquette, fat and glistening. Other frogs croaked and peeped in the courtyards of the deserted town houses behind their shut iron gates.

"Will you ask Mademoiselle Vitrac to marry you?"

January checked his stride, startled at the question. Artois looked up at him with worry in his eyes.

He answered slowly, "In time."

"Why 'in time'?" asked Artois. "Why not now? She cares for you. I can see it in her face, whenever she looks at you. When she took your hand on the road yesterday . . . I . . . she . . . in six months I'm going to be leaving, you see. Going to school in Lyons." And his eyes brightened at the prospect, the joy of leaving this land, this place. Of finding his own place in the world. January remembered, so clearly, how that joy had felt. "She does need someone to care for her, you know. I know it isn't easy for her."

"No," said January, deeply touched. He wondered if Rose had spoken to this boy about the attack on her in Gallatin Street. "And believe me, Artois, it's something I've wanted to do for . . ." For how long? Since first he'd seen her, in the dark inferno of the Charity Hospital, when she'd come in the midst of the yellow fever and cholera, seeking a doctor for her students?

The black weight of Ayasha's death had been heavy on him then. He'd seen that tall, awkward, bespectacled young woman only as someone who didn't deserve to be fobbed off with one of the bloodletting lunatics who worked in the yellow-fever wards, doctors who didn't think they'd given a patient enough salts of mercury until their teeth were loosened, their lips blue, their gums bleeding. A schoolmistress, struggling to nurse the girls who, from being her pupils, had become her friends.

It hadn't been love at first sight, he thought, remembering the wet wind that had rolled through the city that night, flapping her cloak as he'd walked her back to her school on Rue St. Claud. But it hadn't taken long.

"I've wanted to ask her for a long time," he finished. "But you heard her yesterday afternoon in the woods. Every man who's ever said to her 'I want you to be happy' has meant 'I want you to give up what you are.' "

"You wouldn't do that," said Artois, "would you?" And he looked up into January's face searchingly as they passed beneath the flare of the lantern over the intersection of Rue Dauphine, like a child who understands for the first time just how much he doesn't comprehend about the way adults think and act.

"No," said January, hoping that in fact he'd have the wits to catch himself if he started to.

"It's just that . . . you're my friends." Artois hopped across the brimming gutter and resumed walking, the child's tone gone, a careful manliness returning, a little forced, to his voice. "Sometimes it feels like you and she are my family, the only ones who understand." Of his mother, who had disencumbered herself of her son at her earliest opportunity so that she could get on with her own life, he did not speak. "I wish there was something I could do to . . . to help her."

"So do I," said January quietly. "But trust is something each person has to come to on his own—or her own." He thought about taking the knife from Rose's hand, to stab Mathieu with. About Rose walking from the room weeping, to be pursued by Mathieu for the rest of her life. *I'm glad to know you know.* "Some people's roads are just longer than others. They can't take any fewer steps than they have to, just to make me feel better or you feel better."

Artois nodded, digesting this, and they walked in silence for a time through the hot darkness. When they stopped at the corner of Rue Bourbon, he spoke again. "Please let me know if there's anything I can do. Or I'll—I'll tell you if I think of anything. . . . Anything that would help."

January smiled, remembering his own days of youthful optimism, and said, "Thank you, Artois."

"Maybe *I* could go to the Nantucket?" added the boy. "Mulm wouldn't recognize me. I could ask around, find out if there was in fact any word of Jean Lafitte returning. . . ."

"I think we'd better keep to Mamzelle Marie's word on that," interjected January firmly.

Artois looked crestfallen.

"Jean Lafitte has been missing for fourteen years," January said. "I suspect that if he'd changed his name and identity, he'd still have been heard of, either smuggling or slave-trading or leading a band of freebooters or running some huge confidence-trick: he was that kind of man. The fact that in fourteen years nothing has been heard of him—or of someone like him—leads me to believe that he died while he was in temporary hiding, planning how to come back. Probably of fever. It happens," he added, seeing the unwilling wriggle of the young man's shoulders.

The unspoken protest: *Not to Jean Lafitte!*

"You know what they say of white men in Louisiana," January told the boy. "That they come here seeking their fortunes, but all they find is a wet grave."

EIGHT

Rose's note said *Come as quickly as you can.*

"She isn't hurt." Old James spoke in the hesitant tone of one who knows it isn't his place to offer advice, but the valet had clearly seen how January's eyes widened at the scribbled words. "Nor is Michie Veryl, nor Michie Artois. Mamzelle Rose came into the pantry in great haste and handed me this, and asked me to bring it on to you."

January glanced back through his landlady's dining-room to the shuttered gloom of the front parlor. There, one of his two remaining pupils was going through a simplified version of "Catch Fleeting Pleasures" with slow care, while the other—a tiny seven-year-old named Narcisse—followed along, mute and silent, on the edge of the marble-topped sideboard. The clock on the sideboard informed January that there were fifteen minutes to run on the lesson. "Tell Mamzelle Rose I'll be on my way the moment I'm done."

The note hadn't said *Come at once.* And whatever Rose said or wrote was exactly what she meant.

That was one of the things January treasured about Rose.

"You didn't tell me people would be coming." Madame Bontemps popped through the doorway of the back gallery, where James and January stood, like the Demon King in pantomime. "You need to tell me when people are coming. Michie Bontemps doesn't like it."

James opened his mouth, probably to inform her that Michie Bontemps was dead, but caught January's eye. Instead, he bowed himself down the back gallery steps and away.

"I can't have this kind of thing," Madame Bontemps informed January. She had made herself a new dress, acid green with yellow fantasias of appliqué-work and tatted red flowers. Her sewing would have fetched high prices had it been any style remotely wearable in civilized society. Besides her penchant for bizarre colors and complete disregard of current mode, the little woman tended to decorate her quilted, puffed, and padded coats and bodices with designs elaborately worked out in dried chicken-bones or dead and desiccated insects. This afternoon she had an enormous hornet carefully stitched onto the front of her tignon, just above her left eye. It was dead, of course, but January suspected that even so, it wasn't an ornament for which there would be much of a market. "You should have known he was coming."

She retreated to her room to fetch broom and dustpan, with which she proceeded to sweep the gallery and steps where the valet's feet had trod.

January shook his head, and returned to the front parlor, aware that the moment the children departed, Madame Bontemps would take up the straw-matting and scrub the parlor floor—even in the corners and under the chairs, where they couldn't possibly have walked—and meticulously sponge each piano-key with diluted vinegar.

Come as quickly as you can. It wasn't like Rose to panic, to send for him or anyone when they'd be meeting—as they usually did— for supper, when her lesson with Artois was done.

The lesson would run late this afternoon, he knew. Rose and her pupil were setting up a vacuum-bottle for some variety of arcane experiments with spectrums of light. Uncle Veryl, a Classicist to his fingers' ends, had shaken his head over the direction of his nephew's studies, but had arranged to have the air-pump purchased from a supply-house in Edinburgh: *No wonder nobody ever knew what to do with the boy,* January thought.

In six months I'm going to be leaving. . . .
Which would leave Rose out of a job again.

January turned the matter over in his mind as he corrected his little pupils and took them through the pieces they had to learn for next week. Marie-Zange, whose mother was a plaçée, was quite clearly able to wheedle her way out of practice most days and quite clearly did; Narcisse, the child of a free colored grocer, showed real promise. And his parents, thought January, were probably as baffled about what to do with him as Uncle Veryl was about Artois. He could almost see them writing to God: *But we ordered a boy who'll take over the family business!*

It wasn't likely Rose would find a pupil like Artois again.

He knew already she would never accept monetary help, from him or anyone. He'd found that out last summer, when one of the booksellers for whom she did translations died, and for a time it had looked as if she'd lose the room she rented. January himself had had little he could have shared with her, and Olympe's offer of a place to live had been politely turned down: "You have no idea what a bad guest I am," Rose had told his sister. "I'd much rather take in washing and keep you as a friend." And in fact she had scrubbed the floor and fetched wood and water at the Café Venise for three weeks until she'd been able to find work for a professor of Greek.

During those three weeks January had forced himself a hundred times not to say *If you lived with me, at least you'd have a place to live. . . .*

Rose's hesitancy about men aside—if it could ever be put aside—he knew that confined to one room, he and Rose would quickly come to hate one another, and there was no way they could afford more.

Had we world enough and time, he thought, as he walked along Rue Bourbon toward the St. Chinian town house.

And *Love is not love which alters when it alteration finds. . . .*

Neither Marvell nor Shakespeare had ever, apparently, considered love in the light of the money that gave man and woman the independence to choose freely. One's father might lock one in a nunnery for the rest of one's life, but at least one wouldn't end up doing other people's laundry in order to keep a roof over one's head.

After the brazen heat of the streets, the dim gloom of the St. Chinian carriageway was like tepid water. January picked his way around the jumble of old chairs and dismantled carriage-traces to the jungly riot of the courtyard, where Rose, Artois, Uncle Veryl, and James were gathered in front of the open French doors of the laundry-room-cum-laboratory. A wooden crate labeled RENNIE AND SONS—EDINBURGH rested on the courtyard bricks, and great quantities of packing-straw lay strewn about. Space had been made on the laboratory worktable for a stack of china plates, rich cobalt blue rimmed with gold and blurred with straw-dust. A couple of cups, a saucer, and a handsome tureen with a gold fish for a handle rested on the edge of the fountain.

"If you're planning to pump all the air out of that, it looks a little fragile." Facetiously, January picked up the lid of the tureen and peered inside.

The tureen was full of packing-straw. Nestled in the straw was a gun-lock.

He looked back, fast and shocked, at the crate. A dozen gun-barrels glinted wickedly amid the packing beneath the gold-rimmed dishes. Like a nest of savage eggs, six or eight little bundles of greased cloth were visible, one picked open to reveal another lock.

He thought, *The stocks and barrels will be down at the bottom of the crate.*

The hair lifted on the back of his neck. This was definitely something he didn't want to know about.

The label said RENNIE AND SONS, the Scots firm from which Uncle Veryl had ordered the vacuum-pump. It was clearly marked also *M. Artois St. Chinian, 21 Rue Bourbon.*

"I think the label must have gotten wet and come off in the hold of the packet from England." Hands clasped behind his back, Artois sounded more interested than upset, as he had been about the prospect of being electrocuted on Dominique's gallery.

Of course, he had never encountered some of the men who hung about in the Swamp, either.

"You can see the paper's wrinkled and stained. This box, and the pump, must have been the only two things in the hold with FRAGILE painted on the ends of the crates. There isn't another address."

No, thought January. *No, there wouldn't be.*

"My first thought was to pitch it in the river," said Rose.

Uncle Veryl lowered his quizzing glass and regarded her with pained astonishment. "It's quite good china," he protested. He was a small man whose thin arms and legs and scrawny neck combined with a plump little paunch to make him look like a spider. He wore a nip-waisted fiddleback coat so old the dye was turning green, and an immense linen neck-cloth dressed in the elaborate pattern of creases and knotting known as the Mailcoach. "Bow scale-blue if I'm not mistaken, and quite expensive, although of course not up to Wedgwood quality. Personally, I don't think the Bow standards of taste have been what they were. . . ."

"The shipping company will be able to trace the crate here through the carters," said January to Rose, speaking past the old man's perusal of the goods. "It came by carrier from the levee?"

"Yesterday evening. I'd promised M'sieu Songet I'd have the translation of *Helen in Egypt* checked by this morning, or I would have stayed to open it then."

"I believe a letter of complaint is in order," declared old Veryl. "I paid three hundred dollars for that pump, and where is it? It's a delicate piece of scientific equipment."

"We should tell the City Guards, surely," said Artois. "Or—*is* it illegal to import guns?"

"Not in the slightest," replied January. "But if you're arming and equipping people in secret—as Youx did when he traded with the Mexican guerrilleros, or Long when he tried to invade Texas— you're touchy about how many people know you're bringing arms in by the boxload. If you take them to the Guards, you'll almost certainly have to testify in court at some point in time. And the people who *did* order these—and paid for them—know that."

"I see." Artois looked down at the crate again. "So what do we do?"

"Advertise," said January promptly. "Say that you got a crate full of dishes by mistake, and would the real owner et cetera et cetera. When the real owner shows up, you make damn certain to slip into the conversation that you nailed the crate back shut at the sight of the first tea-cup. They know who you are anyway. Or they will the moment they track down the carrier."

"There are times," sighed Rose, wiping her dusty hands on her apron, "when I want to go in and murder those imbeciles at the freight offices."

"I quite agree." Uncle Veryl jabbed his glass in Rose's direction. "In May of 1830 I ordered a set of Legendre's mathematical works from Lampson *et fils* in Paris and they *still* haven't arrived. I'm quite certain the men at the shipping office stole them."

January was silent, contemplating the picture of the illiterate louts at the wharves falling upon a set of mathematical textbooks with cries of greedy delight. In his own way Uncle Veryl was as daft as Madame Bontemps. Then he said, "Let's get these packed up again. Rearrange them so that all the dishes are on top and everything incriminating is buried deep. While we're doing that, Rose, could you compose an advertisement?"

"Be sure to mention the vacuum-pump," insisted Uncle Veryl. "Whoever ordered those guns must have it, and goodness knows what damage they'll do to it."

Perhaps it wasn't the best solution to the problem, January decided, as he and Artois repacked the crate with Uncle Veryl's interested assistance, and Rose perched on a corner of the laboratory table repairing a quill. The crate had been at the St. Chinian town house overnight, worse luck. Were the men who'd smuggled these guns—wherever and for whomever they were ultimately destined—still arguing with the shipping office about their lost crate?

"Who are they smuggling the guns to, do you think? Mexico?" Artois glanced over his shoulder as if expecting a ravening pack of Gallatin Street filibusters to come storming through the carriageway bent on murder—not that anyone could storm through that junk-choked passage without killing themselves. But the courtyard lay motionless in the smothering August heat. From the street the shuttered-up town house had a deserted air, with the paint peeling from its door. Dragonflies hung above the morass of broken bricks and resurrection fern in the yard, thick as burnished fish on a pond.

"I think Santa Anna's got the country pretty well in hand by this time," January answered. "South of the Rio Grande, anyway. These guns may be for Texas. Or for New Grenada. There's still war there in the back-country. Any band of Americans who wants to can go across and try to take those countries for the United States—and incidentally get huge land-grants that they can then turn around and sell to other Americans."

"So much for Life, Liberty, and the Pursuit of Happiness," remarked Rose, and pushed up her spectacles more firmly onto the bridge of her nose as she bent over her notepaper. *"Delivered by mistake* or *Received by mistake,* do you think?"

"Is that always what it's for?" Artois sounded as disappointed as he'd been at the prospect of Jean Lafitte dying tamely of fever in the Yucatán. "Just money and land?"

January started to say *Generally,* then didn't. He had been in Paris in the summer of 1830, when men whispered to one another of the freedom their fathers had died for. Remembered his friends making bullets in cellars, slipping messages to one another under beer-mugs, running through the streets under the stinging snap of rifle-fire . . . dying in the gutters of the Rue de la Chanvrerie. And all to trade one branch of the old Kings for another in the end.

Had that been foolishness?

He recalled, too, the black fog along the Mississippi River, the weight of a rifle in his hands and the ghostly shape of Andrew Jackson's horse passing close by in the fog, the clip of hooves so sharp in the silence one moment, then blending with the first clamor of the oncoming British voices.

And he did not know how to reply.

They stowed the nailed-up crate in the carriageway. A man named Tom Burkitt came for it two mornings later, within hours of Rose's advertisement appearing in the *New Orleans Bee* and the *Louisiana Gazette.* "His address is down on Magazine Street," Artois reported to January. "I thought I should ask him to show me some kind of identification, so it wouldn't look like I thought there was a reason to get rid of the crate as soon as possible." He sat tailor-fashion on the end of January's bed, slitting apart the pages of January's still-unread copy of *Tamerlane and Other Poems* while January transcribed a simple march for the three little Saulier girls. "It's as you said, M'sieu Janvier. Mister Burkitt didn't look much like the kind of man who'd spend a fortune on a scale-blue Bow dinner service, but he looked very much like one who'd be smuggling guns."

"Did you make sure to say you hadn't seen anything but dishes?"

"I got it right in off the scratch," said the boy, pleased with himself. "I was in the laboratory when he came—it's cooler than my room, and I was down there reading—so I saw him across the court when he came through the carriageway. He bent over and examined the box, and I went out at once to talk to him. I was afraid Uncle Veryl would come out and spoil the whole show. . . . That is, Uncle Veryl is a brilliant, brilliant man, but . . ." Loyalty to his uncle struggled in his face with loving exasperation. To the last the old scholar hadn't understood why the guns weren't to be mentioned to whoever came for the crate, or why anyone would ship something as fragile as Bow china in the same box with gun-barrels.

"But there's things he doesn't understand," finished January with a grin, and Artois, relieved to be spared disloyalty, grinned back, and whipped the paper-knife through another pair of pages. January's room—the garçonnière of former times obligatory for white protectors who did not want to sleep beneath the same roof as young gentlemen of color, even their own free colored sons—was reasonably warm in wintertime from being over the laundry, but in the summer, with Madame Bontemps doing daily laundry for her tenants and a number of the surrounding families, it could be suffocating.

In the houses of the whites, of course, garçonnières served a different purpose: there, whatever experimentation the growing sons of the family cared to undertake with the servant-girls wouldn't pass under the white mothers' horrified eyes. It was a mark of how lax Veryl St. Chinian had become, that he gave his grand-nephew a room in the nearly-empty town house itself rather than relegating him to the cobwebbed and leaky quarters out back.

"Anyway," Artois went on, "Mister Burkitt asked if I was Mr. St. Chinian and I said yes; he asked was I the one who'd put the advertisement in the paper and I said yes. He spoke English," he added, "with the most awful accent and he spit tobacco all over the carriageway. I'll have to help James wash it down when I get back, but it'll take hours to move all those chairs and the old chaise-wheels and things like that. . . . I said I was expecting an air-pump and vacuum-bottles, and the labels must have got switched, because when I pried off the lid I saw dishes, and I was afraid I'd break some if I tried to unpack them, so I immediately nailed it up again."

"*Very* good."

"He had two other men with him, and a cart," Artois went on. "They tossed the crate up into the cart and I could hear the dishes breaking; Uncle Veryl had just come downstairs and I had to push him into the house again so he wouldn't go out and take them to task about the pump or the dishes. He's still horrified about the dishes. I left him composing a letter to the shipping company about the pump. I'd probably better get back before he sends it, but I thought you'd want to know." Artois shook his head, trying not to smile.

"Thank you." January gathered up the music-sheets, wiped his pen, and mended the tip before putting it back in the tortoise-shell pencil-box on his desk. His "desk" was in fact a length of plank wedged between the end of his bed and the whitewashed plaster of the wall, with barely room for a chair. Narrow shelves held his books, sheet-music neatly arranged, a small sewing-kit and two candlesticks; an armoire that occupied most of the rest of the available space held his clothes. For some time he'd stored in the bottom drawer of that armoire—along with a box of candles and a japanned tin of coffee-beans—the brass-and-camelbone box that held a gold thimble and thread-scissors, a gold brooch and two or three neatly-bound bunches of feathers, aigrettes that Ayasha had kept to pin in her hats. There was also one gold earring that had belonged to Ayasha's mother.

The gold ring he'd given Ayasha on their wedding day had gone to her grave with her, wherever that grave was. Victims of the cholera had been buried wherever there was space for them, that summer of 1832.

Since his dream of speaking to her on the bridge, he'd brought the box out and set it on a corner of the desk. He'd thought it would hurt him to look at it—especially since his disloyalty in loving Rose—but he found instead that he took a good deal of comfort in seeing it there.

"With any luck, that's the end of it," he sighed after the

conversation had ranged around the chances of recovering the pump, the chances of the pump being unbroken, why Artois and Rose wanted to heat wires of various metals to red- and white-heat in a vacuum-bottle in the first place, and how they proposed to do it if they ever got the proper equipment. "Half the city knows guns are run through here to the rebels against Paez—Shaw knows it, the Guards know it, every banker in town knows it, and the Spanish consulate knows it, and nobody except the Spanish consul really cares. The identification Burkitt showed you was probably someone else's. . . . What address did he give?"

"Nineteen hundred Magazine Street," said the boy promptly.

"I'm willing to bet that was fake as well."

Artois laughed, and triumphantly riffled the pages of the completed book. "Here you are, all ready . . . and of course, Mamzelle Vitrac left your copy of *Mithradates* in the laboratory, and like an idiot I left it there, too. . . ."

"I'll get it on my way to the Cabildo," said January. "Not that I think Shaw has found a single thing about Hesione's murderer, if he's even in town. And the number of men who are about six feet tall and probably American in this town—or even in the Swamp— who've had some contact with Hesione LeGros makes me think that we may have to go down to Grand Terre to find out anything more. But it doesn't hurt to check."

"All we can do is try," reasoned Artois. "If we find it out, and nobody does anything about it . . . well, we did our part." He was practically the only person January knew who didn't add *And what do you hear about the Avocet murder . . . ?*

And January smiled as he walked the boy to the door. "That's true," he told Artois. "And the rest, as my confessor would certainly tell me, is up to God."

By the time January had finished his transcribing, clouds were moving in from the Gulf again, and warm electric winds raced up and down the city's streets. Thunder grumbled, far-off and angry, as January paced along Rue Bourbon; he'd be lucky if he collected his book, talked to Shaw, and got back to his rooms before he got a soaking.

"Michie Artois out at the market," reported Martine as January emerged from the carriageway into the courtyard. She was making up more smudges against the ever-present mosquitoes. "He be back soon, you want to wait."

"I just need to pick up a book." January found it on a corner of the laboratory table—as usual, the old laundry-room's three French windows weren't locked—and as he came out again he noted that the morning's crushing heat had evidently discouraged Artois and James from washing down the carriageway after all. It was still splotched everywhere with expectorated tobacco, and criss-crossed with muddy tracks. Artois' narrow boots, Martine's bare feet . . .

January stopped abruptly, looking down at the heaved, uneven surface of the brick underfoot. The carriageway was already in gloom, but enough light came in from the feverish afternoon sun to illuminate the tracks.

And one of the men who'd been in to pick up the crate definitely had a gouge taken out of the heel of his right boot.

Naturally Shaw wasn't at the Cabildo. "He gone down to Plaquemines Parish again," reported Sergeant DeMezières, who had come to know January over the past two years: a big jolly Spanish Creole with a ferocious black mustache that he waxed into fanglike points. "Why it ain't clear to him it was that brother Bertrand killed Guifford Avocet I'm damned if I know. It was his shirt they found in the woods, all bloody like he stuck a pig. What time the clock in the parlor stopped or what was in the rag-bag in the house that Shaw been askin' about got nothing to do with it all, and so I told Shaw. Blood is blood."

He jabbed at January with an admonishing finger. "If that overseer of theirs disappeared, I'd be askin' questions of the field-hands, not searchin' the parish. That man was a hard one and I'm told the new American fella's worse. Well, stands to reason, them two women needin' a man on the place and takin' on the first one to present himself."

He shook his head, and fished a flint and striker from the drawer of his desk, for beyond the arcade outside the big double-doors the sky had come over black with storm. "Just askin' for trouble, hirin' an American." January wasn't sure whether the sergeant was lamenting the Avocet women's new employee, or Captain Tremouille's decision to hire Abishag Shaw in the first place.

"Thank you," January said, and held out the note he'd come prepared with—he'd half-expected Shaw to be down in Plaquemines. "If he should return this evening, sir, please give him this note for me."

It stormed all night, and in the morning—having heard nothing from Shaw—January walked while it was still cool across the French town and along Magazine Street to number nineteen hundred, which turned out to be the Episcopal Home for Orphaned and Indigent Boys. The servant January spoke to there—he'd taken the precaution of dressing like a servant himself, in a rough calico shirt and shabby trousers—had never heard of a Tom Burkitt. "He kind of a tall white man," explained January, holding out a vague hand to indicate someone around six feet in height and waving, in the other hand, a note addressed to T. Burkitt on the subject of a fictitious sister and her baby. "Chews tobacco."

The servant woman sniffed. "Got no one like that here," she declared in the rough English of the eastern seaboard states. "Father Muldoon tall, but he don't get around much—his rheumatics, you know. And bein' a priest, he don't hold with no tobacco."

This conversation took place in the kitchen doorway, which lay behind the main block of the orphanage. Past the woman's shoulder January could glimpse no sign of gold-rimmed dishes or the smallest trace of packing-straw, which didn't surprise him. It would have been more surprising had Burkitt—or whatever his name was—actually given a correct address.

A likelier avenue of information would be the shipping company. It was early yet to seek out Uncle Veryl—the old man stayed up reading into the small hours under a tent of mosquito-netting, according to his grand-nephew, and didn't emerge from his room until nearly noon. In any case, reflected January as he made his way back along Magazine Street through the cheap taverns, the distilleries and brick-yards and clapboard cottages and boarding-houses of the German and Irish canal-workers, he wasn't entirely sure Uncle Veryl could be trusted to keep his mouth shut about the guns.

Having no students that day, January had contracted to tune the piano in the Milneburgh boarding-house where his mother had her rooms. He'd planned a day of it, arranging to perform the same service for two of his mother's plaçée friends and to take Dominique out for a walk for Italian ices; he returned to town only in time to buy two cents' worth of sausage and a couple of crabs, with an onion thrown in for lagniappe, all of which he and Rose cooked in her stuffy kitchen.

It was a good evening, as most of those long, lazy summer evenings were good. Ti-Louis had acquired half a dozen mangoes at the market, and Marie-Philomène who had the room next to Rose was stewing eggplant; there was talk and a little music and sharing sausage and mangoes and dirty rice around before the mosquitoes drove everyone indoors. But as he walked back home, January felt sadness, and when he slept, he dreamed again of Ayasha.

Ayasha at eighteen, when first they'd met. When first he'd walked her back to her shop and they'd flown together like tinder and flame in the tiny room behind it that had been kitchen and store-room and bedroom all in one. Dreamed of the sandalwood scent of her hair, and her hands, so much older than her face or her body, work-roughened and yet so delicate of touch. He dreamed of waking, and hearing her voice, and going out into the courtyard behind the building where all the *bonnes femmes* of that poor district gathered around the fountain to gossip with their pails of water while their children raced about in play.

There was a peddler there that morning in his dream, a wrinkled old man in long robes, wearing a turban—that wasn't so odd, because it was Paris after all, which had little enclaves of Turks and Greeks and Russians and even Chinese tucked away among its knotted streets. Nobody was giving the old man money, but he kept taking things out of his pockets and handing them to people: to one woman he gave a book, that she stared at in astonishment before bursting into tears; to a young man he gave a girl's blue hair-ribbon; to a boy a sack of money: "Don't lose it," he said.

To Dominique he gave a red rose *(what's Minou doing here in Paris?)*. To Artois, a marigold.

"It's Allah," said Ayasha happily as the old man handed her the gold thimble and scissors that now resided in the camelbone box on January's desk. "He's come with presents for us all."

And the old man turned to January, and regarded him with bright, wise black eyes, not at all the way January had expected Allah to look. "Do you want a present, p'tit?" he asked in a voice like the dark behind the stars. He had something in his work-twisted old hand—*Of course his hand is deformed with work, he made every animal with it, that would be enough to give anyone arthritis. . . .* Held it out to January, hidden in his fist.

"What is it?" January asked, and Allah smiled.

"You won't know till you accept."

January felt a pang of terrible fear about what would be in Allah's pocket for him, in Allah's palm; nevertheless, he held out his hand.

"Benjamin?" Rose's voice.

The rattle of her feet on the gallery.

January rolled out from under the mosquito-bar barely half-awake, caught up his shirt and trousers.

Another woman would have stepped forward when he opened the shutters, would have put her head on his shoulder, clung to him. . . . Another woman's eyes would have borne the marks of tears. Rose had only a kind of tense, small tremor in her hands, as if flailing against fate.

"Artois is dead," she said.

NINE

"He was found in the gutter on Gallatin Street this morning." The morgue attendant opened the door into the long brick-floored room, and stepped aside to let January and Rose pass ahead. Despite truly heroic efforts on the part of the hospital servants, the stink was like a circle of Dante's inferno. Human waste and human blood still clung to the garments dumped on the floor along one wall, where two men and a woman were picking through them. In this heat even the fresh corpses—last night's harvest from the Swamp's tavern-brawls and the drink-fueled arguments of the Gallatin Street gaming-houses—were beginning to go off, and anything riper—like the horrible thing someone had pulled out of the turning-basin yesterday evening—would be unspeakable by noon.

"The woman who sent for the Guards when she came out to close up her place this morning said she saw him there when she went out earlier in the night. Said she thought he was drunk then, and let him lie. Aye, and so he was, poor lad."

From the door January could see Uncle Veryl, standing by one of the line of cheap pine tables that ran down the center of the big room. His sobs made intermittent echoes in the rafters, like a gecko's chirp in the stillness. James stood behind him, arms wrapped around his master's thin shoulders. The valet held and rocked him as he would have held a child, his own head bowed.

"Did the Guards tell you this?" January asked softly. Rose walked ahead of him, her own arms folded tight as if defending her heart from feeling anything, her face like carven wood.

"Oh, aye." The attendant was a little Englishman with a Merseyside accent and a nose like a bottle-gourd. "One of 'em come in with the body, and the ambulance man, to sign it over. I asked did he want to stay for the strippin' and cleanin'—'cause lots of times you'll find stuff that'll tell you who mighta done for 'em, when you strip 'em. But he said no, he had another body to go fetch along Tchoupitoulas by the wharves, and it was damn clear what had happened to your lad. And so it was." The man shrugged. "You could still smell the whiskey in his clothes. Must've passed right out, poor lad, and him not used to it. It's a bad business, goin' down drinkin' alone."

They'd almost reached the table; January hung back, and lowered his voice still further. "Do you know the woman's name?"

"Mackinaw Sal." The man half-grinned. "Like to every man in the town knows Mackinaw Sal—*and* pays for the privilege. Her place is between Hospital an' Barracks streets, near the Water Works. I don't think it has a name."

January checked his watch as the attendant passed ahead of him to Uncle Veryl's side. Barely eight.

How could Artois be dead? Half of him expected that when he and Rose left this place, it would be to return to the St. Chinian town house on Rue Bourbon, to find the boy perched on his high-legged stool in the old laundry-room, full of speculation about whom in New Orleans Jean Lafitte had been disguised as for fourteen years.

How could he be dead?

"It never occurred to me he would go to a place like that," whispered Veryl, clinging to his valet's arms. "He was never interested in gaming, except to calculate the odds on hands of cards. He should have spoken to me if he wanted to go adventuring. Should have asked me. . . ."

Artois' light-blue coat was in Rose's hands. The stench of cheap raw whiskey worked through that of piss and rotted weeds. "Nothing left in the pockets."

Like Rose, thought January, to check the pockets. To look for small clues, small signs. To keep her head. She might have been talking about a rifled sewing-basket.

"Artois didn't drink. Yes," she added, to the attendant. "We do identify this young man as Artois St. Chinian. What arrangements need to be made to have an undertaker come for him? James, maybe Monsieur St. Chinian would be more comfortable outside now."

"Yes, Mamzelle Vitrac." Gently, the valet started to ease his master toward the door. Uncle Veryl clung to his sleeves as if struck blind.

January stepped to the valet's side. "Did you take up a note to him yesterday, or a letter?" he asked, keeping his voice low. He doubted the old man even heard.

James looked surprised that he would have known. "Yes, sir. From the carrier company that delivered that pump he ordered. At least that's what the boy said, who brought it to the door."

"When was that?"

"Yesterday afternoon, sir, after Michie Veryl went out."

I was in Milneburgh, having ices with Minou. Oh, Artois . . .

While Rose signed the papers the attendant gave her—in the name of Veryl St. Chinian—January turned to the body on the table. Death had relaxed the boy's features, and he'd been taken from the water before the crayfish that swarmed in every gutter and pool in town had had time to do damage.

How can that be Artois? Artois can't be dead. I saw him only the day before yesterday. We were going to go up on the roof tomorrow night with his telescope, to search for comets and see the rings of Saturn.

Looking down into the slack, wet face, he knew he should feel something, but didn't. Automatically he crossed himself: *Virgin Mary, Mother of God, pray for us sinners. . . .*

Pray for us sinners.

The attendant had draped a towel over the boy's groin out of respect for Rose's modesty. From some of the questions Artois had asked, January had been fairly certain his young friend was a virgin. He realized he'd been looking forward with friendly amusement to

Artois' initiation into the wonders of sex, the marvels of loving—wanting to hear what he'd have to say about them. How he'd see them at first view, with those clever, delighted eyes.

He tried to raise the boy's right arm, and could barely move it. Like Hesione, he was growing stiff. Not as stiff as she, which meant he'd died sometime between nine and midnight, if the big muscles were only now growing hard. The waxen yellow flesh of the wrist was bruised, and the back of the upper arm, bruised so close to the moment of death as to be barely visible. He lifted Artois' body and saw that the back of the neck, too, was bruised.

Pigs, he thought, laying him down again—observing despite himself that head and neck were already rigid. His whole body felt cold. *Bastard fucking pigs.*

You held him by the wrists, held his head underwater—soaked him down with whiskey so the police would only say, with the morgue attendant, "It's a bad business, goin' down drinkin' alone."

Especially if you were sixteen years old, free colored, and purblind stupid enough to wander down to Gallatin Street.

The cold in his heart was replaced by a rush of heat so intense, he wondered that it did not reduce him to ash.

"I'll wait here with him for the undertaker's men," said January to Rose. "Can you go back to Uncle Veryl's house with him, make sure he's all right? Search Artois' room for that note, if you would."

"You think that will do any good?" Behind her spectacle lenses, Rose's hazel-green eyes burned with the cold, bitter rage of one who has long ago lost the last of her trust. "Obviously the City Guards have already made up their minds about how he died."

"The Guards officer didn't know that Artois had come across a box of contraband guns." January was a little surprised at how even his voice sounded. Why wasn't he shouting, cursing, kicking the walls? He wanted to grab the attendant by the back of his neck and drown *him* in the nearest gutter, to see how he liked it, only because he was white.

"I think even Captain Tremouille will admit that the affairs of *la famille Avocet* should take a back seat to smuggling if it's accompanied by murder. Now, Mister Burkitt—or whatever his name is—

may simply be a bully for hire, working for someone else. That still doesn't answer the question of why someone would hire him to murder a completely harmless woman out by the Swamp . . . much less talk to her for fifteen minutes, and give her a doubloon, first. I'll be along to Uncle Veryl's as soon as I can."

When they were gone, January stood in silence beside the table, his hand resting on the cold curve of the dead boy's shoulder. He should, he knew, do something. Wrap up Artois' clothing. Speak to the attendant. Go out into the streets and tear down the city, brick by brick, that would dare do such a thing to such a boy. . . .

Instead, he fished in his pocket for the much-battered blue glass rosary that never left him, though at the moment God's name was only a word, and the beads only beads. *Hail Mary, full of grace, the Lord is with thee . . . pray for us sinners, now and in the hour of our death.*

Did you pray for Artois when they held his head underwater until his lungs couldn't endure the strain any further? And him knowing all those awful minutes that he'd have to inhale at the last?

Couldn't you have prayed just a little harder?

By the time January had wrapped up Artois' clothing in several layers of brown paper, the undertaker had arrived. He shook his head over Artois: "A terrible thing," he said. "A terrible thing. So full of promise."

"Listen," said January. "When you prepare young M'sieu St. Chinian for burial, would you take note if there is any evidence of liquor in his stomach? I'm told that in spite of the whiskey soaking his clothing, he did not drink. . . ."

"Ah, M'sieu," sighed the undertaker, "boys of that age . . ."

"I understand that some boys of that age make experiments. And I might even think Artois had been so foolish, were it not for these." And he showed the man the bruises on Artois' wrists, arms, and neck. "Would you say that those were consonant with having been held while his head was forced underwater?"

The man closed his eyes, his mouth tightening in pain. "I would, M'sieu. Believe me, I have seen a great deal of such, in my trade. Maybe I'm growing old. The scum—the American animals, coming into this town . . . I cannot believe some of the things that they do." He looked sadly up into January's face. "Particularly to men of our color, M'sieu, to men of our race."

And that, thought January with a wry sting of anger, is exactly what the police will say.

"In any case, M'sieu Quennel," he said. "When you come to prepare young M'sieu St. Chinian for burial, if you should find anything out of the ordinary, anything—however small—worthy of note, please take note of it, and let me know."

"Of course," murmured Quennel in exactly the soothing voice that he must use with all the distraught families, reflected January. The agreement that means nothing, that is just a sound one makes to get the mourner to cease crying.

He knew it well. When he'd worked at the night clinic in the Hôtel Dieu in Paris, he'd used it himself more times than he cared to count.

The undertaker signed to the attendant and laid out his stretcher on the table beside Artois, and January thought, *It is time to say good-by, my friend.*

Grief shut around his throat like a choking hand.

So full of promise. What a hackneyed cliché, he thought, looking down into the young face, waxen and yellow in its tangled frame of wet amber curls. A thousand promises—for love, and sex, and family, for sons unborn and books unwritten—on which life had just reneged. *Oh, my friend, I will avenge you all of this.*

And that assurance rang hollow into the more certain knowledge that Artois was never going to find out, now, the riddle of the old lady's doubloon that had so fascinated him.

January bent and kissed the boy's forehead.

And the undertaker bore Artois away.

"I've written his mother," said Rose when January came into Veryl St. Chinian's library a few hours later. "James had her address in Boston." Her voice was neutral again. So were her eyes. The afternoon rain drummed in the courtyard, chill breaths of air rushing through the open windows and about the mouldering old town house like children's ghosts.

"I've sent to Brancas' Printing for handbills for the funeral. They have a man there who'll post them all around the town. Not that there are many people in town to see. I expect that between them Aunt Marie-Agnes and Theodosia St. Chinian—your Henri's new mother-in-law—will veto burial in the family vault, so I've contacted Père Eugenius at the Cathedral about a wall-vault until Veryl can make some arrangement."

Rose had lit the candles on Veryl's book-cluttered desk, and in the molten light her hands rested on the sheets of cold-pressed paper like a little Dutch still-life: wax, taper, pen-knife, wiper, all laid out across that half-written first line, *Dominique—Something terrible has happened. . . .*

"James tells me Chloë St. Chinian barely had anything to do with her half-brother, but she should be informed at least," Rose went on. "I understand she and Henri are downriver at Bois d'Argent. And I found this." From among the writing-things she brought out a few broken fragments of virulent pink, cracked fragments of what had been a sealing wafer. "They were on the floor of Artois' room. James remembered that the note was sealed with a couple of pink wafers. My guess is there was an address given on it, and Artois simply took it with him so as not to forget."

"Directions to a place, more like." January remembered the boy's facility with numbers. "But yes, he would have put it in his pocket. All his pockets were cleaned out, by the way, not just the jacket. Burkitt, and whoever was working with him, must have searched him—"

He had meant to go on to say *looking for that very thing.* But his throat closed again, and he stood mute, looking down at her, and she, silent, up at him. Then he saw tears track slowly from her eyes, and she turned her face away.

And sat, breathing hard to steady herself, like a statue that knows that it will fly into pieces if once it starts to feel.

January thought, *I can't go to her. If this solitude is what she needs in her pain, how can I break her strength with my own need?*

How can I ever?

She has fought hard for that strength, and it is her victory.

And for a moment, through his grief, he felt a keener pain, as if he saw Rose sitting in the stern of a barge like a young queen of legend, sailing out into a stream and away from him.

Then she held up her hand, reaching out behind her for him, while the tears flowed faster down her face. And January took her hand, and knelt beside her chair, and she turned where she sat and pressed her face to his shoulder, the corner of her spectacles digging into his cheek, her body shuddering with sobs.

Mackinaw Sal proved to be a mammoth-breasted blond slut in a blue Mother Hubbard, sitting at a rough table in the back of her "place" on Gallatin Street, smoking a cigar and having what appeared to be grits and beer for breakfast. The yard stank in the steamy heat of early afternoon, and in the street a man was shouting in German, "You're all pimps in this stinking city! Every shit-eating one of you!" for reasons best known to himself. The grimy building was hemmed in on both sides with the high brick walls of warehouses and shipping offices. In the rear corner of the yard, near the privies, a Chickasaw Indian lay, unconscious or merely asleep—January walked over to make sure he wasn't dead before going to the back door.

" 'Scuse me, m'am." He took off his sorry felt hat and averted his eyes from Mackinaw Sal's heavy thighs, exposed where she'd pulled up the Mother Hubbard to catch the open door's breeze. "I'm lookin' for M'am Mackinaw Sal?"

At least she wore shoes and stockings, and a corset under her dress. Her ditchwater hair was curled and smelled of perfume applied over a general undercoat of cigar-smoke and dirt, and she'd taken the trouble to paint her face. She was probably Dominique's age and looked fifty.

"You found her, Sambo." With one knee she kicked her dress down. She offered no invitation to come in, and January guessed, from her eyes, that he'd better not step across the unswept threshold.

"The folks at the city morgue, they tell me you was the lady who found my boy dead," he said. "I come to thank you, m'am, for callin' the Guards the way you done."

"Well, shit, I wasn't gonna leave him to stink up the street." She took a drag on her cigar, regarded him with hard blue eyes ringed in kohl. "I got customers come in that way."

"Yes, m'am," said January. " 'Course not, m'am. You didn't happen to see—that is . . . You see, m'am, my boy was runnin' with my brother, and my brother's a bad man, m'am. Gettin' money from who knows where and tellin' my boy all kinds of things. . . . Now my brother says him and my boy, they was together up till about midnight—this was down on the levee—and then my boy left to walk home. We live up on Rue Claiborne, up in Tremé. . . ."

"You know, I'm glad you told me that, 'cause I was just fixin' to ask so's I could come callin' on you with a blancmange." Her eyes were red and her voice slurry. Not drunk, thought January, but in the grip of a moderately fatal hangover. He hoped she would die of liver failure.

That they all would die.

"Your brother's a liar, Sambo, 'cause the kid was layin' in that gutter when I throwed Suzy Broadhorn outa here at midnight, the dirty cow. Him lyin' there was the only reason I didn't pitch her *in* the gutter. What's your brother's name?"

"Clarence Horatio, m'am," replied January promptly. "Only he go by a dozen other names, Slick and Red Dog and I don't know how many others. You didn't happen to see—"

The woman raised her head as footfalls thumped on the floor of the barroom. Without so much as an "Excuse me," she got to her feet, slurped a last spoonful of the grits, said "Shit," and walked away through the door behind her and into the barroom that led, January could see, to the space behind the bar itself. "Well, howdy, stranger," he heard her say as friendly and cheerful as if she'd just risen from luncheon after a brisk walk. "You been in these parts long?"

January put his cap on again, and crossed through the dirty yard and out the passway to the street.

Midnight, he thought, looking back at the mean little house. By daylight Gallatin Street looked even worse than it did after dark, swimming with mud from the rain. Planks bridged the gutter before Sal's front door and a dozen others. The gutters here, like those everywhere in the French town, were substantial canals, two feet wide and lined with cypress. Like those everywhere in the French town, they were offensive with garbage, sewage, and deceased animals in an advanced stage of decomposition, overflowing now and running into the street.

At this time of year, of course, most of the City Council were in their cool, pleasant cottages in Mandeville or Milneburgh, eating Italian ices and listening to the breezes whisper in the trees.

A few dozen yards away, at the end of the street, the masts of schooners jutted against the tumble of clouds and daylight. Smoke poured from the stacks of the steam-packets. Liverpool and Le Havre, St. Petersburg and Cádiz and Vera Cruz—all the wide world, where whites wouldn't automatically address him as Sambo or Cuffee if they spoke English, or as *"tu,"* like a dog or a child, if they spoke French. . . .

But where a poor woman could still be murdered in her home, he reminded himself, without the police caring who did it. It would have been the same, for someone like Hesione LeGros, in Paris or Berlin or Peking. Men had been dying on the barricades—or on crosses—for thousands of years trying to make it otherwise, and hadn't succeeded yet.

And if a young man without money or influence were found dead in a gutter, soaked with forty-rod, nobody would go about Paris or Rome or Constantinople asking if he habitually drank, or what he might have been doing in a part of town where he would not ordinarily go.

Boys of that age . . .

What *was* he doing in this part of town? reflected January, and looked around him once again.

M'sieu St. Chinian, please come to the Dead Nigger Tavern on Gallatin Street so that my colleagues and I can talk to you about your missing vacuum-pump.

Boys of sixteen did idiotic things, of course—at the age of sixteen January had thought himself as invulnerable as Hercules. And it was true that he, January, had been out of town when Artois had gotten Mulm's message. But Artois, he thought, at least would have had the sense to ask *someone* for advice if this was where he'd been instructed to come.

So where would the purported finder of the missing pump have set up a meeting where Artois would feel safe?

"Stinkin' yellow pups, the lot of you," screamed a furious voice. "You'd steal the chaw out of a man's mouth if he yawned!" A black woman stumbled from one of the saloons, followed by the curses and laughter of the Oak Cudgel Boys, the gang that ran thievery and violence down at this end of the wharves. In the hot, steamy sunlight she shouted at them, half-drunk and arms akimbo. . . .

Ask her? wondered January.

Or ask the gray-haired sailor, snoring with his back to the wall of the building across the street from Sal's?

He remembered the darkness of the streets here near the market, after the sun went down. No lamps swung above the intersections and few saloonkeepers wasted more on candles than was absolutely necessary to permit their patrons to locate their own drinks. A dray of wine-barrels lurched up the street from the river, one man driving and two others sitting guard on the tailgate, rifles on their arms— the Oak Cudgel Boys made obscene gestures after them, flung horse-shit, and cursed.

Which of them would even have noticed who dumped a beard-less boy here to lie in the gutter?

He went home, and saw beside his bed the book *Tamerlane and Other Poems,* all its pages neatly cut and waiting for him.

Then he cried.

TEN

"That poor kid dead?" Cut-Nose Chighizola's scarred face twisted still further into a gargoyle mask of sorrow and disgust. "And for what? Just what was in his pockets, eh?"

"I think so, yes." January leaned an elbow on the stacked boxes of oranges, the shallow crates of tomatoes and aubergines in the market's blue shade. Passers-by on the Rue du Levee seemed, from here, to be crossing a lighted stage: market-women with baskets on their tignoned heads, sallying forth for one last try at the streets before packing up and going home to their families. Servants with their own baskets hurrying to make up some last-minute deficiency in the dinner menu, impoverished housewives out to bargain for vegetables no longer fresh. The baskets of shrimp had begun to smell strongly fishy. Under the peaked tile roof, flies roared in inky clouds.

"Did you see who he met?"

"Oh, yeah." Chighizola hadn't changed a great deal from the night of General Humbert's ill-fated banquet twenty-three years before. His hair was gray, but he still looked like if you hit him with a cypress beam, the beam would break. When January had come up on him today, the old pirate had been recounting, to three awestruck British midshipmen and an open-mouthed ten-year-old boy, the horrific single-handed battle against Turkish corsairs in defense of the honor of a British countess, that had resulted in the loss of his nose. The mesmerized midshipmen had paid three times the going price for a pineapple before moving on.

"Yeah, I saw your boy." Chighizola nodded toward the coffee-stand between the arcade's square brick pillars. "Right over there at La Violette's. Five or six o'clock yesterday it must have been, I was just wrapping up. You lucky you caught me, I'm hauling my crust back to Grand Isle tonight. Not much of a moon, but the weather's clearing, and this time of year you got to take the weather as she come. Lot of water in Bayou Segnette, I can go straight down to the bay, like a fish swim in the ocean. With that Frank Mulm, the boy was."

"Mulm?" January wondered if Artois had seen the saloonkeeper by chance here, and decided on the spur of the moment to make inquiries of his own about Hesione LeGros. Then he remembered the girl in the dirty green gown behind the Nantucket Saloon, *Sancho Sangre's buying these days. . . . Runnin' guns to the rebels in New Grenada . . .*

But why kill over something that, January was fairly certain, Mulm wouldn't be prosecuted for anyway? There was no law that said a saloonkeeper couldn't buy as many rifles as he chose and sell them to whomever he chose. The only ones who'd get in trouble were those who tried to smuggle them into Venezuela past the navies of those who currently ruled there, and Artois was certainly in no position to get word to anyone who would endanger the smugglers.

Somebody must have panicked.

Or Artois did in fact meet Mulm only by chance.

"That's a bad man, Mulm." Cut-Nose shook his head, unconsciously echoing Marie Laveau. "Have an apple. I grow 'em myself down on Grand Isle. Jean's due in tomorrow with more. These, I give 'em to the Sisters of Charity to make pies for the orphans." He gestured at the dozen fat yellow fruits remaining in the straw-filled boxes.

"He looks like a toff, eh? With them little spectacles and the silver watch and the waistcoat like a Philadelphia undertaker. But you got to watch out for the millipede as well as the serpent and the scorpion. Frank Mulm got the striped eye, like they say, the bad eye. Me, I'd rather have a bad man who carries a cutlass and spits on the police—not that I spit on police myself these days—than a bad man who goes around with a ledger-book under his arm and is all the time waiting for you to turn around so he can knife you in the back with his little pen-knife. Me, I know bad men, eh? I been a bad man myself, though I'm all reformed now, praise the Virgin." He crossed himself.

"When you say *with him,* you mean they had coffee together? Mulm and the boy?"

"No, no, that's what I'm tellin' you." Cut-Nose looked up at January with earnest black eyes like cut jet. "That boy, he shoulda stayed away from him. He woulda if Mulm looked on the outside as rotten as he is in his heart. But he looks like God's uncle, you know? With that soft little voice, and no cussin', and his clean hands." He began to tidy the fruit away into its boxes again, sorting the bruised from the good and stacking the crates preparatory, presumably, to transport to the Sisters of Charity and their orphans.

"I seen him waiting there, drinking coffee by himself, and I think that's a little strange, you know? For one thing, Frank Mulm don't ever drink his coffee here. He buys cheap beans and has a woman make it for him back at the Nantucket. La Violette"—he gestured to the proprietress of the coffee-stand—"she buy good coffee, Havana green, and she got to charge for it. For another, if a man like Mulm gonna drink coffee, he gonna drink it indoors, where he can watch his back. The Café des Exiles is straight across the street. Every time I look over at him, he's lookin' all around him, never sittin' quiet, and whenever a cart come by on the street, it splash his shoes with mud, an' he get out a handkerchief and wipe up the stains and look pissy about it, like a cat under a leak. But he don't move. Just stayed there with his cloak folded up across his lap . . ."

"His *cloak?*" January blinked. *"Yesterday?* It must have been hot enough to bake bread in here. What was he doing with a cloak?"

"Now you mention it, that was funny." The former pirate scratched the scarred stump of his nose. "Bad enough the man was wearing a coat, like an idiot. My daughter, she's always telling me,

'Papa, wear your coat when you go up to town, people gonna think you're some kind of *paisano.*' " Chighizola laughed. Like many of the Americans—the Kaintuck keelboatmen, and the farmers who came south with flatboats full of pumpkins, hogs, and corn—he stood behind his table in shirt-sleeves, and in the faded homespun stripes of pink and blue he did in fact look like a peasant. January was familiar with the adjuration not to go about the town half-dressed. He'd heard it from his mother all his life.

"Well, that's what he had, anyway," said Chighizola. "He got up and walked a few feet to meet this young man, this kid in the light-blue coat, when he come down the banquette. They stand together talkin' right there, between those pillars but outside, next to the street. Then somebody ask me somethin' about my aubergines, an' when I turn around back, they's both gone."

Mulm had a gun. The thought emerged full-grown and obvious, mostly because it was a snatch common in Paris, in the rough districts near the customs barrier. A girl would come in from the country, either for the day or looking for employment in the city shops. A pleasant, harmless-looking man, or more usually a middle-aged woman, would go up to her, sometimes with a shopping basket on her arm, or a big shawl. "There's a gun beneath the shawl, dearie, so get in the carriage. . . ." And a carriage would be there, as if it had dropped from the sky. The victim was usually too confused and shocked to cry out. "We just want to talk to you and you won't be hurt. . . ."

And of course the girl would end up in a brothel. January had never fathomed why, with all the prostitutes there were in Paris, more had to be recruited by force, but apparently that was the case. He'd heard it was ten times worse in London, where men paid premiums to deflower virgins.

But why? he thought. When he'd told Artois to get rid of the guns, to emphasize that he'd never seen them, it had been in his mind only to prevent the boy from a roughing-up by whoever was bringing them in—even if Artois had gone straight to the City Guards and enabled them to trace the smugglers, nothing very much would have been done on either side. Inconvenience to the smugglers, a hitch-up passing them on to Sancho Sangre or whoever was acting for the rebels in whatever southern jungle they were destined for . . .

It didn't make sense.

It wasn't a killing matter, not of a boy who clearly had a wealthy family—be it ever so illegitimate—behind him.

Mulm was an American, but he had lived in New Orleans for several years and he wasn't stupid. He did enough business with the French Creoles to know that the murder of a young man of color connected with one of their families wouldn't be simply shrugged over and forgotten. He would know how close the ties were that bound the shadow-children to their white relatives. Obviously he knew, if he'd taken pains to provide another explanation for the boy's death.

"Yes, you give me a good bad man, an honest bad man," Cut-Nose was saying. "Lafitte, may he rest in peace. . . ." He crossed himself again. "Yes, he stole a little here and there, though he never did sink that American ship like they said he did, that made so much trouble. He wasn't no fool, him. But you know, he treated everyone good. If a man was in trouble, or was ill, he'd support that man's wife and children. If a man died in his service, he'd pay for them to be buried. None of your little wood box stuck in the ground, neither. Candles, and gloves for everybody, and a big spread of food and wine afterward so everyone would remember their friend. There aren't men like Lafitte around anymore."

Given the number of men and women Lafitte had stolen from Spanish slave-ships bound for Cuba and then smuggled into Louisiana to sell to the sugar-planters, that was probably just as well.

Across the street, lamps were lit in the Café des Exiles. Men moved their tables out onto the banquette, to sip their coffee and play dominoes, old men who'd been planters or brokers in Saint-Domingue, before the slaves there rose up in revolt. Men who'd spent their lives telling themselves that it was only a matter of time before the situation there was "cleared up" and they could go back to being the masters.

No white men had slept quite so peacefully since Christophe, and Toussaint Louverture, had led the slaves to revolt. Every few years now, slaves in this land of Life, Liberty, and the Pursuit of Happiness tried to lay claim to the rights promised by its founders, and every few years were beaten down, with greater and greater brutality. Since the last big revolt on the eastern seaboard four years ago, even freedmen and *libres*—people of color who had been free for generations—were regarded with deep suspicion.

Café des Exiles, thought January with a bitter inward smile as servants of the owner came out with flambeaux of gunpowder, cowhooves, and lemon-grass, to drive the mosquitoes away. *As if my mother's mother, and my father, and all those others brought from Africa were not themselves exiles.*

"Did you hear Hesione LeGros was dead?" he asked, blinking hard against the first gust of harsh smoke as it fluffed across the street.

"No . . . Hessy?" The old pirate's busy hands paused. "Hellfire Hessy, we used to call her. . . . That's a damn shame. What happened?"

"Someone came into her place about three weeks ago and slashed her to death," said January quietly. "Someone she knew, I think— And, of course, the Guards are doing nothing."

"T'cha!" Chighizola shook his head, and tucked wisps of straw more firmly around the yellow fruit. "God, what a bobcat that little blackbird was! I remember me the time, down on Grand Terre that was, when she went after old Gambi with a pewter tankard, right in Lafitte's house, when she heard Gambi'd started makin' sheep's eyes at one of the girls we took off a Spanish slaver. Damn near brained him, chasin' him around the room—I nearly fell in the fire, I was laughing so hard. Poor Gambi was givin' Hessy necklaces and earrings for a month, tryin' to get her to forgive him. You'd never think it, a little thing like that."

No, thought January, remembering the crumpled, dirty form dead on the floor among the ants. *You'd never think it.*

"Did she have children, back in the Barataria? Or any family?" he asked.

"Oh, sure. Three daughters, that was raised by the Borgas family over on Grand Isle, and all of 'em married now with kids of their own—what the hell was their names? Somethin' pretty—Marie-Epiphanié works for me, one of the daughters, sweetest little lady you'd care to meet—what the hell was her sisters' names? She had a son, Hessy did, that the Borgases also raised—she loved 'em all but she wasn't much of a mother, and she knew it. But he died of snakebite five, six years ago." He sighed noisily. "She was a spitfire, no mistake. But she hadn't no malice in her, you know. None. She didn't hold no grudges, and didn't make trouble for nobody, once she got over her mad. She'd stab you with that stiletto she kept in her hair one day, wash up your dishes for you the next. She made sure her children went to good families, that didn't mistreat 'em, which is more than some of those bitches did, once Lafitte and his boys moved on."

"And you wouldn't know any reason Mulm would want to harm Hesione? Or have someone harm her? Does he have a man named Tom Burkitt working for him?" he added when Chighizola shook his head again. "Big man, six feet or so, American? Or chews tobacco like an American, anyway?"

"Burkitt? Not that I've heard. There's a fellow Burke that hangs around the Nantucket, Tyrone Burke. Supposed to be a drover, but me, I wouldn't let him touch no horseflesh of mine. Come south on the keelboats, I hear, and got into debt to Mulm. Works thievin' on the docks a little, an' does this an' that for Mulm, keeps order in the place. He's about six feet an' chews. Black hair, light eyes, greeny-brown like dirty water. Black brows that meet in the middle, like my grandma always said was the sign of *malòcchio.*" And he made a quick gesture of aversion with his hand. "That your man?"

"Maybe." January helped Cut-Nose carry his crates through the shining cobalt darkness to the levee, where his pirogue bobbed at the end of an empty wharf. Afterward he returned to the market, where the last of the women were packing to go by the yellow flare of cressets. La Violette confirmed both what Cut-Nose had said and what January suspected. She didn't particularly recall that Mulm—whom she knew by sight and rumor, and detested, having a cousin who worked mopping up at the Nantucket—had had a cloak with him, but she recalled him going over to that young octoroon boy. Standing next to the boy, right up close. She remembered because she'd longed to call out *Step back, son, or he'll pick your pocket. . . .*

Young boys came to Mulm all the time, of course. The saloon-keeper was known to run whorehouses—known, too, for finding out things that young men would pay him not to let their fathers know. Yes, they both got into a carriage. It drew right up where there was a plank across the gutter and didn't pause but a moment. Some gentlemen would have their carriage stop here while they got out and got a cup of coffee, with all the carriages and carts and drays all scrooching around every which way in the street, and she'd seen mules break their legs, being pushed into the gutter and losing their footing.

Not in summer, of course. You could put your carriage sideways right across Rue du Levee today and not inconvenience a soul. . . .

As he left the market, January passed the black-bordered notice pasted to one of the brick pillars of the arcade.

FUNERAL
WEDNESDAY, AUGUST 19
ARTOIS ST. CHINIAN
CHAPEL OF ST. ANTHONY,
NEW CEMETERY

He thought of Uncle Veryl, alone in that empty town house. Of Rose, packing up her student's workroom in the gathering dark.

Lieutenant Shaw wasn't at the Cabildo. He was back in town, DeMezières said, and would be in later tonight or tomorrow for certain. The note January had left him concerning the guns—and Artois' death—still lay on Shaw's surprisingly tidy desk, still sealed, reminding January of the fragments of pink wafer that Rose had found on the floor of Artois' room.

I'll wait for you at the coffee-stand opposite the Café des Exiles . . . I'll be there between five and six. . . . Easy to get a boy of sixteen to slip quietly out of the house without waiting for his guardian, or speaking to his guardian's overworked valet. *I have a gun. . . . Get in the carriage, you won't be hurt. . . .*

January knew how long it took a man to drown. He'd talked to the rough boys, the thieves and housebreakers of Paris, when they'd end up at the night clinic in the Hôtel Dieu. He knew it took a good deal longer to suffocate in water than most people thought.

My boy. His heart ached as he walked back along the hot, gluey silence of Rue Bourbon with the waning moon just lifting above the black line of the house-tops, as if the boy had in fact been the son he'd lied about to Mackinaw Sal. More than the pain of knowing he was dead, was missing him. Wanting to talk to him again. To hear his reactions, his opinions— He would, January thought, have been absolutely tickled to participate in the investigation of his own death. He'd have his own theories, his own ideas to check.

Oh, my boy.

The funeral would be the following morning. Dominique had come in that afternoon on the steam-train, with Thérèse and her cook, and opened her house for the wake. January was surprised at how many of the plaçées, who'd taken cottages or boarding-house rooms in Milneburgh, came that night, bearing blancmanges and cakes, gumbos and étouffés in their finest dishes of French or Prussian porcelain, to lay on the tables in Dominique's front parlor.

"Contessa d'Ernani, huh," sniffed January's mother at the news that Coquelicot St. Chinian had been informed by letter of her son's death. "If Veryl St. Chinian expects that one to contribute so much as a wooden nutmeg toward the cost of a tomb, he'll find his mistake—or to put in money toward the funeral. And *just* like Dosia St. Chinian to forbid the boy to be laid in the St. Chinian family tomb. As if *she* was more than a cousin twice removed herself, before she married Raymond."

"You can't really blame her for that," temporized Catherine Clisson, a lovely, serene-faced woman whose left-handed alliance with a sugar-broker had nearly broken January's heart when he was very young. She waved her black lace fan, for the heat of the candles that lined the tables and glowed from the wall-sconces was smothering. "The way Raymond carried on with Coco was an insult to any wife."

"It's no reason to behave scaly toward the son. And if Dosia St. Chinian thinks that daughter of hers will give her free lodging now that Chloë's married Henri Viellard, I can only say I hope she enjoys the company of the cousins she's been sponging off since Raymond St. Chinian's death—*if* they'll have her, now she's no longer got an heiress with her." Livia Levesque rustled into the rear parlor in a fluffy whisper of black-and-eggplant silk, to find out how much Dominique had paid for the bourbon in the sauce on the tart and inform her that she'd been cheated.

Artois had spoken so often of having been sheltered that January was a little surprised at how many people crowded into Dominique's cottage for the wake. But Coquelicot St. Chinian was the daughter and the granddaughter of plaçées, and related to half the free colored demimonde of New Orleans. In addition, there were many more who had simply known and liked the boy. Dressed in various degrees of mourning black, they passed through the two candlelit parlors, and in and out of the rear bedroom, where Artois lay in his coffin, dressed in his best coat and weskit, a young dandy to the end. Their weeping and cries formed a muffled eddy of sound at the rear of the house, against which the soft-voiced conversations in the front parlor had a gentling sound, like padded silk rolled around broken glass.

"I wish your mother wasn't right so often," sighed Bernadette Metoyer, whose rivalry with January's mother dated to the dim recesses of some antediluvian age. Bernadette had bought a chocolate shop when her protector had paid her off upon his marriage, and had invested the proceeds advantageously; she was dressed in an elaborate fantasia of black crepe that left little smudges of black on everything she touched, and jangling with jet. "I wouldn't want to speak ill of Coco—I've known her longer than you've been alive, Ben, almost—but I'd be surprised if she even went into mourning for the boy. Completely aside from not wanting to admit she has a child, if she's got some other man in tow, which I'll go bail she does by this time . . . she looks dreadful in black. Always did. Did someone write to Chloë St. Chinian?"

And she glanced—rather self-consciously—around as she spoke the name. As if, thought January, Dominique weren't fully conscious of her anomalous position vis-à-vis the boy whose body lay now in the rear bedroom of the house Henri Viellard had bought her.

"Rose did," he answered. "I understand Madame Chloë Viellard is at Bois d'Argent, downriver in Plaquemines Parish."

Bernadette sniffed. "That makes sense. Her mother-in-law is at Viellard Plantation across the lake. I wager if the family had a plantation in Texas, Chloë would find a reason to be there." She bustled off to intercept Dominique on her way to greet yet more guests, to tell her she shouldn't be on her feet in her condition and to inquire about her cook's way of making flan. Five minutes later January saw her on her knees in front of Artois' casket, convulsed with sobs, as if the boy were her own son.

And this was not, he understood, either hypocrisy or hysteria. Bernadette Metoyer's grief—like that of his mother's other friends, of Artois' more distant cousins and friends still more remotely connected—was as genuine as her cheeriness had been only moments before.

This was something else that whites did not understand. He had been hired, many times, to play at the wakes of white people, and had always found them eerily silent and cold. Why stifle your genuine grief, grief at the shortness of life, grief at the vast network of might-have-beens that covers all the earth like a shining nimbus, only because you are not closely connected with the point at which Death has touched this time?

Why not grieve deeply and loudly, sharing your grief with the closer family, letting them know they're not alone?

And if the dead boy's mother hadn't come, all the more reason to let Artois' spirit know how dearly he had been loved.

Even Rose—whom January knew to be a deist, without belief in Heaven or Hell—wept, rocking back and forth in a corner of the bedroom with her arms folded across her breast. She was the closest thing that Artois had had to a sister, perhaps, in all the assemblage: *Sometimes it feels like you and she are my family, the only ones who understand.*

January went into the room again and again throughout the night, to sit beside Rose sometimes, to hold her sometimes, cradling her in silence. Grieving that it had to be Artois' death that had broken that barrier between them. When James brought Uncle Veryl in, January could see the old man struggling to restrain his tears, the way white men did. Saw Veryl's uncertainty, his polite puzzlement, at the intense emotion in the room with the casket, the lighter conversation and copious consumption of tafia punch in the front parlor and outside in the yard.

He cannot understand, thought January even as he went out to shake hands with him, to quietly thank James for bringing the old man to Dominique's house.

And even at that, the wake was quiet compared to others January had attended. The free colored demimonde took many of their ideas of refinement from the whites with whom their blood was mixed. Had the wake been among Olympe's friends—the "respectable" free artisans of color, the less wealthy and less self-consciously "white"—there would have been dancing, and more music than just January playing Dominique's little square pianoforte. Though the liquor flowed more freely as the hot night deepened, no one got really drunk. Most of those present were women, who were, or had been, plaçées.

Had the wake been among Olympe's friends, it probably wouldn't have been over in a single night.

At around two in the morning Agnes Pellicot and one of her daughters walked Dominique to Agnes' house to rest for a few hours; the wake itself went on. January played, sometimes sad tunes, popular ballads, or the gentle complexities of Bach; sometimes dances, light and gay. Others spelled him at the piano, either plaçées or some of the other musicians who'd remained in town through the summer's heat. In the morning the women brought out more food and in time M'sieu Quennel came to the door with his black-carved hearse, his darkly caparisoned sable horses, his choir of eight children, the candle-flames they bore pale as white flowers in the hammering mid-morning sun.

January took the Spanish guitar that was his second voice and the other musicians gathered trumpets or clarionettes, or showed up with tambourines and drums. Dominique came back from Agnes Pellicot's house clothed in simple black ("She shouldn't wear complete black like that," declared January's mother, who'd also gone home to change, "she looks worse than the corpse in it"), to preside over the distribution of black gloves, black scarves and armbands, black mourning-rings with little crosses on them, and the tall, thick white beeswax candles in their paper-lace holders that, January knew, would cause connoisseurs of funerals to proclaim this one "properly done." Everything in Dominique's house was, by this time, smudged with the sooty residue of crepe as if there'd been a fire. Thérèse would be weeks getting it clean. James brought Uncle Veryl, and walked beside the old man and Rose behind the coffin as they made their way along Rue Burgundy to Rue St. Louis, and so lakeward to the New Cemetery through the grilling heat.

Only when the coffin was slipped into the domed "oven" of the temporary crypt, and Uncle Veryl left the churchyard to be escorted home by James, did the music change. The solemn dirges gave place to gayer marches, the reminder that death is not forever, that sunrise always comes. There would be more food, January knew, back at Dominique's—poor Thérèse had been left back at the kitchen with old Martine and Minou's cook Becky to prepare it and intercept what Bella would bring. Stronger punch—tafia and whiskey-laced lemonade—"sweet-beer" made from ginger-water and sugar, pralines and gingerbread and cake. Looking ahead of him at Dominique, walking arm-in-arm with Rose and Olympe, January saw how haggard his sister looked despite the rest she'd been taking as often as she could.

The wake would continue through the day and into the night. It would be tomorrow before he could seek out Shaw again, to tell him what he'd learned from Cut-Nose and La Violette.

That was another thing that a white man would not understand; certainly not the square-jawed heroes of the melodramas that Artois had read and laughed at with Rose, the young men who could not sleep until their wrongs were avenged.

First, you honor the dead. First, you do what you can to care for the living.

Then you take your revenge.

January wondered what kind of wake the Avocet family had given their murdered brother, down in Jesuit's Bend. Guifford's brother was in jail, his wife had been deceiving him, and his "poor little dab of a sister" had been mistreated to a degree that would engender few tears. Would Shaw be able to talk to the house servants about things seen or overheard at the funeral?—for of course a French Creole planter would no more have admitted a Kaintuck to the house than he'd have let in a field-hand. And would the house servants—who had no more use for Kaintucks than their masters did—tell him even if things had been said in the corners concerning the infamous bloody shirt or when the clock in the parlor had stopped?

Walking as he was up near the head of the procession, January was one of the first to cross the cypresswood plank at the intersection of Rue Burgundy and Rue du Maine, closest to Dominique's house. They'd picked up a good deal more of the neighborhood in their return from the cemetery, and the procession straggled behind them for over a hundred feet. Across the street from Dominique's cottage, and a few houses down, stood the town house of the Staël family, a modest building as town houses went, painted a pinkish clay color and shut up now for the summer.

The shop in its lower floor—which sold musical instruments, sheet music, ladies' fans, and silk flowers—was closed likewise; if it hadn't been, January didn't think he'd have taken any special note of the two men standing in the carriageway's arched blue shade.

But he did notice them. And when one of them spit tobacco on the sidewalk, he took a second look.

And for a moment, his eyes met those of Franklin Mulm.

The saloonkeeper stood with hat politely off and hands folded, the sunlight glinting on his little square-lensed spectacles, looking, in his close-buttoned dark coat and old-fashioned stock, more like a Yankee importer than the whoremaster, slave-dealer, blackmailer, and gun-runner that January knew him to be. The other man had left his greasy slouch hat on, but even under its shadowy brim January could see the thick single bar of eyebrow above the broken nose, the pale, wary, vicious eyes.

January's hand stilled on the guitar-strings. His stride checked, the other musicians flowing past him; Pylade Vassage nearly ran into him and came close to swallowing his flute. "What is it, man?" he asked, and January shook his head. "Somebody step on your grave?"

In the sweating glare of the afternoon sun, January felt cold.

Cold and tingling in spite of his exhaustion, and filled with rage, as if he could stride out from among the strutting mourners and cross the street, seize Mulm by his stringy neck and Burke by the tobacco-stained front of his shirt and shove both down into the offal-choked gutter, to hold them there until they inhaled the shitty water and drowned.

What are they doing here?

The first of the mourners streamed between him and the town house: Bernadette Metoyer and her sisters, all sporting black ostrich plumes in their tignons that scattered the banquette with a rain of fluff, like grimy snow. "Benjamin, for goodness' sake, get moving!" snapped his mother, cocking her parasol back to look up at him. "Have you fallen asleep?"

Not, reflected January, *do you have a touch of the sun? Not, are you in grief for your young friend? Not, are you ill?*

He shook his head, making himself smile as he had learned to when his mother behaved like herself; the only way he had learned to dispel grief.

And when he stepped forward, and looked back at the carriageway again, the two white men were gone.

ELEVEN

The wake lasted through that night, and broke up only on the following morning. Dominique had long since gone back to Agnes Pellicot's to go to bed—their mother had returned to Milneburgh almost immediately after the funeral, without, as far as January could see, even acknowledging Olympe's existence. But Rose remained, acting as hostess, and January would not have left her to perform the task alone. Everything that had taken place since she'd waked him at sun-up two mornings ago blurred into a long, single corridor of grief and information and images—colors—the blue of Mackinaw Sal's Mother Hubbard and the green of the resurrection fern that grew in Veryl St. Chinian's courtyard. Rose's head pressed to his shoulder and the shuddering of her breath beneath the hard corset-stays. The taste of bread-pudding and the smell of candlewax and decay.

Artois was gone.

He'd never see him again.

He walked Rose home after the last company had left Dominique's house. Exhausted and numb and only just beginning to feel the real grief, the genuine grief that settles in after the funeral's noise and drama are done. He climbed the stairs with her in the forenoon's pounding heat, meaning only to say, when they reached her door, *Let me know what I can do.*

But instead of saying it, he only kissed her, and her arms went around him, hard, clinging: *Don't leave. Don't leave.*

Life is so goddamn short.

They went in her room together and stretched out on the bed, kissing first, then pulling off each other's clothes, her skin matte silk and sweet-smelling under his wondering fingers, her hair, released from the tignon, handfuls of light, soft, walnut-colored curls. He took her carefully, even in his need for her remembering that the only other time a man had touched her, it had been violent rape. But she didn't shrink from his body, didn't brace herself, didn't react in any of the ways he thought or feared or imagined she would or might. Only held him, tighter and tighter, her breathing thick and deep in rhythm with his. Afterward she wept, the way rocks would weep if they could when an earthquake breaks them apart, and slept almost at once, clinging to him still, leaving him to marvel at the way her face relaxed in slumber, and the softness of her breast above the corset's hard line.

The afternoon's storm woke them both, and he unlaced her corset, both of them smiling now, and disentangled themselves from what seemed to be delicious forests of petticoats, and they made love again. *When I die,* he thought, *if they ask me, What time would you like to have, out of all your life, to be in for eternity, it will be this. With the rain falling, and the far-off lightning flickering in the window, and Rose here beside me at peace with all things future and past.*

"When I was a little girl I used to wonder what made the lightning," she murmured. "Of course there were no books, and nobody to tell me anything about it. But I made myself a telescope out of spectacle-lenses and cardboard, and I went out to the tallest tree in the middle of the island to watch the lightning through it, trying to catch the moment when it first leaped out of the cloud, to see what I could see. I have no idea why I wasn't hit."

"And you still don't believe the Virgin Mary looks after children?"

"In the light of what you say I'll consider the possibility. I still wonder if there isn't some way to divert the lightning enough to make a balloon ascension into a storm. There has to be something one can do." And she leaned back against his shoulder, the fey blue-white flashes from the window outlining her face in the dark.

They talked, and made love again, and dozed; and later walked along the levee to the market in the rain and bought gumbo and dirty rice for a couple of pennies from one of the carts there, and sat in the shelter of the brick arcades, watching the rain fall on the river until it was nearly dark.

"I need to write to Uncle Veryl in the morning," said Rose as they walked back toward her room. The rain had stopped by that time, and queer, warm spooky winds tore the cressets along the levee to streaming yellow ribbons of flame; every awning and abat-vent and gallery along the street seemed to creak and whisper as they went by. "To ask when, or if, he would like help in sorting out Artois' laboratory."

And January was reminded that with Artois gone, the mainstay of Rose's livelihood had also vanished.

It brought home to him like the pinch of a too-tight shoe how precarious his own finances were, how long it would be before he had so much as a dollar to offer toward a life together. . . .

If, he reflected, she even *wanted* a life together.

And he realized that incomparably joyful as the day had been, it had answered him little. He still had no idea what she would say if he asked her now, *Rose, will you be my wife?*

So at her door he kissed her, and said, "Dinner tomorrow?"

And her fleet smile told him that she still valued her solitude; as he himself, he reflected, would value his once he got past that daz-zling surge of need to be with her every single second, to never let her out of his sight. Her eyes thanked him for understanding. "I'll try to finish up the translation of *Helen* I'm doing for M'sieu Songet, and see if he has anything else for me. Madame Vroche tells me that her son-in-law can get me work making cigars if the very worst comes to worst."

January opened his mouth to protest—*Cigars!*—and closed it. It was only through chance and careful saving that he wasn't making cigars himself.

So he only said, "Till then," and kissed her, and his soul went up

in fireworks at the tightening of her hand around the nape of his neck, savoring and prolonging the kiss.

He almost danced his way home, through the hot, sticky night.

In the Rue Condé someone said, "Benjamin," and he turned, to see the man known around town as Ti-Jon spring over the flowing gutter and cross to him, lithe and wary as a big black cat.

Ti-Jon's owner was a man named Dessalines in Rue Bourbon, who rented out Ti-Jon's services to whatever gang of stevedores needed another strong back that week. Like many slaves—far more than the city fathers considered safe or advisable—Ti-Jon "slept out." He found his own lodging, his own food, his own clothing where he could out of the slender wages paid him, returning only on Saturday nights to Monsieur Dessalines' house to hand over the sum agreed upon with Ti-Jon's renter.

This meant that Ti-Jon lived in attics and back-sheds and shacks like those of Hesione's neighbors; that he was lucky if he saved enough over his wages for an ounce of sausage to put in his rice and beans. The shirt he wore tonight was a patched cast-off diaphanous with hard use and, like most slaves in the summer, Ti-Jon was barefoot and likely to remain so until first frost.

But in a quarter of town where every house was an enclosed fortress with but a single gate, where no slave could enter or leave except by passing under the master's eye, this was an acceptable exchange. Ti-Jon had to see his master only once a week, and if Monsieur Dessalines had retreated to the lakefront for the summer, Ti-Jon wouldn't even visit him that frequently. All he had to do was send the money, behave himself, and keep quiet.

Men had paid more for less freedom than that.

"Ti-Jon," said January. He'd heard the Cathedral clock strike ten not very long ago: if the City Guards caught them out, they'd both risk a stay in the Cabildo. And Ti-Jon was smoking a cigar, another infraction of the white man's law. But watching for the City Guards at any time became second nature, whether you were free or not, if one was a man of African extraction in New Orleans. It was understood between them as they both stepped into the shadows of a carriageway, their shoulders touching the wrought-iron bars that closed off the tunnel of flagstone and stucco behind them. From the garden beyond the gate, January smelled sweet-olive, a thick, intoxicating scent in the wet, and heard the peep of frogs.

"That was a fine funeral yesterday," said Ti-Jon. "And a good wakin', I'm told." He had, naturally, not been invited—the free colored, especially the higher class that the demimonde aspired to, had nothing to do with even French-speaking Catholic slaves.

"He was dear to me," said January. "And to my lady Rose."

"I hear tell," said Ti-Jon, "that you've asked questions around the town, and have said as how you know who killed him. Is that true?"

January heard the cautious note in Ti-Jon's voice and narrowed his eyes in the darkness, trying to make out something of the man's face. But he saw only a glint of watchfulness in the slave's eye; the rest of his features drowned in shadow.

"Two days before he died Artois stumbled across a secret, the kind of thing other men have been beat up over, or maybe killed if someone thought they could get away with murder. He was seen getting into a carriage with two men, bad men by all accounts, one of whom at least knew what Artois had learned. When Artois was found drowned, he had bruises on his arms and neck, where his head had been held underwater. You tell me what else to think."

"You thinkin' what you want to think." Ti-Jon's voice was dark velvet coming out of a deeper dark. He stood nearly January's height, African-black, intelligent and wary, and a keeper of his own counsel. Most of the runaways in town went to Ti-Jon for advice about getting along in the cracks and shadows of the white man's world. "There's nuthin' I can tell you about that. But what you've told me is a big jump, from Artois St. Chinian climbin' into that carriage with Franklin Mulm to Artois St. Chinian bein' dragged out of some gutter with bruises on his arms. There's men who saw Artois St. Chinian leave Mulm's house that afternoon on his feet—drunk, but walkin'. Men Mulm told off to go after him, see he got home all right. The boy sent 'em away."

"Who told you this?" asked January, thoroughly taken aback and trying not to let it sound in his questions. "Mulm? Or Burke?"

"Men who was there," answered Ti-Jon, and blew a cloud of smoke. "Men who heard Mulm tell the St. Chinian boy a couple lies about who those guns was for. Small lies, but the boy believed 'em. He wouldn't have gone to anyone. Mulm's no fool."

"I can see that," murmured January, his breath feeling a little strange in his lungs. *Ti-Jon,* he thought. *Why would Ti-Jon ally himself with Mulm?* His acquaintance with the slave wasn't deep, but what little he knew of the man told him that Ti-Jon was no man's lackey.

Had the saloon-owner offered him money to buy his freedom?

But there were other men who'd warn off January cheaper. Other men who'd tell him these lies—if they were lies . . .

But not men he'd believe.

On the other banquette, two indistinct shapes reeled along, their arms around each other, singing in English about the merry month of May. Moments later a third shape slipped out of the shadows, pursuing from doorway to carriageway to the black gulfs beneath the abat-vents, a cautious little drama that would surely end with the two singers slumbering penniless in some dark corner of the levee—if they were lucky, and the robber didn't have to put up a fight for what he wanted.

"Where those guns is goin' is a secret," Ti-Jon went on. "A secret Mr. Mulm—and myself, I might add—would rather your friends at the Cabildo didn't go around askin' questions about, if you understand what I mean. There's a lot at stake here."

"So much at stake that you'd rather not ask yourself whether or not Mulm was telling you the truth?"

Ti-Jon was silent. Behind the cigar-smoke January could smell the sweat in his clothing, the dirt of his body, the smell he was familiar with from his childhood in the quarters when there was no way to wash for weeks on end during the cane-harvest, no time and no energy left at the end of the exhausting day. You could only do so much with swims in the river and basins of cold water in the dark before dawn.

"There's a lot at stake." Ti-Jon's deep voice was slow, as if he struggled within himself. The cigar glowed like a firefly in the dark

with the gesture of his hand. "You can use a bad man to a good purpose, Benjamin. You know that. If you gotta fight for the lives of
your family and the Devil offers you a weapon, you gonna tell him
go away, you'd rather they all die? Burke told Mulm he thought that
boy'd seen what was in that box, and Mulm went out as quick as he
could, to catch the boy before he talked around about the guns and
to convince him it was none of his business. It wasn't hard, Mulm
said. St. Chinian was like all your quadroons an' your octoroons,
wantin' to just lie low an' not make a fuss an' maybe the *blankittes*
would go on lettin' him pretend he was one of them. There was no
reason for Mulm to kill him."

"No." January's heart beat hard, and he knew now where the
guns were going. And he felt angry, and baffled, knowing that
Mulm was lying to Ti-Jon and knowing the slave wouldn't want to
be told it. Knowing, too, that anything he told Shaw would be
countermanded by the same bald lies. Of course Mr. Mulm wanted
to talk to young Michie St. Chinian—a simple matter of business. A
couple of upstanding white gentlemen saw the boy leave Mulm's
house, and such was Mulm's concern that he tried to get young
Michie St. Chinian escorted home. . . . A few too many whiskeys,
how were we to know the boy wasn't used to them? He sent us away,
said he didn't need a nursemaid. . . .

Whoever held his head underwater until his lungs gave out,
then soaked his clothes with whiskey and dumped him in a seedy
part of town, it hadn't anything to do with Mr. Franklin Mulm.

"As a favor to me," said Ti-Jon, "keep this quiet." He blew more
smoke, a mist in the street-lamp glow. "And to yourself."

January drew in a breath, desperate not to say what he was
thinking: *You're a fool. Do you think this is going to do any good? Do
you really think the end justifies the means?*

But he made himself say, "I'll do that."

And walked home through the silent streets with the mosquitoes whining in his ears, trying not to think too much about what
he had just heard.

And wondering why a man like Franklin Mulm—a saloonkeeper,
a part-time slave-dealer, a land-speculator, and a whoremaster—

would risk his money and his freedom by smuggling guns on behalf of a slave revolt.

"What should I do?" asked January.

Olympe replied, "Nothing."

Paul's hammer in the workshop out back tapped, very loud in the doldrum afternoon. The smells of the drying herbs above the cold parlor hearth, the sulfury whiff of the gunpowder she used in her gris-gris, the mildewy scent inextricably tied, in his mind, to every memory of New Orleans—all these impressed themselves on him, like the unspeaking presence of that deity who lived in the black-painted bottle on her shelf. He felt the whole room watched him, and not just his sister with her dark, jeering eyes.

All your quadroons an' octoroons, he heard Ti-Jon's voice again, *wantin' just to lie low . . . maybe the* blankittes *would let him pretend he was one of them.*

He wanted to shout at her, *Just because I know revolt is hopeless doesn't mean I'm its enemy!*

But she hadn't said a word. She was still, like her big gray cat, staring at the swept hearthbricks.

He asked, "Do you know about this?"

"What cause would I have to know about a slave revolt?"

"Because you're a voodoo. You deal in secrets." Olympe had her own reasons for doing things, and January understood that whatever she told him, she would tell him as part of some wider scheme. But as with his torment in his dreams of Rose, there was no one else to whom he could go for advice.

"They killed Artois to protect this secret," he went on. "Everything I've heard about this man Mulm says *Don't trust this man farther than you can throw a medium-sized house.* I don't know what he told Ti-Jon and whoever else is in on it, but if he's bringing in guns for a slave revolt, it's because he's going to end up richer."

"And is that what you're trying to do?" Olympe folded her work-roughened hands. "Save these slaves—if there *is* a revolt bein' planned—from bein' double-crossed by Mulm? Or are you just out to prove Mulm killed Artois?" She regarded him dispassionately.

Their mother had had even less use for her than she'd had for January, and Olympe, January knew, had grown up very much alone. She'd always had a painful skill for going to the heart of events, for separating tangled issues and intents.

"Both. I'd like to pin the murder on him, yes. Artois was my friend and I loved him like a son. Hesione's murder, too. But I don't think I can." When he'd waked, late, after getting Ti-Jon's warning, he'd found in the privy a scrap of paper bearing the torn remains of a note in Shaw's ill-spelled scrawl. His landlady had only regarded him with her unblinking fishy stare when he'd asked if Shaw had left, or sent, a message for him.

"Americans don't know how to write," she'd said. "So I tore it up."

Since Shaw's note—which had come while January was at Rose's—set a meeting time in the market that had already come and gone by the time January found the various pieces, he'd proceeded to bathe and had gone to Olympe's rather than to the Cabildo. At this point he wasn't sure what he could say to Shaw that wouldn't result in generalized reprisals, repressions, and arrests. In the police coming down on whomever they'd suspected lately of making trouble—possibly Olympe and her family as well—whether they had proof of misdoing or not. Like God's rain, the police tended to fall upon the just and the unjust alike.

"I assume Mulm would lie to Shaw as he lied to Ti-Jon, and get his white friends to back him up."

"You're assuming Mulm lied," pointed out Olympe. "You don't have one scrap of proof. I'm not saying Mulm didn't kill the boy or wouldn't have, but for a man who talks about justice as much as you do, you're quick to think ill of an American. Whatever's going on, whatever's being planned, it's more than you know—more than I know. I know what they say about Mulm and I know the things he's done. He buys and sells slaves, and backs the State officials who're stealing Indian land and then blackmails those same officials into giving him tracts to sell. . . . Ti-Jon knows all this, too. You don't think he's checking those guns, to make sure they work, before sending them along? That he's keeping an eye on every move Mulm makes?"

"No," said January. "No, I don't think Ti-Jon trusts Mulm as far as he can see him. I think he's doing what he can."

"Then leave it," repeated Olympe. "You're a bull and you're right on the threshold of the china-shop door, brother. There's a lot of people will die if *les blankittes* start looking for rebels in every cabin and barracoon. Keep your mouth shut till the storm's gone by."

"And you think it'll do them any good?" demanded January. "I don't care if these slaves—these people who're planning revolt—are buying guns, but do they really think killing white men will set black men free? They tried it here in 1811 and the army crushed them before they made it as far as New Orleans. Nat Turner tried it, and Denmark Vesey tried it, and all it got them was hanged. And that's without a Judas like Mulm on their side, waiting to turn a dollar on whatever little plot he's got going on the side."

"So what do you advise?" Olympe's voice was cindery-velvet. "Lay down under the lash? Let *les blankittes* know they can do as they please with us and ours because we're afraid to die as others have died to be free? Wait around till we can find gentlemen who're honest and upright, and willing to sell guns as well? I'm all ears."

She cradled a creamware cup in her hands, eyes like stones holding his, steady and angry and cold. "You tell me what we're to do."

January said nothing.

Her voice was soft, but when she spoke he felt the Power in her, as he felt it in Mamzelle Marie. She was not only a healer, he thought, but a Queen in her own right. "Ti-Jon knows what he's doing, brother. If anyone knows how to trick a trickster, it's Ti-Jon. And if Mulm's the only Judas he's got to worry about, that's all right, because at least Ti-Jon *knows* Mulm's a snake."

As January rose to leave, she said, "There'll be plenty of time to go after Mulm later. If you think you can."

So when Shaw came to the house of Madame Bontemps the following day, with apologies about his absence, January passed on to him only those fragments of gossip about the Avocet family that he'd gathered from Dominique and her friends, most of which he was fairly sure Shaw already knew.

"I had heard M'am Vivienne had an eye to a fine pair of shoulders," agreed Shaw, as he and January crossed the steaming gutters of Rue Bourbon—as usual Madame Bontemps had refused to permit the Kaintuck on her property, though her argument this time was that *"people will know,"* whatever that meant. "That seems to be about all the qualifications that new overseer of theirs has: that, an' the fact that hirin' him put Miss Annette's nose out of joint. He sure don't seem to know much about runnin' work crews or raisin' crops."

"And did Guifford Avocet have a fine pair of shoulders?" inquired January, thinking about Minou's tale of Bertrand's compulsion to romance whatever women his brother attracted.

"Lord knows whether a woman would think so." Shaw spit at a toad on the rim of the gutter; the amphibian appeared to have heard all about Shaw's accuracy with tobacco, because it didn't move. "He was good-lookin' enough, I guess, slim like the sister—the brothers got all the looks in that family. But he was the one who came into town an' lived high an' went to danceables an' drove a match' team. Bertrand was the one stayed on the plantation an' bulled the slave women: him an' Raffin both, sounds like. M'am Vivienne didn't even meet him till she'd married his brother. I learned all this from M'am Vivienne's daughter Laurene, who's so far the only one in the Parish who'll give me the time of day, but every time I speak to her either her ma or her Aunt Annette'll grab an' haul her away."

Scarcely a surprise, thought January. He was astonished the Kaintuck had found the opportunity to get close enough to a young French Creole girl to learn even that much. Shaw looked tired: framed by his long, greasy hair, his ugly face was unshaven, and settled into lines of watchfulness. Like himself, January realized, Shaw understood that there was something about the situation he wasn't seeing, something he didn't know that would make all these contradictory facts make sense.

Yet his own mind kept returning to its anger and grief, and he barely heard his friend's account of finding where cloth had been burned in the woods—"You ever try to burn cloth so's none of it remains? Or get away from other people on a plantation long enough to do it, without bein' missed?"—and of the lawyers' wranglings over Guifford's intestacy and Bertrand's upcoming trial. Again and again he pulled himself back from saying, *Who cares that a thoroughly nasty white man was killed by his thoroughly nasty brother . . . or whoever it was? An innocent woman was killed. An innocent boy was killed. I know who was behind their deaths. . . .*

And Olympe's words, and Ti-Jon's, would clang like shackles before his mouth. *Keep your mouth shut till the storm goes by . . . There's a lot of people will die.* And, *You can use a bad man to a good purpose. Keep this quiet . . . as a favor to me . . . and to yourself . . .*

Oh, Artois my friend. . . .

". . . Artois St. Chinian," said Shaw.

January stopped, blinking in the gloom of the market.

"I am truly sorry," repeated the Kaintuck, "about Artois St. Chinian. I lost my sister when she 's about that age. Is there anythin' I can do?"

Rage blinded him: *You could have stayed in town and caught Tyrone Burke for Hesione's murder* BEFORE *he had time to kill Artois!* They stood twenty feet from the spot where Mulm had put a gun into Artois' ribs, had said, *Get in the carriage, you won't be hurt. . . .*

So angry was he that January had to look past the policeman's shoulder, to the brick pillar behind him where the tattered remnants of Artois' funeral announcement still clung. Someone had already partially plastered it over with another: *The funeral of Mlle. Marie-Ines Nourette.*

Someone's daughter. Someone's child.

Someone he didn't even know.

Maybe she hadn't been drowned in the gutter of Gallatin Street, but she was still dead, and someone's life was still empty. The rage went out of him, though he could not have said why, and he found his eyes burning with tears.

With startling gentleness, Shaw gripped January's shoulders and pulled him to him in a swift hug: rough, almost like the grappling of a wrestler, but light, and as quickly released. January stood for a moment looking at that lank deadly shape, the ugly unshaven face and pale eyes, remembering he had been angry at this man and remembering that Shaw knew he'd been angry.

He put out his hands, took both of Shaw's between his own. "Thank you."

In the white man's eyes, usually watchful and detached as a forest beast's, he saw only concern for him, and compassion for his pain.

He found himself saying, "There's nothing you can do now, but later, yes, we'll talk."

"Later after I find which of those folks down in Plaquemines Parish is lyin' the most." Shaw sighed, and the glimpse January had had of a brother in grief, of a man who had also lost someone he loved *(Where? When? How? What had been her name?)* disappeared behind the gray eyes of a wolf again. A weary wolf, on the trail of elusive prey. "You be all right?"

You couldn't save Artois, thought January. *But neither could I.* He said, "I'll be all right."

Knowing he would get no more information from Mamzelle Marie than he had from Olympe, January returned cautiously to the Swamp twice, to make what observations he could of the Nantucket from the shade of a seedy stand of loblolly pine on the next lot. He dressed in rags, a slouch hat over his face, and cheap rum spilled on his clothing—once a ruffian coming out to piss in the trees spit tobacco on him, but that was about all. He kept clear of the regulars he'd seen there before—Cuffee and Zulime—and left before sundown.

He didn't see Tyrone Burke again, though Mulm came and went in a neat tilbury several times a day. The publican seemed to consult with a steady stream of Americans in the back room of his saloon. Most of these were roughnecks, filibusters, and river-rats, coming in sober in mid-afternoon and only going into the Nantucket later to drink. On one occasion four of them came out, obviously bored, to harass the little group of drinkers in the yard. The male slaves left as soon as they could do so, but the four Kaintucks surrounded Zulime, and though she shook her head and tried to wrench free of their hands, they pulled her into one of the sheds with them. She came out again about a half-hour after the last of them returned to the saloon, stumbling like a drunken woman. Stood leaning against the side of the building, half doubled-over for some time, before at last staggering away down the muddy street.

On his second visit January saw Ti-Jon talking in the yard with Mulm. *You'd better watch your back, my friend,* thought January, shaking his head as he watched carts and drays go out with loads piled suspiciously high over what could have been false bottoms. *You'd better watch it good.*

Whatever Mulm was planning, it would be the worse, he thought, for those who depended on any weapon he sold.

"What do you think is really going on?" asked Rose the night after that second expedition to the Swamp. January had washed off the liquor, the mud of the Swamp, and the filth from his dirty slop-shop clothing, in a tub in her room, with much giggling and splashing; the book-lined room still smelled of wet straw-matting and soap. "How could anyone make money off a slave revolt? If he turned them in for a reward, wouldn't they just say he'd sold them the guns?"

"Not if they don't know it's Mulm who sold them," said January. "He's using Ti-Jon as a go-between, maybe others as well. If Ti-Jon dies—and it may be weeks before his death is discovered, with his owner out of town—all the buyers know is they've got a cache of guns."

"Do you think that's Mulm's plan?" She sat propped on the pillows, her long brown hair, kinked from the strings in which she'd braided it beneath her tignon, catching brass glints from the single candle's light. Outside the mosquito-bar, insects whined in protest; with the coming of evening she'd opened the shutters and the French doors onto the gallery, and the noise of the levee, and the near-by taverns, came faintly to them, even at this hour.

"I don't know," said January. "I don't think so." Her bed was narrow—he lay on his side, his back to the wall, the netting pressed itchy into his skin, and still there was barely room for them both.

"What's likelier is that Mulm's going to have a posse of his filibusters out picking up runaways who don't join the revolt, but who simply take advantage of the confusion and flee. That happens, you know. Slaves hear of a revolt and take to their heels. They figure the local patrols will be too taken up guarding against the rebels. Which they will be. I was seventeen when the last big revolt took place in

Louisiana. To hear the rumors at the time you'd think Spartacus and his army were on the march. There's nothing that puts whites in a panic like a revolt."

" *'Thus does conscience make cowards of us all.'* " Rose blinked past the candle-light to the open cobalt square of the door. "And of course that plan has the advantage that Ti-Jon—and whoever the actual rebels are—won't know about the intercepted runaways at all. It sounds like a great deal of expense for relatively little money."

"Not if Mulm keeps his men west of the rebels. That's the way runaways will go. West, to cross the Sabine into the Texas territories of Mexico. Personally, I think there are easier ways of making a living than gun-running, but what do I know? I'm only a piano-teacher whose last student just quit 'until times get better.' "

Rose slid down into his arms then, and the candle guttered in its holder and went out untended; they spoke no more. But afterward January lay awake, smelling the wax and the woodsmoke from the kitchen below, listening to far-off drunken singing from the direction of Gallatin Street, and the slow chiming of the Cathedral clock, and wondered again, with a kind of tired despair, what he could offer Rose in the way of a future. They'd make it through the summer somehow, of course. He'd pick up a dozen students at the first frost, when the businessmen started coming back to town, and more when the sugar-harvest was done. Enough to save money for the following summer's doldrums, but little more.

And what if Rose conceived? He knew she was going to Olympe for advice—the smell of the vinegar she used was a sharp, lingering fragrance in the luminous darkness—but he also knew that pessary sponges, and lambskins, and the annoyance of *coitus interruptus* all failed as often as they succeeded.

He knew Rose, too, lived in fear of it, and who could blame her? How insane did you have to be to risk everything you cared for, everything you valued, to give yourself to one you loved?

Virgin Mary, he prayed into the shadows, *if what we do is sin, please understand that we're doing as well as we can. Thank you for freeing Rose's heart of the chains of her fear.*

Please show us a way, you who guide wandering mariners home.

Please show us a way.

He slept, like a wanderer in utter darkness lying down on the very brink of a cliff; and the following night the entire question of marriage and money and how they were going to get through the summer became suddenly and hideously moot.

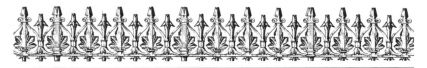

TWELVE

"Benjamin!"

January jolted from sleep. In that first instant—hearing Rose's voice, panting and laced with terror—he thought, *Bad dream.* . . .

No. He was in his own room in the garçonnière. That was last night he'd spent at Rose's.

The door rattled, frantic. He rolled from beneath the mosquito-bar, two strides took him to the door, shutters latched as they always were against his landlady's night-wanderings. He'd gone out to Milneburgh that day, to see Dominique, and the aftermath of the evening rain that had been so welcome on his way home was a tarry swelter now. "Benjamin!" whispered Rose again, and the fear in her voice was clear. He pulled the door open. She caught his arm.

"Run! Get out! We have to—"

He was already grabbing his trousers from the chair, pulling them on, knowing Rose didn't panic and seeing her barefoot, her hair down, a rough skirt and shawl wrapped on over her nightgown and mud and scratches on her face. He didn't wonder even for one second what was going on: he knew.

Mulm.

The men came into the yard like wolves, shadows barely visible in the overcast night. "House behind us is empty, hide in the kitchen," said January as he caught Rose by the waist, boosted her over the gallery rail, held her steady till she could swing herself up onto the roof and so up its tall peak, to the peak of the slave-quarters on the LaPlace property behind. She moved fast, but he scarcely had time to put his head and shoulders back through the door of his room, to grab his desk and heave it at the first man up the stairs, knocking him back. As he sprang up onto the rail himself, he heard the baluster of the garçonnière stairs tear and shatter, heard men howl as they fell fifteen feet to the paving-bricks of the yard.

No one shot at him. The men were professionals, and knew they had no chance of finding their target in the dark. But he heard re-treating boots, knew his pursuers would be around into the next street in moments and they'd better have someone to follow. As he went over the peak of the garçonnière roof, January glanced back and saw the white, ghostly shape of his landlady herself, standing on the back gallery of her cottage, watching the scene unmoving and presumably unmoved.

Then January went over the roof peak, slid and scrambled down slates greasy with moss and lawned with resurrection fern. He knew the LaPlace family had departed, taking their three slaves with them, for the quarters chamber immediately behind his own room was so thinly-walled he could hear their muffled voices when they spoke at night. He turned on the roof, swung his legs over the edge, and slipped down onto the gallery, cast a quick, scared glance down at the yard, half-expecting to see Rose crumpled on the bricks be-low. The moon rode high, a fragile nail-clipping a few days old, and it was so dark in the yard he could see nothing. He couldn't wait to look. Down the stairs, hearing and feeling through the bones of the little building the jarring weight of men clambering over the roof-peak after him. *Please don't let her be hurt. Please don't let them catch her. . . .*

A glance showed him no white blur of nightdress, but that had to be all. He plunged through the breezeway at the side of the house, heard a man curse behind him on the roof and another say in English "Hell, Rob, I thought you said you fought Comanche—"

"Well, there ain't no fuckin' buildin's in Comanche country!"

—and he was blundering through the black pit of the breezeway to the street and praying desperately he'd reach the mouth of it before his way was blocked at the street end. They'd run out of Madame Bontemps' yard and around to intercept him. He had only seconds of leeway. . . .

He saw them, just coming around the corner, by the flare of the iron lantern that hung where Rue de l'Hôpital crossed Rue Bourbon. Four, five—a confused impression of slouch hats, clubs, lead slung-shot probably held in hand, that could crack open a man's skull. He bolted lakeward, up Rue de l'Hôpital, guessing they could see only movement in the dark, and not how many people ran. Praying Rose would wait, would lie quiet in the deserted kitchen till he came. Praying she'd trust.

Virgin Mary, help us get out of this. . . .

He bolted around the corner into Rue Dauphine and instantly, drawing the deepest breath he could, flung himself into the gutter. It was two feet deep and two wide and brimming from the rain and any quantity of chamber-pots, and he stretched out on the bottom as if in a water-filled coffin and listened.

"Fuck, where'd they go?"

"Check that doorway over there. Look in that carriageway. . . ."

Voices dimming. Cursing. He'd heard nothing for a few seconds when he rolled over, raised himself cautiously until he could just feel his face break the surface, opened his mouth, breathed out, breathed in, and went down again. Like a gator in the swamp. This time of year there were baby gators in the gutters, but only in the back of town. Mostly you didn't get them here, though his friend Hannibal claimed he'd encountered a three-footer crossing Perdidio Street one night last summer when he'd been staggering home. Given the number of corpses that ended up in the gutters in that part of town, thought January, one didn't have to ask what it lived on. . . .

He wondered how many men there were. If any had been killed, tumbling in confusion off the garçonnière stairs. If Madame Bontemps would have the wits to call the City Guards, and if she'd let him go on renting from her after tonight.

Virgin Mother, let Rose be all right. . . .

The kitchen door of the LaPlace house was locked. January

whispered "Rose?" and heard the minute scrape of the bolt drawn back. He slipped through the door into absolute darkness. Felt her arms go around him, her hands draw his dripping head down to hers, her lips press his, slime and sewage and all. In spite of every-thing—maybe because of everything—the soft pressure of her breasts against his chest through the thin linen of her nightrail brought his manhood up hard; he turned his hip to her so she wouldn't feel it, forced his voice steady.

"Are you hurt?"

"No. You?" It was like Rose, he thought, not to ask questions, not to panic, not to waste words or breath, although he could feel her trembling—which did nothing to quell the instinctual fire burning so insistently in his groin. At the age of twenty, he reflected ruefully, he'd have had her on the kitchen table and to hell with Mulm and his myrmidons.

"I'm fine."

"What do we do?"

Couple like minks . . . No. "Get out of town. Now, tonight, at once. They'll be back. If either one of us goes to the City Guards, we have nothing to tell them, and they'll be watching your place and mine. Do you have your papers?"

Her hair brushed his arm as she shook her head. "They broke the door in, pulled me out of bed. Told me if I made a sound they'd shoot me. I keep my papers under the mattress; I was lucky I had a pen-knife and a pencil in my skirt pocket." She stepped away from him. He could hear her groping along the tabletop, heard the faint knock of a drawer, and her muttered curse.

Of course the family would have taken anything in the nature of cutlery.

Mulm and his bravos would come back in minutes, to wait by January's rooms. Watching for his return.

It was time to run.

Rose. They'd tried to take Rose. To get him to keep his mouth shut, of course. Or to bring him to them.

The anger that washed over him was so intense that for a mo-ment he couldn't breathe. He could have killed, gladly and unthink-ingly. *How DARED they . . . ?*

The yard behind the house was silent, black as pitch. A blur from the distant street-lamp put a smudge of ochre along the roof-line of the house itself, allowing January and Rose to orient themselves; if they hadn't just come out of the coalsack kitchen they probably couldn't have seen it. Ears strained so that he wondered that he didn't rupture them, January led the way through the hot dark as they made their way among the unpaved streets downriver, past the Esplanade and into the Faubourg Marigny. The foreigners who lived there, for the most part Germans and Italians fleeing the confusion and high taxes of their home principalities, hadn't the money to leave town in the summer. When the fevers came, as they did one summer in three, the people of the district died like flies.

They spent the rest of the night in the hay behind a livery stable, taking turns to sleep. When first light came, January tore a small square off the blank bottom of his own freedom paper and with Rose's pencil wrote a note to Olympe. There was blood on the pencil, a good four inches of it. Rose must have driven it like a dagger into the man nearest her, the moment she judged it safe to do so, in order to get away.

"You've killed him," he said, and licked his finger to scrub the dried blood off the lead point. "Puncture wounds that deep go septic very quickly, even if you didn't pierce an organ."

"Good," said Rose in a voice like a plucked guitar-string wound too tight. Without her spectacles her eyes seemed very large, ringed with dark exhaustion. She said no more about it, but sat stiff and withdrawn as she had been when first they'd met. He thought about what men of that type would have done with a quadroon woman before they killed her or sold her. The anger surged back again, burning heat, making his head swim.

I will kill them. . . .

He'd seen men die of puncture-wound sepsis, and like Rose he thought, *Good. Let's hope it was Burke.*

The Italian boy who came out to clean the stables was visibly astonished when addressed in his own tongue by what were clearly a couple of runaway slaves. He agreed to take the note, and January's watch, to Olympe's house, and even brought them bread and cheese before he went. "They'll give you some money there," January told him. "If they don't, you can keep the watch." It was more than likely the boy would keep the watch anyway and not mention that part of the bargain to Olympe, which gave him a pang. He'd bought the watch in Paris, and it was dear to him. But it was silver, and the only thing of value he'd had in his trouser pockets, and from what he knew of the men he was dealing with, it was a small price to pay.

When the boy came back two hours later, it was not only with the watch—which he returned—but with a friend of Olympe's named Natchez Jim, who had a wood-boat he plied up and down the river: "You tell me where you aim to go," the boatman told them in his deep, mellow voice, "and I take you there."

"Grand Isle," said Rose. She and January had talked about it during the long, wakeful night. "I have family there, my father's family. We'll be able to stay for as long as we have to."

Natchez Jim studied her face for a moment, then looked at January, eyebrows raised under a scraggy multitude of string-wrapped pickaninny braids. He was probably in his thirties but looked older, his face like black oak blasted by lightning. The gris-gris Olympe had made for him many years before dangled among an assortment of ragged beads and chains around his neck: mouse-bones, old keys, a heart-shaped locket of gold. "Your sister say you may be in trouble," he said, switching to the thickest French-African patois, to exclude the Italian boy who still stood near them. *"Les blankittes,* she say."

"That's true." January wondered if Jim also knew about the revolt being planned, and where it would be. He was a small-time trader; his boat went everywhere on the river. Among all those little cargoes of vegetables grown in slave gardens, of bales of moss harvested in hours spared from the master's allotted tasks and of trinkets and toys whittled by firelight in the night, it wouldn't be hard to slip in guns.

"The police in on it?"

He meant, *Are we likely to be searched?* The river traders were the slaves' lifeline to the world outside their captivity and as such they drove the plantation owners crazy. But there was little the masters could do about them beyond giving them whatever grief they could.

January shook his head.

Jim brought money enough to buy Rose a jacket and shoes, and a madras kerchief to tie on her head. The last thing they needed was the police to stop them about her uncovered hair. There was no way of telling who would see them if they were delayed even a few hours in town. No way of knowing which of Mulm's informants would carry word of their whereabouts or destination. The money was probably more than Olympe could afford, and as January washed off the crusted gutter-stink in the livery-stable horse-trough, he made a silent vow that he'd repay every penny. His sister had further found someone, probably her twelve-year-old son, Gabriel, to sneak to Rose's rooms and get her papers and her spectacles.

Olympe included no note, no communication with these items. As he and Rose made their way without appearance of hurry through the muddy streets toward the levee, January wondered how long this exile would last: would he in fact be able to return to New Orleans at all?

At a guess, he thought, slouching his shoulders and wishing he weren't so unmissably tall, if Mulm's scheme succeeded—whatever it was—he would be no danger to the man, although he knew he'd need to walk very carefully for some time to come. He corrected himself: he would be *perceived* as no danger. Mulm was white, Mulm was well-off, and Mulm almost certainly had powerful friends among the more raffish American property holders of the town. A complaint against the saloonkeeper—unprovable at that— would result in nothing but a more determined effort to rid the world of Benjamin January.

He glanced sidelong at Rose. Head up, face calm, she walked as if to the market, while everything she'd built up—the translations she was doing, the network of employers on whom she relied for her rent, the jobs she would not finish—crashed down around her, be- hind her, with an almost audible roar. She would write everyone, of course, from Grand Isle, with some kind of tale. And the second note January sent Olympe via little Giuseppe included instructions about salvaging Rose's possessions from Vroche's. But when Rose re- turned to the city, if she returned, it would be to a welter of broken threads and a bad impression of unreliability, and the long, tedious, painful process of building everything up again.

When a man marries, John Dryden had said centuries before, he delivers hostages to fortune. *And I didn't even have to marry her to put her in danger, to tear a jagged hole in her life. No wonder she kept me at a distance all this time. No wonder she kept EVERYONE at a distance.*

Only when they were in Natchez Jim's boat, struggling to row against the heavy sweep of the Mississippi currents, did Rose say, "Do you think he'll leave town after he's accomplished . . . what it is that he means to accomplish?" She spoke in Latin, and did not mention Mulm's name; held the tiller with the same casual adeptness she'd shown poking around for snakes in the swampy lakeshore. In the Barataria, no one grew up ignorant of the ways of boats.

"*Nonscio,*" replied January. *I don't know.*

Her mouth tightened. Already, out of the city, she was relaxing, though that distant look did not leave her eyes. "He has property," she went on, "so it isn't likely. And if, as you say, he has a scheme of his own in mind, we'll be able to do something with that." And seeing the glance of inquiry January shot her: "We know our young friend wasn't the only person he murdered. We'll find allies. We just don't know where, yet."

They left Jim's wood-boat in Algiers, and walked the three miles or so to the head of Bayou des Familles, through cypress swamps that crowded along the edges of the higher land near the river. For the most part they were entering a land of small hunters, small trappers, and occasional farmers; a land where cypresses towered, clothed in rags of moss, to unbelievable heights; where the airless heat seemed to steam between trees uncut since these lands had risen out of the sea and where the only sound was the steady croak of frogs, the stiff harsh rustle of palmetto-fronds, and the occasional leathery creak of a branch in winds far up in the forest crown. It was slave-stealer country, smuggler country, and as they worked their way by pirogue down Bayou des Familles to Little Barataria Bayou, and from there through the low mazes of the marshlands, January and Natchez Jim took turns sleeping, and never let their hands be far from their completely illegal guns.

Past Crown Point the true marshes began. The ciprière thinned from an unbroken forest to a succession of wooded islands in wide beds of reeds and alligator-grass. The sedges towered head high, navigable only when a man would stand up to look out across the reeds, and not always then. January had never felt easy in this country: here, he was always conscious of how tenuous was man's occupation. The very earth and water and sky conspired to trade places, shallow bayous shelving to mud and flottants—floating blankets of grasses riding unsupported on the water's surface—masquerading as islands to trick the stranger.

No wonder the American Army had never been able to come in and deal with Lafitte.

A world of birds and dragonflies, silent but for the plop and whisper of oars or pole, and the peeping choruses of frogs. Turtles basked on logs, arranged neatly in order of size, largest to smallest, with smaller turtles perched on the larger ones' backs. Now and then the water would slurp and January would look down and see a six-foot gar-fish that could take a man's arm off, sliding so close to the boat he could count the teeth in its ugly undershot jaw, or gators blinking sleepily in the reeds. Olympe had given them oil of citrus mixed with aromatics, which kept some of the mosquitoes at bay, but even in the brutal heat of the day they were everywhere. At night they would settle on Jim's little tent of netting like a thirsty cloud.

The spaces of water got larger, between the squiggly islands of grass and mud. The sky grew huge. Clouds moved across it like traveling cities in the afternoons, and in the mornings the first sun on the water was a sounding cymbal of brass.

Whatever is happening in New Orleans, thought January, *we are out of it now.* Slave revolt and betrayal; Uncle Veryl's grief, and Artois lying in his crypt . . . Whether Henri would return to Dominique, when he came back to town with his bride in the fall, or whether she'd have to raise her baby alone . . . *These are no longer our concerns. They will all go on without us.* He would think this, and look back at Natchez Jim, like Charon poling lost souls across the Styx, brass-gold multitudes of dragonflies hanging in the air about him thick as the falling leaves of Vallombrosa.

On the third day they emerged from among the matted

flottants and passed by Grand Terre, with the open spaces of Barataria Bay on their right and the clean wind sweeping the gnats and mosquitoes and dragonflies aside. January saw the tangles of live-oaks that furred the island's central ridge, the thickets of mimosa and oleander almost hiding old crumbling wharves and the huts of the fishermen. Lafitte's house, he remembered hearing somewhere, lay on the seaward side of the island, where the privateer could lie in a hammock on his gallery through these blazing heavy summer days and look out to sea. . . . Or maybe that was something he'd read in a romance.

"Did you read romances about Jean Lafitte?" he asked Rose, and she turned from contemplation of the porpoises cavorting in the bay and regarded him with sparkling eyes.

"You mean the ones that claim he was the son of noble parents, banished from the familial castle for nameless accusations of wrongdoing? I wouldn't dream of such a thing."

"I guessed your mind was of too elevated a nature for such entertainment. So is mine."

"I particularly liked the one that talked about his castle—"

"On Grand Terre? I take it he imported the stone."

"And evidently took it away with him when he left. I remember in the book it had a dungeon as well. I suppose he could have used it for drowning prisoners in—the water here lies even closer to the surface of the ground than in town, and goodness knows you can't dig a hole anywhere in New Orleans without it filling up."

"Is there anything on Grand Terre now?" asked January, shading his eyes to look up at Jim.

"What you see." The boatman's face creased at the talk of castles and dungeons and wandering scions of the nobility. "Shrimpers and hunters—you see every kind of bird God made, in winter. Trappers. Some of the folks run cattle." He pointed to a small herd, dozing half-unseen under the mimosas. "Now and then men will come down from town, or over from Mobile, and snoop around looking for 'Lafitte's treasure' that's supposed to be buried. But of course Lafitte didn't bury his treasure. He put all his money in the bank, like anyone with sense."

"Cora and I used to sneak over and look for it," recalled Rose.

She brushed back the tendrils of hair from around her face. Though freed of the law requiring her to cover her hair, she'd kept her tignon to protect her head from the sun, but her thick brown braids hung down below it, making her seem younger and more wild. The sun had deepened the freckles on her cheeks and nose. January couldn't imagine living without her and sometimes felt ready to drown Jim, just to have an hour alone with her to make love.

"Madame Vitrac—my father's wife—would have whipped the both of us if she'd known, because of course there were as many slave-stealers about then as there are now. I'm astonished no ill ever befell us. What surprises me still more is that everyone on Grand Isle *knew* there was no treasure—of course Lafitte wouldn't have buried money, he didn't trust half of his captains around the corner! The same way everyone on Grand Isle knows that Lafitte *never* fell in love with a blue-eyed damsel from Charleston, much less married her and reformed . . . but you still find that story cropping up every time you turn around. People in the market get so offended when old Cut-Nose laughs at them for it. And people still come here looking . . . and digging."

January watched the orange-trees and the tiny thatched houses glide past, the grazing cattle and the egrets—white or slate, or those black-and-white birds the locals called *lawyers*—wading among the flottants. On this side of the island there was little in the way of beach, just stringers of shells washed up from the bay floor, and mats of grass, creeping with brown ghost-crabs no bigger than the palmetto-bugs that infested the town. Here and there, rickety wharves thrust into the bay, pelicans perched on the pilings, studying the water like German university professors in grave silence, and gulls yarking and quarreling like an ill-mannered rabble in a lower-class apartment-building in some Paris backstreet. Against the glare of the bay's shining water, the squat shapes of shrimp-boats floated like enormous ducks; closer to the islands, pirogues and luggers appeared and disappeared between the flottants, dark-haired young men lifting a hand in greeting when they saw Jim, or calling across the water in their old-fashioned lilting French, was he back down from town already, hah?

New Orleans already seemed like something decades in the past.

Rose's half-brother Aramis Vitrac owned one of the several small sugar plantations that ranged along the flatlands on the bay side of Grand Isle. Aramis and his flaxen-haired, rabbity-faced wife Alice bade Rose welcome with unaffected joy. They gave Rose and January rooms in the dilapidated outbuilding where the house-servants slept—"I hope you understand," Rose said when January climbed the gallery's tall steps to the doorway a few minutes later, "that I'll always want—I'll always need—a room of my own, just to get away, to be solitary. I can't live cheek-by-jowl with anyone. . . . Why are you smiling?"

"Because I like to hear you say the word 'always.' "

They stayed at Chouteau Plantation, as it was called, among the oaks and the oleanders and the weak, thin, matte-green stalks of Creole cane, for just over two weeks. Rather than idle in a place where others had to work for their keep, January would go out in the mornings with the fishermen whose catches served the whites' tables and the stew-pots in the quarters as well. Rose helped her white sister-in-law Madame Alice in the kitchen—the plantation cook was less than proficient—and with the sewing, or teaching young Hilaire and Liberal and Pierrot and Marie-Rose their lessons. When the afternoons grew cooler, she would take long walks with January along the dunes on the Gulf side of the island, trailed by a floppy-eared pack of the household hounds, observing the clouds and taking measurements of the wind. There was no barometer, but Rose took note anyway of clouds and the feel of the air. Pelicans flew in formation—"I've caught them rehearsing, on the other side of the island," January assured Rose in a solemn voice—and dragonflies hung thick above the tangles of mimosa. They gathered driftwood, breaking desiccated boughs from the long lines of dead gray salt-leached trees washed up along the beaches, to make fires in the sand and sit listening to the waves until late in the night. They set crab-traps, and waded out in the bath-warm waters to harvest them, and got bit on the ankles; later watched the moon come up, lying in each other's arms. January, though he had only a guitar at his disposal—there wasn't a piano on the island—found himself, for the first time in years, writing music again. It was like returning to a house long shuttered, where once he had lived and been happy.

Time was not the same in Grand Isle as it was in other places.

Nothing was. The outbuilding where they slept stood on piers five feet high, and the Big House stood on stilts taller yet. Pigs and cows were penned in the tangle of fern and hackberry beneath. "We're far enough from the sea to be clear of the highest tides, surely?" January said, and Rose raised her eyebrows and looked at him over the rims of her spectacles.

"You've never been here during a hurricane." When he shook his head, she said, "You may yet. This is the season for them. Alice told me there was a bad one only a few years ago."

When a week later the sky grew black and the waves ran higher and higher up the Gulf shore, when wind drove the rain sideways with such violence that January could not walk upright from the door of the kitchen to the outbuilding's stairs to his room, he said, "I see what you mean about hurricanes."

The draft-whipped flicker of the single candle's light—it was two in the afternoon—caught the quirky V of Rose's smile, briefly shown and swiftly tucked away, as if she'd been punished as a child for laughing at things out of turn. "No, you don't," she told him. She folded up her telescope, through which she'd been watching the clouds over the tossing ridge of oak-trees, and struggled to pull closed the shutters, for the rain drove across the gallery and into the room. "This isn't a hurricane. This is just a storm." The gusts caught the mosquito-bar above the bed and made it billow like a gesticulating ghost.

"Then tell me when a hurricane is coming," retorted January, catching the other shutter and hauling it against the wind, "and remind me to go hide in the swamp until it's done." He remembered one of the big storms during his childhood that someone had said was a hurricane. It hadn't been anything like this. Worse, almost, than the wind itself—which was strong enough to make the little building slowly rock, creaking, as if it were a ship at anchor—was the constant brittle roaring of the trees, an animal noise that drowned thought and shredded the nerves.

"If I could tell you when a hurricane was coming," replied Rose, "they'd elect me Queen of this island. Some of the old people claim they can by the way the birds all fly inland, or the way the waves run up onto the beach, or by the greasy look of the sky. But mostly it takes everyone by surprise. And by the time anyone knows it's on the way, it's too late to run. Faugh," she added, taking off her spectacles and trying to wipe the rain from them; impossible, because her dress was wet through from the rain, as were January's shirt and trousers. "Oh, double faugh," as a draft quenched the candle, leaving them in near-darkness broken only by the phosphor-blue madness of the lightning.

And she looked up at him smiling, and there was no more talk of the weather that afternoon.

Thus the days passed for them, loving and coming to know love. January would wake in the night and look at her face in the moonlight, or lie between daybreak and morning listening to the liquid concertos of birds above the cock's sawing crow, and feel joy and love so deeply that he didn't have anywhere to put these feelings. Only wanting them to continue forever. One day they walked around the island finding and talking to Hesione LeGros' daughters, and it was abundantly clear that none of them had or knew anything to do with their mother's death. Hesione had made sure they'd be cared for, then walked out of their lives. January sometimes wondered about the slave revolt, and where Tyrone Burke had disappeared to, and how Franklin Mulm planned to double-cross his luckless confederates, but he really had scant hope of finding such things out until it was too late to do anything about them.

Keep your mouth shut, Olympe had said, *till the storm's gone by.*

Therefore he was as taken by surprise as he would have been by a hurricane when Dominique arrived on the island with word that she knew where the slave revolt would take place.

Trailed by Belle Suzette and Damoiselle—Rose's favorites among the household hounds—January and Rose had gone down to the Gulf beach, three or four days after the storm, and set crab-traps: stakes driven into the shelving sandy bottom where the green waves lapped thigh-deep and warm, and small round nets baited with chicken-necks. They'd walked along the sea-brim, picking up shells, smelling the tepid, salty Gulf winds, then came back and got their hand-nets and waded out into the slow, gentle surge off the waves to take in their harvest. The dogs ran after sandpipers. Dolphins played thirty or forty feet away off-shore. Clouds streaked the sky, dark in the south again. It would storm that night.

Walking back to Chouteau with overflowing buckets of crabs between them, Rose remarked, "Shall we send most of these up to the Big House? Alice tells me my brother's not well today. He used to stand up better against summer heat than he does now. The ague wears him down." She spoke of her half-brother casually, as Artois used to speak of Chloë St. Chinian.

"It isn't a healthy climate for white men." January brushed at the mosquitoes that had already begun to whine in the slow twilight among the oleanders. "God knows why they ever thought they could make a living here, let alone a fortune."

"Was it always so?" Rose hitched the smaller of the two buckets in her hand, to get a better grip on its rope handle. Though she'd tucked her skirts up almost to her thighs to wade, they'd still gotten wet and flapped around her ankles now. With her feet bare and her salt-flecked spectacles and her long hair straggling down from its braid, she had the look of an intellectual Gypsy. "When there were only Indians here, I mean? Every explorer's tale I've read says that Africa is a land of terrible diseases, and I've often wondered whether the yellow fever, and the ague, and the other ailments that strike white men here might have come on the slave-ships."

"Serve them right if they did," said January. "I know the Romans had ague—in Italy it's called mal-aria, 'bad air.' It seems to strike everywhere that the land is low and marshy. Jesuits' bark is supposed to mitigate it, but I've never found—" He halted, surprised, looking toward the dark bulk of the main house. The dogs bounded ahead of them down the path, barking. In the blue twilight the shapes of two women could be made out on the gallery.

"Will you be all right?" he heard Madame Alice ask.

"Dearest Madame, it's so sweet of you to be concerned, but I'm not going to give birth just going down a flight of steps . . . Ben!" The second woman hastened down the gallery steps with startling lightness, considering her condition, and gathered up her skirts of Spanish-brown mull-muslin to hasten toward him. "P'tit, it's so good to see you safe! And Rose, darling, you look beautiful!"

"Minou!" January, who had caught his younger sister in his arms, now held her off from him, looking down at her, unbelieving. "What are you doing here? How did you get here? You shouldn't be traveling in—"

"Oh, p'tit, I'm not going to give birth for *weeks,* and it's perfectly safe! I've got Thérèse with me, and hired three of the most *awful* ruffians—they're cousins of hers, Thérèse's, I mean—to come with us. . . ."

January felt his hair prickle at the thought of his sister, huge with child, traversing the bayous and marshes of the Barataria.

". . . your sister-in-law is the sweetest dear, Rose, and has sat with me there on the back gallery waiting for you. . . . What a *lovely* breeze! After all those days in that horrid boat coming down through the marshes . . . And, darling, you're looking so well!"

"What are you doing here?" January repeated. In the reflected candle-light from the gallery he could see Dominique was as fresh and pretty as ever, her high-waisted brown frock spotless and her tignon of figured brown-and-buff crisp and elaborate as if she were taking the air in the Place d'Armes. A thin strand of pearls circled her throat, and more pearls beaded her delicate ears. "Does Olympe know . . . ?"

"P'tit, it's quite all right." She laid a slim hand, gloved in French kid, on his arm, and urged him toward the outbuilding where he and Rose—and the couple who were cook and valet for the Big House—had rooms. "I mean, you're a doctor, and you can deliver a child as well as or better than Olympe. . . . I left her a note," she added as they climbed the steps onto the gallery. "I told her Henri had gotten me a cottage across in Mandeville, and that Thérèse had found me a midwife there already. . . . Darling, I *couldn't* tell her."

January set the buckets of crabs, the nets and stakes, on the gallery even as Rose brought out a candle and striker to the cobalt twilight. Dominique's room—the smallest of the four in the building usually reserved for the servants of guests—had clearly been tidied and straightened by Thérèse, Dominique's small trunk set at the narrow bed's foot and fresh candles of beeswax installed in the holders of iron and whittled oak. A shawl lay ready for her should the evening grow cool, yellow silk embroidered with butterflies. January tried to imagine it around her shoulders as she drifted in a pirogue through the wilds of the marsh.

"She knows about the revolt, you see." Dominique's voice sank to a whisper, and she glanced around the room as if she thought her maid might somehow be concealed under the bed or inside the armoire—which January wouldn't have put past Thérèse at that. "I mean, it was Olympe I heard of it from—overheard it," she admitted as January stared. "When I came into town to buy stockings— and, p'tit, that *harpy* at the Golden Rose on Rue Chartres charges *sixty-five cents* a pair! I was never so shocked. . . . Well, I went to see Olympe, and she let me in and said she was seeing someone in the parlor, and I thought it was someone just having their fortune told or buying a gris-gris. . . . Which I've told Phlosine a *hundred* times to buy from Olympe rather than go to that *dreadful* Queen Regine on Rue Claiborne—and of course, poor Phlosine is being driven just *distracted* by her friend, who hasn't been with her but a few days this summer and everyone in town is saying he's been flirting with this *dreadful* little hussy—"

"Did you see who was in the parlor?" interposed January, aware from long experience that Dominique's conversations frequently required skilled piloting in order to achieve their destinations.

"Of *course* not, p'tit, I'd never *dream* of prying! But I did hear her say, *They're hiding the guns in the wood-stores,* and something about waiting for a signal to act. And, oh, darling, I prayed Olympe wasn't really mixed up in something like that, that it was just gossip! And I heard her say later, *Ben won't talk*—not that I was trying to listen—and it came over me then that that's why you left town in such a hurry, without a word. And of course Olympe seemed to know all about it when you left, too! But that's how I knew there was a revolt being planned somewhere. So when Thérèse told me—"

"What did Thérèse know about it?"

"Nothing, darling." Dominique glanced around again. Rose had closed up the shutters—it was dark outside anyway and the mosquitoes were growing thick—and touched the candle to three or four more, filling the room with a gentle light. Dominique had settled on the bed, drawing the yellow shawl over her knees. Even eight months pregnant, it was impossible for her to make a clumsy move, or to look less than exquisite. "But you know how Thérèse prattles—I simply *cannot* get a word in! In fact, all the way down here, from the time we left New Orleans, she's kept up the most inane chatter with these—these *bullies* she found to escort us. . . . It was enough to drive me *distracted!*"

"And Thérèse told you where the guns were being shipped?"

"Not in so many words, p'tit, of course not. But she does talk while she's fixing my hair and hooking me up. And she has a cousin who's walking out with a man named Magnus . . . or is it Marius? Maybe it's Marcus. . . . Well, this Marius works for a river trader, and he mentioned—Marcus mentioned—to Thérèse's cousin Lavinnia, I mean—that they were sneaking boxes of rifles down to Myrtle Landing. Now, if a white man were buying boxes of rifles, for one thing he wouldn't have to sneak them anywhere, and for another thing he'd buy them straight from England instead of buying Spanish guns, which aren't nearly as good, I'm told, through Cuba—"

"Myrtle Landing." January tried to recall where that was. Downriver from town, he thought. A considerable distance. There were fewer plantations in that direction, as the river widened and the land along the banks got lower. And he felt a strange, hot quickening in his chest, as he thought, *We can catch Mulm red-handed. If we can get proof he was involved . . .*

"Darling . . ." His sister swallowed hard. "Myrtle Landing is only a few miles downriver from Bois d'Argent. And that's where Henri is."

Henri and his new wife. There were no tears in Dominique's eyes, but a kind of soft, wild grimness, a desperation all the stronger for being ignorant of the enormous odds against her.

"He has to be warned."

Rose shot a quick look at January, across the foot of the bed. Neither spoke. Both understood what would happen to any slaves—or any free blacks—involved in even the whisper of an uprising.

Dominique saw the look, and her face changed. "He has to be warned," she said again, and there was a slight difference in the tone of her voice, an edge of careful grimness. "P'tit, don't tell me—*please* don't tell me—that you're in it, too."

"No," said January. His voice grated harsh in his own ears. "I'm not in it."

But the trust had gone out of her eyes, and the silence returned.

And January saw—as clearly as if he were watching a play at the American Theater in town—that Dominique's reaction to *No* would be *Oh, very well, p'tit, I'll be on my way back to town then. . . .* And Scene Two, Act One would be Dominique, heavily pregnant, poling a pirogue through a swamp somewhere trying to make it to Bois d'Argent herself.

He wished he had the playbill, which would have written on it somewhere whether it would be a tragedy or a farce.

He said, "I'll go." Dominique's face blossomed instantly with joy; he held up his hand. "You stay here—I'll be back well before your baby comes, but I think it would be tempting fate for you to try to make it back to town. All right?"

"*Darling . . .*" She held out her arms to him. "Thank you, thank you. . . ." Enfolding her scented softness, he shook his head at himself, knowing why Henri loved this young woman . . . wondering how the man could be so crassly stupid as to abandon her for any number of thin, pale, tight-lipped heiresses.

And, turning his head, he met Rose's eyes.

For a moment he was back in his nightmare. Seeing her hand closed around the paper-knife, stabbing ineffectively at Mathieu's shoulder. Hearing how she wept when he took the knife away. As clearly as if she'd spoken, he knew her thought, saw it in the blaze of those hazel eyes. *If we can catch Mulm red-handed . . .*

Dear God, she can't be serious! And then, *Doesn't she know what slave-stealers would do to her if they caught her?*

(Of course she does, you imbecile, she's lived in this country most of her life. What do you think they'll do to YOU?)

And it passed through his mind to wonder whether she dreamed of killing Mathieu. Dreamed of winning her own freedom, and not having it as any man's gift.

It all passed in moments, while Dominique was still pressing her cheek to his shoulder and telling him that no brother in the world could be better and stronger and more understanding than he. Then January retrieved the buckets of crabs, caught the six or seven escapees who'd managed to clamber out and were crawling determinedly across the gallery, and carried them down the steps and back to the kitchen while Rose helped Dominique unpack. He heard their voices, that sweet, beautiful chatter of women's friendship, when he returned to gather up the crabbing-tackle—

"Dearest, I'll see you at supper," he heard Rose say. "It would be infamous of me to leave poor Ben to put away the nets after I had all the fun setting the traps." Her shadow crossed the door's tall golden light, and she stepped out onto the dark of the gallery.

They gathered up the stakes in silence, and did not speak till they'd reached the shed. January struck a light, stuck the tallow-stump of the candle on the rough workbench just inside the shed-door, to give them enough light to find the pegs and make sure there wasn't a stray snake or alligator in the black corners. Rose rolled the ropes around her elbow with deft skill, hung the nets in their places.

Then she turned to meet his eyes again and said, as if they'd been talking about it all along, "If we can prove it on Mulm, he'll hang."

Virgin Mary, guardian of women, PLEASE *put the right words in my mouth and don't let me mess this up. . . .*

"You think the testimony of two *libres* will go against whatever lies he cares to come up with in his own defense?" There were two ways this could have been said, and January spoke in a tone of genuine inquiry: *Do you think this can actually be done?*

But what Rose heard was *two,* and he saw the tension leave her shoulders and her face. She blew out the candle and her voice was much more relaxed in the dark. "That depends on what we find. On what happens when we get close to Myrtle Landing. Thank you for not saying anything in front of your sister. She'd be horrified."

"*I'm* horrified."

They stepped out of the shed. She put her hands lightly on his arms, her touch as always going through him like an electric shock, dizzying and sweet. Standing on her toes, she kissed his lips.

Thank you. Thank you.

He took a deep breath, with the sensation of having successfully cleared a difficult jump, only to discover the cliff that lay beyond. *I must be insane. . . .* "What's the quickest way to get to Myrtle Landing?"

Cut-Nose Chighizola loaded a small pirogue into his sloop, the *Little Dancer,* and took them north across the gold-drenched blue stretches of Barataria Bay in the morning, to the head of Bayou Crapaud-Volante. Chighizola *grand-'fils*—who had developed a passionate quixote-like adoration of Dominique—looked with disapproval at Rose's trousers, calico shirt, and slouch hat, but Cut-Nose laughed and told his grandson, "No, no, now and then you'd have a girl who'd go the whole hog; who wouldn't just be a pirate's woman, but a pirate herself. And believe me, if there was a regular mix-up between crews, you'd get out of the way of anything coming at you with tits and a cutlass!"

For January's part, he found the sight of Rose in a man's shirt and trousers deeply erotic—but then, he reflected, what with having been lovers for less than a month, the sight of her hairbrush on the dresser was erotic, and the freckles on her nose. With a broken-down straw hat covering her hair, her lankiness made her a very plausible boy. When she spoke, which was seldom, her gruff alto and slurred, half-African gombo French transformed her further still. His skin still crawled at the thought of her being taken by slave-stealers, but he understood that he could not say so. Even were he her husband, he could not say so.

And would Ayasha have been safer staying in her own rooms rather than venturing about the streets?

"Were there many like that?" asked January to get his mind off his fear. He recalled Cut-Nose's account of Hesione going after her lover Gambi with a tankard.

"More than you'd think." The old pirate drew on the line that controlled the sloop's lateen sail, feathering along the wind past Grand Terre's green maze of reed-beds and shell-ridges. Dolphins leaped in the wake, close enough that the faintly acrid sting of their spray dusted January's cheek, and Poivrette, Chighizola's lean-flanked hound bitch, erupted in a frenzy of barking. "Some of the boys that came along for the adventure, and to learn the ways of the sea . . . Well, every now and then you'd hear of one that was neither man nor maid. Hellfire Hessy was all girl, though, and pretty as a brig in full sail running on a high sea. Greedy, too, like girls are, always asking for this necklace or that ring, and not always from Gambi, either. Sometimes you'd be cutting up a haul and there'd be a necklace or a pair of earrings, and it'd fall to this man or that, and next thing you'd hear one of the girls had stole it from another, and they'd pinch it back and forth half a dozen times. Used to drive the Boss crazy! *Give me two shipfuls of men to command,* he'd say, *rather than a rowboat of girls."*

Cut-Nose laughed, a big, rich, rolling sound, and put the nose of the *Little Dancer* around toward the glittering water northward of the sun. Closer to land a snaggle-haired girl-child poled a raft among the flottants, and with her pole whacked along a half-dozen swimming cows.

"Sancho Sangre had three girls, God knows how he did it; they were just like sisters, washing each other's hair and lacing each other up. But they were island girls. The Saint-Domingue girls like Hessy wouldn't hardly speak to 'em."

A dolphin leaped so close to the gunwale that January saw the wise black eye regarding him, and Poivrette lunged to attack, evidently positive she could bring down this aquatic prey. Rose and January caught her collar, laughing: "Serve her right, she fall in and have to swim to shore," grumbled young Jean at the tiller. "She a *pichouette* like your pirate girls, Gran'père; too strongheaded for her own good."

"Ah, but if they ain't strongheaded, what good are they, eh?" Chighizola smiled, squinting into the sun. "See, originally it was just the island folk," he said, and glanced down at January and Rose. "Ships would land on the beach, and they'd trade a little, and run the stuff up to New Orleans by Bayou des Familles. Sometimes just up as far as Round Lake and put the word out in town, and people would come down quiet-like to have a look and buy. Gold, wines, slaves, whatever was going—they had a system of signals, so the alcalde's men couldn't get near them, nor the American Navy, after the Americans took over in '03. And Lafitte was their man. He was working out of that blacksmith shop he had on Rue Bourbon. The back room was stuffed with loot, though he kept the slaves down on the old Indian Mound at Little Temple in the swamp. He was probably the only blacksmith in town who never got his shirt dirty."

The scars on his face all bent with his gargoyle grin, and he fished in his pocket for a blackened pipe, holding the rope wrapped in one hand while he squished tobacco into the bowl with his thumb.

"The English were always fighting the Spanish around Cuba and Saint-Domingue anyway, and raiding each other's ships, and it'd all end up here. Most of the corsairs put up around the far side of Saint-Domingue, or on Guadeloupe or Martinique, though we'd go drinking in Havana, bold as paint. What were the *sbirri* going to do against a hundred of us, eh?" He laughed again. "But then the British captured Guadeloupe. So we came here." He gestured toward the flat green shimmer of Grand Terre, already dropping behind them, and January saw the reflected fire of burning towns, transmuted by memory in the old man's eyes.

"And there'd be fights between us and the Grand Isle boys. Over girls, or sometimes we'd clean up on a Spanish ship and they'd be waiting in luggers around behind the island and try to take us as we came through the pass. Bad for us, bad for them, bad for business. Finally it got so ugly, we had to parley, and that's when Lafitte got called in. Before he was just the broker, but he was a special man, Lafitte. I never met another like him."

"No," said January softly. He thought of that tall form in black, with the general who'd fought in Napoleon's army weeping on his chest. "No, I don't think there was another such."

"Well, what started out as Lafitte getting us to agree with each other ended with him taking over the whole show . . . us giving him the whole show, both sides, because that's the kind of man he was." Cut-Nose curved his heavy shoulder to the wind to strike flint and steel. January would have bet money that no fire could have been made in the sharp breeze off the bay, but he'd have lost, because a moment later the former pirate was drawing contentedly on his gruesome old pipe, black and shiny with the residue of a hundred thousand lightings. "That's what it means—*barataria*. In Portugee. When the master of a ship turns around and embezzles the cargo . . . and didn't he just, Lafitte! But we didn't mind. He had more brains than the rest of us, and we knew it—or everybody but Gambi knew it. Gambi always thought he was as smart as Lafitte. That Hesione, she saved Gambi's life two, three times, when he'd disobey Lafitte, and she'd have to go make the peace."

He shook his head, leaned to unwrap the rope from the belaying pin: "Hold course for that chenier, would you, Jean?" He pointed to the mound above the waterline, a clump of oaks whose roots held the soil, dark against the light-drenched sky. "The bottom here gets a little close. One night . . ." He laughed. "One night Lafitte and I, we were coming back from town, across the bay in a lugger like this, and he ran it aground on a bar. We could see Dominic Youx, out in the brig from the *Pandora,* and Lafitte, he's saying, *No, no, don't call out! We'll wait for the tide to get us off! I'll never hear the end of it!* But that Gambi . . ."

January remembered the hard-faced little man, striding into the hotel dining-room a few paces behind Lafitte's other captains. Remembered how he'd glanced around at the silver and the crystal—at the women, too, the free plaçées of the town men—as if all things were only cash to be pocketed and spent.

"Gambi never liked to take Lafitte's orders. Thought Lafitte was soft for not taking the Americans, when most of the rich ships were under the American flag by then. But Lafitte knew what side the bread was buttered on. I never believed he sank that ship, that *Independence,* that everyone got so hot about. . . . Put her around, Jeannot, point her toward the head of Bayou Fevier. And of course the girls were worse than the men, always stealing each other's jewelry, and hiding it . . . that's the only buried treasure anyone's likely to find on the island, that is! Hesione must have had six or seven caches of earrings and pearls, stuck away under the huts or in thatch or in some tree or other out in the marsh. . . . Then like as not she'd give them away. We were all like that. They were good days."

He smiled, the wicked, contented smile of an old man who has lived lushly. "They were good days," he repeated.

If you didn't happen to be merchandise yourself, reflected January. At a guess, the hot, lazy days at the pirate camps on Grand Terre looked different from the barracoons than they did from the deck of a pirate brig. And different still if the pirates didn't happen to get you unchained from below-decks before the ship they were robbing went down.

Chighizola put the sloop about near the mouth of Bayou Crapaud-Volante, and while Jean and January off-loaded the pirogue into the chop, took Rose aside and went over with her the map he'd made of the whole river-front between the head of Bayou St. Roche and Myrtle Grove. Clumsy-looking, of shallow draft, and fifteen feet long, the pirogue would, as the island saying went, run upon dew. January heard the old pirate rattle off a whole string of signs to look for, to tell Rose how high the water was likely to stand in any of a dozen of the small bayous in the marsh country; Rose nodded, leaning on the jib sheets, her spectacles glinting in the hot light.

Athène was what Hannibal would call Rose in jest, after the intellectual warrior-goddess of the Greeks, meaning sometimes her erudition, and sometimes her spectacles. January understood now that it meant other things as well.

"I suppose it won't do me any good to make you promise to run if I yell *Run?*" he asked as he helped her down into the pirogue. "Run and hide, and don't make any attempt at rescuing me if I get into trouble?" He poled the pirogue away from the *Dancer;* beached her up against what he thought was an islet but which turned out to be a flottant, as he discovered when he stepped off onto it to adjust the lie of the provisions in the boat and went down instantly crotch-deep in the bay. Something moved under his bare foot, and he scrambled back into the pirogue, fast. Though the water was too brackish for alligators, a snapping-turtle or gar-fish could do tremendous damage if annoyed.

"Now, you don't worry about smugglers, hear?" Cut-Nose called down to them from his deck. "I tell Captain Chamoflet, *These folks are my friends, hear? You let them alone.*"

"I appreciate it," January called back, though he wouldn't have been willing to bet ten cents—much less his own and Rose's freedom—on the good-will and forbearance of Chamoflet, the current chief of what was left of the Barataria smugglers. Gnats hung over the water in stinging clouds. As far as the eye could see, the world consisted of blue, shining water, speared by armies of waving reeds and dotted with flottants, as if someone had thrown a hundred thousand shaggy green blankets down off the deck of a boat. It was noon, and January prayed they'd make it to relatively dry land before the night came on.

"You go careful, eh?" The old pirate-captain gathered the sloop's jib-sheets in hand, while his grandson leaned over the side with a long pole, thrusting off the muddy bottom to angle the boat toward clear water and home. "And good luck."

We'll need it, thought January, looking around him at the shimmering world of green and reflected gold. *Two free colored, journeying through the Barataria country alone . . . We'll need it as few have needed it before.*

FOURTEEN

At one time the head of Bayou St. Roche probably came to within a mile of the river. With the low water of summer it finished in a sort of shrub-choked flatland of deep grass, sugarberry, palmetto, and mimosa, but its high-water course was marked by an intermittent line of cypress and magnolia, leading to a thin belt of trees that screened the higher ground. Though there was less cover in the marsh than among the trees of the cypress swamp, there was also more air, and fewer mosquitoes. Among the trees, January knew, the summer stillness would weigh like a barber's steamed towel.

A mile or two before the bayou's end, January first heard the swish and rustle of movement, and the voices of men singing: a soft humming murmur, rising now and then to words in a tongue he did not know, if they were words at all.

"Afa ya-ya, afa ya-ya, iyé-wo, ya-ya. . . ."

He grounded the pirogue deep in a stand of alligator-grass, and left it to circle toward the sound, walking warily for fear of snakes. He came on a trail, winding among tussocks of harsh, muddy grass. A file of men followed it back toward where the plantation fields would lie, each bearing on his back a load of wood more suitable for a donkey. All were naked but for madras loincloths, and slick with sweat. The smell of their bodies drifted pungent over the sappy odors of mud and reeds, like clean animals well-kept. Even the overseer, a slave like themselves, wore only a loincloth, though in keeping with his elevated position he carried a whip, and wore a top-hat, the privilege of overseers throughout the district. Walled in by the tall grasses, cut off from sight of the plantation buildings by the trees, the scene was startlingly African, as if neither America, nor France, nor slavery, nor the nineteenth century had ever existed for these strong singing men. January stayed kneeling in the green twilight, and watched them out of sight.

They're hiding the guns among the wood, Dominique had said. A moderate-sized plantation would burn thirteen hundred cords of wood to render its harvest down to sugar, sometimes more; there was never a time when gangs weren't out cutting trees. With the ciprière mostly lying to the north, they'd be cutting on the cheniers, and what stands of woodland they could find.

Was it his mother who'd said of the Avocet slaves that they'd spend half their work-time getting to and from the wooded swamp? And Avocet lay north of here.

Rose waited by the pirogue, in her right hand the red bandanna that meant *All is well, come into camp.* If it was on the ground, or in her left hand, it meant *All is not what it seems.* They had a system of whistled signals based on the first few bars of "Eine kleine Nachtmusik" for how many ambushers had taken the camp.

"I think this is as far as we'd better try bringing the boat." January took off his straw hat to wipe the sweat from his face. "There's a pretty fair trail out to the cheniers, probably from St. Roche Plantation. Shall we go back to that shack we saw about a mile ago? It looked deserted. Then when the moon rises we can go have a look at St. Roche itself."

The shack did indeed prove deserted, containing only dusty muskrat-traps and crabbing-nets, several families of rats, and some shovels. January concealed their rifles along the rafters, hung the food sacks in the corners, and tucked the blankets on which they slept, and the little tent of mosquito-bar, into an old box of pulley-blocks behind the broken door. He felt weary enough to drop after the day's journey. But the moon would rise soon, just past full, and he needed a look at the wood-sheds of St. Roche. He smeared more of Olympe's citrus oil on his face, neck, and arms, then passed the gourd to Rose.

"This is where your mother would come in useful," she remarked, tugging the brim of her hat down more snugly over her forehead and readjusting the pins that held it to her tight-coiled hair.

"You mean to poison mosquitoes with her malice?" he asked, and Rose laughed.

"I'm sure she could tell us which planters treat their slaves poorly enough to make buying guns from Franklin Mulm sound like a good idea. It would save us checking."

"You wrong my mother," returned January in a shocked voice. "If we sat her down and asked her, I think we'd find every single planter between here and Jesuit's Bend to be stingy, cruel, capricious, and a practitioner of unspeakable vices."

They ate bread and cheese and oranges from Cut-Nose's orchard, and drank the ginger-water from the gourds they'd brought, and waited for the moon to rise. January hooked a couple of the empty gourds to his belt, to fill up at the plantation well, if possible. Like Coleridge's Ancient Mariner, they had moved all day surrounded by water, with not a drop of it potable. Only closer to the river would there be wells, and water that was not brackish.

Like the Ancient Mariner, too, they had moved through stillness—*Alone, alone, all, all alone*—seeing no other soul. The land was too open here, and the river too closely patrolled, for there to be much traffic of slave-smuggling from Captain Chamoflet and his boys: their usual routes lay north and west in the direction of town. Still, it was in January's mind that Mulm would be lying in wait west of the river when the revolt began, to pick off runaways. It was perfectly possible that Mulm had made a deal of some kind with the smugglers.

Or did the American think himself too powerful to need to divide his profits with Chamoflet? *He'll catch cold at that,* January thought. Both the British and the American armies had learned, at different times, that if the trappers and fishermen of the marshes were against you, you were in trouble indeed.

When the moon turned the indigo world to silver, he and Rose left the shack and followed the line of the old bayou. It had clearly been passable farther up a number of years earlier, to judge by the wharves that jutted out now into sluggish pools of mud and quicksand. The path along it passed through the thin belt of cypress and palmetto to the fields of St. Roche Plantation, where cane stood already shoulder-high. From the back of the fields January smelled the smoke of the quarters, the pungence of privies and livestock. He and Rose easily followed the cart-paths to the edge of the homeplace, the familiar pattern of cow-barns and pig-houses, stables and kitchen garden, plantation shops and, set among its trees facing the river, the Big House itself.

The sight of it, in the ghostly drench of the moonlight, filled January with uneasiness. Nature was ravenous in this countryside; every planter along the river waged constant war against its overnight incursions of seedlings, fern, and elephant-ear. While the ground around the quarters, and the "shell-blow grounds" where the slaves raised their own food, was relatively clear, seedling pines and swamp laurel grew in thickets right up to the back of the house. And where, on every other plantation January had ever seen, a barbered lawn stretched to the river, this one grew rank with weeds.

The overseer's cottage was dark, its shutters and doors and windows hanging slackly open, like an idiot's gaping mouth. In the quarters, the gay rattle of drums and banjos sounded, and voices called and answered in song. But the Big House was dark. A single candle marked one window at the back on the upstream side.

Owner in Mandeville, January thought, trying to brush away the cold sensation that crept on the back of his neck. *Or Pass Christian, or one of those other pleasant little towns along the Gulf Coast. Looks like he spends most of his time there. Well, I'd be drumming and singing, too.*

And, maybe, plotting revolt.

Knowing what he knew of the quarters on hot summer nights, he waited until the sounds of singing died away before touching Rose's hand to move on. From the fields, couples emerged, shadows who kissed, and giggled, and slipped into their stifling cabins, shut up against the inevitable mosquitoes. In spite of the citrus oil, January and Rose were bitten everywhere. It was only a few hours until dawn.

But some nights, reflected January, you have to dance. You have to make love in the hot musky pungence of the cane. Or if you're a child, you have to run madly with your playmates in and out through the cane-rows, forgetting everything your mama ever told you about snakes. You have to do it or you'll die, inside where it counts. The darkness settled closer around the home-place and the cicadas throbbed like the beat of the sea on the Gulf beaches. Beneath those drumming waves sounded the peeping and booming and warbling of a half-hundred separate kinds of frogs, all singing like Aristophanes' chorus, guarding the road to the land of the dead. His father had given them names, January recalled—Monsieur Gik and Monsieur Big Dark, and little Mamzelle Didi of the tiny silvery voice. Who had made those names up? And beneath those names, he heard the darker names of the secret gods who lurked in that African midnight, watching over those who slept.

Handfast, he and Rose moved along the edge of the cane until they were nearly opposite the sugar-house. Here, at least, the ground had been kept clear. The tall chimney brooded in the moonlight and the smell of burnt sugar and cane-sap lingered, even during the five-sixths of the year when it stood quiet and empty. It was an old-fashioned kind, with the roundhouse where the mules would walk standing separate, so that the green, sticky juice had to be collected in buckets and carried across to the receiving-trough in the sugar-house itself. Behind all this, the four wood-sheds stood, open-sided and steep-roofed, containing blackness thick as velvet. Coming close, January saw that one was filled with wood, a second nearly so.

The quarters were dark now and silent. Silence, too, shrouded the overseer's deserted house. That single candle on the upstream side of the Big House had gone dark shortly after the drums in the quarters had ceased. Odd, for planters to keep such late hours in the country when they had to rise and ride their acres before it grew light.

Did someone know or guess—or fear—something about the drums? Most planters forbade them, on pain of whipping.

From his pocket January took striker and flint, and raveled a wisp of tow around the two smaller fingers of his hand. The sound of steel hitting flint was like a hammer in the night, the sparks appearing to him as sky-wide lightning. He touched his candle's wick to the burning tow, pinched the kindling out. The smoke seemed, for a moment, to fill the night with its smell.

Without a word, Rose stationed herself by the corner of the shed closest to the Big House, where she could watch the open ground. Warily, trying to keep the light concealed as he studied the dirt around the front of the filled wood-shed, January searched for marks of coming and going. Nothing unusual. Not, he reflected, that he knew exactly what he was looking for, and the dim light of a single candle wasn't exactly optimum for the task. Hefting the snake-stick he'd carried since leaving town, he slipped into the second shed. Napoleon could have marched half his army up to the shed under cover of the cicadas—January nearly jumped out of his skin at the sudden eruption of a cat.

A moment later he heard Rose's two-note warning whistle— *Run for it. . . .*

The cat, he thought.

And then, *Maybe not . . .*

He blew out the candle and slipped out the side of the shed almost into the arms of a man with a gun.

"This here a shotgun," said a warning voice in gombo French, "and I can't hardly miss. Serapis . . ."

Lantern-light. The hiss of a metal slide. A tall silhouette, the top-hat and the way he held his shoulders identifying this second man, Serapis, as the driver from the trail. He still wore only a loin-cloth, no better than those of the other slaves, unusual in a driver. Most of them liked the distinction of wearing a jacket and boots, let alone trousers. He carried a shotgun like that of his companion. Both lowered their weapons when the lantern-glow showed them they weren't dealing with one of Captain Chamoflet's smugglers.

"You just passin' through?" asked Serapis—meaning, *Are you a runaway?* The driver might have been twenty-five, but he looked older. Between overwork and never quite enough to eat, never quite enough sleep or rest, men generally didn't grow old in the quarters. His condition was good, and he carried himself proudly. Whoever owned these slaves, January found himself thinking, must have skill in the handling of men.

"My brother and me, we lookin' for a place to sleep, 'case it rains later," answered January. "That's all. We be gone by mornin'."

"Best you be gone now." Serapis had a deep voice, mellow and soft. January guessed him to be pure African, like the younger man beside him. He wore a juju-bag tied around his chest and neck with string, a dark splodge like a cicatrice between his arm and his ribs. Close-up, January could detect the frailest whiff of the whiskey that the bag was soaked in periodically, to "feed" the spirit—a ball of intricately knotted string, most likely—within.

"I swear to you, we ain't out to steal anything," January said. "Just that out on the marsh, we seen folks about we'd rather not run onto in the dark."

"Best you be gone now," the driver repeated. "There's a shed out on the marsh, under an oak by the old bayou. Roof don't leak too bad. But we don't have strangers comin' around St. Roche. That's your warnin'." He touched the lock of his shotgun. "You won't get another."

January held up his hands, palm-out, placating, "I didn't mean to offend. . . ."

"You didn't."

"Thank you for word about the shed. We'll sure sleep there, and like I said, we'll be gone by daybreak."

"See you are, then," said the driver. "Igi and me, we'll see you and your brother to the head of the bayou, make sure you don't get yourselves lost. The slave-stealers, they mostly keeps away, or works to the north. You be all right. Whistle for your brother, and make sure he knows not to come back here."

"Alejo," called January softly, the name they agreed on. "It's all right. We goin' to a shed on the bayou to sleep, not comin' back here."

And he saw a flickering wisp in the dark that was Rose, and a gleam of the sinking moonlight on her spectacles. He guessed she'd heard every word.

Only when they were alone in the shed—with dawn only an hour away and every bird on the marsh giving tongue like Judgment Morning—did he ask, "What the hell did you make of that?"

"At a guess," she murmured—barely more than a murmur against his shoulder in the dark—"he thinks we might be working for M'sieu Chamoflet. This close to the Barataria they must get slave-stealers now and then."

"Or he's heard something," suggested January. "We were looking for guns, and there they are."

"Only a fool would buy shotguns for a revolt if he could buy rifles instead," pointed out Rose. "Shotguns are what a master would let a trusted slave handle, for hunting—or guarding. Or what men would take to hunt if their master was away. And as you recall, rifles is what Artois found in that box."

"Maybe," said January. But something about that deserted house, those weed-choked grounds—about the tribal marks cut into the faces of both young men—lay on his heart, like the stain of bad dreaming. When Rose lay down to take an hour's sleep, January slipped outside the shack and into the indigo world of water and moonlight. It might have been his imagination, but as he listened to the frogs (*M'sieu Gik over there, and Mamzelle Didi and all her pretty sisters answering like a chorus of miniature silver hammers from the other side of the bayou*), he thought there was one direction—back toward St. Roche—where no frogs sounded at all. Nor did the birds, twittering like an opera-house orchestra tuning up, touch those few dark cheniers.

His rifle across his knees, he settled down to watch in that direction. He saw nothing move there—not humans, but neither birds nor foxes nor rabbits, either, when all around him the marsh flickered and whispered with wakening life.

When they went on in the morning, January found himself glancing repeatedly over his shoulder for the first mile or so, until the sensation of being watched was left behind.

FIFTEEN

They followed the narrow zone of cypress and palmettos between the marsh and the cane-fields, a band of country that had been extensively logged already to feed the ravenous fires of the winter harvest, picking their way among the flat, reedy islands, the summer-shrunk pools and muddy tussocks. It was slow going— back-aching, too, for the grasses were seldom higher than four feet. But they could hear the strike of axes in the trees, and the singing of the men. Gnats and mosquitoes swarmed despite all Olympe's medicaments, until Rose was driven nearly frantic. White cattle-egrets regarded them with amiable yellow eyes, and water-moccasins, dark-striped gray like tabby cats, glided sinuously through the pea-green duckweed in the pools.

January talked to a herdboy from Plaquemines Plantation, watching over the cows in the marsh: "They just strange, over to St. Roche," the boy declared. His name was Tibo and he looked about ten, a wiry, cheerful boy who seemed to accept a couple of probable runaways making their way through the marsh as a welcome change from the company of cows. "Michie Joffrey there, he don't let his folks marry off St. Roche, or go off, much, an' he sure don't let no-body come on. They ain't had a overseer for as long as I can remember. Just Serapis, an' Serapis' daddy before him. They like still Africans over there, you know? They don't hardly speak no French, and they go hunt in the woods with blow-guns."

He shook his head, clearly afraid of the place. "Crazy. My mama say, Michie Joffrey crazy, an' his sons crazy, too. They ain't been off that land in twenty years. Michie Pierre up at the Big House here, he goes up to town all the time, and his daughters they go to school with the nuns there, and the nuns whacks 'em over the hand with a ruler when they mess up." He sounded pleased about that.

In the course of the conversation, which ranged over the usual gossip of the quarters, January got no sense of the touchfire rage that fueled rebellion. Only the petty griefs and tyrannies of bondage itself: Tibo's aunt Josie was whipped for being insolent, when it was Michie Gerard's wife who didn't like the way Michie Gerard looked at Josie; Michie Pierre was making everyone work in the wood-gangs and nobody could tend to their gardens so everything was full of weeds. A cow got sick from eating loco-weed and Tibo had got blamed. Always more work than could be easily done; never quite enough time to rest, to sleep, to watch the flotillas of clouds that rolled up over the flat, monotonous land from the Gulf. Three of Michie Pierre's children sick down with the fever, and had to be bled, and M'am Helaine blaming their nurse for not watching them well.

Only once did Tibo say, "There's talk, if there's trouble, some of the folks runnin' off, hidin' in the marsh. But Nate—he the main-gang driver—he say that's a stupid idea."

"What kind trouble?" January tossed a pebble at a lizard on a deadfall log, and the boy shrugged.

"Nobody sayin'. But they kind of look at each other"—and he aped the tucked-chin, eyebrows-raised face of We-won't-say-this-in-front-of-children—"and say, 'If there's trouble.'"

At Myrtle Bank, where January and Rose begged lunch with one of the wood-gangs, there was definite talk of trouble: "But it may all be rumor," said a slave named Zeno, and cast a quick glance at the trail that led back to the plantation fields—watching for Michie Turnbull, the overseer, about whom every member of the wood-gang warned January and "Alejo." "You hear all these rumors, that somebody's broad-wife hears from one of her friends she sews with, that somebody she's walking-out with heard. . . ."

"What may be rumor?" asked January, and tried to look like a man who, since he's running already, would at least like to know what direction to avoid.

"Big trouble." Zeno sank his voice. "Killin' trouble."

"Trouble that'll get the army and the militia down here, you mean," retorted another of the gang. "You remember back a couple years ago, when Michie East hear about some slaves risin' up an' killin' their masters in Virginny. He hired about three new overseers, just to lock all of us in at night—put locks on the doors of all the cabins. . . ."

"Like we couldn't get out the windows," added another man, laughing.

"Nuthin' came of it," said Zeno. "But there was talk of shootin' people just for the kind of back-talk you do when you get mad enough. Trouble is, when things get bad like that, and everybody's sayin' *We're doin' this so's you won't rise up in arms* an' *We're doing that other so's you won't rise up in arms . . .* Well, pretty soon you think *Hell, I guess I'll rise up in arms.*"

"Like when you start gettin' jealous of your woman," added a sour-faced man. "An' once you start doin' that, then *she* starts thinkin' *Hey, he all over me about it already so I might as well.*"

The presence of a white overseer with the wood-gang at Autreuil Plantation prevented January from approaching them later in the afternoon, but at a guess, had the trouble been at Autreuil, the slaves at Myrtle Bank would have known more. "You find most of the broad-wives and husbands, or the men and women walking-out with each other, within one or two plantations up or down the river," he told Rose as they watched the lights moving around the Autreuil Big House and quarters, waiting for all to sleep. "Nobody had much to say about discontent on Autreuil, either. . . ."

"You call that tale Tibo told us about the woman here getting whipped, 'no discontent'?"

"No," said January tersely, "I don't. And they didn't, either. If

there was real trouble here, real anger, they'd have heard of it there."
He glanced sidelong at Rose, nearly hidden in the gloom among the
cane-stalks. There was no dancing in the quarters as there had been
at St. Roche, but someone was playing the banjo, "My Beautiful
Suzette," a popular tune in town.

> *Ah, Suzette, you do not love me,*
> *Why do you not love me?*
> *I will go to the bush for you,*
> *I will cut cane for you,*
> *I will make a lot of money,*
> *And I will bring it all to you.*

January sighed, studying that long, delicate profile and wondering if it was ever that simple.

> *I will make a lot of money,*
> *And I will bring it all to you. . . .*

Not as romantic as the golden apples of the sun, he thought, but
it would certainly help.

The Big House showed lights in half a dozen windows, blotted
out now and then as people walked about the gallery. A flurry of
barking sounded from the household dogs.

"Damn," muttered January, and fished in one of the food-sacks
for the scraps of salt-pork he'd cut for the purpose. "I'll draw the
dogs. When you hear them barking, get in fast, look around the
back and sides of the wood-sheds for scraped wood, as if cords or
bundles had been pulled out and pushed back in, then get out as
quick as you can. We'll meet back at the magnolia at the far edge of
the fields. But I'll bet you find nothing."

"Nothing would be fine," said Rose. She settled her spectacles
more firmly onto her nose, and adjusted her hat. "No guns, no
snakes, no overseers, no dogs who might be smart enough to ask
themselves *Why's this man leading us into the woods with salt-
pork . . . ?*"

No slave-stealers waiting in the marsh for you when you leave, January added to the list as he circled wide around the quarters, approached the house from the side away from the sugar-mill and sheds. *No slaves with shotguns and top-hats and reasons why they want you off their master's land. No quicksands, in those black-shadowed reedy pools, to leave me to wonder forever why you didn't make the rendezvous. . . .* Ayasha's death of the cholera had done something to him, he realized then. Had broken his trust in a way he hadn't even been aware of at the time. True, he and Ayasha had lived fairly quietly in Paris—no hare-brained treks through slave-stealer country in quest of rebelling slaves. . . .

Not that Ayasha would have hesitated for so much as a heart-beat to put her life in danger exactly as Rose was doing.

It occurred to January for the first time that Ayasha would probably have gotten on very well with Rose.

The dogs behaved exactly as he'd hoped the dogs would behave, bounding off the gallery in a barking pack and chasing him across the ground upriver of the house, and into the dark of the fields. He had to move quickly to elude them, listening to them sniffing and barking—they weren't watch-dogs, but just the household hounds, as ready to turn back and settle again on the porch as they were to continue pursuit. As he led them farther and farther afield, running in the flooded ditches to lose his scent, he had to use the salt-pork to keep them interested. When at last he judged Rose had had time to investigate as much wood as she could deal with by the light of a single candle, he retreated beyond the territory that the dogs considered their own, and made another wide circle through the cane-rows in the dark, heading for the damper ground inland from the river, for the cypresses and the palmettos. Certain that he would reach the rendezvous and find no one—that Rose would be taken from him as Ayasha had been—he came near the white-starred black cloud of the magnolia-tree and whistled his two-note inquiry. He heard the soft flicking bobble of Rossini—the overture of *Barber* for *All's Well*—whistled back.

The next plantation upriver was Bois d'Argent, and there was a white overseer there, too. From a distance, through Rose's spyglass, January observed the layout of the place in the next morning's clear light: large and prosperous-looking, with a lot of cattle grazed on the marsh, and extensive stables. "According to my mother—and to Dominique—they run this place mostly with an overseer," January told Rose. "Since the Viellards seem to run to girls, you don't have here the phenomenon you find in so many French Creole plantations, of three and four families sharing a single house. The Viellard branch of the clan alone has four plantations, for one thing, and only one of them is occupied by an uncle and his family."

"And God forbid a mere uncle's worthless bastard should lay hands upon the family's sacred account-books." Rose lifted herself to her knees and took the spyglass from him—they were concealed among the cane-rows, about two hundred yards from the Viellard house. Between guarding each other's slumbers and coupling like rabbits in the ciprière all night, neither had had much sleep— January felt like his eyeballs had been breaded and deep-fried and his heart infused with brandy and champagne.

"Not to speak of a son-in-law's child, whose other grandmother Madame Viellard undoubtedly despises . . . And there he is. The man behind all this to start with."

She handed the spyglass back.

Henri Viellard, tall and fat and dandified, took off his spectacles to wipe his sweating face, and nodded at something being said to him by a cool little wisp of a girl in celery-green voile. He looked unhappy, but bent to give her a dutiful kiss.

Chloë St. Chinian. Now Chloë Viellard. Artois' sister, and the woman who would be responsible, if Henri left Dominique to fend for herself, to bear his baby alone. With a curious, bitter despair January studied that flat-chested, girlish shape, the flaxen hair, and precise movements. Chloë Viellard paused as if she would have said something else to her new husband, then turned and went briskly into the house. Henri stood for a time, gazing at the river in silence.

"Ben." Rose's voice called back January's thoughts from Dominique. "When we do find where the rebellion is—if we find it— what are we going to do?"

January folded up the spyglass. The air was moist and stifling and alive with gnats. The cicadas kept up their metallic beating in all the oak-trees between the field's edge and the house. Though no wind could be felt, the cane rustled and whispered all around them, splashing their faces with occasional blades of hot light; the smell of the earth was overpowering, and the sticky smell of the sap.

"Henri—and certainly Chloë—won't heed a warning to get out, unless we give specifics. And if we warn them, who knows what reprisals will take place?" Beneath the brim of her dilapidated hat, Rose's face was streaked with nearly a week's dirt and grime, freckled with the sun and dotted with the puffed swellings of insect-bites. Her hazel-green eyes looked tired, haunted by the dilemma at the core of who and what they were.

"Where we find the guns," said January, "we'll find Mulm—or with luck, enough of his tracks to have him caught and probably hanged. For the rest of it . . . We won't know what to do until we see what the circumstances are."

"But you know Mulm's going to talk," countered Rose. "You know he'll thrust the blame onto the slaves who're buying the guns."

"He can't do that without admitting to complicity himself. Either way, people have to be warned, somehow. Maybe the warning itself will abort the rebellion. But we won't know the shape of it, we won't know the circumstances, until we find where it's being planned. And who's planning it."

Rose was silent, turning the telescope over in her hands.

"I want the men who murdered Artois to die," said January quite softly, thinking of that young face, that young body with its bruised arms and bruised neck, so still on the mortuary table.

The memory was always like a knife in his guts.

"And I want the slaves they're deceiving—and I don't know how they're deceiving them—to get clear of whatever it is Mulm's planning. But how that's going to happen is still in the hands of God."

"You truly think God concerns Himself with such things?"

January stood, and held out his hand to help her up. "If I didn't, Rose, I don't think I'd have lived as long as I have."

But at the next plantation, Boscage, the men they met gathering Spanish moss in the ciprière were clear. There was trouble in the wind, they said, and people in the quarters were murmuring of rebellion near-by.

"The broad-wife of one of the men here, she say they even got guns," whispered one of the moss-gatherers, a young man called Griff.

"That's bad," said January with a look of horror and a glance back up the narrow trail through the stifling gloom of the cypresses, toward where the plantation would lie. At this point the ciprière had widened from a narrow belt of trees into the swamplands with which January had been familiar in his childhood. "That's crazy! The *blankittes,* they'll bring in the army, like they done before."

"It sure sound crazy to me," agreed Griff. "But they say they got guns, and they got boats waitin' on 'em, and they're gonna get clear out of this country and go straight to Mexico. And what I hear of what's happenin' on that plantation, I don't blame 'em."

"That bad?" January knew better than to ask *What plantation?*

"Man, it's crazy." The other gatherer set down his basket on the pile of harvested moss. "That new overseer there, he's like a crazy man. It was always bad, 'cause the two brothers that owned the place was always fightin' and blamin' the folks in the quarters for what they'd do to each other. But now one of the brothers got himself stabbed to death, and his wife and the new overseer and one of the lawyers is tryin' to make out it was one of the field-hands that did it, and the new overseer's sayin' as how this ain't done right and that ain't done right, and nobody gets food unless the work gets done. . . . You keep clear of that place when you head out from here," he warned.

"Hell, yes." Griff's face creased with anger and concern. "That new overseer, he whipped the potter there pretty near to death, just for talkin' to a river trader. Says there's too much carryin'-on with people off the place. Says he won't have it no more, and Berthe— that's my friend Amos' broad-wife—says she's scared she won't be let come to see Amos down here no more. That they'll all be forbid to have wives and husbands off the place."

"Damn!" January put shock into his voice, which indeed he felt, shock and anger at the stupidity of whites who thought their slaves were no more than livestock, to be controlled for the convenience of their owners. But he felt satisfaction, too: for now he knew where the guns were going.

Indeed, he thought, he should have seen it before. If he hadn't been half-blind from annoyance and frustration, he could have guessed.

He and Rose stopped briefly at the next plantation upriver, Soldorne, to gossip with the moss-gatherers in the ciprière—the harvest of Spanish moss was a major source of spending-money for the slaves during the slack summer season—and gleaned more information about the new overseer's iniquities, and the power the man had gained during the chaotic weeks of uncertainty since the mysterious death of Guifford Avocet. But by the deepening of the long August afternoon, they were making their way with increasing caution through the ciprière, sticking close, now, to the edges of the cultivated fields, watching and listening.

Mulm would have heard, thought January, of the troubled conditions on Avocet Plantation, probably through one of the river traders who bought everything from garden produce to pilfered tablecloths. Like Mamzelle Marie, Mulm was a gatherer of secrets. Or else the "troublemaker" of the plantation, whatever angry soul it was who demanded to know why he must be enslaved, had somehow gotten in touch with Ti-Jon—maybe he'd originally come from town?—asking about guns. And so the word went to Mulm. . . .

And Mulm and his men would be watching for their chance. That was why he hadn't seen Burke in town at the Nantucket. The overseer—Raffin, had Shaw called him?—had dropped out of sight immediately after Hesione's murder. Burke must have been sent out here to wait for the trouble to start, for the lunatic martinet who had replaced Raffin to push too hard. At Soldorne they'd whispered there would be trouble soon, that the slaves were arming. A number of the Soldorne slaves had been getting ready, not to join, but to flee in the confusion. January had to bite his tongue not to say *Don't*. . . .

It was time, he thought, to retreat and take stock of what could be done.

At January's size, he had never been much of a tree-climber, either during his early childhood on Bellefleur Plantation or later, growing up within a street or two of the cow-pastures and ciprière that in those days lay just beyond the city's old walls. But in the flat riverine terrain there was no other way to get a view of Avocet Plantation by daylight, and by all accounts it would be far too dangerous to try to creep in along the cane-rows by moonlight as they had done at Autreuil and St. Roche.

If for no other reason, he thought, there was the added danger that they'd run into Abishag Shaw. The men at Soldorne and Boscage had spoken of a skinny white man with a rifle, who moved with uncanny silence through marsh and swamp—"He lookin' for somethin', but damn if I know what, and he trouble. You can tell by his eyes."

Given Shaw's sense of duty, January didn't feel himself up to explaining what he and Rose were doing themselves, snooping around Plaquemines Parish. Shaw was too good a guesser, and there was no telling what he'd learned about the rebellion so far.

January boosted Rose to the lowest branches of a big magnolia on the edge of Avocet's cultivated land. She untied the coil of rope she wore around her waist and let it down so that he could scramble up beside her. They climbed another thirty feet, to two branches that would bear their weight at a little distance out from the trunk, and stretched along these like leopards, trained the spyglass on the house by the river.

The layout was a common one for plantations of this kind. The U-shaped house, bright yellow and green in the Creole fashion, faced the river, its wings extending back to funnel the breezes on hot afternoons. The upstream wing would be for the males of the household, the downstream for the women—the reverse of the pattern that existed above New Orleans.

A woman stood on the gallery, trim and fair-haired, as Guifford Avocet had apparently been, though her mourning gown in no way marked whether she was the dead man's sister or his widow. *The boys got all the looks,* Shaw had said: with little beauty, and apparently scant hope of a dowry from the impoverished property, what hope did that "little dab of a sister" have of getting away from a family who made her mend clothing and remain in the background?

And if one of her brothers was hanged for the murder of the

other, what then? An isolated plantation, a run-down house, slaves on the point of revolt?

A short distance downstream, the sugar-house stood. January identified the marshy clump of laurels and oaks behind it where Guifford's corpse had been found. Past that, brick piers and a straggle of lumber marked the second house that had been begun, and stopped, and begun again a number of times in the course of the enmity between the brothers Guifford and Bertrand Avocet, snaggy now with fern and undrained pools of standing water. At one point, Shaw had told him, Guifford had had his slaves tear down what Bertrand had leased slaves from New Orleans to build, which couldn't have done the family's already precarious finances any good.

What had Annette Avocet thought about that?

The wood-sheds stood well upriver from both of these buildings, perfectly situated to hide things in: so close to the edge of the cane that January wondered how they kept them from catching fire when they burned the fields after harvest, and very near also to the river's edge. A sand-bar above them made a perfect landing-place for illicit cargo on a moonless night. It would be fairly easy, he calculated, to make his way through the cane-rows to the sheds to confirm that guns were indeed hidden there, and to get enough information about type, quantity, and caliber to match up with whatever records could be found of Mulm's purchases. Fortunately they were far enough from the house to be out of immediate range of the household dogs.

For the rest, the place was much as Shaw had described it. The infamous bloodied shirt—Bertrand's? The missing overseer's?—had been found there in that clump of swamp laurel—and Shaw was right, Bertrand would have to be an idiot to think the shirt wouldn't have been seen immediately, that close to the house. And that window would be the ladies' parlor, where Madame Vivienne, her twelve-year-old daughter Laurene, and Mademoiselle Annette had been sewing together when the murder took place. . . .

"And what the fuck do you think you're doing?"

January nearly pitched out of the tree. He froze, not moving, as the man's harsh voice repeated in garbled French, "You think you done for the day, Sambo?"

"It's sunset, sir." The slave's voice, replying, spoke English, and fairly good English, too. And January thought, *Of course.* He looked down to where the voices were, a dozen yards off, although they'd sounded at first to be almost under his feet.

The "troublemaker" had indeed been bought from town. The educated speech was unmistakable. Which was how the leader of the rebels would know Ti-Jon, that nexus of information among runaways and would-be runaways. Any river trader would have carried him a message, for a price. . . .

"If you ask Madame Avocet . . ."

The leathery thwack of a riding-whip cut off the slave's words. Below and to his left, January saw them: the wood-gang standing on the path, the overseer beside the horse he had just dismounted. The "troublemaker" still bore his load of wood on his back, a young man, like most field-hands, but lighter-skinned than most. Quadroon, thought January. Almost certainly an import from town. With his hands gripping the cordwood's ropes, the young man could not wipe the blood running down his face.

"Mrs. Avocet hired me 'cause she didn't want nobody runnin' to her every five minutes askin' this and that, *Hy*acinth." The overseer's voice jeered the name, a perfectly usual one—if not common— among the French: Jacinthe. But, January knew, such names were regarded with scorn by Americans of the rougher type, as all things French were regarded. "Now I told you that before. And I told you, too, we need twenty cords of wood here. I count only sixteen."

"There are but the six of us, sir." Jacinthe's voice grated, very slightly, on that final honorific. "We have been working—"

The whip lashed out again; Jacinthe barely flinched. "If I can count to sixteen, you think I can't count to six, boy?" The man was nearly spitting with anger. "Now, you boys put down that wood here by the path and bring me what I asked you to bring me and don't give me no more back-talk. And that goes for the rest of you shit-eatin' niggers!"

There was a dangerous silence, and even at that distance January could feel the anger like the eerie moan of a wind-harp before a storm. But they put down their burdens and turned back silently into the woods. The overseer took off his wide-brimmed hat to strike the nearest man on the back with it as he rode by.

And January felt his breath catch again, this time with bafflement and shock.

Because the overseer was unmistakably Tyrone Burke.

SIXTEEN

"The *whole revolt* couldn't have been contrived?" Rose set her rifle against the trunk of a cypress, settled tailor-fashion beside it, and uncorked her water-gourd as January slung the bundle of their food to the ground. "Could it? From the *start?* When did Burke replace the old overseer here?"

It wasn't a thought that had occurred to January, and the scope of the scheme appalled him. "Raffin disappeared two days after Guifford's murder," he said. "The day after Hesione LeGros was killed." He frowned, trying to recall details Shaw had given—details to which he had been paying less than close attention, owing to his own anger over the neglect of Hesione's murder.

There's a lesson in there somewhere, he reflected dryly. *And it's probably Don't mess in ANYTHING that doesn't concern you.*

"By Burke." Rose shook her head. "So there was time for Mulm to get word that the old overseer—who appears to have contributed considerably to the climate of resentment in the first place—was gone, and to send Burke here to take the man's place. To exacerbate an already volatile situation, and push the slaves into armed revolt, so that Mulm could sell them guns. Does that make sense?"

"No," January said bluntly. "It's lunatic."

Darkness was coming on, dense as doom, and though the

stifling heat remained, the queer electric wildness of the air had increased, the cypresses fidgeting around them, whispering of a storm. Far off, January could still hear the strike of axes. He hoped Burke had sent back to the quarters for torches. Trying to cut chunks of wood into pieces small enough to be bundled and carried would cost someone a hand. The extra work would come out of the time slaves had to work on their own patches of vegetables and corn—shell-blow grounds they'd been called in his time, when the sound of a conch divided the day into what the slaves owed their master, and what little time they had for themselves. With a storm coming that night there was even less time to spare.

No wonder the slaves were angry. What the weeds choked, or the birds got, was food they wouldn't have, come winter. Masters who provided land for their slaves to work themselves did so in preference to doling out food from a central store. A man like Burke, put in charge of that store, would often sell it to the river traders, robbing the slaves of even that pittance.

Maybe Burke was doing that, too, reflected January angrily. Just for the pocket-change.

"Can you think of another reason Burke would be here? Deliberately antagonizing the field-hands? He can't be *that* stupid, can he?"

"I wouldn't want to put money on either his good sense or his good manners." January tore a hunk of the bread they'd bought the day before from the Myrtle Bank gang, and cut slices of cheese with his knife. "But it explains why I didn't see him at the Nantucket. Mulm must have sent him away the morning after he killed Hesione. Maybe *because* he killed her, though I can't imagine either of them would think there'd be the slightest inquiry made. . . . It doesn't make sense."

Thunder grumbled, a counterpoint to the strike of axes, the uneasy cicada thrum.

"Mamzelle Marie said Mulm collected information for blackmail," January went on. "So he'd know about the dissension in the Avocet family. Building the foundations of the house and tearing them down again; duplicating work; selling off each other's favorites."

"That situation must have been a joy to work in." Rose wet her bandanna, wiped her grimy face.

"You never were a slave, Rose. It's hard to explain to anyone who hasn't lived like that. The . . . the sense of fragility about everything. Even at the best of times, you never feel that anything is certain. Anything can be taken away at a moment's notice. People—*blankittes*—talk about how slaves are 'lighthearted' and 'lightminded,' living only for the day. But the day is all they have. Whites make jokes about how slaves gossip—"

"*They* should talk."

"Yes, but it's more than that. We—slaves, I mean—we had to keep an eye on what *les blankittes* were doing up in the Big House, even if we were just field-hands, because the decision to send Mamzelle to finishing-school in Paris instead of to the Ursulines in town could translate into somebody you know losing his wife. A new overseer, or a new wife, or even a tight-fisted aunt coming to stay meant that the way you got along in life, and got enough food for your family, was thrown into jeopardy: *Oh, you feed those niggers too much, they're eating their heads off doing nothing. You don't need to give the men two suits of clothes, just one is fine and we can save seven hundred dollars on the cloth.* And that's little things, Rose."

He tore hungrily into the bread and cheese with the sense of feeding the firebox of a machine on the coarse fare and having but little time to work up enough steam to continue to move. The day had been a long one, struggling along soggy and difficult terrain.

"You get a major feud in the family—and God knows I'm astonished it doesn't happen more often, with Creole families all living under the same roof the way they do—and the whole atmosphere of the place turns to poison. Everyone starts telling tales, trying to score off each other or gain some halfpenny-worth of imaginary victory. And all the petty vengeances fall on the slaves. We're—they're—the ones who pay for everything sooner or later. And it doesn't take much, under those circumstances, for someone to start asking *Why put up with this?*"

In the silence that followed, the strike of the axes rang loud. Where the marsh lay, visible through the trees from where they sat, the frogs' peeping rose to a clamor. The smell of smoke unfurled like a dirty ribbon from the direction of the river, then veered away with the veering of the unfelt winds beyond the ciprière.

"The folks at Boscage said the family lawyer was trying to put the murder on one of the slaves."

"Probably our friend Jacinthe. The fact that they haven't jailed him already must mean he was in plain view of several people at the time of the murder. Maybe he was locked up in the plantation jail. That's the only alibi I can think of that would hold. But now with a new overseer, and the plantation not doing well, and no one knowing whether everything will be sold, the uncertainty will be a thousand times worse. And with Bertrand in jail in town, and Guifford's widow without experience and not taking advice from the one family member remaining, Burke must have a free hand, to put pressure on an already raw nerve. . . ."

"Pig," Rose declared. She folded her arms around her knees and regarded him sidelong in the thickening light. It would be pitchy black once the sun set—January extracted a new candle from his bundle, fitted it to the lantern, and turned his back to the wind to strike light. "That brings us back to where we were this morning, Ben. What do we do now with what we've learned? How do we trap Mulm without killing the innocent? Because I'm willing to bet you that at least half the people on that plantation are innocent, and have no more desire to rebel than I have."

"Are you? You're giving a lot of people credit for forbearance. Myself, I think the first thing we must do is learn one more thing: that the guns are, in fact, in the wood-sheds. Are you willing to do that tonight?" He stood, slung the meal-sack, and his rifle, over his back.

Rose swatted at a mosquito whining in her ear. "That's a pretty stiff storm coming up."

"I know. But we may not have another night before things break. And even if the slaves don't rebel tomorrow or the next day—and I wouldn't put any money on Jacinthe's Christian forbearance—the longer we stay near Avocet, the more chance we have of being seen by someone or of running into Shaw. As it is, the rain should cover our tracks and keep any observers indoors."

"Hmn." Rose didn't sound any too pleased, but uncorked the gourd of citrus oil to smear on her face and arms. "And I don't even want to think about the number of things that can happen between now and tomorrow's sunset. Maybe not half the people on Avocet are in favor of holding on," she added as they set off through the wind-thrashed gloaming. "I'm not sure what the ratio is, of women with children to men on a place like that. But any woman with young children, who is aware of what's being planned, must be in the most ghastly state of terror right now. Possibly frightened enough to go to the whites and tell all she knows, just to save her own skin and her children's. And what happens after the first shots are fired, and the whites are killed, and the slaves are free to go where they will—or where they can? What then?"

"That moss-gatherer back at Boscage said they'd arranged not only guns, but boats."

"I seem to recall Spartacus being promised something along those lines when he tried this same thing with the Romans."

"And I think Jacinthe is going to find exactly what Spartacus found when he gets to the rendezvous: a lot of empty water. Especially if he's dealing with Mulm." A sky-wide flare of dry lightning silhouetted the trees at the edge of the sugar-fields. Though the dark afterward seemed more dense, it gave January a direction; his gear on his back, and Rose's hand slick with oil in his. "Which is why the first thing we need to do, after we get back to Grand Isle," he continued, "is get word to Ti-Jon that Burke is working for Mulm. I tried to warn him before that the whole thing was a set-up. He said that didn't make a difference, but this may change his mind."

"Will he trust you?" asked Rose. "Will he believe the message is from you? Especially if he doesn't want to?"

January was silent, knowing she was right.

She went on. "And do you think that, having the guns in hand, Jacinthe will simply disband his conspiracy? He can't, you know. Not if the guns are already there, waiting to be found. And if they're not, of course, you and I have no proof of anything."

Again January could find nothing to say. Another burst of far-off lightning showed him her face, boyish under the hat-brim and under its coat of grime, save for the curious firm line of her mouth.

"Logically," Rose said, "the only thing we can do is fire the sheds."

That stopped him in his tracks. *"What?"*

"It's not like they're near anything but the sugar-house." She hitched her rifle on her shoulder, then went forward toward the sullen iron-black of the twilight sky. By now the trees were barely visible, great columns of darkness, the leaf-matted earth no more than a suggestion of gray. Between flares of lightning only a frieze of darker-gray slats, like a sort of edgewise jalousie, indicated the open sky. But the wind, cold and eerie, flowed over them, and January could hear little over the surging clatter of the cane.

"The quarters are on the other side of the Big House." Rose had to raise her voice to be heard. "There must be two hundred yards of open ground between the house and the mill. I think the fields are too green to burn, don't you?"

He did, but he also didn't give a spitball in a gale whether the white man's crop went up in flames or not. Guifford and Bertrand Avocet sounded exactly alike to him, both contentious, greedy men who didn't care what befell those around them so long as their precious Creole honor was satisfied. He and Rose darted across the path that divided the fields from the ciprière and plowed straight into the cane-rows. January had to unsheath the lantern's light to distinguish his way between the rows of leaves that flailed at them like razors. The wind would cover their movements, but it would cover those of an enemy as well. If the time of the rebellion was near, Mulm would have men in the ciprière, waiting for those frightened ones of whom Rose had spoken, those who dared not rebel but feared to stay.

And in truth, January thought, raising his arm to shield his face, he could think of no other way of averting the rebellion that must end in disaster for Jacinthe and all who took up arms at his side. But his stomach churned at the thought of simply stepping in and destroying the guns. What Rose suggested was exactly like him saying *You can't come with me because it's too dangerous. . . . You'll only get hurt. . . .*

Even if he had known she would get hurt, had known for a fact that she would be killed, to make the decision for her was to dishonor her courage and her choice. And to simply burn the sheds would insult men who would rather be free than live safe. It would make a mockery of his own beliefs that people were free to choose.

Damn it, he thought, hating the choice: did he really, REALLY believe these men—and a certain number of inevitable innocents—would be better off dead than dishonored?

Except, of course, that he didn't *know* they would die.

As he didn't know, *for certain,* what Mulm was planning.

Only God knew that.

So he fought his way along the rows toward the sheds, the sharp leaves cutting at his hands, turning on the horns of the dilemma and wondering how one would start a fire in a gale like this anyway.

Rose, he reflected with an inner sigh, would inevitably know. She'd been experimenting for years with ways to make a fire underwater.

Halfway across the fields, spits of rain hit them, then huge, juicy drops. By the time they reached the sheds, the downpour had begun in earnest, the winds whipping the rain now into January's eyes, now against his back, and though the cane-leaves sliced at his face he could only be thankful that they shielded him and Rose from the worst force of the blow. Lightning silhouetted the mill chimney in ghostly white, like a scene in a nightmare, and January remembered the storms of his childhood: lying in the single bed in the half-cabin where he'd been born, clinging to Olympe when the walls swayed and the pots and gourds hanging on them clattered like the champing of demon teeth. . . .

Listening to his mother's soft snores. It would take more than a storm to keep Livia awake.

Feeling his father's arms warm around them both.

They came out of the cane a few yards from the sugar-house. The wind blew so fiercely, it made January stagger and nearly swept Rose off her feet. So dense was the darkness, so blinding the rain, January could only guess where the wall of the sugar-house lay; he dared not uncover the light. Gripping Rose tight around the waist with one arm, he leaned into the wind until he reached the wall, and worked his way along it in what he hoped was the right direction. Lightning steadily punctuated the rain up until this time, the thunder like the splitting of rocks—so naturally, Jove of the Thunderbolts decided this was the time to rest up a little, and they clung to the corner of the sugar-house for what felt like an hour and a half but was probably no more than ten minutes, until the next bolt showed them where the wood-sheds lay.

Never trust a damn blankitte *Greek god.*

The stillness in the shelter of the wood-shed was profound, the noise of the rain on the thatch like water being poured from a bucket. Wind whined through the cracks, but unlike the shelters at St. Roche, these were proper sheds, like small barns.

"And if you tell me you let the lantern go out," whispered Rose out of the darkness, "I will succumb to a case of the vapors."

In spite of the danger, January chuckled. There wasn't much smell here of cut wood, and a great smell of dirt. At a guess the shed was empty, or nearly so. A flashing quick scutter of sound—rats, he thought. Or snakes. Or a six-foot alligator waiting for its dinner. He wiped the rain out of his eyes with a bleeding hand and fumbled at the lantern's slide. "I wonder if Jacinthe and his gang got—"

He raised the slide just in time to see a slave come at him with a knife.

He made a noise like *Yuh!* and felt the lantern slip from his hands. The ground, though covered with wood-chips and shreds of bark, was also soggy, sliding under his feet as a body hard and strong as a panther's collided with his in the ensuing dark. He felt the knife-blade skin his biceps, grabbed for the man's shoulder, twisting and rolling and knowing he dared not lose contact with the arm. A powerful hand grabbed at his cheek, fingers gouging for his eye; the thumb raked his lips and he bit with all the force of his jaws. Salt blood in his mouth. The man screamed; January slammed his knee up into his opponent's groin and hurled him back, hearing the wall creak with the impact. The shed door rattled sharply and he yelled, "Look out, Rose!" as wind and rain came roaring in.

An indistinct, dark shape against lighter darkness, and then a hollow, deafening boom, yellow muzzle-flash, and the stinging sear of shot ripping arm, calf, cheek. A clang, a curse, and Rose's voice shouting, "Out!" January plunged in the direction of her voice and tripped over someone rolling and scrambling on the muddy floor, fell himself, came up like a bullock from a mire with hands grabbing at his legs, his shirt, his ankles. "Here!" Rose yelled again. It sounded like she'd been near enough the entrance to thwack the gunman over the shotgun barrel with the butt of her own weapon. January ripped free, fell through the door into Rose's steadying grip and pattering, blowing handkerchiefs of diminishing rain.

They hit the cane-rows, plowing and swimming through the churning blackness, only the straightness and direction of the rows leading them back toward the ciprière two miles away. The shotgun roared behind them again—two barrels or a very fast loader—and Rose cried out, lurched forward, January catching her in the crook of his arm.

Her back was so wet, he couldn't tell how much blood there was in the rain-water, but he smelled it, strong.

She was breathing—panting, each gasp a stifled moan—and still trying to keep on her feet and run. January swung her into his arms and strode through the mud and wind and slashing cane-leaves, and cursed the rain that lightened and dwindled—*DAMN it, can't you keep up long enough to cover our traces at least?*

Mulm and his men—or Jacinthe and his sentries—would be waiting, out in the dark of the ciprière.

January rammed himself crosswise against the cane-rows. He stumbled in the rain-filled ditches, staggered up the mounded rows, and fought through the hedge of razor-leaved cane. Rose's arms went around his neck. She'd lost her hat, and her long hair hung thick and wet against his breast beneath the torn calico of his shirt and caught on every leaf of every cane of every row. . . . She never made a sound. Her blood felt hot on his arm.

Four or five rows upstream he turned again, heading in the direction from which they'd come, praying he hadn't miscalculated, that this row would go clear down to the water. Praying that the storm wouldn't raise the level of the river, that there'd be enough of the tree-covered batture to follow, so they wouldn't have to risk going in the water itself. In summer, the batture would be dangerous enough.

Don't let her die. Virgin Mary, don't let her die.

His own wounds smarted, but they'd been glancing, he'd been

rolling aside already. Rose had caught part or all of a charge straight on. No telling how close the marksman had been, or how much of the shot had broken up or spent before it found its target, or what kind of shot it had been. Fear made all the soak of rain that drenched her clothing into blood.

Wind struck him hard as he came out of the cane, though not as hard as before. The rain had eased, no doubt to facilitate pursuit. In his arms Rose shivered violently, and murmured something indistinguishable when he spoke her name. No lightning had struck for many minutes, and he saw only the vaguest blur that was the shell road along the river. Beyond that, the levee and the sky were a sightless abyss, but he could smell the river.

Don't let her die.

And in his mind he saw Mathieu in his dream, grinning as he thrust her legs apart.

The batture was a solid granny-knot of brush, saplings, weeds, and snags—a nearly-impenetrable snarl of desiccated roots and branches, occupied by birds, turtles, snakes of every variety, alligators, and upon occasion runaway slaves. Carrying Rose and thanking God for the size and strength that made most Americans look at him with that dismissive glance that said *field-hand,* January stumbled along the outside of the levee, shivering himself now, until he estimated they were clear of Avocet. Then he stooped, and set Rose down, fumbling in his pockets for flint and steel even as he realized there was absolutely nothing dry in the entire world to light.

"Rose," he whispered, bending over her, touching her hair. "Rose."

He felt her nod her head.

Useless to ask where she was hurt, or how badly. His ear to her lips, he could hear her breathing, and it sounded steady, if shallow and swift. He had no idea how many men might come after them, or whether those would be Mulm's bravos or guards set by Jacinthe himself—in the end, it would come to the same thing. If they were still anywhere in the vicinity of Avocet at first light, they were doomed.

So he gathered Rose into his arms again and moved downstream. He stayed as close to the top of the levee as he could, and prayed the rain would be enough to keep the snakes under cover. They had lost both rifles, and all their food and drink. He found himself desperately calculating how far out of Burke's reach they must go against how much cold and exposure Rose could endure.

The rain seemed to fill the universe with water; the darkness before Creation, when God moved upon the surface of the deep. What time it was January had no idea, but far off, ahead of him and to his right, a light glowed through trees. He thought it must be a steamboat, seen around a bend in the river—there were steamboat captains mad enough to navigate on a moonless night in a storm, though not generally this far below town.

Still, he made his way along the shell road; in time the tossing oceans of dripping cane on his right gave place to rough open ground, dotted with native oaks whose leaves sounded wetly under the rain, and it was clear to him then that the light was indeed shining from the window of a house.

A Big House, but that would mean that at least a few servants were still awake. He came down off the levee and circled among the trees toward the kitchen yard and the outbuildings where the house-servants slept. As he passed the dark shape of what he guessed to be the overseer's house, a chorus of barks resounded from the gallery, and January stood still, to let the dogs come up. From the porch a voice called out in thickly Hibernian French, "Och, who's out there, then?"

January called back, "I'm a free man, sir. But the woman with me is injured, and in desperate need of help."

He spoke in English, and in the same language the voice exclaimed, "The de'il you say!" And over his shoulder, back into the house, "Bide, Aggie, 'tis all right." The overseer sprang down the steps and strode toward them, a lantern swinging from his hand and showing him to be a fat, sandy man with a face like a petrified potato and a mouth like a penciled line under a stiff red mustache. "Christ," he added when the light fell over Rose. And well he might, thought January, utterly aghast: her blood soaked her clothing as if she had been butchered. "This way, man, get her to the hospital! What in the name of God . . . ?"

"I don't know if it's as bad as it looks, sir. But she was shot, buckshot, I think—by slave-stealers, men we couldn't see." January followed him as he spoke, toward a brick building near the kitchen.

"Lucy!" the overseer bellowed in a voice like Capitoline Jove. "Lucy . . . !" And, when a woman emerged, shawl-wrapped, from the little cabin built off the rear of the kitchen, "Get Sapphire and be quick about it," he snapped in French, "we've an injured woman here. . . . Damned slave-stealers." He switched back to English as he led January into the cabin designated as the plantation hospital. The lantern-light showed one of its two beds occupied by a boy of eight or so, tossing restlessly with fever. The other was empty, mosquito-bar tied neatly back behind its rough head. "And what were you doin' abroad to be shot at like that, me buck? Water over there." He pointed toward a jar in the corner. "Rags in the cupboard." Under a shelving jut of bleached eyebrow, his pockmarked face was hard but not cruel.

January was so glad just to be indoors, and able to lay Rose down on a bed, that he simply did as he was told. He had had considerable time, in the past few hours, to meditate about honor, insult, and death.

"Christ," said the overseer again as he pulled the remains of Rose's shirt off her, exactly as he'd have stripped harness from an injured horse. Two or three pellets had lodged in her shoulders, a few more in her back. By the tears in her ragged breeches, more had struck her buttocks and thighs. "Bird shot, thank God, and hit her at a distance." He cocked a very sharp hazel eye up at January. "Free, you say?"

Without a word January produced his own and Rose's papers. While the overseer was angling them to the lantern's dim flare, the cook, Lucy, came in, with a taller woman who was clearly the head woman of the plantation, presumably Sapphire.

"January, is it?" The overseer held out his hand. "Colin Perth. And Miss Vitrac?" He pronounced it as an American would, with the emphasis on the first syllable rather than the last. "Where is it you were bound?"

"Grand Isle," said January. "My friend has family there." Past Perth's shoulder he could see the woman Sapphire gently mopping the rain-diluted blood from Rose's back, and nearly cried out with relief. The wounds, though bloody and obviously very painful, were clearly superficial. "We came ashore at Myrtle Landing. We were told there was a way down Bayou St. Roche. . . ."

"Gah, no wonder you ran into them de'ils. You should have ta'en a packet, and gone clear 'round by sea."

"We hadn't the money for that, sir," said January baldly.

"And I suppose you *had* the money to buy your ladyfriend back from the likes of old Chamoflet out in the marshes, eh? You couldn't . . ."

A light step creaked on the gallery; shielded candle-light flickered in the rain. "What is it, Perth?" asked a cool little voice like a porcelain bell and, turning, January saw Chloë St. Chinian Viellard, framed in the doorway.

SEVENTEEN

"You are Mademoiselle Vitrac," said Chloë Viellard. "Artois' tutor. Uncle Veryl told me about you."

Rose fumbled for the spectacles that Sapphire had taken off her and said, in a voice weak but surprisingly even given the circumstances, "Yes, Madame. I am Mademoiselle Vitrac."

"My dear Mademoiselle, this is dreadful." Even dressed as she was, in a flowing wrapper of Italian silk spotted with rain, Chloë Viellard moved with the precise grace of a woman gowned for a Royal ball. Her pale blond hair, like raw silk around a precise little heart-shaped face, had clearly been brushed out and braided for the night, before being coiled swiftly into a loose coronet; and she wore spectacles, the lenses round and thick as the bottoms of wine-bottles. "What happened . . . ? No, never mind that now. Just rest. . . . Are you hungry? Thirsty? Lucy, wake Marie and have her make a tisane before you come back and help Sapphire if she needs it. . . . M'sieu . . . Janvier?" She removed her spectacles, looked up at January with those enormous pale-blue, myopic eyes. "You are a friend of Mademoiselle Vitrac's?"

"I am, Madame, yes." He'd lost his hat, and inclined his head respectfully. "I was escorting Mademoiselle Vitrac to her family's home on Grand Isle." The top of Madame Chloë's head barely came up to his breastbone. It was like talking to a child.

"Of course," she said. "It must have been as grievous for her as it was for me. . . . I think everyone loved Artois. Would you object to occupying the room where my husband's valet stays when he is here? My husband returned to town only yesterday, so the room is still made up. Lucy will get you something to eat."

"If you please, M'am," answered January, "I'll remain here with Mademoiselle Vitrac, should she wish it." Sapphire seemed to know what she was doing, removing the bird shot swiftly and deftly with a bullet-probe and cleansing the wounds with an astringent aromatic. Lucy, a stout woman with a gap between her prominent front teeth, returned with Rose's tisane, and at a sign from Perth unlocked the corner cupboard and brought out half a dozen more candles, to add to the lantern's smoky light. Their clear, bright radiance and the faint smell of honey filled the long room.

"Ben . . . you're tired." Rose's voice was tight with pain. Her fingers lifted to sign him to go; January returned to the side of the bed and drew over one of the room's two or three low stools, to sit on as he took her hand.

"Sapphire, would you show M'sieu Janvier where the room is when you're done here?" asked Chloë. "Or if Mademoiselle Vitrac wishes it, would you get Marie to bring some blankets for him here? Thank you." And she took her departure like a diminutive queen, trailed by the overseer Perth and by the somewhat disgruntled Lucy, in quest of clean sheets and food. Rose's fingers tightened hard around January's. When Sapphire's face was turned away, bent over the wounds on her back, Rose brought his hand to her lips and kissed it. She made no sound as the slave-woman continued her treatment, and fell asleep almost as soon as it was done.

January ate some of the congris and sausage Lucy brought, and made up a bed in the corner, under an old mosquito-bar the cook tacked to the wall for him. His own wounds ached damnably—Sapphire had washed them with her astringent before she thriftily pinched out the candles and left—and he thought he'd lie long awake, but he got as far as *Blessed Mary ever-Virgin . . .* in his prayer of thanks and then it was daylight and he was wondering who had pounded him with hammers while he slept.

"I could have wept with envy when I heard Uncle Veryl had hired a tutor for Artois," Chloë's sweet, silvery voice was saying as he woke. Steamy morning heat filled the room, and diffuse light from the western windows, and the heavy green scents of summer in the country. Through the open door January could see sunlight glaring beyond the building's shadow on the unscythed grass. "Up until Papa died I used to spend most of my days at Uncle Veryl's, you see, reading in the library. The nuns at the convent were so *stupid,* and there was nothing to read there but edifying sermons and the lives of the saints. Uncle Veryl taught me Latin when I was eight, so he couldn't very well object when I'd read Suetonius or Tacitus, or even Procopius, who must have been part American, I think. . . . I could always tell him I was practicing my Latin. I don't think he believed me. *Just don't tell your mother,* he'd say." Her imitation of the old man's voice was loving, and nearly perfect.

"Someday I should like to lay hold of the man who started this rumor about women being unfit to study," sighed Rose. She still lay on her stomach, but she'd eaten, to judge by the tray set aside near the bed, and the whitewashed room was fragrant with coffee. In the other bed, the sick boy slept deeply under the mosquito-bar. The two women kept their voices low, lest he or January wake.

"I imagine you would need a spade," said Chloë thoughtfully. "He's certainly been dead a good many centuries, and serves him right, whoever he was. I do remember reading the advertisement for your school, you know, the one you had a few years ago, if you're the same Mademoiselle Vitrac. . . ."

"I am."

"I thought you had to be. Papa was horrified—he was spending a fortune keeping me with the nuns—and Mama of course would have had a palsy-stroke at the mere mention of me studying in the same classroom as *filles du couleur.* I said it was *infamous* that young French ladies should be denied the teaching those girls were getting. . . . Which I still think it is."

"As do I," agreed Rose, propping herself a little on one elbow to sip her coffee. "But I couldn't teach both, you see." Her hair had been braided, and pinned to her head. Her back was a criss-cross of plasters and dressings, the flesh between them blackened and swollen. "Surely you could have gotten a decent education in France."

"I could have, were I not an heiress." The girl's voice was crisp with a matter-of-fact exasperation, where another girl might have gloried in that state. "My mother was Jean-Henri Duquille's only daughter, and he died young, you see. His older brother, my uncle Joffrey, has two sons, but neither of them ever married. . . ."

"That's odd, isn't it? In a Creole family?" Rose was clearly thinking of Chloë's new husband, the hapless Henri.

"They're an odd family." Without her spectacles, Henri's wife looked forbidding—curiously so, for a girl of her delicate appearance. She was as neatly turned-out here on Bois d'Argent as she would have been in town, in a simple gown of shell-pink sprigged muslin and her ivory hair smooth as moonlight. Her frown of puzzlement made her human.

"Uncle Joffrey's wife, my aunt Felice, committed suicide when the boys were fifteen and seventeen: they're in their forties now. I think it must have affected Uncle Joffrey's mind, for he never left St. Roche after that, and neither did his sons. My husband and I attempted to pay a bridal visit, both before and after the wedding—we were married only last month—and both times, my letter asking could we come was returned. I have it on good authority that my uncle has his slaves turn all visitors off the property."

Rose opened her mouth to comment on the truth of that rumor, then obviously remembered that she and January were supposed to be traveling down from New Orleans, not the other way. She said instead, "How very Gothic."

"I've always thought so." Chloë settled back on the stool January had brought up the previous night. "Though you know, if a woman chose to immure herself like that after a husband's suicide, no one would give the matter a second thought. Unless of course she happened to be an heiress, in which case her mother would be serving up male cousins and eligible bachelors with breakfast, lunch, and dinner. I used to make up stories, you know, I and my Picard cousins, about Aunt Felice's suicide. About what drove her to it, I mean, and why Uncle Joffrey never could be free of it. Sometimes I favored Cousine Musette's theory of a long-lost former lover—who was sometimes called Florizel and sometimes Werther, but in either case had spent the years between Felice's betrothal and her son's fifteenth birthday rowing in the Dey of Algiers' galley."

Rose, who had undoubtedly spent many nights listening to the chatter and tales of the girls under her care at the school—to say nothing of Chighizola's widely-varying tales about how the old pirate happened to lose his nose—nodded with the air of a connaisseuse and said, "That's a good one."

"But I also liked my own tale of the ghost of Mad Juana of Spain. Mad Juana was the daughter of Ferdinand and Isabella, you know, and the mother of the Emperor Charles V—which would make her the aunt of Bloody Mary of England." Chloë folded her lace-mitted hands on her lap. January, who had come to think of her as some kind of matrimonial monster, smiled a little at this trade of schoolgirl confidences.

"When Juana's husband, Philip le Bel of Burgundy, died, she did the same thing Uncle Joffrey did—went insane and refused to leave his side. She traveled with his corpse in her baggage for years and years. . . . I suppose she paid her porters bonuses."

"She would have to," remarked Rose.

"In any case, I deduced that one of the necklaces she wore during all of this had ended up in a pirate treasure, buried on Uncle Joffrey's land—for there was a pirate landing there, before Uncle Joffrey built the house and started to grow sugar there. . . . In fact, I believe he bought most of his original slaves from Jean Lafitte at a suspiciously low cost. They were friends, of course, Uncle Joffrey and Lafitte, and there was all sorts of contraband run across his land by various sinister gentlemen with names like Red-Hand and Turkish Jack and Cut-Nose. So of course one night while she was out walking, Aunt Felice happened to tread upon ground where a treasure was buried, and was possessed by the ghost of Mad Juana, and went mad and hanged herself. . . ."

"I think I've seen that opera. And Uncle Joffrey keeps her embalmed corpse—I assume M'sieu le Bel's corpse *was* embalmed?—in his parlor?"

"Either that or he buried it beside the treasure."

"It has a certain neatness to it." Rose's eyes sparkled appreciatively. "I'm sorry, Madame," she added. "This is your family we're speaking of. . . ."

"My mother would remind me of that." Chloë's own impish smile faded. "In the most tragic voice. And my nurse had her own ways of punishing me in the name of propriety of thought." Her voice flexed a little, like a steel swordblade, at some recollection, and she rubbed half-unconsciously at the small triangular scar of a burn on her wrist. "Not that Father would ever hear a word against Nurse—who was quite young and pretty.

"But in any case I've never had much in common with my Picard or Viellard cousins, and most of my life has been lived with Julius Caesar and Alexander the Great and the heroes of the Peloponnesian War. So it's very difficult not to . . . to see one's own family legends in that same light. It is one of the few things," she added, rising, "that I have in common with my husband." Again that momentary flaw tightened her voice, as if at the memory of conversations aborted, of silent dinners and civil good-nights.

She laid a testing hand against the coffee-pot, and poured out a little more into Rose's cup. "I hope that we may . . . you and I . . . continue our acquaintance when we return to town. Or . . . will you be returning? You said you were bound for Grand Isle . . . ?"

"For a visit only."

Something about those narrow, bird-fragile shoulders relaxed. "Mama never would let me meet my half-brother—whom I liked very much, on the occasions when I *did* encounter him, at Uncle Veryl's. But she is forever telling me that a married lady may go where she pleases, and do as she wills. The only incentive I have seen so far for matrimony—that, and not having to deal with spiteful nurses. Perhaps you and I can meet at Uncle Veryl's? He spoke so well of you, and would grieve if . . . if the connection were to end now that Artois is gone."

"In that case," said Rose, "let us definitely meet there."

When Chloë was gone, January stirred and rolled over, and Rose turned her face toward him, and groped for her spectacles. "I'm sorry. I hope we didn't wake you. . . ."

"You couldn't have." January slipped from beneath the make-shift mosquito-bar, and knotted it back, his shoulders and arms stabbing him at every move. "Not if you'd pounded me with a plank, which somebody appears to have done." He limped to her bedside, and despite the red-hot ramrod with which someone seemed to have replaced his backbone, knelt to kiss her. "God, I can't tell you how good it was to wake up hearing you laugh."

"Ah, then you woke after Madame Sapphire came in to change the dressings; you would have heard some choice cursing if you'd opened your eyes then. There's coffee, if you don't mind using my cup. Madame Chloë was here. . . ."

"I heard." By the soft slur in her voice it sounded like Rose had been dosed with a small quantity of laudanum, something he usually mistrusted but was grateful for now. He sniffed the dregs of her coffee-cup to ascertain this wasn't where it had been administered, then sipped the unsugared brew gratefully. "Trading Gothic tales of pirate treasure and suicide . . ."

And he stopped, holding the cup suspended halfway to his lips. "Dear God," he said, blinking, as if someone had suddenly opened a window into morning sun.

"Dear God," he said again.

With a grimace of pain, Rose put her folded hands beneath her cheek. "You've had sudden inspiration for an opera about Jean Lafitte and Mad Juana's necklace?"

"No." January set the cup down, still feeling dazzled, as if like Jesus he'd been taken up to a high place and seen all the world lying before his feet. "I know why Mulm wants a slave revolt—and what Tyrone Burke talked to Hesione LeGros about before she died. What he paid her to tell him . . . and then missed one doubloon when he took the money off her body with the candle guttering in the near-dark."

Their eyes met, and he saw Rose's comprehension, as complete and certain as his own.

They said, almost in unison, "Jean Lafitte's treasure is buried on Uncle Joffrey's land."

"That's ridiculous," said Rose a moment later. "Jean Lafitte didn't bury any treasure."

"No," said January. "But one of his captains did."

"Gambi. Of course. Cut-Nose said Lafitte never trusted him. . . ."

"With good reason, I suspect. Now that I look back on it, I'm almost sure that it was Gambi who sunk the *Independence* . . . the American slave-ship that caused all the trouble on the night of that wretched birthday party. Gambi was there, and I remember he had fresh cuts on his face, the kind of splinter-wounds a man gets in a sea battle from shot hitting the gunwales. And Hesione was Gambi's mistress."

"And Sancho Sangre—the fellow you said is running guns to New Grenada with Mulm's backing—knew Hesione then, and could have told Mulm that her tales of treasure and piracy could well be true. Those shovels we saw in the shed near the head of Bayou St. Roche . . ."

"They had to have been left by Mulm. All ready, when the slaves come through. I thought they looked awfully clean. It doesn't matter, really, whether the slaves themselves burn the house and kill Uncle Joffrey and his sons or not, though at a guess Mulm has told Jacinthe that the boats will be waiting for them at St. Roche. When the army finally reaches St. Roche and finds the house burned and Joffrey and his sons dead, it'll be Jacinthe and his rebels who'll take the blame." January turned back to his makeshift bed to collect his boots.

"What are you going to do?"

"Exactly what you suggested we do," returned January. "I'm going to go back to Avocet and fire the wood-sheds."

January's first instinct—to return to Avocet immediately—was tempered by second thoughts, and he did end up persuading Lucy to heat water for him to get a much-needed bath in the tin tub behind the kitchen. In return he fetched water and wood for her, not only for the bath but for the general use of the kitchen: he regarded the cook as much more his hostess at Bois d'Argent than Chloë Viellard was. It was Lucy, after all, who did most of the work.

In doing all this, he gave the impression that he would remain at Bois d'Argent with Rose for as long as she lay in the hospital. This, according to the healer-woman Sapphire, who came in to help Lucy in the kitchen, would be at least another day or two. Rose had lost a good deal of blood, and was still weak and in a good deal of pain. When the young slave-boy—Samson was his name—went back to his parents' cabin that afternoon, his fever having broken in the night, Lucy put fresh blankets on the cot for January, should he elect to spend another night at Rose's side.

"Acting as if you're staying will come in handy," remarked Rose when January fetched in luncheon for them both: rough fare, beans and rice and greens, "if anyone asks where you are at any given time. Will you go back to Avocet tonight?"

"I'll travel tonight, yes," said January. "The moon doesn't rise until nearly ten, but I should have enough light after that. I'll lie hidden on the batture until the men go out to their work in the morning. If Burke is overworking everyone, there shouldn't be a guard kept on the sheds in the daytime. I've offered to help Lucy bring up firewood this afternoon for the kitchen, and that should give me time to wrap up and hide enough kindling to get a blaze properly started, once I find which shed the guns are actually in."

"Be careful." Rose held out her hand to him. She still looked ashy, and the drowsiness of laudanum slurred her voice. The night-gown she wore, though old, was of the lightest cotton lawn, far finer than any slave-woman would have worn. Too big for Chloë, it had undoubtedly come out of the stores of old clothing in the Big House's attics at Chloë's request. An interesting aspect of generosity, thought January, in a young woman who already had a reputation as a sharp and heartless trader.

January helped Sapphire change the dressings on Rose's back that night, and saw that the wounds seemed to be healing clean. "I'll sit with her awhile, before I go to bed," he said, and the healer-woman nodded. With any luck, and with Rose to back up any story he told, he should be able to account for his whereabouts at the time the sheds at Avocet burned. Not that it would do him any good if Burke caught him anywhere in the vicinity—at his size he might well have been recognized in last night's jarring maelstrom of lantern-light and darkness. But if no one remarked on his absence, there was a better chance of getting out of the area unmolested.

He set out at moonrise, traveling along the batture with his two sacks of kindling. He kept close to the water, among the snags, prodding and testing the brush before him with a stick. Some god or saint must have been watching out for him and Rose the previous night, he reflected. Five times in the course of the journey his probings dislodged hissing and disgruntled serpents from the tangle of branches underfoot. Though it was hard to make out in the shadows and moonlight, at least one of them bore the black bars of a water-moccasin.

Rose, of course, ever the skeptic, would argue that it was only last night's rain that kept them deeper in shelter.

He smiled.

There was more bad weather coming in. He could feel it in his skin, hear it in the dead silence of the air. The cicadas were hushed, the air indescribably eerie. Bars of cloud gathered before the moon, then fled, racing visibly, like the insects and birds—seeking to flee. Moving along the batture, January felt as if he were the last man living on a silent earth, left behind by some unimaginable catastrophe.

He saw a light or two on the river, where steamboats bound down for the Belize forts and village on the Gulf rode the current, hugging the banks as close as they dared, for below town the river was a monster of strength. Below Myrtle Landing the plantations were few. Other lights shone from the masts and prows of the ocean-going packets, the New England clippers, and the coastal steamers, working their way stolidly upstream to the New Orleans levee or heading down fast for the open sea. There had been a time, he thought, not terribly long ago, when he'd only counted the days, and his earnings, to take one of them, to go back to France, or to

Italy, or even England. To go anywhere that men would address him as *vous,* like a man, instead of *tu,* like a dog or a child; to make his home in some land where Americans didn't look at him with calculation of price in their eyes.

To go to some country where the thought of a slave uprising had the arcane absurdity of something one only read about in novels of ancient Rome.

It's the nineteenth century, he thought. *In Paris, and London, and Lisbon, the streets are lit by gas-lamps. Steam-ships cross the ocean in six weeks and men have made balloons to fly in through the sky. Slave uprisings?*

But there was nothing of the nineteenth century—its gray stone cities, its up-to-date mills and factories, its railway trains and glass windows and pianos—in the dense, sweaty silence along the river, in the hot green stink of the cane-fields in the velvet night.

The wind was rising.

No lights shone at Boscage.

None at Soldorne—it must have been Chloë's bedroom light, as she sat up late reading Tacitus or Herodotus, that he had seen in the deeps of last night's stormy darkness. Avocet, too, would be wrapped in darkness, though he dared not climb the batture at this point to see.

Guifford's twice-widowed young widow and her daughter would be sleeping, so newly members of the family that the man she had married had not yet made provision for her in a will. What would become of her, if Bertrand were to hang? And on the other side of the house, Annette Avocet would likewise sleep: a woman Vivienne had hired a good-looking American to spite, a woman she had pushed into the position of mending her clothes. Yet with the well-worn enforced amity of isolation, the two of them had been sewing together at nine-thirty, when someone had stabbed Guifford in the side.

And Franklin Mulm, with his blackmailer's ear for gossip, had unerringly picked the situation as the one that could be most quickly escalated to a slave revolt, the moment Tyrone Burke had broken it to him that Lafitte's treasure lay buried on land they could not get to any other way. Maybe he'd had his eye on the place already, as a weak spot whose potential for chaos could be taken advantage of, the way a puma can tell by scent which deer in a herd will be slowest to flee.

Certainly Tyrone Burke had arrived at Avocet—according to Lucy, who knew his name as Burkitt—the afternoon following the overseer Raffin's disappearance, leading the horse that had disappeared with Raffin.

Found him wanderin' in the woods and remembered as how I'd seen Mr. Avocet on him at Jesuit's Bend t'other day, somebody said he was from here. . . . Me? Just passin' through, lookin' for work . . .

With Raffin gone, Guifford murdered, and Bertrand in jail, the two women had needed another overseer, and quickly. Without a doubt, Raffin's body would be found in one of the near-by bayous, chewed beyond recognition by crawfish.

Moonlight outlined the shape of Soldorne's landing, a weedy wharf standing high above the sunken river, a flight of crude plank steps leading up the levee. Cypresses shaded a bench where passengers could wait once a steamboat hooted its approach, and a flagstaff to signal for a ride.

St. Roche would have been a perfect place twenty years ago, thought January as he left Soldorne behind, for a small-time pirate captain to bury loot pilfered from—or in spite of—Jean Lafitte's unilateral command of all corsairs in the area. It might not even have been Gambi who did the stealing. Hesione herself could have stolen the money—and presumably the fictitious, accursed necklace of the accursed Mad Juana of Spain—from Gambi, and come up Bayou St. Roche to keep it safe from her fellow women in the camp. There would have been no St. Roche Plantation in those days, only a landing at the head of the bayou and another on the river's edge, an easy portage of a mile or less.

And there it had lain. January thrust his stick into the blackness beneath a deadfall, heard something swish and scramble as it fled unseen. Mosquitoes hummed sullenly; he slapped at them with arms that had grown tired of slapping.

There the stolen fortune had lain, while Hesione went from a corsair's jeweled mistress to a tired, blowsy slattern, turning tricks in the sheds behind the Nantucket to get her the price of a bottle. He recalled hearing that Gambi had been murdered by his own men not too long after Lafitte had been chased out of his colony by the U.S. Navy. Had Hesione been part of the little settlement of Campeche? Or had Gambi—or whoever had succeeded him in her affections—already put her aside?

Had she tried to get the treasure herself as her money ran out? Crept out of the ciprière some night, only to be met by the eccentric Uncle Joffrey's African overseer with a shotgun in his hands? *We don't have strangers here on St. Roche.* How many times had she tried, before returning, penniless and angry, to town and to her bottle, and to her memories of past glories on the hot beaches of Grand Terre?

Men accused the plaçées of being greedy, especially as the women grew older. Of saving and scraping and making demands on their protectors, of feathering their nests in whatever way they could.

And why not? thought January. One had only to look at his mother, with her investments in cotton presses and town lots and steamboat companies, with her comfortable house and the sturdy health that lingers into old age only with adequate care, and compare her to Hesione, who gave away and spent every sou in her hellfire youth. The free women of color understood, as perhaps no one else did or could, how precarious life was for those who had only their beauty and their bodies to sell.

And Dominique?

She'd come south to warn the lover who might very well have already promised his new wife he would give her up. Come to save, not only Henri, but that chill, pale little child-bride who read Thucydides until two in the morning and wore spectacles when she didn't think anyone could see her. Who was notorious for selling her nurse who'd had "her own ways of punishing me . . . not that Father would ever hear a word against her . . ." and made up tales about why her eccentric uncle had become a recluse. . . .

Smoke stung his nostrils.

His first thought was *A steamboat at a landing.*

But into the deadly hush of the night a clamor rose. Confused voices shouting, snatched by the wind and flung away.

The crack of a shot.

January scrambled up the levee and saw the wildfire glare of crimson through the trees.

A house burning. Two buildings, maybe three . . . A woman screamed.

He began to run.

EIGHTEEN

Men pelted back and forth among the oak-trees by the light of the burning Avocet house; January could see them from the levee where he stood. The rising winds that lashed his clothing against his flesh fanned the flames into yellow banners among the thrashing oaks. A salvo of gunflashes spouted out of the windows of the garçonnière wing; a moment later two figures burst through the French doors, sprang and scrambled over the gallery rail, fleeing for the brick sugar-mill.

Men closed on them, men clothed in the rags of slaves, or naked, sweat shining with the firelight, long cane-knives swinging in their hands. The howl of the wind drowned their cries. The shirt-sleeved figures fired, a rifle and then a pistol. Then they were cut off from the mill and could not re-load, and January glimpsed an old-fashioned white pigtail: the family lawyer, Diacre. Was the other man Bertrand's dandyish attorney Rabot? At the same time four white-nightgowned forms, long hair whipping in the storm, dropped from the gallery in the company of a single white man and bolted for the levee, while out of their sight the slaves hacked the two decoys to death.

Even at this distance, and by the chancy glare of the wind-whirled fire, January recognized the tall, lanky form of Abishag Shaw.

January had the sense to duck down behind the crest of the levee and run along its riverward slope. Shaw would never recognize him at this distance in the fire's wild glare—all he would see was yet another ragged, black-skinned man racing toward him, and January had enormous respect for the policeman's aim, even in this wind-lashed darkness. There was a pirogue tied at the landing, and the fugitives would have to come over the levee near there. He strained to hear what was happening, but there was too much noise from the rush and surge of the wind in the snags of the batture, in the trees beyond the levee, in the hammering air itself. The clamor blanketed everything in the bizarre illusion of silence, and he had the impression—when he saw a dozen men in the garments of slaves emerge from the tangled growth of the batture below him—that they did so without a sound.

They were armed, as the slaves of Avocet were armed, with cane-knives and clubs. Coming from some plantation upriver, alerted by rumor, and ready to fight.

The nightgowned women came over the top of the levee, veered when they saw this second group of slaves swarming up toward them. Shaw appeared a moment later, head bare and long hair snatched and torn by the wind. He fired a shot into the batture group with the Kentucky long-rifle in his hands, trying to open a gap to the landing. January barely heard the report. Shaw tossed the spent weapon to one of the women and unslung another rifle from his back and fired again. He was pulling the third long gun clear when the Avocet slaves mounted the levee behind him and fired. Shaw dropped to his knees, hand pressed briefly to his side, then brought up the rifle again to fire into the mob that was now only yards away.

January broke cover and reached Shaw in two strides, wrenched the rifle from his hand and at the same time fetched Shaw a kick in the ribs that hurled him down the river side of the levee, into the dark where the light of the burning house did not penetrate. Only his appearance stopped a volley from the slaves' rifles which would have shredded the Kentuckian—as it was, one shot whipped past January's ear. Praying his aim would be true, he pointed Shaw's rifle down a foot or so to the right of Shaw's head and fired.

It was too dark to see if the ball hit dirt or skull. Shaw, who even then had been trying to rise, twisted and fell limp into the inky shadow of the levee. The Avocet slaves, clothes and bodies bloodied from the killing of the men, reached the crown of the levee as January knelt beside Shaw, ran a rough hand through his hair in the darkness, then pressed a finger to the pulse in his neck. It was hammering, though Shaw didn't breathe; January stood, spit on him, and turned to the Avocet slaves and the other rebel group who'd come from the batture.

"He dead." He had to shout the words.

He was afraid they'd check on Shaw themselves, but at that moment the four women were dragged back from the landing by the arms, the necks, the hair. The homely blond one January knew by Shaw's description to be Annette Avocet, the darkly pretty one had to be Vivienne. Her daughter—Laurene?—was like her, petite and fairylike, terrified but silent, which was more than could be said of her mother. There was a young woman of color, nurse or maid or companion, as well. The rebel leader Jacinthe strode up the levee, pistol in hand, and grabbed Vivienne Avocet by the arm. His loincloth, arms, and belly were slick with blood. He put the pistol to her head and she screamed, her knees collapsing beneath her, spoiling the shot. January reached him before he could drag her to her feet again.

"The hell you think you doin', fool?" he demanded as he swatted the gun barrel aside.

Jacinthe stared at him. "Who the hell are you?" he yelled over the bellowing of the wind.

"My name's Sam and I heard folks here was gettin' boats an' gettin' guns." If the slaves at Boscage had heard it, it was a safe bet others had as well. "Who the hell are *you?* Fucked if I wouldn't have broke out on my own if I knowed they was fools here who'd throw away hostages, for the U.S. Navy to let you past the Belize fort." And he jerked his hand at the woman whose arm Jacinthe gripped. The other women clung together, trembling in their nightgowns;

the daughter and the nurse shedding silent tears, the square-faced blond Annette impassive as an Indian warrior from the Texas plains. Jacinthe's gaze rested thoughtfully on January's face for a moment, studying it, then slipped sidelong to the women.

"We're traveling under the storm," he said. Cane-leaves and the broken branches of the oaks blew past them as he spoke, striking with stinging force. "By the time we get down the river, neither army nor navy will even have heard of us. We movin' fast."

"Well, excuse me all to hell," retorted January. "You know why I got sold this last time?" He turned to the men, raising his voice above the rattling of the cane. " 'Cause the sorry bastard who owned me said just that: *I got two good horses an' there ain't no reason for me to take extra money with me when I ride up to Natchez—I ain't gonna need it.* So when one of them horses throwed a splint an' the other got stole from the stable, guess who ended up goin' home with the first man who came along with five hundred dollars in his pocket? Sure is nice to have to do with folks who know the future."

While he'd been speaking, another man came up the levee, small and thin and walking with the halt stride of the old, though January guessed this newcomer wasn't too much more than his own forty-two years. He carried a torch; its wild light showed the tracks of illness and hardship on his face, and a body so emaciated that January could have named each of his bones. "What you think, Doctor?" asked Jacinthe.

Vivienne Avocet, still kneeling on the ground, screamed again and rocked on her heels, crossing herself repeatedly—the man called Doctor paid her no heed at all, and only regarded January for a time, as if gauging who he was and what he might bring to the rebel group. Then his sunken eyes went past, to the non-Avocet slaves. Beyond the burning house January could see horses being led out of the barns and loaded with stores. "I think a damn sight too many people knows too much about us breakin' out." The Doctor's voice was the voice a vulture would have, could vultures speak.

More slaves crept out of the threshing dark tangle of the river's edge, women leading children, or with babies at breast. The flames showed gold in their eyes.

Jacinthe pointed toward the confusion around the barns. "Get down there, get whatever food loaded up you can," he ordered the newcomers. He included January in his gesture. "We move and we move fast. Somebody tie Mesdames"—scorn flicked from his voice as his eyes ran over the adult women—"and their pretty little girl behind a horse. . . ."

"Put them on that horse." The Doctor raised a hand against the ripsaw wind. "Tie them good. They slow us down else. Storm, she be bad, killin' bad. We gotta get to where the boats is, be ready to put out the moment the sky clear, if we gonna make it past the fort 'fore they hear we comin'."

"Best you pray"—Jacinthe jerked the widow to her feet and shook her, her head lolling—"that all go well, M'am Vivienne." And he thrust her back at the others so hard that she fell again.

"Virgin Mary, save me, a sinner!" Vivienne screamed, but the fair-haired Annette Avocet merely watched her, heavy jaw set and eyes dry and wary.

"Because I'm tellin' you," Jacinthe went on, "whoever slows us down, whoever tries to run, whoever causes trouble, we get rid of. I don't need the four of you. Haran—what'd you find in the house?"

He strode down the levee to speak to a new-come messenger, followed by the Doctor, and the men dragging M'am Vivienne, her sister-in-law, her daughter, and the nurse, all the newcomers and the rebelling Avocet slaves trailing behind. January followed but fell back through the straggle, dropping at last behind one of the oak-trees and letting himself be swallowed by the whirlpool of the night. He watched Jacinthe shout orders to men loading up the horses with provisions, watched the slave-women run from the quarters with their few small possessions, holding their children by the hand. In his mind was Plutarch's account of Spartacus and his rebels, and what had befallen them in their quest to be free.

He turned back and climbed the levee again.

Shaw was gone.

Behind the levee, away from the flame-light of the house, the darkness was abyssal. The river surged and churned in its bed, but January could see nothing of it; cold rain spattered him as he groped his way back to where he thought Shaw had fallen.

Damn him, thought January savagely. *He's got to be Leatherstock-*

*ing and try to go back to save those women from death or, presumably,
worse fates. . . . As if Jacinthe is going to let his men indulge themselves
in even the most speedy of rapes, when they have only the duration of the
storm to get the whole mob down to St. Roche and onto whatever boats
they think will be there.*

He yelled, "Shaw, damn it!" but the wind yanked the words
from his mouth and flung them upriver, and whacked him over the
head with a torn-off tree-branch for good measure. He groped a little farther along the batture, and nearly put his hand on a four-foot
snake that went whipping from beneath a downed tree. "Shaw!"

Nothing. And the longer he remained, the greater the chances
of someone either coming over the top of the levee again, or coming
down the batture from upriver, drawn by rumor of the rebellion. He
had called Jacinthe's attention to himself once already, to his face
and voice and mostly his size. The rebel leader was intelligent, he
was suspicious, and January knew better than to think that he,
January, wouldn't be watched if he crossed Jacinthe's path again.

Even if, reflected January, Jacinthe didn't join up with Mulm at
some point between there and St. Roche. And if he did, there was
no chance of talking his way around that.

They'd be heading out soon, and moving fast. And between
Avocet and St. Roche lay Bois d'Argent.

Bois d'Argent, and Rose.

Any advantage the pirogue might have gained from running
downstream was nullified by the brute force of the wind. At least,
thought January when he got to the little boat, he was poling in the
same direction as the snags, tree-limbs, and other flotsam that
heaved all around him in the blackness. There was a lantern in the
prow, and he even managed to light it: it did absolutely nothing for
him. Only the tangles of flooded brush to his right kept him ori-
ented, he couldn't even see the levee, and the rising millrace of the
water roared among the snags. It would be far too easy to drift into
the main current and find himself swept away to the sea.

There'd be a landing at Soldorne. He strained his eyes for the
flagstaff that would signal it, rising above the levee—waited for the
ghostly blue flash of the lightning that more and more often lit up
the sky. Strained his arms and his back, too, fighting that hell-bent

current, and keeping to shallower water. Once he delivered a warning to the people on Soldorne, he knew, the warning would spread downriver. If the whites weren't able to hold against the rebelling slaves, at least they would have plenty of time to flee, or to make enough resistance that Jacinthe would simply abandon the straight track down the river road, and move inland. January had almost concluded, despairingly, that he'd missed the flagstaff and landing in the dark, when he saw it, silhouetted against a lightening, a reddening in the storm-black sky.

Firelight that caught the flying rain like burning jewels.

The house at Soldorne was in flames.

He tied the pirogue at the wharf and ran up the plank steps, head bowed against the slashing rain. At the top of the levee the wind nearly took him off his feet, screaming around him as if it would skin the clothes off him, nearly blinding him as he looked down. The rain kept the Big House roof from catching, but every French door that opened onto the encircling gallery was a furnace-mouth, scarlet light showing the gallery planks themselves scattered with the debris of flight. January descended the levee, disbelieving—*they couldn't have gotten on the road that quickly!*—and thought, *The slaves here saw the flames at Avocet and knew what they meant. They rose up, without waiting for Jacinthe to arrive.*

Had the owner and his family had time to flee?

Leaning against the wind, driven aside from the path again and again, he climbed the gallery steps. He had to shield his eyes against the glare from those broken doors. Furniture within had been tossed and tumbled, drawers yawned in the parlor secretaire. A woman's jewel-case lay at his feet, a single ruby earring catching the flame-light. Then a gust caught it, and the case, and batted them away into the darkness.

Though he walked all around the burning house, he could see no bodies. The rain was too heavy now, and the wind-jerked crimson fire-glare too uncertain, for him to tell whether there had earlier been blood. Stable and mule-barn both showed flames within, but the shrieking wind and deafening rattle of trees and cane drowned any sound. Beyond the holocaust glare was only tumbling blackness—whether anyone remained in the quarters or even in which direction they lay was impossible to discern. If they were smart, they'd flee whether they had anything to do with the rebels or not, thought January. Once the army heard of Jacinthe's rising, few distinctions would be made between slaves who rebelled and slaves who concealed their suspicions about what their friends and family members might be up to.

Which was exactly what Franklin Mulm would be counting on.

But it was curious, he reflected, recalling the jewel-case, that the fleeing Madame Soldorne would have removed the jewels from the case. That was much more the action of a man, to take the jewels and cram them in his pockets.

There was no question of taking to the pirogue again. He set off along the shell road along the levee's top, leaning against the wind and staggering when it veered, the force of it almost twisting his nearly-useless lantern from his hand. Branches, leaves, and uprooted cane-stalks smashed him as he walked—once a bird, dead and soaked and very solid, crashed into his temple out of the darkness—and below the road, the threshing of the cane-fields had the note of a sea in storm. Midnight? One o'clock? Only the wind existed, bludgeoning him like a flail and bellowing in the trees.

Rose was at Bois d'Argent. He remembered Ti-Jon's scornful words about the free colored; remembered, too, how the free colored had been massacred by the slaves of Saint-Domingue in the great uprisings of the 1790s, who had seen in them only the lackeys of the whites. Vivienne Avocet's light-skinned servant had stayed with her mistress rather than flee or throw in her lot with the slaves. She would very likely be killed without compunction, a fate that would almost certainly befall Rose if she fell into Jacinthe's hands. And if she fell to Mulm and his filibusters—wherever they were in this maelstrom—she would likely be passed along to an unscrupulous dealer, taken out of the state, and sold, freedom papers or no freedom papers.

Unless Mulm recognized her as January's friend, of course.

The house at Boscage was burning. A fool's action, January thought, with the certainty of the army's arrival . . . He recalled the moss-gatherers, Griff and Nate, and tried to recall what they'd said of their master and his family. He would not have thought there was sufficient anger there to fuel this kind of reaction, but knew from his own days in the quarters how such anger underlay every aspect of the fabric of life.

That was the great fear the whites lived with, day in and day out. The thing they would deny, and lie about to others and to themselves: that their slaves were angry. That their slaves actually did not like to be treated like animals. That the people whom they bought and sold, whom they told who to marry and who they had to let into their beds, the people who ate congris and salt-pork while they—the whites—consumed chicken and jellies and coffee with dessert . . . that these people had their own opinions about what was done to them. About the life that they were forced to live by threats of physical punishment or of separation from their families and friends.

Speak of rebellion, thought January, standing on the levee with the wind hammering him, and nine whites out of ten would become instantly irrational. Angry, blaming everyone from Quaker bleeding-hearts to ungrateful slaves.

Terrified of this. Of the gold flames streaming in the stormy darkness.

The next house down the river road was Bois d'Argent.

The wind grew worse. The rain grew worse. January heard Rose saying *This is only a storm,* and tried to remember, tried to imagine, a time when he thought water was a soft thing, or gentle. This was like being peppered continuously with small shot, hammered and drowned and driven again and again to his knees until sometimes he simply crawled, groping with his hands like a blind beast. When the wind veered the rain into his face, he felt he was drowning, unable even to tell up from down. His body ached from the effort of fighting to stay upright, never mind move forward. The roaring of the wind in the cane-fields below the road passed beyond the sea-boom of ordinary storms and rose to a constant bellowing roar, like a live thing uncaged and ravening; the river level was rising, and when January was able to see anything at all in the dark, he could glimpse only surging chaos.

Dante, he thought, must have gone like this into Cocytus, the frozen Hell where Satan's wings churned the air to storm. Jacinthe and his troops couldn't be far behind him. They were obviously gaining strength by the hour, if even a few of the slaves from the other plantations joined them in their flight. He thought of Vivienne Avocet and her stoic sister-in-law, of the quadroon maid and the young girl clinging to the back of a horse in this shrieking inferno of waters, wondering how this could possibly have happened to them. Thought of Shaw, somewhere in the wet, churning woods on their flanks, wounded and watching for his chance . . .

Or, likelier, dying of shock and exposure when he could no longer continue with a bullet-wound in his side and whatever damage January's kick might have inflicted. Or stumbling off the batture in the blackness, to be swept away in the river's flood.

The wind eased, like Jupiter taking a breath. The rain poured straight down like an upended ocean. Firelight through the trees again, glaring from every door and window of the house at Bois d'Argent and transforming to blood the water sheeted among the oaks. The overseer's house was burning, too—January could see it—and the stable beyond. A body lay on the gallery: a man's, it looked like, when January fumbled Rose's telescope from his pocket.

And on the shell road of the levee itself, where the path ran up to cross over to the landing, lay the red bandanna Rose had used as a signal that all was not safe to go into camp. That all was not as it seemed.

It was fixed to the road-bed with a horn-handled kitchen knife.

January stood for a long time, looking down at that bandanna, by the glare of the burning house.

There was no way the slaves here could have seen Boscage burning. Not unless someone had come and told them. Conceivably Jacinthe could have arranged with slaves in every plantation along his proposed route of flight to all rise on the same night—the night of the first storm heavy enough to delay the whites' communication with the army—but the Doctor's comment seemed to indicate that that had not been the case. On every plantation there were men willing to risk their lives—and the lives of everyone around them—for freedom. But equally, on every plantation one could find men and women both so eager to curry favor for themselves, or so malicious about their neighbors, that they'd betray their fellow-slaves. And Jacinthe, he thought, did not seem to be a trusting man.

More movement in the dark. January's lantern-light briefly spangled what was almost certainly pale cloth, snagged in the branches of the batture. He struggled down to it, knee-deep in rising water that dragged at him like a riptide. He wrenched it loose: a thick silk shawl, flapping like a sail. Chloë's, without a doubt. She had fled this way, then, down the road, instead of inland across the fields to the small farms that would be located somewhere in the ciprière. Just as well, with escaped slaves—probably armed with cane-knives—wandering that roaring darkness, not to mention Mulm . . .

He reached the top of the levee, held the shawl where the firelight would fall on it, and drew breath as if he had been punched in the gut.

The wet yellow silk, the embroidered butterflies, blue and red . . . it was definitely Dominique's.

It can't be. January staggered, the wind nearly taking him off his feet. Below the levee, trees were not only bending, but rocking, cracking under the rage of the storm. Huge boughs and young trees flashed past like spirits, appearing out of nothing, violent and deadly. For a moment he wondered if Henri, in a sudden attack of poor taste, had bought identical shawls for his wife and mistress, but remembered that Dominique generally bought her own clothing with money her protector gave her—often bought Henri's gloves and waistcoats, and chose his presents to his sisters as well.

What the HELL is she doing here? At Bois d'Argent . . . Had she truly come there herself? Thinking Henri was there, thinking to warn him . . . Olympe, or someone, must have sent him—January—word at Grand Isle, word that Dominique intercepted.

He tied the shawl around his waist, stumbled in the wind, and went on.

The house at Autreuil was burning. From the levee, through the telescope, January could see shadows moving against the flame. Water lay three and four inches deep below the gallery, and the men clung to the stair-rails and the trees to keep on their feet. They led horses out of the stables, as the slaves had at Avocet, but these figures wore coats like white men, and slouch hats tied on their heads with bandannas. January recalled the jewel-box on the gallery at Soldorne—had it only been a few hours ago? Mulm was looting and burning the houses himself, he realized, in addition to picking up escaped or straying slaves. After warning the inhabitants to flee, of course.

And Jacinthe and his people would take the blame for it all.

January staggered on, feeling as if the storm had lasted for days. As if he'd been condemned to struggle through it forever, punishment for some sin that had seemed right at the time. His confessor, without doubt, would have told him that his duty lay in remaining with Jacinthe's band to protect the four Avocet women—one of whom, he was almost certain, Shaw strongly suspected of murdering Guifford Avocet. And indeed, there was every chance that none of those women would come out of this alive.

But he knew, too, that to try to rescue them—to show himself too willing to stick by them—would have been the quickest route to a cut throat, and no good either to them or to Rose and, now, to Dominique. He could only push on, in the hope of catching them at St. Roche, or of organizing some kind of resistance strong enough to bargain.

But the house at Les Plaquemines was shuttered fast and locked, and no amount of pounding could rouse response from within. He felt his way along the wall from door to door, hammering with his fist and calling out. Near the doors of what would have been the parlor, he felt fresh bullet-holes in the wood. *They'll see my lantern,* he thought, but didn't dare put it out, knowing he'd never get it lit again and would be lost indeed without it. Something crashed into the other side of the house—an oak-tree uprooted in its entirety. A second crash, and the whole house shuddered while buckets of rain sluiced onto the gallery, and he felt like a lone mariner on the deck of a derelict ship, abandoned and sinking in the night-wracked abyss of the sea.

There had to be an overseer's house out in that blackness somewhere. There had to be quarters. If he could find them, they'd be somewhere out a good half-mile beyond the house. . . .

He came around the corner of the house just as lanterns bobbed in the wet blackness below the gallery.

Numb with exhaustion, January could do no more than swiftly flatten himself to the wall, shield the lantern with his body, and pray the darkness would cover him. The men had to shout to one another to be heard: he heard one yell, "You sure those niggers going to come on, in rain like this?" but did not hear a reply. Footfalls clumped on the wooden planks, then the house shivered with a crashing blow to the shutters. January risked a peek around the corner, and saw Franklin Mulm and a dozen others, standing huddled together while Tyrone Burke ripped at the lock on the shutters with a crowbar.

January's aching body was filled with a huge irrational unwillingness to move, but he guessed that in these few moments—when the men were intent on getting into the house—lay his best chance of disappearing into the screaming wet darkness unseen. He crawled down the back gallery steps on hands and knees, and away into the darkness again.

The last two miles, from Les Plaquemines to St. Roche, were the worst. He had long ago ceased to judge the physical violence of the wind, or the intensity of the rain that slammed into him, but he could hear the changed note of the noise in the trees. It had risen to a steady, eerie drone that made his skin creep, like a sound heard in nightmare. He fell, not far beyond Les Plaquemines, and though he struggled to his feet he knew he would fall again. Blown branches pummeled him, and once something huge whipped past him—he didn't know what and didn't want to guess.

Shortly after that he realized he was wading and staggered toward his right, seeking for the way up the levee again. But he was already on top of the levee. It was the river coming over, where that barrier was low. The fear clutched him that he would miss St. Roche completely and go stumbling on, like a soul forever damned, until he staggered off into the sea where the river ended. At times he thought he did dream, struggling and half-drowned. That he dreamed finding Dominique's shawl, and Rose's bandanna . . . That he dreamed of Rose loving him . . .

That he dreamed of light down to his right, nearly hidden in the trees.

He stood gasping. Rather to his own surprise, he was still on top of the levee, and still alive.

Water stood knee-deep in the snarly jungle of weed and saplings below. The wind was marginally less here, though all the trees around him in the darkness writhed as if trying to work their roots free. At least the saplings, the random stalks of degenerate cane, gave him something to cling to, to haul himself along. He wasn't sure he'd have made it, else. Something brushed past his leg, and he wondered if it was a snake, flushed from its hole by the flood. Last year Olympe had taught him a charm against snakes and he tried to remember it, calling on the Virgin Mary and Damballa-Wedo. As he waded toward the light, it seemed to him that the water was alive with serpents, wriggling like maggots wherever his lantern-light struck it.

Every door and window of St. Roche was shuttered, but light shone between the cracks.

Had Rose made it? he wondered. Had she warned them?

How bad had the wind been when she and Dominique struggled along the river road? Had they been swept bodily off the levee to drown? Or been brained by a flying branch? He could have walked by their bodies and not known it, walked by them trapped in the flooded batture, with them screaming his name not ten feet from him, and would not have heard . . .

He pounded the shutters, shouted, "Let me in! In the name of God, let me in!" Wind scoured the gallery; the house seemed to creak and sway as if it, like the trees around it, were trying to twist itself loose of its moorings. Was old Aunt Felice's ghost out there in the screaming blackness, walking toward him with Mad Juana's accursed necklace glittering evilly about her throat?

"Rebellion!" he shouted. "The slaves are up in arms! Up the river at Avocet! Let me in!"

"We heard all about this slave revolt." January turned his head: to see the overseer Serapis near the end of the gallery, shotgun in hand, the muzzle leveled on January's chest. "And we heard what happened to the folks that fell for that story and went runnin' out into the night."

"No, it's all right!" The shutters of the women's side of the house opened and a figure stood silhouetted in the blackness. The gown she wore, gauzy white and high-waisted in the style twenty years gone, floated about her like a shroud in the wind. Dark, streaming hair caught the wind, too, gleaming in the slits of light from the windows near-by, framing her beautiful face like a stormcloud. "P'tit, is that you?"

Dominique.

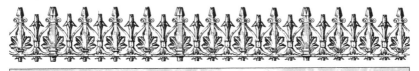

NINETEEN

"P'tit, it was horrible—just ghastly!" Dominique draped a quilt around January's shoulders. Another man who by his shabby, elegantly-cut coat January guessed to be the household butler brought in another blanket, to lay across his knees.

"This is clean," the butler told him. The flicker of the parlor's two candles danced ghoulishly over the neat geometry of tribal scars, over hair elaborately braided in a fashion January hadn't seen since childhood and never on a house-servant. But the butler, under his elegant coat, wore only a loincloth. *They Africans down there,* the little cow-herd from Plaquemines had said. It seemed he was right.

Even in the house they had to speak loudly, over the howl of the wind. Drafts whipped through the open doors between parlor and dining-room, and into the women's side of the building; everything stirred with unholy life and the whole place rocked and creaked sullenly in the wind. "It's been in a chest in the attic many years."

January could have guessed this by the smell of cedar and mildew that impregnated it and the quilt over his back. He understood the man's need to reassure him on that score, however. Like the outside of the house, the inside showed the last extremities of emptiness and neglect. Cobwebs draped the parlor walls, old and white and so thick with age that the tunnels the spiders wove could be seen boring away into their cloudy fastnesses—the fleeting drafts made the webs lift and seem to paw at the shadows. The divan on which he sat, with its ornate lotus motifs and carven crocodile feet, was gray with dust and reeked of mold. In their high-waisted, pale gauzes, Dominique and Rose recalled January's youth, while Chloë's flat, immature form was rendered more schoolgirlish still by the sashed frock of some forgotten young lady not yet out when Napoleon was still in military school.

The rifle she held was taller than she was. "Thank you, Kitanga," she said to the butler.

"Mulm came just after dark, with the warning that the slaves were rising all along the river road." Rose brought January coffee from the pot on the sideboard, her brows very dark against the ashen pallor of pain. "I saw him ride up, but I was afraid to cross to the house and warn them inside, in case I was recognized. I wish I had. Because a few minutes after he left, Mr. Perth came out the front of the house and was shot on the gallery. . . ."

"M'sieu Perth told that *beastly* M'sieu Mulm that he was . . . that he didn't believe the slaves on Bois d'Argent would rise up," put in Dominique, her eyes flashing suddenly hard. "M'sieu Mulm waved his arms and swore that the slaves were on their way down the road from Avocet right that very second, that he had barely escaped with his life, and M'sieu Perth only said, *We'll see about that, then.* . . ."

"I shall never believe that it was the slaves that shot him," declared Chloë, her voice quiet but her eyes cold as ice.

"Nor was it." January tried and failed to find an alternative *mise-en-scène* to the obvious one: if Dominique had heard Perth's words to Mulm, she must have been in the Big House—that is, talking to Chloë—at the time.

"Of course it wasn't, darling." Dominique put her arm around Chloë's shoulders. "If they were killing white men, they would have killed M'sieu Mulm when he rode away from the house, to keep him from spreading the alarm."

"On the other hand," said Chloë to January, her arm around Dominique's waist, "it was quite clear that *somebody* was shooting. . . ."

"I was halfway to the house when Mr. Perth was shot," said Rose. "Oliver—Madame Chloë's butler—went out to the quarters. He said most of the hands there had fled, probably because of the rumors of revolt. But Oliver and Lucy stayed with us, when M'sieu Chighizola brought us here. . . ."

"Captain Chighizola agreed to bring me to Bois," explained Dominique with her sunniest smile. As if, thought January, *bring me to Bois* didn't involve a day's slogging in a pirogue through marshes infested with slave-stealers . . . "I hoped to catch you here, because Mimi Rigaud—she lives just past the mimosa grove near Rose's brother—heard from a trapper that the guns were going to Avocet. The Captain is the sweetest old gentleman. . . ."

"Cut-Nose and Oliver are guarding the nursery wing," explained Rose. "Lucy is there, too, with poor Madame Perth, as loaders." She glanced at Serapis. The driver stood in the doorway that divided the front parlor from the downstream front bedroom, the bedroom presumably inhabited by the ghost of Aunt Felice. Through the doors that opened to the darkness of the dining-room, January could see the St. Roche butler Kitanga, relieved of his task of fetching "clean" blankets, keeping watch at the rear of the house. In the eerie flickering of the candles, in that disused chamber of dust and cobweb, there was no sign of anyone besides the three girls, the two slaves, and January. He looked inquiringly at Rose. "And M'sieu Duquille . . . ?"

"Michie Joffrey Duquille doesn't speak to company," said Serapis, glancing out from the dark of the bedroom. The pattern of printed flowers on his loincloth was like the mottling of an animal's hide in the gloom.

Sudden pounding on the shutters of the parlor window made them all jerk. The house was swaying, groaning as it swayed; the screaming of the wind nearly drowned a man's voice shouting, "The slaves! Rising up . . . murdering . . . burned Autreuil and Boscage and Bois d'Argent . . ."

"*Opuró,*" muttered Kitanga, crossing to the dead Madame Duquille's bedroom and opening the door onto the gallery— January recognized the word the old aunts of his childhood sometimes used, meaning *liar.* "Who are you—"

The blast of a pistol on the gallery was like a thunderclap; the impact of the ball slammed Kitanga back against the doorjamb, and the butler was slumping to the floor as Serapis sprang over him. Feet thundered on the gallery outside. Serapis caught up the pistol that had been in Kitanga's pocket and fired out the door, Rose grabbed a pistol from the mantel and shoved open the shutters before January could so much as draw breath. She fired out, slammed the shutters again, ducked as a bullet crashed through in an explosion of wood-fragments and glass, and all around the house boots crashed on the gallery, guns fired, thunder louder than the wind's howl.

There were three pistols on the marble-topped cabinet, perhaps the only objects in the room not silver with dust. January caught up one, Rose another, pushing open the brisé to fire through at the men kicking and hammering at the shutters of the door that Serapis had just slammed closed. In the confusion January glimpsed a man lying on the gallery, blood mingling with the rain-water to make a black flood around his head. January fired and ducked, slammed the shutter against the return fire and threw the pistol to Dominique to load—she had powder-flask, bullets, and patches ready on the divan beside her, near to hand. A bullet plowed into the mantel beside her head, and Dominique said, *"Bleu,"* and dropped to the floor, keeping pistol and ramrod with her. A ball tore splinters from the shutter beside Rose, and Rose said something considerably stronger.

Rank powder-smoke clogged the air, burning January's eyes and mingling with the dead butler's blood to give the house the reek of a battlefield. A voice somewhere called, "We all right in here!"

More shots, and something struck the house, a giant's kick, a tree uprooted by the tempest. The building shuddered in its bones. "Watch out, sweetheart," warned Chloë, setting her rifle against the *faux marbre* mantel to carefully tip the divan over on its side, where it would protect Dominique from stray bullets.

When she put her hand on the door that led into the front bed-room, the men's side of the house, Serapis called from the other bedroom door, "Don't go in there, m'am. Michie Joffrey and his boys, they got that side of the house covered."

Chloë looked startled, and drew herself up to reply, but a crash and splintering from the rear doors of the dining-room cut across her words. She whirled, caught up her rifle, and fired through them, the shot and muzzle-flash like thunder and the stink of powder thicker yet on the gloomy air. January ducked, crawled back through the dark dining-room to fire again, but wasn't sure he hit anyone. When he reached the shutters he heard nothing but the bellowing of the wind and rain.

"Well, at least they can't fire the house." Crouching next to the downstream brisé, Rose slammed the ramrod down the barrel of the pistol she held with neat strength. "Is there a chance of sending to the navy at the Belize fort for assistance?"

"Not in this." Serapis slid his own pistol, and the one Kitanga had been holding, back to Dominique. Another salvo of shots tore holes in the shutters, sprayed the parlor with glass, and all in the room flattened to the floor. "Flood's already over the fields. When the big flood-wave come, whoever we send gonna be swept away."

"Have you enough men in the quarters to make a sortie around our attackers?" Chloë spoke from Kitanga's old position in the butler's pantry, where a ladder ascended to the attics above. "Or are M'sieu Mulm and his men too widely scattered?"

Still on his belly, January pressed his ear to the floor. "Do you hear anyone?" whispered Rose, leaning close.

"Not on the gallery, no. Movement somewhere else in the house. But that would be Chloë's butler—Oliver, you said his name was?—and Cut-Nose and their loaders in the nursery."

Rose nodded. Blood marked a number of the wounds that had opened again, giving her the horrible air of some blood-boltered spirit from a bad Gothic novel. "Madame Perth's as formidable as her husband was. Can you hear M'sieu Duquille and his sons in the garçonnière as well?"

"I can't tell." January raised himself on his elbows, glanced to the shut upstream doorway beside which Serapis waited in the shadows, and switched to Latin. "If there is a M'sieu Duquille. Did you see him when you came here?"

Rose's eyes widened behind their oval lenses. "Kitanga made us welcome, fetched us clothing from the attics—which he assured us was clean, meaning, I suppose, that it isn't covered with mildew like everything else in the house. I don't know what he thought we expected: calico loincloths? Which seem to be all they wear here . . .'"

"That's exactly my point," said January softly. "How long has it been since anyone has seen Uncle Joffrey Duquille? How long has it been since there was another white person on this plantation, to tell whether Duquille was alive or not? Think about it, Rose."

His hand moved, taking in the dust-filled parlor, the cushions breathing of mildew, the indigo-washed plaster of the walls sheeted with cobweb and the portrait of a woman, beautiful and sad, looking down on them from beside the locked door of what had been the gentlemen's side of the house. "Freedom doesn't have to mean escaping in boats to Mexico or Africa. Maybe it only means having Africa *here*—having your village *here*. Your freedom *here*. Raising enough sugar to sell for a little profit, having one or two people on the place who can write a hand sufficiently like Duquille's to fool his factor in town . . . And who's to know? Who's to know if the man hasn't been alive for years?"

She glanced toward the doorway again, at Serapis' lean, dark shadow in the dimness. "Until someone wants to come dig for Jean Lafitte's treasure on his land."

"Until someone wants to dig for treasure on his land," agreed January.

More gunfire outside made them all tense. Chloë tucked her diaphanous skirts tight above her knees and crawled to the fireplace, to pick candles from the tin box there and gingerly replace the nearly burned-out stubs in the holders on cabinet and mantel. January guessed Mulm's filibusters were all around the house, firing into the lighted rooms, but he dreaded still more what would happen when the candles gave out. He heard Chloë whisper, "Are you all right, darling?" leaning over the tipped-up sofa.

"Fine, thank you. Not," Dominique added, "that any of us could do anything about it if I *did* go into labor . . ."

"Don't even *say* it," returned the younger girl with such comic alarm in her voice that both women giggled.

In Latin, January asked Rose, "Does she know?"

Rose shrugged helplessly. "I haven't the faintest idea. The first I knew Dominique was at Bois d'Argent was when I ran into the house after seeing Mulm. I almost fell over when I came on the two of them sitting together on the back gallery. . . ."

The house shuddered again, as something struck it—*That HAS to be a tree.* A moment later, from the upstream side of the house—from the locked garçonnière side—came the snap of gunfire. Serapis slipped into the parlor, whispered to January, "Take the parlor window, if you would, Michie," and from a cord around his neck took the key to the locked door. Despite the crash of the wind and the hammering rain, January heard the door lock behind him.

It made a bizarre kind of sense. He'd heard of runaway villages, little fragments of Africa out in the siprière. Such villages were rare now, but he'd visited one not far from New Orleans itself, where slaves raised their own crops, tended their pigs and their chickens, set watchers in the marsh, and pulled up stakes and moved on when the patrols started coming too close. How difficult would it be, he wondered, to take that one step further? To dispose of a master known for his eccentricity, to take over an isolated plantation. *Michie Joffrey doesn't speak to company.*

A line of men, singing an African song as they carried wood in from the marsh.

We don't have strangers comin' around St. Roche.

And the shotgun in Serapis' hands.

He pressed his ear to the boards again, listening for the thud of invading boots, and the storm shrieked and rocked the house—empty for how long? he wondered. Haunted—inhabited—not by the specter of Madame Duquille, as Chloë and her cousins had imagined, but by the much more useful ghost of Joffrey Duquille himself. By the legal fiction of his continued existence that enabled his slaves to live in security and peace.

Serapis slipped back into the room again, locked the door behind him. "Wind gonna stop," he said softly, and dropped another couple of powder-flasks down into Dominique's little fortress of up-ended divan. "When it does, they'll make their try. It's light, when the clouds break."

January glanced at the mantel clock, covered so thick in cobweb that it was hard to see the hands at all. He pulled his own silver watch from his pocket. It was twenty minutes to seven. "Can we make a sortie and take them from behind? You, me, maybe Oliver or one of the . . . one of M'sieu Duquille's sons?"

"No." Serapis moved from the divan to the cabinet, then across to the bedroom door again. His back, January noticed, was unscarred as a child's, something you seldom saw in a slave with that proud carriage and watchful eye. Certainly not in a slave who bore tribal scars on his face. "It's death to go out when the wind stops."

"Good heavens, no!" said Rose. "In hurricanes like this there's a stillness of perhaps ten or fifteen minutes, then the wind starts up from the opposite direction, harder than before. Redfield wrote that it was because of the cyclonic nature of such storms. It hits without warning. . . ."

"There speaks a lady from the islands." Serapis' eyes glinted approval. "The men from the quarters, they're all hid up in the sugarmill." He nodded in the direction that January recalled vaguely that the mill would lie. "I doubt any will come out during the stillness. Not against men in the woods with guns. We'll have to hold them, keep them out of here until the winds come again. When the winds come, and the flood that will follow on them, we'll be rid of those evil men."

When the stillness came, the silence was shocking. He felt, for a moment, a strange elation, a kind of relaxed peace, as if the night were over and they were safe. . . .

Then Serapis slammed open the shutters and fired through, and January, throwing back the jalousie nearest him, saw men pushing through the tangled brush and weeds, knee-deep in water and struggling to reach the house. Men with rifles, water splashing around their boots; at least a dozen of them. He recognized Mulm, black close-buttoned coat shiny with wet, and Burke beside him with his slouch hat still tied to his head. January fired, and the men scattered, vanished into the tangle of laurel and sugarberry that grew too close around the ruinous house. He settled his sights on the top of the gallery stairs, but knew they'd likely climb up some less obvious way.

Gunfire sounded on the other sides of the house.

Then, breaking from the brushy thickets along the rim of the sugar-fields, he saw four running forms in white. Three women and a girl, long hair soaked, wet nightgowns sticking to their bodies and impeding their flight; stumbling, falling in the water, dragging one another up to run on.

And behind them, wading grim, mud-smeared, and bloody as the platt-eye devil from childhood fable, was Abishag Shaw.

He still had two rifles with him, and two pistols around his neck on ribbons, the way the pirates used to wear them, stuck through his belt to keep them from flopping. His right side was one huge rain-diluted bloodstain over the torn rags of his shirt. He fell against the corner of the nearest building, a sort of shed that had probably been a laundry or pottery or cooper's shop, and turned back to face the fields—all this January saw in seconds. The running women blundering through half-submerged brush, Shaw bringing his rifle to his shoulder like a man near the end of his strength, and then the black, loping shapes of the pursuers. Angry men, frightened men, appearing and vanishing among the half-drowned foliage, cane-knives gleaming in their hands.

Shaw fired once, and the pursuing slaves took cover—January was less astonished that Shaw had tracked the rebels and freed the women than he was that the Kentuckian had kept his powder dry through the storm. *They'll creep up on him at their leisure,* thought January—if snakes didn't get them in the water first. January heard Mulm's high nasal voice yell an order: two men broke from the trees and splashed toward the women to intercept them, pistols waving in their hands.

Still moving carefully, leaning on the shed for support, Shaw fired at the approaching filibusters, and as usual Vivienne Avocet stopped dead in her tracks, clutched her hair, and screamed. From his window January fired, too, and the men ducked for the nearest trees. In a single long spring January crossed the gallery; another stride took him over the rail, praying gators hadn't come up from the river with the floodwaters. He landed with a monumental splash on something that rolled underfoot, almost spilling him off his balance. Someone shot at him from somewhere and he heard men yelling in the cane-fields, Jacinthe's slaves closing in on Shaw.

Vivienne Avocet screamed again at the sight of January and tried to break from her companions and flee, but her daughter shouted, "Mama, he's from the house!"

January yelled, "Make for the house!" and fired at Shaw's rebel attackers, breaking their charge. Bullets slapped the water near him and one of the slaves launched into him from behind with a cane-knife; January grabbed the man's wrist, wrenched his arm around, and pulled him into a punch that snapped his head back and buckled his knees. Dropping him, he waded toward Shaw without turning to see if the man he'd struck drowned or not.

Shaw fired off his last shot—January was counting—just as January reached the shed. If Jacinthe's men were counting, too, they'd come on again soon. He wrenched one of the pistols from around the Lieutenant's neck, flipped open the patch-box in its handle, and dumped out ball and wad as Shaw wordlessly placed a pinch of perfectly dry powder into his hand.

"Sorry I kicked you." He rammed the charge home and handed the gun back to Shaw, who he knew to be a far better shot than himself.

"Had to be done." Shaw brought up his own rifle, and scanned the muck of hackberry seedlings and weeds and water, watching for the movement that would tell him the rebel slaves were working their way around under cover. His breath labored and his gargoyle features were taut under streaming lines of watered blood. "I'll get over it."

His right arm would barely move, something that didn't seem to affect his aim much, or his speed at loading. A bullet tore a chunk off the corner of the shed between them, and they both ducked, made a dash along the side of the little building, and vaulted through a window. More shots cracked outside. Looking back, January could see the gun-flashes in the two windows in the front—Serapis and Rose, he thought—and counted three on the garçonnière wing. There was no sign of the four Avocet women and presumably they'd made it to the gallery in safety. He found himself thinking, *If they'd been shot they'd still be floating. . . .*

It was a hundred yards to the house. The shed offered little protection, Jacinthe and his rebels would . . .

Movement in the water that stood in the doorway, men swimming, trying to stay beneath the surface. January caught up a rifle and strode to the door, slammed it down, heard at the same instant a grunting howl from the window and guessed others had come up there. God knew how much longer Shaw was good for. January cursed himself grimly as he smashed one attacking slave across the face, seized the cane-knife from the attacker's hand, and slashed at another—for himself, he didn't care if the Avocet women lived or died, and resented being put in the position of protecting them. Not when Rose and Dominique needed his presence in the house.

He stomped, kicked, thrust a bloodied slave back through the door, risked a glance over his shoulder. Shaw was clinging to the window-frame to keep himself on his feet, gasping for breath, and past him, January could see more of Jacinthe's rebel slaves dashing through the water toward the shed, and toward the house beyond.

We'll never stop them. . . .

Like the drop of a theater curtain, darkness fell. January saw, a split-second before he felt it, the crawling turmoil of wind race across the floodwaters in the overgrown yard, saw the trees buck and heave and lean. Heard the bellowing clash of leaves, of canes, of wind.

Then rain hit, like Noah's flood; the deeps broken up, the skies emptied. The shed which had seemed to be so stable a few moments ago creaked and swayed like a drunkard; January contemplated for a moment trying to make it to the house and looked out the door in time to see an oak-tree pinwheel past in the rain.

Shaw said, "Fuck me," and pressed his hand to his right side. At a guess, the bullet that had taken him down on the levee had lodged against—and probably broken—some ribs. The window beyond him had turned into a cinder-colored sheet of streaming water. The slaves that had been only a dozen yards away never arrived.

The water began to rise. In the gloom January saw now the rats clinging to the shed's rafters, or swimming madly in the corners; something that he thought was a deer swam past the door, antlered head cleaving the flood like a floating snag. Branches slammed into the landward side of the shed, and now and then something softer that had to be a bird. January couldn't imagine where Jacinthe and his slaves would go, not to speak of those who had fled Boscage and Autreuil and Les Plaquemines. No wonder Serapis had said that no one would dare emerge from the sugar-house long enough to attack Mulm and his filibusters.

"Who-all's in the house, Maestro?" Shaw waded to the corner where January stood, away from the bending, creaking landward walls. Bloody hair hung in his eyes—he groped for the wall's support.

"One or two house-servants, a woman named Chloë Viellard—the niece of St. Roche's owner—along with Rose and my sister Dominique. Supposedly Joffrey Duquille and his sons are there, too, but I haven't seen them."

"Right inhospitable of 'em." Shaw had to shout over the screaming winds. "Seems like nobody's seen 'em. Not for years."

"You know anything about his wife's suicide?"

"Only it was hushed up." His words came in broken fragments. "Miss Laurene told me Felice Duquille's family bought new altar-cloths for the Cathedral . . . new vestments for every priest an' altar-boy . . . she was wrote down as havin' died of a fall down the gallery steps. Fact is she hanged herself. Most of the parish knew it . . . though I 'xpect the altar-boys did need new duds that year. When I was a kid . . . woman the next place over from ours did the same . . . but it was a two-day ride to Nason's Corners *if* you had a horse, an' that woman was the only female in fifty miles, barrin' the squaws—women needs other women to be with. . . . But St. Roche is only a few hours from town on the steamboats."

"What'd Joffrey Duquille have to say about it?"

"Not much. An' what he said, he said by letter to his factor. But this was right after the British . . . things was a bit unsettled." His breath caught and the muscles bunched along his jaw. "I think . . . M'am Felice was buried here. . . . We gonna get outa here, Maestro, we better do it."

The water had risen breast-high, pouring in through window and door. The corpse of a fox washed by. "Can you swim?"

Shaw glanced at the fresh blood that dyed his palm. "Not far."

"Here." January hooked an arm around the Kaintuck's body, worked his way around the walls to the door. Even in that few minutes the water-level had risen, so that he had to duck his head under water to get through. Coming up, rain pounded him, beat cold on his head and his arms as he dragged himself and Shaw up to the shed-roof. "Rose tells me the water sometimes gets as high as ten or twelve feet," he yelled. "I make the shed to be about that at the peak."

"How high's the house?"

"Six feet above the ground on piles." January started to turn, to strain his eyes through the whirling iron-gray maelstrom of the air toward the house, but the shed beneath them lurched, staggered like a foundering horse, then sagged sideways, nearly tilting them from the roof. He flung his arms wide, worked his fingers through the plank roof's cracks, pressed his cheek to the soaked wood. Rain flayed him. The shed jerked a few more times, spun slowly around its northwest corner—probably the only corner-post still attached to whatever slight foundation it had had—then steadied, rocking in the bleak, dark waters and tugging with every floating deadfall that rammed it. "Bastard better hold or we'll be swept out to the river. We'll never swim to shore."

Something that January thought was a floating branch bumped his leg—he kicked at it, and a moment later it bumped him again. He turned, squinting through the rain, and saw that it was a sixteen-foot alligator.

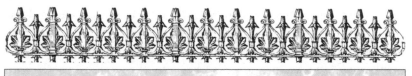

TWENTY

January wasn't conscious of rolling and flipping himself over the peak of the shed-roof, but by the time the gator opened its pink mouth and hissed, January was over, and Shaw—who had seemed only barely possessed of the strength to cling like a drowned water-rat to the planks—was beside him. The gator heaved itself up farther, glad of the room. The shed jerked at its uncertain mooring.

January pulled up the pistol on its ribbon and fired at that blinkless yellow eye, hoping that the powder was still dry, but of course it wasn't. He caught Shaw's rifle, reversed it, and began club-bing the gator on the snout, shouting against the wind and not dar-ing to raise himself up enough to get leverage lest he be blown bodily off the roof. God knew what else was swimming around. The gator backed, hissed again, but clearly wasn't about to plunge back into the current. The huge tail lashed, the shed lurched, and then they were floating free.

For an instant January thought the gator would lunge up over the roof-peak at him. He'd seen even six-foot gators spring the length of their own bodies in seconds. The floating shed rocked, turning ponderously as it blundered among the submerged trees, headed for the sweeping gray vortex of the river, and there wasn't more than a space of six feet by eight or so in which he and Shaw could maneuver. But the unsteadiness of the footing may have kept the big reptile where it was. It snapped at the rifle-butt, its eyes expressionless as beads in their crusts of gray-green armor; January hammered it, shouted, glanced hastily over his shoulder and saw that they were approaching the upstream side of the house.

"Get ready to jump!"

Shaw, clinging grimly, lifted his head a little to see, but January wasn't sure that he'd be able to move when he had to. The water swirled only a foot or so below the Big House's eaves. Above that pale churning, the high peak jutted like an island. *They'll be in the attic,* January thought—narrow dormers projected from the hipped roof, the windows shuttered against the storm's hammering. An oak twenty feet from the upstream end of the house made another island in the heaving near-dark, funneling the water between them, and toward this chute the floating shed swept. January struck again at the gator to keep it from gathering itself enough to lunge, and snatched a handful of Shaw's drenched shirt by which to inch him painfully toward the edge of the shed-roof—

Then the shed spun a leisurely forty-five degrees and snagged in the oak-tree, wedged between it and the roof of the Big House. January and Shaw were on the tree side, the shallow peak of the roof between them and the gator, and the gator on the house side.

Silent under the sluicing rain, the gator lunged. January grabbed Shaw, scrambled, and rolled backward. The current was stronger than he'd thought, slamming the two of them onto the half-submerged wall as he worked his way along it, praying the shed wouldn't dislodge until they'd reached the house-roof, and the gator wouldn't decide to drop into the water after them. Eyes, nose, mouth filled with water, blinded by wind and rain, he could only grope as nameless things rammed into his back and head and the current dragged at his limbs and at the limp body he supported.

The shed lurched, tore loose of the oak, and disappeared just as January caught the overhanging eaves of the house. He'd have sworn Shaw was unconscious, but the Kentuckian got one arm up onto the roof, and with the current tearing at him January braced himself on a beam, boosted Shaw, then fought his own way up. Wind nearly scoured them off the wet slates, pinned them flat, not daring to move, and January thought, *Now the Big House comes loose of ITS foundations and we all get swept out to the river, and down to the sea. . . .*

The shutters of the dormer were fastened on the inside, but only with a latch. January considered pounding on them and shouting, but the noise of the wind was so enormous, he doubted he'd be heard, even if Rose and the others happened to be at that end of the attic. Dragging himself little by little into the shelter of the projecting dormer, he worked his knife from his boot, slid it through the crack and up, easy movements enough if one's hands weren't wet and shaking with exhaustion and shock, if one weren't being lashed by the rain and torn by wind. He dropped the knife twice, the second time barely catching it before it slid away off the roof slope. A branch struck him like the bolt of an arbalest, numbing him as he pushed open the shutters, dragged himself through . . .

A gunshot roared in the narrow gap of the dormer, the yellow explosion of muzzle-flash blinding him. Pain lanced his arm like the sting of a giant hornet, and he plunged into darkness.

"Don't even think about it, my girl," said Franklin Mulm's nasal voice. "Just do as I say, and your mistress will take no harm."

There was a candle. January opened his eyes.

He couldn't tell if the rocking was still the wind that pummeled the house, or the waves of dizziness and nausea that swamped him with the mere movement of his eyelids, the mere intensity of that single small gold light.

He'd been hit—arm, shoulder, he couldn't tell. Nausea. Searing pain and the weakness of shock and lost blood.

He lay where he'd fallen in the narrow space beneath the slant of the roof and the dormer window, where the smell of dust and mildew was overwhelming. Cobwebs thick with dust caught the dim yellow glow. Mulm was between him and the main attic, his arm hooked around a girl's throat and a pistol pressed to her head. It took January a moment to realize that the white blur of her clothing was the old-fashioned schoolgirl dress that Chloë had been wearing, and not young Laurene Houx's nightdress.

He blinked, consciousness battling its way back to focus. Candle-light revealed faces, past Mulm's narrow silhouette. Serapis, blood on his forehead and his flesh ashy-gray beneath it, slumped in a corner with hands bound. Beside him Lucy, the Bois d'Argent cook, watched the proceedings with wary eyes. Her tignon was gone and her hands were also bound. A skinny little bald man whom January recognized as one of Mulm's filibusters from the Nantucket was tying Annette Avocet's hands with strips torn from an old dress—a trunk thrown open near-by showed where it had come from. Tyrone Burke stood near a shut door into a farther attic, almost hidden in the shadows of the great beams, his pistol trained on the rest of the occupants of the dim-lit room: Dominique, Rose, the quadroon maid, and Laurene Houx, all gathered around the unconscious Vivienne. It was to Rose that Mulm had spoken, Rose who'd half-risen from among them.

"We don't mean anyone here any harm." Mulm spoke in the soft, reasonable voice January remembered from the yard of the Nantucket. "We want only one thing here, and when we've got that, we'll be on our way. We never intended to harm anyone—"

"Except Madame's brother Artois." Dominique's voice shook. With her dark hair hanging wet over her half-bared shoulders, her wet, gauzy gown tattered and clinging to her swollen belly, her eyes wide in a face hollowed and gray with fatigue, she looked more than ever like some spirit, if not of this place, then of the flooded marshes all around them. "Except poor M'sieu Perth, back at Bois, and his wife, and Kitanga the butler downstairs, and Madame's butler Oliver, and how many others who got in your way."

Rose touched her arm, warning, but Dominique shook free of her hand.

"What does it matter? He's going to kill us anyway! He knows we've seen him, can identify him—"

"My dear girl," interposed Mulm softly, "whoever gets killed here, it wouldn't be a valuable nigger like yourself. And so far in pup, too."

"Oh, *en effet!*" cried Dominique passionately. "Whisper words of love in my other ear, *cochon!* They want to believe you, Serapis and Lucy and Melisse, because they think, *Oh, I'll be sold, I'll get away, I'll still live.* . . . But you no more plan to let any of us live than you plan to shave your head and become a monk!" She turned, wildly, furiously, to the Avocets' maid, and the girl Laurene, both huddling in the shadows among the cobwebbed trunks and ancient chairs. "He will kill you, too! He kills just to silence whispers, the way he shot that poor fool rebel who only seeks to come out of the storm. . . ." She gestured at January.

"Burke," said Mulm. "Shut her up."

Burke moved toward Dominique, his free hand reaching with a man's casual anger at a troublesome woman, the pistol still in his right hand but lowered. The bald man, clearly under the impression that none of this had anything to do with him, continued to tie Annette Avocet's hands . . . and January flung himself full-force into the backs of Mulm's legs.

Mulm yelled, the gun flying—it hadn't been cocked and January suspected the powder was wet. He'd formed a pretty good idea of Chloë's level-headedness, watching her during the earlier fighting. He tried to grab Mulm: pain ripped through his left arm. Mulm reared over him with a knife in his hand and January seized his wrist in his right hand, twisted him one-handed, and slammed him, hard, against the corner of the roof where the dormer formed a sharp angle. The saloonkeeper went down like a schoolboy—January was very powerful, and very angry. In the same instant he heard a gun fire—*Burke,* he thought, *so much for my theory their powder would all be wet*—and as Mulm slipped down unconscious, blood and hair leaving a huge dark smear on the rafter, January turned and saw Burke sprawled on the attic floor, twitching in a pool of gore.

Chloë was just picking herself up from between two trunks where she'd dived the moment Mulm's grip had loosened. The bald man scrambled up—Annette Avocet had kicked him in the belly like a mule and was herself on her feet now with a paper-knife— goodness knew where she'd gotten it—upraised in her hands. Baldy dashed for one of the dormers but another shot cracked from the shadows of the inner door near which Burke had stood, yellow gun-flash silhouetting for an instant the two forms that stood there. January had a momentary impression of dark faces, calico shirts—an overwhelming stink of camphor, sulfur, rotting flesh. . . .

Baldy flung out his arms and fell. At the same time a voice from the dark of another dormer called out, "Hey, in there, watch the shootin', eh? I woulda take care of that American. . . ."

Cut-Nose Chighizola dropped down through the dormer as he spoke, cutlass in hand and dripping with rain, and stopped, blinking at the two shadows in the inner attic's dark door. Vivienne Avocet, rousing herself from her faint, looked, too, peering through the wreaths of powder-smoke and candle-glow. Her eyes widened and she scrabbled backward, screaming now in good earnest.

"Shut up, Vivienne," said Annette Avocet, and Laurene whispered, "Mama, please," her own eyes huge.

"There should be a knife in that man's boot." Serapis spoke into the silence that followed. Rose went to Burke's side, took the weapon. The filibuster moved his hand, made one final, horrible sound, and died. Rose didn't spare him a glance. January dragged himself upright against the nearest trunk, Chloë coming to help him.

"Shaw's on the roof," he panted, and Chighizola backed uneasily from the two newcomers in the shadows, and went to the dormer through which January had come, using the lid of a trunk to scramble up. Annette Avocet and her maid grabbed for the candles as the wind and rain bellowed in again. The movement flung light into the shadows, the yellow glow failing and uncertain but confirming what January suspected. Neither of the men in the shadows moved.

"Oh, dear God," Vivienne Avocet was gasping, "Oh, dear God . . ."

"Got him," January heard Cut-Nose say from the roof. A moment later the pirate lowered Shaw through, unconscious and bedraggled, blood and water dripping down onto the floor. Once the storm was shut out, and the light steadied, Dominique came around the truss-beam that separated her from the newcomers, and extended her hand.

"Messires, thank you. . . ."

"Stay back!" cried Serapis.

And the taller of the two shadows said, "No closer, Mamzelle, please." His voice was mumbling and muffled. "It is a sickness that takes long to spread, but still it is best that a woman with child not see our faces."

"If it makes you more comfortable, of course, M'sieu." Dominique stepped back, lowering the candle she held. "But I assure you the only faces I see are those of men who saved my life, and those of my dear friends, and of my child. Those faces are beautiful to me."

"Madame, hush," said Rose to Vivienne Avocet, who was having hysterics in her arms. "Hush! Minou is right. They saved our lives."

But Vivienne Avocet would only sob, "Oh, dear God! Oh, dear God!"

From the shadows the gleaming eyes turned toward her. Wind leaking through the shutters flared the candle's light, showing up the hands of the man who had spoken. The hand holding the pistol with which he'd shot Burke still had two fingers and a thumb, the nails hard and hooked like claws, the other, only part of the little finger.

All this January saw as his hands worked automatically, seeking the pulse first in Shaw's wrists and then in his throat. The Kaintuck was barely breathing, waxen and still as a dead man as January stripped the remains of his shirt off him, checked the roughly-bandaged wound in his side. As he'd guessed, the rifle-ball he'd taken on the levee at Avocet had broken three ribs; his whole bony torso was dark with bruises. Serapis, when Cut-Nose severed his bonds, silently brought blankets from a trunk; Chloë handed January a gourd of very strong rum with which to clean the wound.

"I assure you, M'sieu . . ." Joffrey Duquille's thick voice broke the grip of muteness that seemed to have settled on the attic, ". . . that nothing in this part of the attic—or in the main portion of the house—has been touched by either myself or my sons since our illness began."

He wasn't looking at Madame Vivienne, who had pulled Laurene to her and perched on a trunk-lid with the appearance of a woman trying not to touch either it or the floor.

"I had no fear of that, M'sieu." January looked up from the makeshift dressing he was binding in place. His own left arm throbbed and he felt lightheaded from the shock of the wound. The whole conversation had a dreamlike quality to him, as if he'd already had it once before, as if he'd known all along why neither Joffrey Duquille nor his sons had been seen in twenty years. "I am well aware the disease infects only slowly; that one exposure will not transmit it. I am a surgeon," he added, "trained at the Hôtel Dieu in Paris, but I have had some training in medicine as well. My name is Benjamin January. If I can be of assistance, to you or to your sons . . ."

"Thank you, my friend," said the old man. "I doubt there is much that can be done for my younger boy, Philippe. He is blind now, but otherwise as well as can be expected. We are quite well cared for, here. Gontran's eyes have thickened, too . . ." he touched the arm of the man beside him, ". . . and my own, a little. But we can still shoot."

January finished with Shaw—the rifle-ball was lodged in the broken ribs and January felt too shaky himself to try to extract it by the light of a couple of candles—and sat back as Rose bandaged his own arm. While she worked, Joffrey Duquille went on.

"When first we found the discolorations on the skin of one of the slaves, we burnt everything she might have touched, and confined ourselves to the part of the house where she had gone least. None of those who worked in the main part of the house since that time, until we closed it up, have shown symptoms. And we have been careful over the years."

As surely as if Duquille had said it, January knew then why Felice Duquille had hanged herself. He only wondered whether she had found the darkening discolorations, the areas of numbness, the first nodules on her own skin, before her husband and her sons had found them on themselves.

Rose whispered, "It is leprosy, isn't it?"

January nodded. "I've heard of it—very rarely—among slaves."

"I understand it's common in Africa. One finds mention of it in European histories, but it seems to have died out of there now. I suppose it was only a matter of time before a slave passed it along to his masters. Will he . . . is there anything that you can do?"

While she spoke her hands worked deftly, probing at both wounds—the bullet had passed through the meat of his left arm, missing the bone—and daubing on the stinging rum from the gourd. Chighizola went over to Mulm, and checked the back of his head with the matter-of-fact familiarity of one who's survived a hundred battles himself.

"Let him lie," snapped Annette Avocet when Cut-Nose announced that the saloonkeeper was still breathing. The maid Melisse went to fetch a quilt for him, but hesitated in the face of her mistress' frown. Dominique took the quilt from the maid's arms and laid it over Mulm.

"He ain't gettin' up," January heard Chighizola mutter to her. "Back of his head's like a smashed cantaloupe."

Chloë's soft voice could be heard below the screaming wind, making introductions—*The proper Creole matron,* thought January. Even in the midst of chaos and flood and slave revolt and death, she had taken the earliest convenient opportunity to make known to her uncle the names and stations of those who had invaded his house.

". . . I believe the first gentleman you shot is named Tyrone Burke. The bald gentleman whom Lucy and M'sieu Chighizola are hauling over into the corner, I have no idea of his name, not that it matters. . . ."

"I'm sure we can think up one for him if we need to, darling," said Dominique. "We're going to boil water, p'tit—should we put up enough for you to work on M'sieu Shaw?"

"Serapis informs me that the man Mulm was the one who killed your half-brother, Madame," said that slow, muffled, mumbling voice to Chloë. "Is this true?"

"I believe so, yes." Chloë glanced over at Mulm, whose breathing rasped stertorously in the shadows, without a flicker of emotion in her face. "Dominique tells me it was because Artois learned of the slave revolt they were planning, the revolt M'sieu Mulm was aiding with guns in the hope that it would force you to flee St. Roche. And if you didn't flee, the slaves could take the blame for it if M'sieu Mulm and his men simply killed you and burned this house. It was quite a good plan, actually. Artois just . . . just happened to stumble upon it."

"You were fond of him." Duquille said it gently.

"Everyone was, who knew him. He was . . . that kind of person. Are you all right, sir? Are you comfortable here?"

"We are as comfortable as Serapis and his tribe can make us," said the planter. He and his son were seated on a trunk, nearly invisible in the darkness. Chloë had dragged up an old footstool, just before the threshold of the open door, a white shimmer in the gloom.

"Serapis—and his father Gende—have taken great care of us. It was Gende's sister, who was a housemaid here, who first showed signs of the sickness. Of course I had her quarantined—I had a house built for her, separate from the quarters, and made arrangements that she be cared for. And at the same time we . . . we went into a quarantine ourselves. Your aunt, my sons, and I. And waited."

And how many men would have done that? wondered January. Most other planters would merely have slapped a bandage over the first of the sores and told the next buyer, *Oh, she burned herself on the lamp-oil—she's a likely wench, but clumsy.* As, undoubtedly, the last seller had said to Duquille.

He'd heard of sales like that, and of much, much worse.

January leaned back against the wall after Rose finished bandaging his arm, sick and weak with reaction and blood loss, and knowing as soon as the wind slacked he'd have to dig the bullet out of Shaw. Now that the danger was done, he was grateful only to be warm and more or less dry. Lucy brought him some water, dragged up in jars from the butler's pantry below, and knelt to sponge the blood from the unconscious Shaw's face. The house still swayed with the pounding of the wind, but the roof didn't leak, and the roar of the rain seemed almost soothing. Chloë's voice was a gentle murmur, telling over the account of how Sancho Sangre had probably identified Hesione LeGros to Mulm, and how Burke had bought from her some account of where Lafitte's twice-stolen treasure was hidden. Once when Dominique went over to say something to her, Vivienne Avocet caught her by the skirt and whispered, "My dear, do you think it's wise?"

"I'm afraid I don't know that, Madame. Perhaps I'm not very wise." The graceful shape of the outdated gown she wore suited her condition like the robe of a fertile goddess, her sable hair, hanging in damp curls to her waist, like some Renaissance painting of Eve. She moved to the blackness of the inner charnel-house door, and said, "May I bring you anything to make you comfortable, Messires? Darling"—this to Chloë—"Lucy tells me she brought up some biscuits from the pantry as well as the water jars, when we came up here in all that confusion. Would you like those with your tea?"

Of course Minou would make tea in the middle of a hurricane, thought January, closing his eyes. It would probably do everyone a lot of good.

A noise jolted him from sleep—from dreams of alligators and mad queens' necklaces, and of Artois St. Chinian eating Italian ice beneath the willow-trees on the lake's marshy shore, watching the hurricane from afar with delighted enthusiasm and making observations of the clouds. For an instant he lay breathless, trying to identify what it was.

Then he heard it again and thought, *A bird.*

It was a bird singing in the silence.

Someone had laid a quilt over him. His arm throbbed as if it had been cut off. Dappled light filled the attic, with a great swampy smell of water. The festering smell of sores, the stink of camphor and medicines, had faded. A yellowthroat sat on the sill of the dormer through which January himself had fallen—he could see the bullet-scar in the wood now, by the soft, clear evening light. For a moment he thought, *How beautiful. That that little bird could take refuge here from the storm; and now that it is over, can sing its happiness, a message to us all from God.*

The bird hopped to the rafter directly over January's head, dropped a generous dollop of guano onto his hair, and flew away.

January sighed, wondering if Noah had experienced similar indignities following the Flood. Then he laughed, thinking how much more preferable it was to be shat on by a bird than to be devoured by an alligator, drowned by a hurricane, or shot by a slimy piece of work like Franklin Mulm. Close beside him Shaw still slept. January wondered whether he himself looked that bad.

Neither Burke's body, nor Mulm's, was anywhere in sight.

January sat up.

The attic had been partitioned while he'd slept. Sheets had been tacked across the nearest rafter to form what was—judging by the three other heaps of quilts between the trunks—a general quarters for the men, both black and white. A strong smell of woodsmoke permeated the air, and wraiths of it drifted in the failing sunlight, accompanied by the scents of coffee and frying meat. Presumably, thought January, Dominique *had*, in fact, rigged up enough metal or potsherds to form the base for a fire.

From the other side of the sheet he heard Cut-Nose say, "Nah, you didn't want to bury it in the sand, see, 'cause the sea, she's always piling up more sand or carving it away. I seen whole forts that the Spanish built just collapse in the sea, 'cause the waves cut in under 'em. Even them places where they say they dug these pits, with boards over the top of the treasure, an' coconut-mats, an' that . . . Most the time they was dug for somethin' else, to found a gun onto or somethin'. 'Least, the Boss never did that. Sometimes you got the navy, or the Brits, right comin' down on top of your ass, you gotta get your stuff an' get outa there, you can't spend two days cuttin' around with logs an' coconut-mats an' that. . . ."

"Oh, thank goodness," said Minou's voice from farther off. "Lucy, you're a darling—garlic *and* sausage as well as the rice. But what we'll do about boiling drinking-water after the wood runs out. . . ."

"Virgil's bringing charcoal across on the next boat, m'am," said Serapis. "And herbs, to clean the wounds of those who're hurt. Those up in the mill, they say the flood went up nearly to Jesuit's Bend. They'll bring across what we need till the water goes down. That'll be tomorrow sometime, by the look of it."

"Thank God!" moaned Madame Vivienne in shattered tones. "I will never, ever be the same after this; I don't think I will ever sleep again. . . ."

"Mama, you slept three hours this afternoon before the storm stopped."

"Hush, Laurene, I did not . . . and what effect this will have on my poor child . . ."

"While you were asleep M'sieu Serapis showed me how to make a block and tackle, Mama, to get the food in from Virgil's boat. . . ."

"Don't say *M'sieu,* dearest, about a slave. . . ."

The sheet was put aside, and Rose ducked through, shaking dust from her bedraggled skirts. "How do you feel?" she asked January.

"Thirsty. Hungry. My arm hurts like the devil. Not bad."

"Well, I'm pleased to hear that, Maestro." Shaw turned his head a little on the worn pillow; his voice was barely a whisper. "I hear right, Miss Vitrac, in that the waters of the earth are bein' called home an' we'll be able to get out'n here by morning?"

Kneeling between them, Rose handed January a gourd of weak and lukewarm tea. "It's what Serapis says. From the windows you can see the level of the flood has already sunk. We'll be here for the night, it looks like—hence the Walls of Jericho." She gestured to the partitioning sheets. She had washed her face, and her hair was braided, smooth and neat. As she held the gourd for Shaw to drink in his turn she lowered her voice and went on, in English instead of French, "The Avocet ladies have insisted upon a separate section for themselves and Chloë—they'll share quarters with lepers if they have to, evidently, but God forbid they should do so with women of color."

"Have they, now?" Shaw moved to fold his hands over his chest, but let them slip back to his sides. Sunk in dark circles, his gray eyes had a speculative light.

"The boat coming across from the sugar-mill with food and drinking-water is three or four feet below the eaves now," Rose continued, going to the open dormer. "There's also a sort of raft in operation. But I wouldn't advise trying to go down into the house before it's fully light tomorrow. Floods like this flush snakes out of their holes. There was a three-foot water-moccasin on the steps about an hour ago when I looked."

Shaw looked interested. "Still there?"

"Would you like me to check?"

"Iff'n you would, Miss. An' ask Cut-Nose in here for a word with me, if you would . . . I recollect as you speak Italian?"

Rose nodded.

"An' the Avocet ladies don't? Nor English? They wouldn't speak English around me, but then they wouldn't speak much of anythin' around me. . . ."

Rose shook her head. January had already guessed this: tart-tongued though Rose might be, she would never exercise her bitterness in a language that its targets might understand. "Laurene told me her mother had to communicate with Burke through M'sieu Rabot. Would you like me to speak to M'sieu Chighizola in Italian?" Behind the spectacle-lenses her eyes twinkled, as if she guessed what Shaw was up to.

"Iff'n you would. Maestro," he said, as Rose departed through the curtain again, "thank you. You didn't have to do what you did."

"There's been many times," said January quietly, "that you didn't have to do what you did."

"An' bein' that you saved my life—an' a lot of others besides," Shaw went on, "we'll sort of pass over what you was doin' Johnny-on-the-Spot at Avocet when things sort of blew up there."

"I appreciate it," said January gravely. Then, "You know I had nothing to do with what happened."

"Oh, I figured that—Jacinthe didn't seem to know you, anyways. But iff'n you would, I do have another favor to ask." Between fatigue, shock, and loss of blood, his voice was barely more than a scrape; January had to kneel close beside him, for at the other end of the attic Madame Vivienne was loudly complaining about the food.

"Fact is, Maestro, I ain't forgot why I was lurkin' around Avocet to begin with when the shootin' started," breathed Shaw. "In the household rag-bag I found the took-apart pieces of a woman's dress: the skirt, the back of the bodice waist, an' the left sleeve, all in good condition, not much worn. The front of the waist an' the right sleeve was missin'—the parts of the garment that'd catch the blood, if a woman were to stab a man up close to her. Now, it was M'am Vivienne's dress, right enough, but a dress can be wore by more than one woman, specially if she ain't particular about the fit because it's dark. So it may be, Maestro, that I'll be needin' some help tonight, 'long about the time everyone's snorin'."

By the time full darkness fell, the water level around the house had sunk almost to that of the house floor itself. The quarter moon's thin light barely filtered through the attic dormers as January carried Shaw to the ladder, bore a nearly-covered dark-lantern down the trap to the floor below to check for snakes, then re-ascended, silent as a cat, to carry the policeman down. "You're a fool for doing this," January whispered, as he guided his friend's feet to the rungs and maneuvered Shaw's good arm around his shoulders. Before full darkness fell he'd cut the rifle-ball out of Shaw's side, bound a dressing as tightly over the wound as he could, and had told him to rest. He went on, more loudly and in French instead of the English in which he usually spoke to Shaw, "Whoever did the murder, what does it matter now?"

In the same tongue Shaw replied, "It matters to me. You fetch the boat, an' leave the rest to me."

For all Shaw's rangy height, he was thin, and in his years working in the clinic at the Hôtel Dieu, January had learned the knack of carrying bodies, though he'd never had the occasion to carry a man of his own height down a ladder in near-pitch darkness before. Moreover, the dead have few opinions about their own comfort. Try as he would to be gentle, twice January had to shift his grip around Shaw's ribs and wrung strangled oaths of pain from the Kentuckian's throat. Shaw was barely conscious by the time they reached the bottom of the ladder. January's injured arm ached damnably in its sling, and he felt sick and dizzy as he lowered the policeman at last to the butler's pantry floor.

"Are you all right, sir?"

"I'll live." Shaw's voice struggled to remain steady. "Lord, that hurt. Just get me out to the gallery, an' get the boat." January could hear the thready gasp of his breath in the dark. "An' hurry."

January cracked the slide on the lantern a trifle more, shone the light around the dining-room. Furniture, books, candle-stubs, and bibelots strewed the slimed floor. A silver needle-case gleamed in the middle of the room; a snake slipped around a woman's shoe and fled. Curtains bloated with wet and dark with mud draggled from their rods. Newspapers clung like lichen to everything in sight, washed from some giant cache where they must have been accumulating for decades. January had taken the precaution of wrapping his legs from boot-top to groin in strips of leather cut from a trunk-covering, yet he stepped carefully when he gathered Shaw up in his arms again and carried him out to the gallery. There were more snakes out there. He only hoped their friend the alligator wasn't lurking somewhere.

The raft Virgil had used to tow supplies from the sugar-house still lay tied to one of the porch colonnettes; January hauled it in on its rope and looked around for another piece of flotsam to use as a pole. "I don't like to leave you here like this, sir," he announced, more loudly perhaps than the silence would bear and still in French. He knelt next to Shaw. "There's no telling how many of Mulm's cut-throats survived."

". . . take that chance. Need . . . to get men quick. Just get the boat."

January straightened up, and stood for a moment looking down at the prostrate form in the dark of the gallery.

"Hurry," whispered Shaw again, his eyes sliding shut. He started to gesture with his good hand, but it dropped back to his chest.

January turned, straddled the raft—which was only a section of planking—and cast off, paddling toward the sugar-house, invisible beyond the dark trees. He glanced back once, to see the tiny glimmer of the covered lantern and the dim shape of Shaw lying motionless near the door of the butler's pantry. Though Shaw had coached him mostly on what he must say in order to be clearly overheard, he had meant it when he said he thought the man a fool.

Or else, he thought, a more dedicated servant of justice than himself.

Ahead of him the floodwaters were a sheet of silver patched with the dense black of trees. The ruins of the kitchen, stable, laundry, and workshops formed a sort of blighted archipelago against the quicksilver gleam. Not a roof remained of the slave cabins, and most of these humble dwellings had vanished. January guessed—and later confirmed—that the quarters upriver for miles were so ruined. A number of plantation houses had lost their roofs as well, and orchards, crops, barns.

The moment he passed the corner of the house, instead of continuing on toward the sugar-mill he paddled around the corner, tied the raft to the rail again, and climbed back onto the gallery.

Nothing struck at him as he eased his way into the inky house.

He could not have said which made him more uneasy, paddling through the floodwaters with his legs dangling, or tiptoeing through the snake-infested house. He stepped carefully, not only because of snakes but because he had no idea where furniture had washed up, and he moved with breathless silence.

Somewhere above him, he heard the stealthy creak of a foot on the attic floor above.

Shaw was right, he thought.

He timed his next footfalls carefully, matching creak for creak when he could. Advancing across the lightless parlor with his plank-paddle stretched out before him like a blind man's cane. Listening. Seeing in his mind the man still lying by the lantern in the blackness of the gallery, too weak with blood-loss and battering, almost, to move.

The shutters had all been opened downstairs, that the house might more quickly air and dry. At least, in the aftermath of the storm, there were no mosquitoes, though they'd be back soon enough and worse than ever.

Another creak, tiny in the immense silence. There was another ladder and trapdoor in Duquille's office, but that, he knew, would not be used.

Twenty years. The thought of the planter and his sons made him shiver, though the night was thickly hot. Twenty years.

And in those twenty years, Joffrey Duquille and his slaves had settled into an agreement. *You care for me and my sons, and you can live as you please.* Sugar was a cash crop, enough to buy tobacco and coffee for everyone on the place. Enough to replace tools and kitchen pots, to buy bright-colored loincloths, beads for the women, new shirts for the shabby, desperate old man and his sons. To buy books—hundreds of them seemed to have washed out of the library, plus those that had been salvaged into the attic above the in-fected garçonnière wing.

You care for me and my sons, and no one will be sold from here. No one will come to break up your families and your village and your lives.

We don't have strangers here at St. Roche.

Would they have made that bargain, January wondered, had Duquille not offered sanctuary and care to the headman's infected sister? If he'd simply tried to pass her along as she'd been passed along to him? Dealers dyed the hair of older slaves all the time in order to claim them young and fit. Dealers had also been known to plug the anuses of those suffering from dysentery or enteritis, to get them off their hands, not caring what the consequences would be.

As Mulm had not cared.

What some nameless dealer had done to Duquille and his sons made Mulm look like a boy pilfering apples in the market.

Twenty years.

And in all that time, the treasure that Hesione LeGros had stolen from her lover—who had stolen it from Lafitte—had lain . . . somewhere.

January slipped through the archway between parlor and dining-room. The faintest stain of light outlined the doors onto the gallery. In the silence he heard the ladder creak again, just the tiniest bit.

Then a shadow passed across the door.

For a moment January couldn't tell whether the woman who stood in the doorway of the butler's pantry, looking down at Shaw, was Annette or Vivienne Avocet. Both women were much of a size, and in the frail thread of the lantern-light it was nearly impossible to distinguish individual features. Both had changed from their soaked clothing into garments once worn by Felice Duquille, out of fashion and laid up in trunks long before the disease took hold.

Only when she stepped forward did the light catch for an instant on her blond hair, and on the blade of the knife she held in her hand.

She struck fast. She had a pillow in her other hand and this she slapped down over Shaw's face, muffling any cry he might have made. When he caught her wrist in his good hand, fighting the descending blade, she rammed her knee with all her strength into the bandages that covered his broken ribs. Then January was on her, dragging her back, and she kicked and fought and, when she saw he was a black man, began shrieking, first "Murder!" then "Rape!"

"What, you gonna rape somebody here, eh?"

Cut-Nose Chighizola appeared out of the dining-room also— January had to marvel at the man's silence, for though he knew the pirate had to be somewhere in the house, watching all that transpired, he had heard not a sound from him in the darkness.

Annette Avocet stared at him, panting, her square, homely features a mask of rage. Shaw pushed the pillow from his face and asked, "Now, was it Ben who was gonna murder me, Miss?"

She looked wildly around, from one man to the other, recognizing January at last. Within the house, feet scrambled and creaked on the stairs, and voices called out—"Annette?" "Mademoiselle Avocet . . . ?" "What's going on?"

"You care to say what's goin' on, Miss?" Shaw tried to prop himself up a little and held out his hand for the paper-knife Annette Avocet had dropped. January knew it—he'd borrowed it to get the bullet out of Shaw's ribs. He recalled suddenly what Shaw had said about the wound that had killed Guifford Avocet being too small for a regular dagger, specifically the one that his brother habitually carried.

This weapon was thin-bladed but very sharp, and long enough to have been lethal. Shaw's chest was slashed as if with a razor above the heart. "Miss Chloë," he said when the other women appeared, blinking and confused, in the doorway, "would you be so good as to look in Miss Avocet's dress pockets an' tell me what's there—? That should be it."

Chloë was unwrapping a little wallet of oiled silk, containing several letters: these she unfolded and held close to the light.

Two of them were from a M'sieu Marius Motier—"That's M'sieu Guifford and Uncle Bertrand's uncle in Marseilles," said the girl Laurene in a tone of surprise. Vivienne had retreated into the butler's pantry, where she was having hysterics in Melisse's arms. "Quite a wealthy gentleman, Uncle Bertrand always said . . ."

The third was from a Cousin Catherine Motier. Dated the second of July, it informed Annette Avocet that Uncle Marius had died a few days before Guifford's marriage and had left quite a large sum of money and the controlling interest in his shipping firm jointly to herself and her two brothers.

"Maestro," said Shaw as Rose bent over him to stanch the bleeding wound in his chest, "Mr. Chighizola, I'll be askin' you two to come to court an' tell the jury about what you seen."

TWENTY ONE

"According to Cut-Nose"—Rose balanced herself with her snake-stick on a tufted green flottant and stepped gingerly over the rill that surrounded it—"one had to be careful about burying treasure. Any place where there's ground high enough to get a hole dug, that isn't likely to get drowned when the river shifts course, is going to be a long way from whatever boat you brought the treasure on in the first place."

"I bow to his expertise." January put his foot on what appeared to him to be the exact same place where Rose had put hers, and sank to his crotch in muck.

The flood had renewed the marshlands behind St. Roche Plantation. Bayou St. Roche now extended far up between what was left of a line of tupelo trees, those that survived the winds, stripped of most of their branches; the chenier on which the little hut had once stood was again an island in a reed-prickled lake. A few white egrets had returned, and regarded the party of explorers with disapproval, as if they knew perfectly well that the bespectacled boy in rough breeches was actually a young woman, and that Serapis and his two black village-mates were secret partners of their master back at St. Roche rather than subservient chattels.

No sign had been found in this wet wasteland of Jacinthe or any of his rebels. In not very many days, January guessed, the army would come, to be dealt with by Chloë, who had already sent Viellard Plantation word that she was well. She would remain on St. Roche, she said, living in the overseer's house, until the Big House was made livable again, the shops and quarters rebuilt, and "things were straightened out." January had seen her that morning already marshaling the St. Roche African villagers with a terrifying degree of efficiency that had nothing whatsoever to do with the fact that she was a slaveowner or white. Had she been African herself, she would still have been ruthlessly running the lives of everyone around her.

The plantation, January gathered from the bemused Serapis, was going to be financially as well as physically reorganized and renewed, the better to protect both Chloë's relatives and the villagers who had taken them into their care.

The body of Franklin Mulm had been found in the woods a short distance from the house. He had drowned, January guessed, without regaining consciousness, although Joffrey Duquille and both his sons assured him that they'd seen the man get up and sneak out through a dormer window (*With a deep concussion?* January wondered, glancing at the little smear of blood and hair on the rafter). All three—including the blind Philippe—signed a deposition to that effect, which they'd given Shaw.

At a guess, the police would make no more inquiry about Mulm's death than they had about that of Artois St. Chinian or Hesione LeGros. January didn't know whether that made the whole situation more just or less just in the abstract sense, and wasn't about to argue the point with himself or anyone else.

"The best way to dispose of treasure in this kind of country"— Rose held out her staff for January to flounder to marginally drier ground—"was in water itself." She moved along to the higher ridge of the old bayou, prodding carefully among the cypress-knees and uprooted tupelos. A turtle paddled indignantly from the hollow among the roots. Dragonflies filled the bright air. January kept wanting to turn and look over his shoulder, to see if Artois was keeping up with them. To see that laughing young face, the blue eyes drinking in the whole treasure-hunt with unalloyed delight. He felt the boy's presence keenly, like a cheerful ghost.

Or maybe that was only his wish, born of light-headedness from his wound.

"No telltale hole," Rose went on. "No drag-marks for your inquiring colleagues to find. No sweaty lifting . . ."

"I'll go along with that," said Serapis. Hands clasped behind his back, he looked like some minor voodoo deity in his blue calico loincloth, bare feet, and top-hat.

"And no transporting who knows how many hundredweight of metal and pretty ornamental rocks on your back over rough country. This looks promising."

Rose poked a little more around the roots of a huge old oak, then knelt in the long alligator-grass and brushed aside the matted mud and leaves. January saw a chain passed clear around the trunk. With the stick he poked for snakes as Rose followed it with her hands to the edge of the bayou itself.

"A tree to anchor the loot from sinking indefinitely into the muck—and any number of limbs overhead to which a block and pulleys can be affixed."

"Which you just happened to bring along." They were in the bundle of things—along with rope, chisels, a blacksmith's saw, and a couple of carrying-poles—that Rose had assembled from the tools salvaged by Igba, the plantation blacksmith, in the mill.

The oak itself didn't look capable of supporting much weight, but Igba, Serapis, and January rigged the pulleys to what remained of its stoutest bough, which coincidentally overhung the water at exactly the point where the chain went in. Awkward with his injured arm, January waded into the bayou, following the chain down with his good hand as far as it would go. It lost itself in the mud, but a little careful digging brought his fingers to where it wrapped something cylindrical. The other men brought shovels to scrape and clear as much as they could. The bottom was treacherous, the more so from having been stirred up, and January guessed that Rose was right. Had the cylinder not been held by a chain, it would have sunk irretrievably into the mud and been lost.

Even with their digging, which clouded the murky water still further, it took all their strength to haul the cylinder clear. When tugging on the pulleys served only to bring the damaged tree down into the bayou with a splash, Rose waded out around it and drove the stout carrying-poles down under the cylinder, straining on them like levers and getting herself covered with water and mud. At last, with a horrible squishy lurch, the thing shifted, the suction unbalancing Rose and dumping her backward into the water. She scrambled to her feet and up the bank, and slowly, slowly, the coffin-shaped lump of mud and weeds emerged dripping from the marsh.

It was a ship's cannon, plugged with what turned out to be about eight inches of tar, rope, and fiber, hardened by time almost to the consistency of stone. Igba worked at it by turns with chisels, hooks, and a scroll-saw over a low fire built on the bayou's edge, which softened the tar slightly, while Rose sat on the bank and talked to Serapis about hurricanes, African tales told him by his father, and Chloë's suggestions for financial and legal arrangements to better utilize the land.

"Michie Joffrey, he said to me many a time how he doesn't want to leave. I heard from my cousin, that's on Les Plaquemines, how there's priests in France that make it their gift to their god to look after lepers. But Michie Joffrey said no, he'd rather live as he is, where he knows those around him. Which is fair," Serapis went on, nodding, "there being no cure. Can she be trusted, this Madame Chloë?"

Rose frowned, chin in hands, brows drawn together over her eyes. Possibly putting together the tale of selling her own nurse with the burn-scars on the girl's arm: *Father never would hear a word against her.* . . . It had been a long time, January realized, since she'd completely trusted anyone. "As much as anyone can be trusted in this world," said Rose slowly at last, "I rather think she can. The arrangements she's proposed for selling the sugar, and for keeping any St. Roche slave from being disposed of by the family corporation, certainly don't sound to me like something that can be casually violated, not even by herself. And you understand," she went on, "that in any case, Chloë is Michie Joffrey's ultimate heir."

Afternoon light streamed long and golden over them when the last of the tarred plug was finally scraped and wrenched from the old cannon's mouth. The clouds that had sailed in from the Gulf dispersed without rainfall—*Thank you, Virgin Mary*—and the late sun mingled water and grass and sky into a huge blended shimmer of bird-stitched glory. Igba and January rolled the cannon off the fire, and going around to its butt-end, tipped it up, so that its contents spilled out onto the grass.

"Well, the gods do watch out for their children after all," Serapis said into the silence that followed. He held up one of the coins to the light. "This is Spanish, I think. I have seen some like it, in Michie Joffrey's strongbox."

"Mexican," said Rose, kneeling amid the gold and wet grass. Small heaps of coins all jumbled together—six or seven gallons all told—spilling out of the cannon's mouth and flashing from her fingers as she scooped them up, let them fall just to hear the jingling they made. Mingled with Spanish gold and Mexican silver and golden American eagles and half-eagles, there glinted necklaces, rings, gold chains, bracelets; loose jewels pried out of former settings; strings of pearls like dusky moons. There were gold buttons, intricate with filigree and set with gems; an embroidered scarf, blackened and rotting, held pieces of carved Chinese jade.

Rose picked out a coin. "They don't make small half-eagles like this anymore, but they did in 1812—it may well have come off the *Independence*. Of course, Gambi would have wanted to hide it from Lafitte. Oh, how beautiful!"

She held up the necklace of sparkling topaz, the necklace January had last seen around Hesione LeGros' neck in the dining-room of the Marine Hotel.

January dug his hands into the pile. Coins slithered and clinked in the weeds, a sound like music.

Music that said *You are no longer poor.*

Music that said *You no longer need to fear.*

Music that lifted his heart like a bird, like the long lines of pelicans sweeping the golden sky.

He closed his eyes and prayed, *Guide me. Show me the best way to use this, for the highest good of everyone concerned.*

". . . half to Michie Joffrey," Rose was saying. "It's been on his land all these years. Goodness knows if Mulm and his brutes hadn't been attacking the house during the storm, so much more could have been salvaged. Just the gold and silver here alone, not even counting the jewels, should be enough to restore the house and the quarters. There will be plenty left over for him to invest."

"And the rest is yours, Mamzelle Rose."

January opened his eyes, to see Rose wearing Hesione's flame-bright necklace over her old red calico shirt, the dirtied jewels catching the light. Kneeling amid the marsh-grass and the coins, she'd put another chain of jewels around her sorry old straw hat, and bracelets on her wrists, heavy bracelets of pearls and gold and emeralds.

"Yours and Michie Ben's." Serapis was smiling, the other two men looking at the coins with a kind of detached curiosity: happy, but without greediness, knowing their needs were going to be met anyway. Free of the metal that was life and death to those who lived in towns.

Rose's eyes were sparkling, delighted and at rest. January thought, *Her days of poverty are over, too. Her days of fear.*

We are both free.

"What will you do with your share, Ben?" she asked.

There was a gold ring among the coins and his hand went to it as if drawn there, as if he'd always known it was there, waiting for him. He picked it up, a plain pure circle, and said, "Give it all to you if you will take this as well." And he held out the ring to her.

Rose's eyes met his, now filled with a calm, sweet joy. "Keep it," she told him. She reached out and took the ring, kissed it, and slipped it onto her forefinger, where ladies in France wore the rings that marked their betrothal. "This is all I want. And this I will be honored, and very pleased, to wear for all the days of my life."

Benjamin January married Rose Vitrac in the St. Louis Cathedral on the twenty-sixth of September, five hours after he assisted at the birth of his sister Dominique's child. Dominique and Henri Viellard, who was also present at the birth—his wife being still downriver at St. Roche—named their daughter Charmian. After that time Dominique took the name Viellard for herself.

The hurricane had caused considerable damage in New Orleans, though the main force of the storm had passed the city by. Many of the pride-of-India trees along the levee had been felled; three steamboats were wrecked at the wharves. The Nantucket Saloon—and many other ramshackle buildings in the Swamp—were completely carried away, and others de-roofed or flooded several feet deep. Most people felt that the town had gotten off easy.

Bertrand Avocet was tried the week before the wedding for the murder of his brother Guifford, and acquitted. Shaw—barely a day on his feet and with his rib cage still in plaster—made his case well, pointing out the discrepancy between the size of the wound and the extent of the bloodstains. It was likelier, he argued, that the incriminating garment had been soaked with the blood of a chicken, and placed where it would be found so that the one brother would be hanged for the murder of the other, leaving their sister Annette in possession of the fortune left to the three of them by their French uncle Marius Motier—a fortune of which, by her cousin's letter, only she was aware.

However, when he made the nearly identical case at Annette Avocet's trial—which took place on the twenty-fifth, the day before January's wedding—the jury simply looked at him. Painstakingly, Shaw reconstructed how the despised and neglected sister had decoyed Bertrand from the house with a forged love-note purporting to be from Vivienne, and had lured Guifford to what he thought would be the illicit lovers' assignation: how she had worn her sister-in-law's dress so that the enraged Guifford would believe her to be Vivienne in the darkness behind the sugar-mill, and come close enough for her to strike. By setting back the parlor clock—the only clock in the countrified house—she had convinced Vivienne and Laurene that the three of them were together from nine until ten, when in fact they were together from eight until nine, giving her plenty of time to accomplish the murder; later she had burned the bloodstained portions of the dress, easier than burning the entire voluminous garment.

January and Cut-Nose Chighizola both testified that Annette Avocet had attempted to murder Abishag Shaw rather than let him return to New Orleans with the fragments of the forged love-note that he'd found.

Altogether, January thought, it was a convincing case. Freed of the resentment which had blinded him to its details—he realized he couldn't very well be angry at the police for not bothering to track down Hesione's murderer when they weren't going to bother to track down Mulm's killer either—he had to admire Shaw's attention to anomalous detail, down to the half-dozen mosquito-bites Annette Avocet had acquired waiting for Guifford in the wet darkness behind the sugar-mill, which had first drawn Shaw's attention to her as a suspect.

If the jury hadn't been largely French Creole, they might well have convicted her.

But they didn't.

January felt genuinely sorry for Shaw, because the moment he'd stepped into the courtroom in the Cabildo he'd foreseen the outcome. The jurymen were mostly French and Spanish Creoles—men of families who had lived in New Orleans for generations, and who, if not related to the Avocets, did business every day with them and with the entangled ramifications of their family. They weren't about to convict one of their own on the testimony of a tobacco-spitting Kaintuck river-rat.

They acquitted her, and ascribed Guifford's murder to "person or persons unknown": most probably the vanished overseer Raffin, whose body was in fact never found.

By Christmas, Annette Avocet had the good taste—and the funds—to move to New York, whence litigation over their uncle's fortune proceeded against her surviving brother and his new wife Vivienne for years.

But to January, the affairs of *les blankittes,* except insofar as they touched his life or the lives of those he loved, were more and more like some huge, gaudy theatrical performance. He would watch, from the third-tier gallery where he and his friends were obliged by law to sit. It was sometimes an entertaining show, but there were more interesting things for him to do.

He and Rose bought a house the week before their wedding, a ramshackle Spanish structure back on Rue Esplanade, large enough—when first frost brought the well-off free coloreds back into town, and the wealthier plaçées—to be made into a school.

"You'll do better to invest in slaves," said his mother when he encountered her at Dominique's the evening after the trial. "Or land. They're talking about splitting the city into three, and let the American animals run their own affairs—good riddance, I say—and town lots are going like hotcakes. Or set up a contracting business. You'll coin money—"

"I'm not a contractor, Mama," he interrupted gently. He passed her the coffee-cup with her two lumps of sugar—he couldn't imagine how Rose could drink hers black. "I couldn't push a work-gang from can't-see to can't-see, and argue with some rich white man about the price of roof-slates."

"I don't see why not." Her lips pursed in impatience. In the chair by the little hearth, Dominique caught his eye and smiled. Since her return to town, Henri had virtually lived in this peaceful pink cottage on Rue Burgundy while his wife saw to her uncle's affairs. Dominique never mentioned what had passed between herself and Chloë, or whether Henri's wife even knew that Dominique was her husband's mistress, but Rose told January that Chloë had said that she was aware that it was not in her to make a husband happy.

But that's no reason why he shouldn't BE *happy,* Chloë had said. *And I would like him to be. For I do like Cousin Henri, useless as he is about money.* Chloë sent Dominique a little gold cross for the baby to wear, and grapes from the arbors at St. Roche.

"Mama," said Dominique now, "one cannot be a contractor and write music. And Ben has written some beautiful things since he's returned from Grand Isle."

"Music." Their mother sniffed. "And what does music put on the table, pray? What does music put over your head?"

"The sun and the stars, Mama," said January, taking her hand, with its old cane-stalk scar that she told her friends had come from a scratch with a hat-pin. The doors stood open onto Rue Burgundy, and over the stillness of the town and the thrumming of the cicadas a market-woman cried her gingerbread in a long sing-song wail. "Besides, I know Rose, and Rose would never have married a man who built houses."

"Then she's as foolish as you."

"Yes." January smiled. "That way we know we'll be happy."

And his mother looked up at him, puzzled, and for one moment he saw in her eyes that she genuinely did not expect happiness to come from the person she gave her body to. That it was not something that had ever crossed her mind. Her gaze met his blankly, as if she'd put her hand on what she thought was a painting, and felt under her fingers the true scented velvet of flowers.

Then she pulled her hand away from his, her half-closed eyes masking whatever it was that she felt, or thought, or might have said had she been seventeen and alone with the man who had been January's father. The man from whom St.-Denis Janvier had taken her—and her children—without a moment's thought.

St.-Denis Janvier had given her the rose-colored silk she'd worn on the night of General Humbert's birthday party twenty-three years ago, and enough jewels to shine down even the gaudy Grand Terre women. He'd taken her to bright banquets with the ladies of the demimonde and let her meet the rich men who came there, and had bought her a house like this one of Dominique's, and had paid for the education of her son.

But he'd never asked her if this was what would have made her happy. Had never asked her what she dreamed.

She said, "You're a silly boy." And she swept into the yard, calling for Thérèse to come close the shutters before the mosquitoes devoured them all alive.

January kissed Dominique, and returned to the echoing, nearly-empty house on Rue Esplanade, where he'd moved his bed and his books and his piano the moment the place was his. Rose had been staying at Uncle Veryl's town house, where the old man—to the shocked horror of the entire Viellard and St. Chinian clan—was insisting on holding the wedding reception, having claimed the right to give the bride away in the church. That night, however, Rose came to the Esplanade house, too, and the two of them cleaned out the kitchen hearth and cooked their first supper together. When Henri Viellard knocked on the door at midnight, flustered and panting with the news that Dominique had gone into labor, Rose was still there.

"I'll have Thérèse to help me, and Olympe," said January, kissing her as he dressed. "There's no sense in both of us falling asleep at the wedding Mass tomorrow."

Charmian was born two hours before first light. Coming out of Dominique's house into the steamy darkness, January started to turn inland, to his own house, then, on impulse, went the other way, riverward. Even at this hour, when he crossed the Place d'Armes, he could see torchlight and movement on the levee; men's voices called out, and from the gambling-halls the jangle of music came, softened with distance to something almost resembling beauty. He felt wakeful in the warm thick-scented night, aware that he'd pay tomorrow for every half-hour's delay in returning to his bed, but knowing there was something he must do.

The Cathedral doors were open. The two nuns keeping prayer-vigil before the Host glanced back at him as he made his way down the side-aisle, but either he looked sufficiently respectable, or their faith upheld their courage: as he took a taper from the box and lighted a candle before the Virgin's image, they merely returned to their prayers.

A candle for Dominique, and a candle for tiny Charmian.

And a candle of thanks, for the wedding to come.

"If you are there, Artois," he said—for the longer he stayed around Olympe, the closer he felt to those no longer in this world—"I hope you will be with us, too, later on today, as I would have prayed you be, had things been otherwise. And maybe had you not been killed—had Rose and I not had to flee together to the south—she and I would not be wedding. We would only have gone on as we were, to come together differently, or not at all. If that's the case, I'm sorry. I would not have traded your life for this, sweet as this happiness is."

And in the dark of the Cathedral the candles flared up bright, the light consuming the wax, and glowing on the face of God's mother, bent down over them and watching all the earth with her benevolent secret smile.

January knelt there for a long while, and in time, his thoughts of what might have been, or could have been, dissolved only into the scent of the incense, and the honey perfume of the wax, and the starry brightness of the flame; and that was enough. "Artois," he said, "I love you."

And the flame and the dark both answered, in the voice of the boy and the man he would not grow to be, *And I you, my friend.*

January went out into the hot night with peace in his heart, and walked down the blue streets of the French town with his soul full of music, knowing Rose waited for him.

In the winter of 1835 a man named Murrel organized a conspiracy to foment widespread slave rebellion, with the intention of looting plantation houses in its wake all along the lower Mississippi valley when their owners fled. Murrel was arrested on another charge— slave-stealing—before the plan could go into effect, but others were tried and hanged.

The island of Grand Terre, where Jean Lafitte had his pirate settlement, is now completely occupied by a government research station. Most houses on the near-by Grand Isle sit on fourteen- foot piers, fourteen feet being the height at which flood insurance kicks in. Numerous Chighizolas still inhabit the island, and a blacksmith shop—said to be Jean Lafitte's—stands to this day on Bourbon Street in New Orleans, though it's now a rather pleasant little bar.

If you dig among the flottants that make up the northern shore of Grand Terre Island, you'll find, mixed with any amount of mud and broken clamshells, fragments of china dishes. These are the remains of the resort hotels built from the 1860s to the 1890s—a period of relatively few hurricanes in that area—on the barrier islands that divide Barataria Bay from the Gulf of Mexico. It's understandable why people would want to vacation there: the islands of Grand Isle and Grand Terre and the little peninsula of Chenier Caminada have an indescribable sleepy magic that's ex- tremely seductive. By the 1890s a number of large resort commu- nities had joined the original small populations of fishermen, shrimpers, and trappers.

In 1893 a massive hurricane came ashore at Chenier Caminada and wiped out most of the population and nearly all of the resort hotels, killing over 1,900 people.

Approximately where Jean Lafitte had his camp, the United

States government later built Fort Livingston, which is itself slowly collapsing into the Gulf of Mexico as tidal forces erode the island from beneath it. Grand Terre, Grand Isle, and the lesser islands of the Barataria are much smaller now than they were in the 1830s, gradually being chewed away by the sea as the ecological balance of river silt and tides is altered for the convenience of shipping.

There are a lot of stories about Jean Lafitte, who became a figure of romance almost as soon as he disappeared, and I am indebted to the papers of the Jean Lafitte Society for a whole spectrum of fact and theory. Lafitte seems to have come to prominence primarily as a broker of smuggled and pirated goods, only uniting the various factions of the Barataria pirates in 1812 into a single operation. In 1814 he threw in his lot with the Americans against the invading British, and won his niche in American history. But whichever side won the battle—and with it, control of the entire mid-section of the North American continent—Lafitte's freebooting days were numbered, since neither the Americans nor the British would tolerate organized piracy in the Gulf. Lafitte's camp of over one thousand men was burned out in 1816, and he retreated to Campeachy on the Texas coast. In 1821, out of consideration for past services, the American navy gave him twenty-four hours to give up that headquarters also, and he sailed away, presumably to the Yucatán, though I have encountered those who argue that he gave up piracy and settled in Missouri and lived to a ripe old age.

He appears to have been the last of the organized pirates in the Caribbean.

Louisiana is the only state in the United States where leprosy—almost certainly imported with the African slaves—was endemic. The only leprosarium in the continental United States still exists at Carville.

BARBARA HAMBLY attended the University of California and spent a year at the University of Bordeaux, France, obtaining a master's degree in medieval history. She has worked as both a teacher and a technical editor, but her first love has always been history. Ms. Hambly lives in Los Angeles, where she is at work on the next Benjamin January novel.